Denial

By

Paddy Magrane

Fahrenheit Press

For Kimmo Evans

1972–2014

'Security is mostly a superstition.'

Helen Keller

Chapter 1

Creech Hill Immigration Detention Centre, Essex – 11am

For one brief, blissful moment, Zahra Idris understood what it was like to feel free.

She and ten other women had been selected for what the governor called 'a special treat' – to try out a recreation room in the new wing of the detention centre while a group of important people were shown around. They'd been chosen, he said, because they weren't trouble makers and could be trusted to enjoy the room's facilities, if only for an hour, without the need for guards.

The room was huge and – bar the noise of ping pong balls hitting the table as two burly women in hijabs played a clumsy game, and the surging music and quick-fire dialogue of the soap opera the Nigerian girls had found on the Africa Channel – quiet, at least by Creech Hill standards.

Zahra was used to people screaming or crying out in anguish, arguments between detainees and guards interspersed with vile language, heavy metal doors slamming shut and keys turning in locks.

Here, you might have imagined you were in a hotel. In the corridor the signs that read 'LOCK IT, PROVE IT' had been removed and all the doors were wedged open. Inside the room, instead of the posters depicting happy, photogenic guards and the slogan 'The Team That Works Together

Succeeds Together', there were prints of abstract paintings. Bright, cheerful blocks of colour.

The Nigerian girls were grinning insanely at the prospect of watching an entire episode of Tinsel without another detainee grabbing the remote and swapping the channel, and the ping pong players were giggling like schoolchildren at every dropped shot.

But the cheery, holiday mood had not infected all the detainees in the room. An olive-skinned girl with lank greasy hair who was taking advantage of the wifi – a signal that was clear and, compared to the main building, almost exclusively hers – to tap and swipe furiously at her phone looked as miserable in here as she did on any other day. And a Russian girl, her hair cropped and bleached, who was using one of the brand-new computers, was wiping away tears as she caught up with her emails.

Zahra returned to the screen. She'd sat with the Nigerian girls before, watched snippets of the soap opera. From what she could gather, it centred on two rival movie studios in Abuja. The men were tall and handsome, the women slim and glamorous. Everyone wore designer clothes. Given their present situation, Zahra could see why the girls loved it so much.

When she looked back on that morning later and thought about what made her turn, she concluded that all humans carry in them an innate instinct that responds to the proximity of threat, even if that threat cannot be seen or heard. It was certainly not a noise. And it wasn't a change in the light. Winter sun poured into the room from floor-to-ceiling windows on the opposite side, so there was no disturbance in that way. No, what made Zahra turn was a feeling of dark dread placing its cold hand firmly on her shoulder.

At first, she was bewildered by the gut sensation. There before her was the promised group. Smartly dressed men and women quietly assembled at the open door. They were glancing around the room, jotting down notes on pads.

All except one man, who was staring right at her.

Zahra blinked then narrowed her eyes to focus on him. And as she did, the gut feeling became something solid, a lump of hard terror in the pit of her stomach. Terror so pure, she felt she might pass out.

Chapter 2

Creech Hill Immigration Detention Centre

As their eyes met, Sir Harry Tapper, CEO of Tapper Security, felt his throat go dry. His torso prickled with sweat, gluing his shirt to his chest and back.

She had recognised him, he was certain.

He turned to edge out of the room, the group he was showing round the new wing of Creech Hill Immigration Detention Centre – a mix of hacks, charity workers and local councillors – taking his lead and following.

He moved down the corridor, trying to walk at a normal pace even though he wanted to sprint, convinced that at any minute the woman would scream out.

They passed the base of a staircase.

A female voice spoke out. 'Excuse me.'

Tapper froze.

'What's that for?'

He turned and saw a woman pointing up to a blue net that hung just below the first floor to the wall opposite. Tapper remembered being introduced to the woman at the start. She was dumpy, dressed in all the colours of the rainbow, and worked for a charity that supported refugees and asylum seekers.

Tapper swallowed hard, attempting to moisten his dry mouth. 'Very occasionally, detainees, when faced with the prospect of being sent back to their country, try to harm themselves.' His voice, with its faint trace of Essex, was normally soft and deep, but it sounded cracked and high-pitched to him now. 'We do everything we can to ensure the vulnerable ones are supported. But the most determined are hard to stop. So we've taken some precautionary measures.'

A murmur of approval rippled through the group. Tapper ran a sweaty hand through his thick grey hair. He'd chosen a white shirt and pale blue tie that morning to highlight his tan, but he imagined his skin was ghost-like now. Surely someone would notice?

'Shall we?'

He led on, reaching the starting point of their tour. It was time to say goodbye. He stood as they filed past him. Some of them shook his clammy hand. There was a peck on the cheek from a journalist at The Mail. He tried to smile – to maintain the façade. The CEO in a tailored suit from Richard James – a suit that accentuated a trim figure for a man in his early fifties. A man of health and success. A man who'd built a security empire from scratch.

But at that point he felt as if he were sixteen again. And in the dock.

He had to do something. He couldn't just stand there.

Tapper had the beginning of an idea.

The last of the tour shuffled past and he turned to his PA, Jenny. 'Change of plan. Need to talk to the governor.'

Jenny, dressed in a black skirt and jacket, hair tightly arranged like an airline stewardess, tilted her head. 'Are you OK, Sir Harry? You look a little poorly.'

'I'm fine,' he said, already leading the way back to the administrative wing, Jenny and their escort of two guards trailing in his wake.

The governor's secretary waved Sir Harry and Jenny through the door. The governor, a tall wiry man, stood to greet them.

'Sir Harry,' he said, 'I thought you were heading straight back to London. How did it go?'

'Well,' said Tapper tersely.

'They saw the healthcare wing, gym, library, garden and vegetable patches, and all those large windows bringing in the light?'

The tour had been designed to dampen recent criticism from a number of human rights organisations that immigration detention centres were nothing more than glorified prisons. So they'd specifically avoided the Heron Wing, where violent detainees were locked in soft-walled cells.

'Yes, all of that,' said Tapper. 'The thing is, I want to see more.'

He heard Jenny tapping on a tablet behind him.

'I'm not here often. Might as well see a working day.'

'You have a 2pm appointment, Sir Harry,' said Jenny.

'Then shift it.'

The Governor signalled to his secretary through the open door.

'Pauline, can you get some lunch in here? Anything you'd like, Sir Harry?'

Tapper, who could not stomach the thought of any food, said: 'A sandwich is fine. And water.'

They had lunch in the office. Tapper took two bites of his tuna sandwich but the fish tasted like bile. They talked about Creech Hill, Tapper half disengaged as he racked his brains for a way forward.

It was her, he was sure of it.

The woman, her curly hair drawn back in a ponytail, had the same sculpted face. The same scar above her left eye.

He had to discover her name.

'So, Sir Harry,' said the governor, as Pauline brought in a tray of coffee, 'what would you like to see? I guess the big event this afternoon is visiting time.'

Tapper saw an opportunity. The woman might just show her face, though if she was talking to anyone, that wasn't good.

'Is there any way I can observe from a distance? Don't want to intrude.'

'Know just the place,' said the governor.

Tapper felt a tiny trace of hope before it quickly drowned in despair.

Seeing the woman brought that terrible night last summer crashing to the front of his mind in hideous clarity. Bar the occasional nightmare from which he'd wake, heart hammering so hard he thought he might have a massive coronary, he thought it was in the past.

But now it was back.

There was a witness.

Alive and well. And she'd been staring right at him.

Chapter 3

From the moment Sam Keddie spotted Zahra enter the room, he could tell that something was different today. That something was wrong.

She shuffled quickly past the other tables, her head darting from side to side, as if wary of being watched.

The cavernous, high-ceilinged space echoed with the sounds of dozens of conversations in as many languages. Guards in white shirts and black trousers, bunches of keys hanging heavily from their belts, shuffled between rows of tables occupied by detainees and their visitors – counsellors, healthcare professionals, social workers, solicitors, barristers, family members, translators.

Zahra perched on the edge of her chair, as if ready to bolt at a moment's notice. Her eyes were bloodshot. She looked around the room agitatedly.

Such evident change, as Sam had been warned by his supervisor at Creech Hill, was not uncommon. A letter from the Home Office, bad news from home. It didn't take much to upset the delicate status quo of the detainees.

'Are you OK, Zahra?' he asked.

A hand shot across the table and grabbed one of his, gripping with surprising strength. Sam felt a shot of electricity up his arm. Other than a shake of hands when they'd first met, they'd never touched. And then the voice, normally soft and even despite her worries, uttered words that made him swallow hard.

'I have seen someone,' she whispered. 'A face I remember. I feel scared.'

The hand slowly slipped from his, as if the emphasis it had provided were no longer needed.

Sam edged forward in his seat. He'd seen her stressed or worried about things before – twists and turns in her asylum claim, hassles at the centre, sadness and longing for the child she'd left behind in Eritrea, the husband from whom she'd become separated on the boat trip from Africa – but this was different, a fear that had contorted her face.

'Has this person done something to you?'

'I think so,' she said. Her face crumpled up in pain and confusion. 'But I'm not sure.'

When Zahra had emerged from the back of a Polish lorry full of cabbages at Dover and been screened at the port after claiming asylum, there was one part of her story that had not impressed the interviewing officers. When asked how she'd entered Europe, and whether she'd been fingerprinted anywhere else (which would make her the responsibility of the country in question), she stated that, while she remembered leaving Libya in a boat, she had no memory of the next stage of her journey until she found herself wandering the streets of Catania in Sicily. It was this flaky answer that had landed her in Creech Hill, her detention considered a fast-track case that would result in deportation. But as the medical staff at Creech Hill had discovered, Zahra Idris's case was by no means cut and dry.

'That period you cannot remember,' said Sam. 'Does it feel as if you might have met him then?'

Zahra nodded.

'Can you describe him?'

There was a visible shudder, as if revisiting the man's face caused genuine revulsion.

'He's white. He was wearing a suit. He came into the new recreation room with some others. He has grey hair. About your height.'

Her eyes had glassed. She was shaking.

'You can't remember what he did to you. But you're scared.'

She looked up. Face stony. 'When I saw him, I felt terror. Like he'd done something evil.'

Sam's heart had begun to beat faster, as if over-empathising with Zahra. Beneath this anxiety was a sadness for her. He thought of all she'd been through. And now she was facing this.

'Evil,' he repeated.

Zahra's mouth opened but the sound that came out was a dry croak. As if her brain were not able to formulate the words.

'Have you told the guards?'

Zahra broke her stare and looked at her hands resting on the table, the fingers splayed wide. Her head moved rapidly from side to side.

'Do you want me to talk to someone about it?'

'Please,' she said. 'Help me.'

Then, in a sudden movement, she was on her feet. She wiped her eyes with the back of her hand, looked at Sam one last time, then moved as swiftly out of the room as she'd entered.

Chapter 4

Creech Hill Immigration Centre

Watching them through a one-way mirror that looked down on the visitors' hall, Tapper felt his heart pound against his ribs like a jackhammer. He couldn't be sure, but he had the horrible feeling that the woman had told her visitor.

She was now walking away, her face stricken. Tapper glanced at the man. He looked like he'd seen a ghost.

Fuck, thought Tapper.

The one-way mirror looked down on a hall and several rows of tables, most occupied by detainees and visitors.

The governor was wittering on about confidentiality, and how tables were spaced sufficiently to allow a degree of privacy.

'All the tables are pre-booked,' he added. 'Otherwise it would be a right bloody bun-fight.'

'I see,' said Tapper, his body cold.

Some naively optimistic part of him had begun to wonder whether he hadn't simply locked eyes with a paranoid detainee who happened to look like the person from his darkest nightmare. But then a woman had walked into the room below, her back to them. She was black, a ponytail of curls bouncing as she moved, shoulders hunched. She wore jogging bottoms, trainers and a t-shirt. She sat down at a table, opposite a white man. It was then she looked to her side and behind, and Tapper realised, with a stabbing sensation in his stomach, that his initial impression had been absolutely right. It was her. A face he could never forget.

To his side, a guard was sitting in front of a pair of monitors. Tapper noticed that one screen was filled with row upon row of columns and boxes, each filled with names and times.

'What's that?' he asked, though he'd already guessed the answer.

The governor nodded to the guard. 'It corresponds to the booking system,' said the man. 'Tells us who's at which table.'

Tapper looked down at the hall. The man was pulling on his coat, readying to leave. Tapper made a mental note of the table's location.

'Interesting. May I have a look?' Tapper was already resigned to the prospect of never discovering her name. Her meeting was over, after all.

Another nod from the governor. The guard shifted his seat a little so that Tapper could move closer. He rested his palms on the desk and leaned in to look at the screen.

'This is excellent,' he said. His eyes scanned through the columns till he found the box that corresponded with the woman's table.

'We have to allot thirty minutes for each meeting but they're often over quicker than expected,' explained the guard. 'Even if the table is empty, it remains booked and we can't use it.'

'Another human rights issue, I'm afraid,' muttered the governor. 'Wastes so much time.'

Tapper stared at the information in the box. Zahra Idris, it read. And Sam Keddie, psychotherapist. 1.10pm – 1.40pm.

He looked down at the hall. The table was empty. He glanced at the time in the corner of the screen. 1.16pm.

So that was her name. Zahra Idris. And she'd told her shrink, he was sure of it.

His mind raced. Who else might she tell? Other detainees was one thing – they were less credible – but what about professionals?

'I'm interested in how you vet visitors,' he said, winging it. 'Presumably you don't let anyone in.'

'There's an assessment process,' said the governor. 'Professionals tend to sail through. Family members can take a bit longer. Often we discover people are not who they claim to be.'

'I can well imagine.'

The guard by Tapper's side spoke up. 'You can hover over the detainee's name for a full list. Look.'

The guard moved his cursor slowly across the screen. As it passed over the detainees' names, boxes containing anything between two and ten names appeared.

'This is marvellous,' said Tapper. 'May I?'

The governor laughed. 'Be my guest, Sir Harry. Glad you're impressed. We try and keep a tight ship.'

Tapper leaned in again and began moving the cursor across the screen. Feigning general interest, he paused three times before he reached Idris. Touching her name with the cursor, he hoped to God the list was small. There was only so much he could remember and Christ, if she was telling the world, then he was truly fucked.

A small box opened. Just two names. The shrink's he already knew. The other was a solicitor, Thomas Fitzgerald.

He played with the mouse for a moment longer, mulling his next move. If he was right, Keddie already knew. And there was nothing stopping her telling Fitzgerald, too.

He slid the mouse back towards the guard, then glanced at his watch.

'Damn,' he said to the governor. 'There is something I need to get back to London for. So sorry to mess you around.'

'I cancelled your appointment, Sir Harry,' said Jenny, as they made their way across the car park. 'We could have stayed.'

'It's fine,' said Tapper, knowing that his PA would not pry. She was used to managing both his diary and occasional mood changes.

Jenny fell silent and Tapper began thinking again. Idris was a no-one. A terrified, vulnerable asylum seeker. In an ideal world, he'd sabotage her claim and send the bitch packing to wherever she came from. But he couldn't possibly show interest in one immigrant's case, and certainly not without arousing suspicion.

So what did that leave him with?

And then it hit him. He needed to ensure that she understood she could not speak about this any more. So even if she had already told her shrink, solicitor and God knows who else, she would not mention it again, and any further investigation into her story died there and then.

This effectively meant threatening her. And how did he achieve that without compromising himself?

Ahead, a black Mercedes was waiting for them, the engine purring.

Accompanied by a brief heave of nausea, Tapper had the answer. It was discomforting, to say the least. He hadn't even had a parking ticket since his spell in Ipswich Young Offenders. But then, he countered, this was hardly the crime of the century. Just a short and sweet solution. One that Zahra Idris would, if she had a grain of sense, understand fully.

It was time to contact an old friend.

They reached the car. Tapper held a finger up to Jenny, indicating that he wanted a moment. As Jenny climbed in, he walked to the rear of the vehicle. Pulling his mobile from his pocket, he searched the contacts, then tapped on a name.

The phone rang. A man's voice answered.

'Pat,' said Tapper, 'it's Harry. We need to talk.'

Chapter 5

Basildon railway station, Essex

Sam huddled with the other passengers in a small waiting room at the station, no one saying a word as they stood as close to the one electric heater as they could without touching.

A ferocious winter had the UK in its grip, which meant that being outdoors, even for a short time, was a deeply unpleasant experience. The latest forecast suggested a heavy downfall of snow in the coming days.

Sam caught a glimpse of himself in the glass. A head poking out of the upturned collar of his pea coat. Short hair turning silver and a jaw that needed a shave. He sorely regretted not wearing a hat.

A train flew past. The journey was normally a good place to write up Zahra's notes. But today Sam couldn't shake off the image of her stricken face. He'd never seen her like this before. On the one hand, the recognition was a good sign. Memories might be returning. But this particular recollection was clearly terrifying.

Until now, her memory loss had been no hindrance to therapy. There was plenty to talk through besides that brief lost period – life living under a repressive regime in Eritrea, where Zahra had been imprisoned twice for speaking up against the government. The hell of her journey through

Africa – crawling through trenches into Ethiopia, hiding from government gangs in basements in Khartoum, passing out from thirst in the stifling rear of a truck crossing the Sahara.

Besides, Sam had been told by his supervisor that Zahra's retrograde amnesia was in all likelihood induced by a head injury – she'd described 'waking' in Catania with a splitting headache, a crust of dried blood to the back of her head – which made psychotherapy all but redundant. Had the amnesia been the result of emotional trauma, Sam knew of interventions that might have helped. But in this instance, time and rest were the only possible treatments.

Now, if Zahra was right about that man, the lost period was significant.

What had she said? An evil man in a suit. It sounded crazy. Perhaps the pressures were getting to her. Given what most immigrants had gone through, mental illness was always a possibility. Either way, he was sure of one thing. Zahra needed protecting.

He inched out of the waiting room into the cold, pulled his phone from a pocket and called his supervisor at Creech Hill. It went straight to voicemail.

'Linda, it's Sam. I'm worried about Zahra. She's seen someone at the centre – a white man in a suit, about my height, with grey hair. I'll give you more background when we next meet, but in a nutshell, Zahra is convinced the man is a threat to her. She even used the word "evil". Can you ask the guards to keep an eye on her?'

Sam ended the call. The tannoy was announcing the arrival of his train. He'd soon be in the warmth of his home. There was dinner with Eleanor to look forward to.

But even as he thought of the evening ahead, he couldn't shake the image of Zahra's terrified face.

Chapter 6

Tapper pulled tight the cashmere scarf around his neck. A wind that seemed to have blown direct from Siberia was whipping through the basement of the multi-storey car park. He stamped his hand-made shoes, desperate to generate some heat.

He hated the cold. It reminded him of his father's pitiful existence. How he'd stood, chilled to the core, selling fruit and veg from a stall in Romford Market. As a teenager, Harry Tapper had vowed to live a life as far removed from the man as was humanly possible.

Most people would have acknowledged that Tapper had achieved just that. Thanks to the substantial security empire he'd founded, he pocketed over £1 million a year, and that was before all the dividends. He had properties in London, New York, Cape Town and the Cotswolds. There was also a 50-metre superyacht.

And yet here he was in a car park in the middle of the night trying to ensure that the empire he'd so carefully built did not get reduced to rubble.

'Harry.'

Tapper turned. Dressed in a bomber jacket and tight jeans, Pat Wallace stood before him. Wallace had always been powerfully built, but since leaving the army, much of it had turned to fat. The years had been unkind in other respects. They were both in their early fifties, but in contrast to Tapper's clear skin and abundant hair, Wallace's head was shaved, his once-handsome face now creased and lined. Above the collar of his jacket were the remains of a tattoo, now a grey-blue blur.

'I probably shouldn't call you that,' said Wallace with a nervous smile. 'You being the CEO and me a humble guard at Creech Hill.'

'It's fine, Pat,' replied Tapper.

'You look well.'

'So do you.'

Wallace emitted a sad little chuckle.

'So,' he said, 'if this is an Ipswich Young Offenders reunion, where are the others?'

Wallace was no fool. The clandestine nature of the meeting suggested an exchange that was not to be witnessed – or recorded.

'I'm in a bind, Pat. I need to ask a big favour.'

'Name it,' said Wallace.

Tapper had a fleeting glimpse of the cell he and Wallace had shared all those years ago in Ipswich. He often thought of that time as a comforting period, when his daily concerns were a lot simpler – certainly compared with now.

Faced with the prospect of actually asking the favour, Tapper felt his jaw clench.

'I want you to chat to a detainee at Creech Hill. Tell her not to talk.'

Wallace's eyes widened a fraction. 'About what?'

'What she saw. She'll know what you're referring to.'

Wallace stared at Tapper, doubt written all over his face.

'I need this thing very badly, Pat. You have skills. Stealth being one of them.'

Tapper was referring to Wallace's spell as a burglar, which he'd fallen into after leaving Ipswich. He had a real flair for it, but one evening he broke into a house and was confronted by the owner, clutching a wrench. The man hit

Wallace with the tool, but Wallace managed to disarm him. He then attacked him so violently, the man nearly died. He was sent down for eight years.

Wallace slapped his belly. 'I'm not so stealthy these days, Harry.' He frowned. 'Christ, you know I'd do anything for you, but this could get me in a whole pile of shit.'

Released in his late twenties, Wallace was determined to go straight. He joined the army, saw action in the Gulf, which Tapper suspected was a useful outlet for the violence that was never far from the surface. But after cuts to the armed forces, he found himself unemployed. Despite his time in the army, people were reluctant to take on an ex-con. So he came to Tapper for help, and his old cellmate, who owed Wallace a debt of gratitude that dated back to Ipswich, gladly secured him a job at Creech Hill.

'I really need this, Pat. The woman has something on me.'

Wallace's face grappled with doubt. He seemed about to ask a question, then changed his mind.

'It's going to be tough getting into the women's wing.'

'You know the place. Its rhythms. You'll find a way.'

'And what if I get caught?'

Tapper, anticipating Wallace's reluctance to get involved in anything that might jeopardise his job, dipped a leather-gloved hand into the inside pocket of his coat and pulled out an envelope in which he'd placed £1,000 in cash. He handed it to Wallace.

'I wouldn't ask if I wasn't desperate, Pat.'

Wallace tore the envelope open with a fat finger, staring numbly at the cash.

'There's a grand in there,' said Tapper.

'Christ, Harry,' said Wallace, apparently moved. 'Thank you,' he said, stuffing the envelope inside his bomber jacket. 'So when do you want me to do this?'

'Tomorrow, if possible.'

'That doesn't give me any time to prepare.'

'It's rather urgent.'

'What's the name of this woman?'

Tapper heard a rustling noise behind him and turned, spooked. A plastic shopping bag was flying across the concrete floor of the basement, caught up in the wind. He breathed deeply, then turned back to Wallace.

'Zahra Idris,' he said.

Having said the woman's name out loud, Tapper felt a rush of fear and paranoia, as if a poison had been injected directly into his veins.

'Let me know how it goes,' said Tapper.

Wallace nodded again.

'And thank you, Pat.'

They shook, Wallace's hand strong and cold. Tapper caught a stench of body odour at war with cheap aftershave – a smell that was both acrid and strangely comforting.

It was odd, thought Tapper, that he felt more at ease with Pat Wallace than he ever did with the people Yvonne invited round.

Wallace turned on his heel. Tapper watched the hulking figure retreat across the car park, aware that his former cellmate was, in effect, his only hope.

Chapter 7

Creech Hill Immigration Detention Centre

As one of Creech Hill's longer-serving detainees, Zahra had seen room-mates come and go. Her current one was a Pakistani girl, who was due to be deported in a matter of days. Zahra spoke Tigrinya, Arabic and English. The Pakistani girl spoke only Urdu. So they nodded and smiled at each other, miming anything that needed clarification.

The girl was a devout Moslem, who prayed the obligatory five times a day, starting with Fajr dawn prayers. Although her mobile phone alarm, which went off at around 5.45am, always woke Zahra, the girl tip-toed around the room like a mouse, exiting in near silence, turning the key in the lock with the lightest of touches.

But this morning Zahra could not get back to sleep. The man's face appeared before her in the darkness, as it had repeatedly in the night. She felt a shudder of horror run through her, and longed to know why he caused such a reaction.

A few minutes later, she heard the key turn. For some reason, the girl was back early. Perhaps she'd forgotten something. The door eased open and a shaft of light from the corridor sliced into the room.

Zahra froze. It was not the girl. The silhouette framed by the open door was a man. A huge figure with broad shoulders. Zahra sat up in bed, pulling the duvet up around her, feeling naked despite the t-shirt she wore.

She'd heard of this happening. The male guards who sneaked into the women's wing. One had been caught masturbating while watching a girl shower. Another had forced himself on a young Somali girl who was due for deportation the next day. Nothing had happened to that guard. Was this him? She felt her skin prickle with fear.

The man moved into the room, but did not close the door. Zahra pressed back against the wall behind her. She looked for a weapon of some sort. Anything to beat him away with. There was a book by the bedside table, a small metal table lamp. She reached down with her left hand, unplugged the lamp, then grabbed its shaft.

He stopped by the bed, sat down, seemingly unperturbed by the sight of her hand on the lamp. The springs creaked under his weight. In the dark, his face was in deep shadow, his features hidden. But she could smell him. The light changed fractionally and Zahra noticed another figure at the doorway. Someone was keeping watch.

'I've come to give you a message,' the man said.

He was so close Zahra caught a whiff of his stale, early morning breath, too. Her hand tightened around the lamp's shaft.

The figure at the door spoke. 'Need to get a move on.' It was a woman's voice. 'There's a gang heading this way.'

The man looked in the door's direction, distracted for a second. Zahra lashed out with the lamp, striking him on the side of the head.

The man cried out in pain. 'Bitch!'

He reacted with a speed that belied his weight, twisting on the bed and grabbing Zahra's biceps with both hands, pinning her against the wall.

Zahra screamed out. 'Help! Help!'

There was a noise from the corridor. A sound of voices raised.

'We've got trouble,' said the woman at the door.

The man hissed his next words, his bitter breath hot against her face. 'You need to keep your mouth shut, bitch. Understand?'

Zahra, though physically paralysed and all too aware of the damage a man his size could inflict, felt the blood rush to her face. 'Get your hands off me!' she screamed.

The door was pushed open wide, light from the corridor pouring in. There were other figures there. The Moslem girls back from prayers, taking in the scene before them.

'Understand?' the man repeated.

The woman at the door – now visible in her guard's uniform of white shirt and black trousers – was pushed aside and Zahra's room-mate and four others barged in. The Pakistani girl began barking at the man in Urdu. The man unclasped Zahra, stood to his full height, hoping to intimidate. But Zahra's room-mate, with deportation so close, clearly felt she had nothing to lose. Her voice grew louder. The others were joining in, ranting angrily.

'Girls!' shouted the female guard, who'd moved into the room, 'we all need to calm down here.'

The women turned to the guard, momentarily distracted. The man spotted an opportunity and tried to slip out the door into the corridor.

'Where are you going?' Zahra shouted, leaping out of bed and pulling on a pair of jogging bottoms.

The girls immediately turned on him, blocking his path. They circled the man, jabbing at his chest with their fingers, voices hurling abuse in languages she was sure he wouldn't understand.

Finally he cracked, slamming a mighty slab of hand into the Pakistani girl's face. She dropped to the floor like a discarded toy. The man and his female sidekick rushed out of the door and to the left. Zahra helped the women pull the Pakistani girl, whose nose was now bleeding, from the floor. The assault had done nothing to shut her up. She was raging at the top of her voice and, having steadied herself, led the group, Zahra included, in pursuit of the guards. They were not going to get away with this.

Women had emerged from their rooms in the corridor. The Moslem girls shouted down the hall. Whatever was said was enough to rally a further handful of women.

Ahead, the female guard was fumbling with a key in a lock, the man at her side. Finally she opened a door and the two of them disappeared inside. But there was no time to lock it behind them. Zahra and the women were there in seconds.

They emerged into a large laundry area. A bank of washing machines was ranged along one wall, while industrial presses and dryers lined the other side. The two guards had raced to the far end of the room, but Zahra could tell something was wrong. The woman was trying to open the door with a key but it wouldn't budge. The man was now pounding on it with his fist.

The girls began moving down the room, a collective anger – at past humiliations and abuse from guards, at the injustice of their situation – growing with every step. With a matter of metres between them, the man grabbed at a laundry cart on wheels and pushed it at the women. The cart, weighed down with sheets but shoved with all the man's strength, came flying at them like some enormous missile. Zahra and the others just managed to scatter in time, leaving the cart to crash into a washing machine, the glass window at the front shattering.

The man then grabbed a large plastic container from a shelf and hurled it at them. There was a cry as it hit the Pakistani girl on the head, splitting on impact. She began screaming and clawing frantically at her eyes and cheeks. The liquid was burning her face.

In seconds, another bottle came flying in their direction. This one exploded on the floor, where most of the liquid from the first bottle had pooled.

They were exposed, in danger, and Zahra and a group of others rushed to take shelter behind the laundry cart. As they huddled down, she caught sight of two women leading the

Pakistani girl back towards the corridor. Zahra could hear the sound of the man's fist hammering on the door, and the girl's wailing.

The air began to fill with a sharp smell, as if the two liquids had combined to become something more deadly. At first, it irritated Zahra's eyes, but then she could feel it burning. She had to get out of the room.

She looked behind. As the women helping the Pakistani girl were now discovering as they wrenched at the door handle, they had locked themselves in.

Zahra glanced to her right. Above a bank of dryers there were windows. Without hesitation, she ran to the nearest dryer, climbed on top and turned the handle. It opened, blasting her face with icy air. The window frame was rectangular, wider than the average person. Below, about six feet, was a bed of shrubs. Beyond was a car park and, in the distance, a break in the wire fence that surrounded Creech Hill, where there was a security office and a barrier that was now lifting to allow a car in. She looked down the room where the two guards had been. They were gone. But their door now stood ajar. Just to her left, the women hiding behind the laundry cart were coughing. If escaping the gas was the only priority, they could all have simply moved through the open door. But Zahra knew she was no longer safe inside Creech Hill.

'If you want to leave this place, now's your chance!' she shouted at the hacking women. Some were too weak to stand, but five moved towards her.

As Zahra helped the women clamber through the window, there was a shout from the opposite end of the room. She shot a look in that direction. Guards were spilling through the doorway. By the laundry cart, the remaining women were wheezing, gasping for air. At the other door, the Pakistani girl collapsed to the ground. The two women helping her were crying out. Zahra wanted desperately to help but knew it was a matter of seconds before the guards reached the dryer and grabbed at her legs.

The woman in front of her eased through the window. A guard was running towards the dryer, arms outstretched. Zahra placed both hands on the window frame, pulled her body up, then leaned out of the opening until momentum tipped her forward, and she dropped.

She landed on her belly, the shrub's small, sharp branches tearing at her t-shirt, cutting her stomach. She cried out but was soon being pulled to her feet by two women. They ran as a group into the car park, weaving between stationary vehicles. Overhead lights cast an orange glow over the space, the tarmac sparkled with frost. One woman slipped, but was soon dragged to her feet.

Ahead, the security office had been alerted. The man who emerged was in his sixties, overweight. He raised a hand helplessly at the women but they simply sped past him, ducking under the barrier and running out of the open gate.

Chapter 8

Stoke Newington, London – 8am

Sam flicked the kettle on to make coffee. Eleanor was already gone. She had a meeting in Birmingham that morning and had left just after 6am.

The radio was on and the news was being read. The kettle came to a boil. Sam spooned granules into the mug, added milk, then poured water in.

'Reports are coming in of a riot at Creech Hill Immigration Detention Centre in Essex,' intoned the newsreader.

Sam froze.

'There are suggestions that two detainees have died during the incident, which took place early this morning. It's believed that several inmates have escaped. Creech Hill is one of three immigration detention centres run by Tapper Security in the UK. More details on this story as soon as they become available.'

The item was over, the newsreader now talking about a speech by Prime Minister Gillian Mayer about a more joined-up approach to tackling what she described as 'the morally repugnant issue of human trafficking'.

Sam began feverishly processing the implications of what he'd just heard. Was the riot anything to do with Zahra's fearful statement yesterday? Was she safe?

He went upstairs and grabbed his jacket, which was lying over a chair in the bedroom. He rummaged through the pockets until he found his mobile. He phoned Linda. It went straight to voicemail, so Sam called the charity's office at Creech Hill, but that was engaged. Still gripping his mobile, he went back downstairs to the sitting room, hoping the television would offer more details.

The item on Creech Hill that he eventually found showed a reporter outside the centre's gates. The woman was wearing a thick coat and scarf, her breath turning to vapour.

'According to a source inside the centre,' she said, 'the riot broke out at around 6am shortly after a woman in her 30s displaying violent behaviour was restrained by guards. The guards were set upon by other detainees and forced into a laundry area, where they became trapped. Cleaning fluids were used as missiles and it's believed that spillages of ammonia and bleach combined to form the potentially hazardous gas, chloramine. It's now confirmed that one detainee has died from inhalation of the gas, another has suffered severe facial burns and a guard is being treated for injuries. Six detainees have escaped.'

Sam drew slim comfort from the fact that there'd been only one death, not two as originally suggested. But mention of a woman in her 30s made his stomach pool with anxiety. Was it Zahra? And if so, had she been injured? Christ, what if she was the fatality mentioned?

Sam tried the office number again. This time, to his huge relief, it rang. A woman's voice, harried, answered with the charity's name.

Sam explained who he was and asked to speak to Linda.

'I'm afraid she's tied up, as you can imagine.'

'Can you just confirm whether a client of mine is safe? An Eritrean woman. Zahra Idris.'

There was a pause at the other end. 'We're still struggling to piece things together.'

'Of course,' Sam said. He felt chastened. They had better things to do.

'Hold the line a moment. I'll see what I can find out.'

Sam's ear filled with a slow-paced and crackling piece of muzak. Then, a minute or so later, it abruptly ended and the woman's voice came on again.

'You asked about Zahra Idris.'

'Yes.'

'She's escaped.'

'Shit,' he said. 'And was she the woman being restrained?'

The woman paused. 'I'm not able to talk about that,' she said, with evident discomfort. 'There's going to be an investigation.'

'Can you ask Linda to call me back?'

'I'll ask, but I can't guarantee it'll be today. It's mayhem here.'

The phone call over, Sam realised that he had less than fifteen minutes before his first client showed. His head was spinning with the morning's news. It was too late to cancel but he had to call his other clients. There was no way he'd be able to sit calmly through the rest of the day.

The woman had neither denied nor confirmed that Zahra was the one who'd been restrained, but her voice said it all.

Had Zahra spun out, become violent, as the news item suggested? Or was something more sinister occurring?

One thing was certain. Whatever happened had convinced Zahra that she wasn't safe inside Creech Hill, and escaping was the only option.

From what Sam had gathered, Zahra's case for asylum was compelling. What had begun as a fast-track detention leading inexorably towards deportation had changed course when scars – the signs of repeated beatings – were found on her back by Creech Hill medical staff. She refused to talk about them, but did speak about her incarceration in Eritrea's most notorious prison. Her identity, as the daughter of a prominent critic of the regime – a former senior army officer – was confirmed. Her lawyer began arguing that sending her home would without doubt put her in grave danger. Despite Home Office grumbles about what was referred to as

Zahra's 'selective memory', the omens began to look positive. Zahra dared to hope. To dream that asylum would be granted, that she'd start a new life in the UK, that her son would be able to join her from Eritrea.

If Sam knew Zahra at all, then she would only have thrown that away if she was bloody terrified.

He had to find out about the man in the suit. It started with him. Of that, Sam was convinced.

Chapter 9

Basildon, Essex

'What happened this morning?'

It was midday. Tapper stared out of the front window of his Range Rover on to a field still covered with the morning's frost, the ploughed earth rigid in the cold.

The warm air in the car began to fill with his old cellmate's smell, as Wallace's version of the story slowly unravelled.

By the time Wallace got to the part about flying missiles and his escape back into the men's wing, Tapper felt his bowels loosening.

He now had two crises on his hands. A very public fall-out from the riot at Creech Hill. And, more importantly, Zahra Idris. She had not responded as expected to a threat from the intimidating bulk of Pat Wallace. Quite the opposite, by the sounds of it. The woman was, by all accounts, feisty, head-strong, angry. And now on the loose.

'So,' said Tapper, his mouth dry, 'plenty of witnesses to your presence in the women's wing.'

'There's going to be an investigation, isn't there? And I'll get called in. You don't exactly get promoted after something like this.'

Tapper continued staring at the field. He could feel a headache developing above his eyes. With a thumb and forefinger, he massaged around the bridge of his nose. What the fuck had he been thinking, sending Wallace – with his predilection for violence – into the women's wing?

A press conference at Tapper Security's HQ in Southampton Row was scheduled for the afternoon, by which time a soothing message about the Creech Hill incident was needed. He'd heard that the PM was fuming.

'You're right,' Tapper said, thinking out loud, 'there will be an investigation. But I can delay that. In the meantime, perhaps you need to have a bit of sick leave. Call it stress. I'm sure we can spin this. Say you were called in to help with the restraint of a violent woman. Blame the riot on a bunch of crazies who were already baying for blood. But I think it's probably best you don't return.'

Wallace's eyes were fixed on an indeterminate point in the bleak field ahead. Tapper could see he was wounded. The man had just lost his job – his one-and-only hope of employment after prison. They went back a long way, but would bitterness get the better of him? Would Wallace start mouthing off?

And what did he do about Idris? The woman was dangerous. With the right allies – a solicitor being one – she might just start a fire. They'd been careful, destroyed the evidence. But all it took was a strand of fucking hair.

Tapper felt a rising panic at the thought of what this demanded, the steps that were now required, the line that would need to be crossed. But desperate times called for desperate measures.

He glanced at his old cellmate. Tapper knew that, if he was going to pursue this matter to a satisfactory conclusion, he needed assistance. Things hadn't gone well at Creech Hill, but Wallace could not be wholly blamed for how it had turned out. Now very much available, he was the obvious candidate. And there was another advantage to keeping him on board. Paying Wallace would take the sting out of his sudden redundancy – placating him, lessening the chances of him blabbing out of anger.

'How about you work for me now?' said Tapper, a new course of action taking shape in his head.

'I'd appreciate it, Harry.'

'But on an informal, cash-in-hand basis. This Idris business needs tidying up.'

Wallace turned in Tapper's direction, a question forming on his face. There was a cut and a bruise on his left temple from where he'd been struck by the lamp.

'You gave me a chance when no one else would, Harry, and I really appreciate that. And last time we met I didn't ask too many questions 'cos I could see you wanted to keep everything under the radar. But, given how things have changed, I think I'm entitled to know what I'm involved in.'

Tapper understood. Wallace had lost his job and the mention of cash suggested more dodgy activity. But there was no way he was incriminating himself by telling the full story.

He felt the bile rise in his stomach at the thought of revealing even a snapshot of what had happened.

'I was involved with something last summer. Something that went horribly wrong.' A shiver of disgust ran through him. 'Idris witnessed it all.'

Tapper hoped it was enough to satisfy Wallace.

There was silence. Then: 'We all make mistakes, Harry. Christ, I'm no angel.'

'I will tell you the rest, Pat. But it's a long story, and now's not the moment.'

'In your own time, Harry.' A smile spread across Wallace's face. 'The pay at Creech Hill was shit anyway.'

Tapper felt his eyes well, not just with gratitude, but at Wallace's lack of judgement. The man knew him when he was nothing, a terrified young convict. He had always accepted him. How could he have doubted him?

They locked eyes for a moment – an unspoken message passing between them – before Tapper broke away, the intensity of the moment deeply unsettling.

He thought of his next request, and now anxiety began spreading queasily in his gut. He breathed in, steadying himself. His hands were sweating as he pulled a leather Smythson notebook from his pocket, opening it to scribble down a couple of names. He peeled the sheet from the pad and handed it to Wallace.

'I need you to search their places,' Tapper said. 'Both their homes and offices. Find anything that links me and Zahra Idris. Keddie's a shrink and Fitzgerald's a solicitor. You OK to find the addresses?'

Tapper could see that whatever Wallace had been expecting, it wasn't this. Just yesterday he'd been in legal employment. Now that was over and he was being asked to break into people's property.

'Shall we say a grand per address?'

Seconds passed, then the doubt dissipated. 'Appreciate it, Harry.'

'Can you get going as soon as possible? Time is not on our side.'

'I'm right on it.'

'Sort this out and I'll find you something more –'

'Legal?'

The two former cellmates from Ipswich exchanged a smile. 'Quite,' said Tapper.

*

They drove back to Basildon in silence. Tapper dropped Wallace off on a street corner, then took the A127 back to London. It meant a journey through his old turf in Romford.

The traffic was painfully slow as he circled the roundabout in front of the town hall, the market place to his left, where his dad had sold fruit and veg. He watched a stall holder dancing on his feet to keep warm, the punters thin on the ground. How much would he earn today in such pitifully cold weather?

Strange how our destinies pan out, thought Tapper, in the warm interior of his Range Rover. From the son of a feckless market trader to a multi-millionaire CEO.

Tapper had started out providing humble security systems like CCTV, ?re detection and intruder alarms for high street shops. The firm's clients now included huge multinationals across the globe. For them, security also meant monitoring and response units, and mini armies to provide dense layers of protection, both static and mobile.

Other Tapper offerings included highly-skilled operatives for close protection of celebs, exiled despots and paranoid oligarchs. And of course they ran secure facilities, such as Creech Hill and a handful of young and adult offender institutions, including some in Eastern Europe, India and Israel.

There was a new area too, one which he was certain would, eventually, transform Tapper Security from a firm with a profit of around £240 million last year (not bad when some of his rivals couldn't give shareholders a bean by way of a dividend) to the stratosphere.

He remembered the firm's first prison contract and how the media had been all over him, dragging up the crime that had landed him in Ipswich.

Thanks to his formidable PR machine, the story that stuck was of a loving teenage lad who'd been defending his mother against the blows of a violent, alcoholic dad when he'd pushed him hard against a wall. Not that it wasn't true, of course. But Tapper knew that, in the wrong hands, the story could easily have been one of a young, feral killer.

Tapper drove on, putting distance between him and the town centre. It had always been about controlling the narrative, shaping the story. And that was exactly what they were doing now. Ensuring one particular strand never saw the light of day.

Chapter 10

Stoke Newington, London

Sam spent the day glued to the news, learning nothing. Late in the afternoon, Linda finally called back.

'Sam,' she said, her voice strained. 'I got both your messages about Zahra Idris. Though I suspect your concerns are rather academic now that's she escaped.'

Linda was clearly exhausted, the day's events evidently overshadowing everything. But Sam wasn't letting this one go just yet. 'I mentioned Zahra's description of the man.'

'Most days, this place is crawling with white men wearing suits. They're called lawyers.' The words dripped with sarcasm. 'Besides, there was a tour of Creech Hill that morning. A bus-load of suits – journalists and local councillors mostly. It could have been any one of them. If indeed it was any of them.'

'What do you mean?'

'I can't comment on her mental health – she's your client, not mine – but what she said to you doesn't bode well.'

Something flared in Sam. 'And that's your line, then?'

'I'm sorry?'

'That she was losing it. And therefore needed restraining.'

'As you've already been told,' said Linda, her voice prickly, 'there's to be an investigation. I can't discuss the day's events. But I think you may be over-stepping your responsibilities as her therapist. Now, if you'll excuse me, I've had a bloody awful day and I need a bath and a glass of wine.'

The line went dead.

It was late afternoon, dark outside. Sam stood to draw the curtains. Perhaps Zahra wasn't who she appeared to be. Perhaps her mental health was more fragile than he realised. Perhaps she had got violent.

Whatever the truth of the matter, he knew one thing. Eleanor was expected back at any minute, and he'd promised to cook.

Outside, Sam pulled his collar up and yanked down his beanie so that as little of his face as possible was exposed to the biting wind that whipped down his street.

How would Zahra fare now she was out? In all likelihood, she'd head to London. Pinched by a deeper, colder winter than anyone could remember, the city felt far from welcoming. A couple of weeks ago a riot had erupted outside a mosque just down the road in Clapton, supposedly a newly gentrified area. Cars had been set on fire, shops looted. It was not an isolated incident. Aggression aimed at immigrants rarely seemed out of the news.

Emerging on the high street, Sam headed to a Turkish Cypriot supermarket. He was looking forward to seeing Eleanor and was determined not to let his musings ruin the evening. He smiled at the prospect of greeting her as she came through the door. He imagined her shedding her thick coat and them kissing, a whiff of her citrus-based scent and the heat of her body filling his nostrils.

Over the last year or so, he'd often wondered whether their relationship would survive, forged, as it had been, in such adrenaline-fuelled circumstances. And would the secret he knew about Eleanor's family worm its way to the surface, its poison corrupting their love? So far, his concerns had proved unfounded. But he had the strong sense that his knowledge was not buried forever.

He bought vegetables and herbs and cut down a small alleyway to his street. The wind was now behind him, clawing at his coat's thick material.

In the distance, he saw a figure emerge from a house near his, a broad barrel of a man, a dark silhouette in what looked like a hoodie. But as Sam got closer, he realised it had been his house. With a lurch in his stomach, he saw that his front door was wide open, the light from the hallway illuminating the path. Sam picked up his pace. Had that been a burglar, seeing Sam nip out and chancing his luck?

The last few steps were taken at a jog before he turned into his path and up to the front door. It was there that Sam froze, his world turned upside down by the sight that greeted him.

Eleanor was slumped on the floor, her back resting against the radiator, eyelids closed. Her head had flopped forward. The bike she'd been riding lay discarded like an unwanted toy against the base of the stairs.

Something snapped in Sam and the bag of groceries dropped from his hand. He ran to Eleanor, collapsing to his knees by her twisted body. He was about to pull her torso away from the radiator but stopped, some trace of first aid knowledge sounding a warning. If her neck was in any way damaged, then he didn't dare move it. He fumbled in his pocket for his phone and, with a shaking finger, dialled 999.

'Emergency services – how may I direct your call?' asked a calm male voice.

'Ambulance.'

'One moment, sir.'

The call was transferred. A female voice this time. Sam was asked for his location and mobile number.

'Can you explain what's happened, sir?'

'My girlfriend has been attacked.' Sam realised he should also have asked for the police, told them about the man he'd seen. 'I need the police too.'

'We will contact them, sir. Now, can you describe what you can see?'

As Sam began to paint the scene before him, he felt the emotion rise up from his stomach like an unstoppable wave, one that threatened to drown him. His breathing started to race, his speech stumbling with every word.

'An ambulance is on its way, sir,' reassured the woman. 'Is your girlfriend conscious?'

Sam looked at Eleanor. Were it not for the awkward angle of her head, she might have been sleeping. Her eyes were closed and there wasn't a trace of fear or trauma on her face.

'No.'

He touched her face gently, whispered her name.

'Please hurry,' he said, his eyes flooding with tears, the emotion finding an outlet even as everything else seemed to shut down. 'Please hurry.'

Chapter 11

Stoke Newington Police Station, London

The interview room was cold, its walls a dull green. The man opposite Sam, who'd introduced himself as DI Carl Emery, rubbed his stubble and sighed. His bloodshot eyes were ringed with grey.

'How would you describe your relationship with Eleanor Scott? Any recent disagreements or arguments?'

Sam shot Emery a withering look. He'd been in the room for over an hour and had told his story at least five times. It was clear the DI was working on the assumption that Sam was the most obvious suspect.

'It's just fine, thanks. I've told you. I was shopping –'

'And you came back to see a large mystery man in a hoodie vacating your home.'

'There's a bag of shopping in the bloody hallway.'

'Which proves nothing. You could have come back and then assaulted your girlfriend.'

'I'm no expert on these matters, but doesn't violence occur in the heat of an argument, perhaps after a drink? Not when two people have just walked in the front door from the cold?'

'You're right, you're not the expert. I am. So let me tell you what I know. In situations like these, it's almost always a male partner or ex-partner who's committed the crime. So until I have evidence that suggests otherwise, it's you I want to speak to.'

There was a knock on the door and a younger man with short, balding hair poked his head into the room.

'Can I have a word, sir?'

'DC Phil Corr has entered the room,' said Emery. He stood and went to the door. There was a hushed conversation, a piece of paper passed from the younger policeman to Emery. The DI looked at Sam with an expression he could not read. Then the other policeman nodded and left the room, closing the door behind him. Emery sat.

'Right, Mr Keddie.' The DI's tone had changed. It was less combative, more appeasing. 'We've made some progress. We now know you were on the high street at the time of the attack. We have a statement from the shopkeeper you mentioned,' he paused to look at the piece of paper, 'Mr Chalayan, as well as CCTV footage of you in the store between 6.12pm and 6.26pm. We also spoke to a neighbour who saw your girlfriend return at around 6.15pm and then, moments later, a man in a hoodie leave.'

'So he was in the house when she arrived?' Sam hadn't thought about how the attack might have happened. He felt a swell of nausea as he pictured Eleanor literally walking into it.

'It would seem that way. We can only assume he was a burglar, who saw you leave and took his chances. But if these timings are right, he was disturbed before he had the opportunity to turn your house over.'

'Nothing was damaged or missing,' Sam said, remembering the dazed inspection of the house he'd been asked to make.

'I'm guessing you hadn't double-locked the front door. So much easier for a skilful burglar to pick.'

Sam buried his head in his hands.

'Mr Keddie,' said Emery. 'At the end of the day, this is about the actions of a violent man, not a slip-up you might have made with your household security.'

Sam emerged from his hands. 'Can I go?'

'You were free to go at any time.'

Sam looked wearily at Emery. 'But it wouldn't have looked good if I had left, would it?'

Emery shook his head. 'Not great.' He paused, attempted a conciliatory smile. 'You understand we have to devote resources to interviewing the most obvious suspect. Which, in this case, was you.'

'I get it,' said Sam flatly. 'But you'll start looking for the man now?'

'We will.' Emery's face softened. 'As soon as your girlfriend regains consciousness, we'll talk to her. And hopefully whatever we find at the house will help. By the way, the crime scene officers will be there overnight, so if you can keep out till the morning.'

Emery stood, his chair scraping the floor. He fished in his pocket, pulled out a card and handed it to Sam. 'Anything you remember, or think is significant, give me a ring.'

Sam took the card.

Emery pursed his lips in a tight smile. 'I wish your girlfriend a speedy recovery, Mr Keddie.'

*

Eleanor lay motionless on her back, a coiling blue tube running into her mouth and industrial levels of wiring and machinery around her bed. Her face looked peaceful yet everything else suggested life clinging on by its fingernails. Sam held her limp hand in his, rubbing his thumb across her smooth skin. Her scent had disappeared, swamped by a hospital whiff of disinfectant.

There was a movement behind him. Sam turned to see a tall Asian man in a white coat.

'Are you Mr Keddie?'

Sam nodded. The Asian man proffered his hand.

'I'm Mr Khan.'

They shook. Khan's handshake was strong and reassuring.

'For obvious reasons,' said Khan, 'Miss Scott has not named her next of kin. But we have discussed the matter with her aunt, who was here earlier, and we would like to keep the two of you informed of Eleanor's condition. How does that sound?'

Sam thought of the fragile remains of Eleanor's family. Eleanor an only child, her mother in the final days of Motor Neurone Disease, her father dead.

'That sounds fine. Thank you.'

Khan led Sam into a seating area opposite Eleanor's room. A few dog-eared magazines lay strewn across a low lying table. To their side was a vending machine packed with chocolate bars and cans of drinks. In another corner was a television, the sound muted. A rolling news programme was on, the screen showing a man in a suit delivering a press conference, the occasional flash of photography illuminating his features. Underneath the image Sam caught the words 'Tapper CEO promises full investigation of Creech Hill riot'.

They sat. It was just after 11pm, the lights dimmed in the corridor beyond.

'Do you know anything about the Glasgow Coma Scale, Mr Keddie?'

Sam shook his head.

'It's a neurological scale. It tests certain responses, helping us record the conscious state of a patient.'

'Right.'

'Eleanor is a three.'

'Sorry,' said Sam. 'But is that good or bad?'

Khan smiled gently.

'It's not good. But we need to do further tests to assess the true extent of her injuries. For now, all we have is her CT scan, which came back clear.'

'Surely that's good news.'

'Not necessarily,' said Khan. 'We'll need to do a little more investigation – an MRI in Eleanor's case – to be really sure of what's going on.'

'I see,' said Sam, numbly.

'Once we have a clearer picture of the nature of her injury, we can talk about treatment.'

'But she'll wake up, right?'

'Let's wait for the results of the MRI,' said Khan.

Sam thought he saw the tiniest flicker in Khan's gaze, as if the consultant couldn't quite maintain eye contact.

'In the meantime, why don't you go home and get some rest?'

'Home's off limits right now. The police are all over it.'

Khan smiled sympathetically. 'Of course.' He looked around the seating area. 'Given the circumstances, why don't you curl up here? I'll let the nurses know.'

Sam opted instead for the chair in Eleanor's room. His body felt leaden, ready to drop, but his mind was wide awake.

A little later a nurse passed the room and looked in. He disappeared for a second then returned with a pillow and blanket which he handed, silently, to Sam. As he exited the room, the nurse left a faint trace of body odour, some suggestion of a long, arduous shift.

In that instant Sam was reminded of the ghostly trace of a presence he'd smelt at the house when he'd arrived to find Eleanor on the floor. It was one that he'd completely failed to tell the police about because of the flood of emotion that had subsequently overwhelmed him. And of course because, with the door wide open and the cold air sucking the heat out of the house, the smell had rapidly evaporated. He tried to recall its constituent parts – it was unpleasant, of that he was certain – but as he struggled to bring it back to life, he could feel it quickly retreating.

It was immaterial in the end. A smell wouldn't identify Eleanor's attacker. Only Eleanor could do that.

And only if she woke.

Chapter 12

Islington, London

Zahra stood in a ragged overcoat she'd found in a shed in countryside near Creech Hill. The material was thin, scant insulation against a wind that seemed to have penetrated her bones. She'd never known cold like this.

In front of her was the canal, the water sluggish and black. Behind was a high wall, beyond a terrace of tall houses, lights on in windows. She'd seen a couple arguing, the man jabbing his finger at the woman. In another, an elderly man shuffled between rooms, his back bent. What she would have given to sit, or better still lie down, in one of those warm homes.

She had made it clear to Fitzgerald that she would not meet anywhere public. So he suggested the Regent's Canal, at the point where St Peter's Street crossed the water to Wharf Road. It had not been easy to find.

She'd tried Sam Keddie three times, but he never answered his phone. He must have heard about the riot. So where was he?

There was a click of heel against stone and she jumped. Turning in the noise's direction, she saw a figure in the distance. She relaxed a fraction. The person coming towards her, difficult to make out at this distance, was certainly not the big man from Creech Hill. He was leaner, taller. Could he be Fitzgerald?

He raised a hand, as if to say hello. Zahra tentatively returned the gesture.

As he got closer, she could see it was Fitzgerald. He smiled, and she felt herself relax further. At last, an ally. Someone who would help her.

The solicitor stopped before her. 'Zahra,' he said, placing a hand gently on her arm. 'Thank goodness you're safe.'

Zahra noticed that his nose and cheeks were a bluish colour.

'What happened today?'

But just as she was about to speak, she caught a glimpse of another figure some distance behind Fitzgerald. The tension that had momentarily dissipated came back like a huge electric shock. He was tall, built like a wall, wearing a hoodie, and jogging in their direction. Was it the man from Creech Hill? She couldn't be sure, but she wasn't hanging around to find out.

Zahra turned and began to run.

'What's going on, Zahra?' shouted Fitzgerald in her wake. 'Come on, we need to talk. I can't help you if you don't speak to me.'

Zahra had reached some steps and briefly turned to look back. Fitzgerald had heard the sound of the approaching figure and was now looking in his direction. The man reached him, moving at a pace.

'Who the hell are you?' called out Fitzgerald.

The man's response was brutal, machine-like. He lashed out with his right hand, the palm outstretched, slamming into Fitzgerald's chest. The solicitor lost his footing, his arms grabbing at air as he tipped backwards. And then there was a splash, as he fell into the water of the canal.

Zahra gasped, as if the breath had been sucked from her lungs. She saw the large man briefly peer over the edge of the towpath at Fitzgerald. Then he looked up at her, a shadowy face under the lip of his hood, and began running again.

Zahra mounted the steps, three at a time, then turned right, sprinting across the bridge. As she ran, she caught the briefest glimpse of Fitzgerald. His mouth was open in a silent cry and he was flailing, as if in slow motion, in the water. She knew what those sluggish limbs showed, that the icy chill of the canal was draining the strength from his body. That soon he'd slip beneath the surface.

She could not stop, could not help him, could not even cry for him. She was being hunted like an animal and the only way to survive was to keep moving.

On the other side of the bridge, she dared to look behind. The man had reached the top of the stairs and was turning on to the bridge when he slipped, his great bulk tumbling to the pavement.

'Fuck!' he shouted.

Zahra seized her advantage, put her head down and sprinted.

It was ten minutes later, when she'd reached the comparative safety of a busy road, that she dared to slow her pace and look again. Her lungs and muscles were screaming out in protest, begging her to rest.

The man was gone. For now. But somehow Zahra knew he would find her again.

Chapter 13

Notting Hill, London

Tapper closed his study door as quietly as possible, placed a glass of Armagnac on his desk, and sat. He drew his mobile from a dressing gown pocket, searched his contacts then tapped a name on the screen.

It was 2am, but the man he was calling needed to know.

It rang six times.

'Yes,' a weary, muddled voice answered.

'It's Harry.'

There was a pause. 'Christ, do you know what time it is?'

'There's something you need to know.'

Another pause, then: 'Wait a sec.'

There was a sound of movement, a muffled apology. Seconds passed, a door closed. 'This had better be good.'

'It's about the riot.'

'You've handled it well. Word is, the PM is appeased. Just make sure the investigation is tied up pronto, the detainees are blamed. You know the score.'

'There's a bit more to it.'

'Go on.'

Tapper started from the moment he'd seen Zahra Idris, then explained how the riot had been entirely of his own making.

When he'd finished there was a moment of silence, then the man on the line hissed: 'You're telling me all this happened because you thought you saw the girl. Christ, Harry. What the hell were you thinking?'

'I tell you, I saw her.'

'But how can you be sure?'

'It was the way she looked at me. It was her, damn it.'

Silence.

'She had that scar,' added Tapper.

'She can't be the only African woman with a scar like that, Harry.' The man's voice had risen a notch. 'It might be some tribal thing.'

'A raised scar above one eye?'

'Really, what are the chances of this?'

'I don't give a shit about odds,' snapped Tapper, his voice louder. He closed his eyes. He had to stay calm. 'It was her, I tell you. If you'd been there, you'd have recognised her too.'

The other man's voice was quieter when he next spoke. 'So what are you going to do now?'

'Don't you mean "we"?'

'Sorry. We.'

'I'm looking for her.'

'What do you mean?'

'She escaped,' said Tapper.

'Oh fuck.' The man's voice sounded choked. 'Do you think she intends to hurt us?'

Tapper thought of the look she gave him. That narrowing of the eyes, what he could only describe as hatred. 'If she could, I think she would.'

There was a deep intake of breath from the other man, as if he were summoning strength. 'Let's be rational about this. What could she really have on us?'

'I'm not prepared to sit on my arse and wait to find out.'

'But who would believe her – an illegal immigrant with a far-fetched story? And even if anyone did, would they have the motivation, let alone energy or resources, to investigate it?'

Tapper took a swig of Armagnac, the liquid tracing a warming passage to his stomach. 'That's what I think when I'm being rational. When I'm not, I think about what she saw.'

'I take it you destroyed the film.'

'Christ. Need you ask?'

The other man paused, weighing up his next words. 'We can't have any more PR disasters, Harry.'

'I notice you're not telling me to stop looking for her.'

'You know I can't get involved.'

'But you'd sleep a lot more comfortably if you were sure she was out of the picture.'

There was silent assent.

'This can go one of two ways,' continued Tapper. 'Either the whole thing dies and we pursue our shared agenda. Or a scandal that would make WikiLeaks sound like office gossip is going to crush us both. I am going to do everything in my power to prevent that from happening. You need to understand that.'

Chapter 14

The Royal London Hospital, Whitechapel

Sam woke. A dull light was leaking through a small gap in the curtains. He was momentarily lost, the grey room around him alien. But then he turned to his left, saw Eleanor, and knew, with a sickening lurch in his stomach, exactly where he was.

He rose from the chair, turning his head from side to side to ease the stiffness in his neck. He went to the window and drew the curtains. It was snowing outside, heavy flakes forming a small wall against the window sill. The hospital rooftops below were covered with up to three inches, save where ventilation shafts puffed steam into the air, leaving a damp patch around their bases. It was as if the capital had been given a benign white cloak, beneath which all manner of dark activities might hide.

'It's snowing,' he said. 'Just as they said it would. This'll slow everyone down.'

He turned to look at Eleanor. She lay still, her eyes closed. She could have been sleeping, just like the night before last when he'd turned off her bedside light. He could feel his eyes prick with tears, and walked out of the room.

In the seating area where he and Khan had spoken, Sam bought a coffee from the machine. A cup dropped into a small compartment and a steaming, grey-brown liquid spat into it. Sam took the cup and sat. A large man snored in a seat nearby, his shirt loose and bunched up, revealing an expanse of hairy belly.

The breakfast news was on, the sound turned down low. Sam moved nearer the television so that he could hear it, desperate for something else in his head. The anchor was talking about the snow. There was an image of Westminster Bridge and a cab skidding on its surface.

Then the anchor was back, saying something about a body found in the Regent's Canal in Islington. There was footage of the scene, police tape stretched around an area of snow on a towpath. Behind, high walls and the backs of Georgian townhouses. Sam knew the spot well. He and Eleanor had shared a bottle of wine there one summer evening. They'd chatted to an old man who'd been sitting in a deck chair, the line of his fishing rod dangling in the canal's murky depths.

A reporter on the scene, bunched up in a puffa jacket, was talking about the person who'd been dragged from the canal. 'The man, Tom Fitzgerald, is a forty-eight-year-old solicitor. Police are still unsure how Mr Fitzgerald ended up in the freezing water but according to sources close to the investigation, officers are following up a number of leads, including the solicitor's most recent phone contacts. Fitzgerald was an immigration specialist, who worked with refugees and asylum seekers.'

Sam's stomach twisted. He and Fitzgerald both worked with the same client group. He might even have crossed paths with the man at Creech Hill. Was Eleanor's attacker also behind the solicitor's death?

Sam rubbed his eyes. He was exhausted, not thinking straight. He began arguing with himself. Bar that one connection, the two events were very different. Fitzgerald had drowned in a canal, who knew how or why. Eleanor had disturbed a burglar. And yet when he factored in Zahra's fears, the riot and her escape, he couldn't shake a feeling of deep foreboding in his gut. That the man who'd thrown Eleanor against a radiator was really after him.

He glanced at his mobile, desperate to distract himself from the dark thoughts in his head. It was 8am. He cursed. His first client arrived in an hour and a half. He needed to cancel – he couldn't work while Eleanor lay in a coma. Sam noticed he had three missed calls from the previous evening, all from the same 0208 number. He'd call back later. Right now, he couldn't face talking to anyone. He needed air.

He stepped back into Eleanor's room – barely able to look at the woman he loved, once so animated, now lying so still – and grabbed his coat. He would walk round the block and use the time to call his clients.

He exited the warm hospital reception area. On the pavement, a narrow footpath had been carved out of the snow and he joined a shuffling file of people battling against a similar line moving in the opposite direction. A bus passed by. The snow had already been churned up by vehicles and the double-decker sent a thick wave of grey sludge on to the pavement and over Sam's shoes.

'Shit,' he said, feeling icy liquid penetrate the leather to his feet. He thought again of Fitzgerald in the canal, and how the same sensation had spread, fatally, through his body.

His mobile began vibrating in his coat pocket. Sam fumbled with a numb hand to pull it out, saw a number he did not recognise, and answered.

'Sam Keddie.'

'Sam.'

At the sound of the softly spoken voice, Sam's skin tingled. It was Zahra.

He halted on the spot, prompting groans of protest from those who'd been walking directly behind him. He dodged to the side into a pile of ankle-deep snow.

'Where are you?'

'I can't tell you.'

'Are you OK?'

There was a pause. 'I didn't kill him.'

'Kill who?'

'Tom Fitzgerald.'

Sam ran a hand through his hair. 'I'm sorry, Zahra, but I don't understand.'

He could hear that she was crying. 'I asked Tom to meet me.'

Sam felt as if the temperature had dropped another degree.

'I was there when he was murdered.'

Chapter 15

The line went dead.

Sam tried the number again. It rang for over a minute, but no voicemail kicked in. He left it a minute, then tried once more, with the same result.

He stood in the snow, the lines of pedestrians moving slowly past him in both directions.

With frozen, lifeless fingers, he began rooting in his pockets, trying to find the card the DI had given him at the police station. Finally he located it. Realising that he didn't want to conduct the conversation within earshot of dozens of people, he edged further into the snow that had been piled up against the side of the makeshift footpath.

The number he called went straight to voicemail. 'This is Detective Inspector Carl Emery. I can't take your call at the moment. If you have an urgent matter that needs attention, please call the incident room on –'

Sam left a message. 'It's Sam Keddie. I've just heard from someone called Zahra Idris. She was a client of mine at Creech Hill Immigration Detention Centre. Until yesterday, when she escaped. She said she was with Tom Fitzgerald when he was murdered. She got cut off and I can't get hold of her now.'

Ending the call, Sam's head began to fill with thoughts, none of them pleasant. Events were beginning to connect and he didn't like where they were leading one bit. His client had talked of feeling terrified of a man at Creech Hill. The next day she escaped during a riot. Hours later, his girlfriend was attacked and then, that same evening, another man linked to Zahra was killed. Sam felt sweat break out on his skin as his earlier theory solidified. Eleanor's attacker was after him.

He stood rooted to the spot, the idea taking hold, poisoning him with its implications. He had brought this on Eleanor. He had put her in that coma.

But why would someone be after him and Fitzgerald? What possible danger did he and the solicitor present? The man who'd terrified Zahra was clearly the key, but without his identity, neither Sam nor Emery would be any nearer finding him. And only Zahra could help with that.

Sam tried Zahra's number again. It rang for about thirty seconds.

'Hello?' A man's voice, slow and deliberate.

'Can I speak to Zahra?'

'What?'

'Zahra Idris. She just called me on this phone.'

'You called me, buddy.' He sounded drunk, his throat rattling like a heavy smoker's.

'Who are you?'

'Terry, mate.'

'And where is this phone?'

'What am I, the fucking operator? Fuck you.'

Terry hung up.

Sam tried again. Minutes passed. He gave up.

As Sam felt frustration building, his mobile began ringing.

'Sam Keddie.'

'Mr Keddie, it's DI Emery.'

Sam repeated everything he could remember about Zahra's phone call.

'She was emphatic about it not being her,' Sam said when he'd finished describing the brief conversation, suddenly aware that, in his haste to contact Emery, he might have implicated an innocent woman.

'We need to discuss Ms Idris urgently, Mr Keddie. Where are you now?'

'Whitechapel. Outside the hospital.'

'Stay where you are. I'm sending a squad car now. Keep out of sight until it arrives.'

Chapter 16

Whitechapel, London

The squad car arrived fifteen minutes later, pulling up outside the hospital entrance.

In the back of the vehicle, the warm air spiked with an acidic note of vomit, Sam wiped a window free of condensation to look out. While traffic moved smoothly enough on treated streets, Londoners were struggling on the pavements. He saw an elderly woman being pulled by two teenage boys off the ground where she'd slipped. Long queues snaked away from bus stops, faces bluey-pink and beaten.

In all likelihood, Zahra was already on Emery's radar. If she'd contacted Fitzgerald, left a message, then they had a record of her asking to meet. She would only be eliminated if there were witnesses to the murder – and in the middle of the night that was unlikely – or she came forward.

In the eastern edges of Stoke Newington the car picked up speed before turning left on to the high street. Five minutes later Sam was deposited outside the police station.

Emery led him to an interview room, identical to the one he'd been in the night before.

'Apologies about the room,' he said. 'No third degree, I promise.' He smiled rather unconvincingly. 'Can I get you a coffee?'

Sam shook his head.

'Right, first things first.' Emery clasped his hands together. 'We need to speak to Ms Idris. Do you have the number she called you from?'

Sam found the number on his mobile and turned the screen to Emery. The DI scribbled it on a notepad then used his own phone. 'Paul, it's Carl. Need a location on this number.' He repeated it twice.

He laid his mobile on the table. 'Can you tell me what you know about Zahra Idris?'

'She's my client.'

'Well before you get tied up in issues of confidentiality, can I remind you how important she is to this enquiry? We have one man dead and your girlfriend –'

Sam raised a hand. 'I get it.'

He gave Emery a pen portrait of Zahra, a brief description of the oppression she was escaping in Eritrea, her journey to the UK, the amnesia, the ups and downs of her asylum claim, and her encounter with the man in the suit. Sam felt grubby, like he'd betrayed her. But the image of Eleanor in that hospital bed soon brought him back to the importance of the task in hand.

'Any previous issues with her mental health? Signs of paranoia?'

'None.'

At this, Emery frowned. 'So, we have an escaped immigrant with amnesia, real or otherwise, who says she saw an evil man in a suit. But she doesn't know why he seemed so threatening.'

'Yup.'

Emery blew out his cheeks. 'Well, we know she contacted Fitzgerald. Left a message begging to meet. But beyond that, there's nothing.'

He leaned forward. 'One thing I do know, Mr Keddie, and it's this. You need to avoid your home for the time being. I don't know how Fitzgerald ended up in that canal or what involvement Ms Idris may or may not have had, but we need to assume you're in danger.'

Sam's heart, which had begun to calm, began hammering again.

Emery's phone rang.

'Paul, what have you got?'

A voice rattled off some details. Emery ended the call.

'It's a payphone on the Holloway Road apparently. So a dead-end.' He scratched the stubble on his jaw.

Sam remembered Terry. He was probably some pisshead stumbling out of a pub.

'Have you got friends or family nearby, some place you can stay?'

'No family,' said Sam, with rather more emphasis than he'd intended. 'And I can't face friends right now.'

'Then check into a hotel. There's one in Stamford Hill which I'd recommend. Not because I've stayed there,' he said, smiling weakly, 'but because it's close. Needless to say, if Idris calls, please tell her to get in touch. We need to speak to her. Now she will understandably think that if she comes forward, she's going to be in shit whichever way it goes. That even if she's cleared of Fitzgerald's death, she'll be going back to Eritrea.' There was a pause. 'So please tell her we will look favourably on any co-operation she can offer.'

Sam nodded. 'I need to go home. Get some clothes.'

'Of course. But you're going in a squad car.'

*

At the house, Sam noticed the torn ends of police tape still attached to the gate. He took his keys and opened the front door.

The police officer who'd accompanied him went first. He peered into the consulting room, sitting room, then kitchen. Re-emerging in the hallway, he mounted the stairs. Moments later he came back down.

'All good.'

Sam went upstairs to his bedroom. He pulled a bag from inside the wardrobe and, numbly, began packing. As he was zipping the bag shut, his phone began to ring. It was another 0208 number. With his pulse gathering speed, Sam answered.

At first there was silence at the other end. Then breathing.

'Zahra?'

'I'm ringing to say goodbye,' came her hushed reply.

Sam swallowed hard. Wherever she was planning to go, he had to stop her.

'You must talk to the police, Zahra. Tell them what you saw.'

'It's not safe to do that.'

Sam thought of Emery's comment about Zahra fearing deportation. He'd been right. 'They said they'd treat your co-operation favourably.'

Sam immediately regretted his words. He thought of the way Emery had paused before making that offer, as if he'd just thought of it. Who was he to make such promises? Only the Home Office could do that. But Zahra's reaction surprised him.

He heard a short, lifeless laugh.

'I'm not scared of being sent back to Eritrea,' she said, some hint of strength in the words. 'I'm scared of them.'

'Who?'

'The police.'

'They're not the same as they are in your country. There are laws in the UK. A justice system.'

'Men in uniform are the worst.'

'I promise, Zahra. The police are different here.'

'I'm leaving,' she said, her voice trembling.

'Please.'

'I can't stay, Sam.'

He paused, aware that his pleading was getting nowhere. 'Where are you going?'

'The last place I felt safe,' she said. 'It wasn't perfect. But it was better than this.'

'Don't do this, Zahra.'

'Goodbye, Sam.'

And with that, she hung up.

Sam called back. Again, the phone rang endlessly. Sam pictured another payphone, Zahra walking rapidly away.

Something about her phrasing triggered a memory. He ran downstairs, into the study. He pulled open a filing cabinet labelled A–J and began sifting through the files. When he got to clients with surnames beginning with 'I', he exhaled. Zahra's file and case notes were still there.

He laid the file on his desk. Opening it, he began leafing through the case notes. A minute later, he found the one he was after. He called Emery.

'Mr Keddie.'

'I've just spoken to Zahra Idris.'

'And?'

'She said she's leaving.'

'Did you tell her we'd look favourably on her co-operation?'

'She's not interested. She said she doesn't trust the police.'

'Bollocks.' There was a pause. 'Did she say where she was heading?'

'That's just it. She said she was going to the last place she felt safe. I've just looked through my case notes and found a mention of Amsterdam, where she lived before coming to the UK. She described a kind of community. A mix of East African immigrants and Europeans. She didn't exactly spell it out, but it was clear some of them worked in the sex trade. She said they looked out for each other – and that she felt safe. Believe me, she's never used that word to describe the places she's been since.'

There was a loud exhalation. 'It's not enough.'

'What do you mean?'

'Let's say she does manage to get to Amsterdam without a passport. The only thing we can do is get a photo and description alert out to Strasbourg, who'll hand it over to the Dutch Bill. But, like I said, it won't be enough.'

'I don't understand.'

'Every year, people with National Insurance numbers, passports, bank accounts, Facebook profiles, jobs, friends and family disappear in the UK and all over Europe. Tracing them is hard enough. Zahra Idris is an immigrant, living below the radar. The only way they're going to find her is if she turns up for another reason.'

'So we just let her disappear.'

'No, Mr Keddie. We continue to look for her. Right now, my colleagues are making enquiries within the capital's Eritrean community. We are also analysing everything we found at your house. Hoping that your intruder has slipped up, left some trace of DNA. There are numerous lines of enquiry. In the meantime, I strongly urge you to book into that hotel.'

Sam hung up, too irritated to continue the conversation.

It was then that his eyes drifted to the desk.

Numb with shock the previous evening after discovering Eleanor, he hadn't noticed it. But now he could see a conspicuous gap next to a pile of paperwork. His laptop was missing.

It had been a gift from Eleanor, who couldn't believe that Sam still wrote up his case notes by hand. But her attempt to change his behaviour had failed. He preferred the way his thoughts emerged and solidified while putting pen to paper. The laptop was only used intermittently – for research or the odd email. And now, like Eleanor, it was gone.

He paused, surprised more by his reaction, than what he'd discovered. The missing laptop should have compounded a sense of violation, rekindled his fear. But the truth was, he didn't feel violated or frightened. He felt furious. There was a monster on the loose yet the police refused to act on his lead.

He couldn't sit in a hotel room waiting. He had to do something.

An image halted him in his tracks. Eleanor. He couldn't walk away, abandon her. But then he heard her voice. Thought of her resolve. That well of strength she seemed to draw on whenever she was tested. She would understand how important it was to do something. Besides, he would check in regularly. And be back soon.

Sam knew what he had to do. He would add one last item to the bag he'd been packing upstairs. Book into the hotel, as expected. Call his clients to cancel their appointments.

Then he'd leave and start searching for Zahra himself.

Emery's words about crossing the Channel without a passport rang in his ears. But Zahra had already escaped her own country, crossed the Sahara, Mediterranean, Europe and the Channel. Given what she'd achieved, would getting back across be so difficult?

The nearest ferry port for the Netherlands, if he remembered right, Harwich. And it was entering the UK, not leaving it, that seemed the goal for most illegal immigrants, so would that route be as heavily scrutinised as, say, Calais to Dover? He had no idea. One thing was certain, it would not be simple. But whatever challenges she faced, Zahra was fuelled by fear and a fierce determination – and they'd not let her down yet.

Chapter 17

The Cotswolds

Sir Harry Tapper's house in the country was a twelve-bedroom rectory set on the crown of a gentle hill amid forty acres. Behind the house, arranged around a manicured vegetable and herb garden, was a set of converted stables which housed a huge games room, indoor pool and gym, and four more bedrooms, each with lavish en-suite bathrooms.

Inside the rectory, the rooms were dressed with expensive furnishings sourced at huge expense by Yvonne's Notting Hill interior designer. A dull palette of grey wall colours was offset by brighter autumnal hues – Persian rugs, African drapes and kilims, silk lampshades, abstract art.

It was fair to say that none of it spoke to Tapper; none of it seemed a representation of what had led him to this point. There were no paintings of rural Essex or the marketplace in Romford. No studies of life in Ipswich Young Offenders.

But of course the point of this house was to eradicate that life and present a glossy picture of today. Sir Harry and Lady Yvonne Tapper – friends of the great and the good.

Tonight in the games room, in between rounds of pool and darts, the 200 or so friends glugging Bollinger and eating canapés included, among others, a member of the Cabinet, two junior Ministers, an acerbic right-wing broadcaster, a supermodel, a retired Indian fast bowler, a Turner Prize-winning artist, one Hollywood B-lister and a scattering of the local landed gentry.

'Friends' was how a newspaper might have described the gathering. But in truth the Tappers' annual Valentine's Day party, when high-end food and drink were wittily paired with more down-to-earth games, was an ordeal for Tapper. A time when he charmed and gurned for those gathered, but every moment was a mini hell of maintaining front – the façade of an incredibly wealthy man, a man with a dark past which no one ever mentioned.

Tonight such concerns were the least of his problems. All day he'd been desperate to contact Wallace – a part of him terrified by what he'd discover when they spoke – but a dense schedule of meetings and then preparations for the party had eaten up every minute and ensured he was never alone.

Finally, at 9pm, an opportunity presented itself. He escaped into the kitchen – thanked the chef they'd engaged at huge expense from the local, much-feted gastropub – and stepped through a heavy door outside.

It was bitterly cold, a refreshing change from the warm, perfumed air of the games room. Above him, the night sky presented itself like a vast black cloth glittering with diamonds. A full moon cast defined shadows across the snow-covered fields that dropped away below him.

Tapper's mobile began vibrating on the hour.

'Pat.'

Wallace recounted what had happened. As the story slowly unravelled, Tapper began to feel breathless, as if he'd climbed a mountain and the air at the summit were thin.

'Christ,' muttered Tapper, when Wallace had finished. As soon as he'd heard about Fitzgerald on the news, he guessed something had happened and the thought had chewed away at his insides all day. But confirmation was something else. He'd set in motion a process that had left a man dead and a woman unconscious.

Wallace's weakness for violence cast a long shadow over the account. But by sending the man into Keddie's house, there was always a chance he'd encounter someone. And Fitzgerald had been talking to Idris, hearing the truth directly from the horse's mouth. At least now the solicitor would not be repeating what he knew.

His pulse accelerated with the realisation that he was already finding ways of rationalising what had happened.

'I took precautions,' Wallace said, as if anticipating Tapper's next thought. 'I wore gloves at the house, and a hoodie on both occasions. Doubt there were any witnesses to the solicitor's death. As for Keddie's girlfriend, she only saw me fleetingly.'

But Tapper could see countless ways in which this might blossom. Some overlooked detail, some trace of Wallace at the crime scenes – a microscopic particle of DNA. Was Wallace's DNA still held? Course it was, he realised, dread slicing like a blade across his stomach. DNA in adult convictions was never bloody destroyed. And what if the girlfriend was able to describe Wallace when she awoke?

If the police homed in on Wallace, his old cellmate was hardly likely to simply fall on his sword, take one for the team. If it came to that, he'd pay Wallace off royally, help him disappear. Even as the idea came to him, he ridiculed his thinking. What did he know about helping someone disappear?

Bile rose up from Tapper's stomach as each loaded complication surfaced in his mind. He swallowed hard, remembering another strand to this business.

'Had a chance to look at their computers?' he asked.

'Not yet.'

'They'll be password protected.'

'I've got a bit of knowledge in that department. From my burgling days. Cracking them is not as hard as you'd imagine. People are very unimaginative when it comes to passwords.'

Tapper took a deep lungful of the wintry air – so cold, it almost hurt.

'And what about the police?'

'From what I hear, they're looking for Idris in connection with Fitzgerald's death.'

Tapper's skin prickled. What if they found her? What if she talked?

'And the shrink? His laptop's been nicked and his girlfriend's taken a beating. He's going to want answers.'

'I'm keeping tabs on him. He's staying up the road from his place at a hotel.'

'Ring me if there's any news.'

Tapper hung up. He stared at the landscape before him, processing Wallace's update. His former cellmate had gone from ex-con forging a new life to murderer in a matter of days. But there'd been no fear in the man's voice. Which was a comfort. At least Wallace wasn't panicking. And while Tapper's heart hammered away in his rib cage, he knew that what Wallace had done paled when compared with what had happened last summer. And the fact was, the two of them were locked into a course of action that could not be derailed, now more than ever. They had to finish the job. If that was bloody possible.

He heard a cough behind him. He stiffened, aware that whoever was there would have heard the whole conversation.

'Who was that on the phone?

Tapper exhaled.

'Best you don't know.'

'I suppose you're right.' The man paused. 'And how are things?'

'"Things"?'

'Don't be so bloody coy, Harry. The death of a solicitor wouldn't happen to be anything to do with you, would it?'

'Do you really want to know?'

'Probably not. But at least reassure me that there's nothing to worry about.'

'There's everything to fucking worry about,' he hissed, turning to meet the other man's gaze head on. 'Our woman is somewhere out there and it's very unlikely that we'll ever trace her. She also has an ally, who has every reason to feel pissed off and not a little curious.'

The man's face visibly paled, as if reflecting the moon's chalky features. Tapper was almost enjoying this.

'But looking on the bright side, it's very cold and she is now all too aware of the threat she faces if she causes any trouble.'

The man took a step back.

'Christ,' he said in a choked voice. 'You did kill the solicitor.'

'I told you I would act,' Tapper whispered. 'You understood. Besides, you're hardly Mother Teresa.'

Just then the door flung open and Phoebe Eastman, a supermodel whose face had graced the covers of Vogue, Elle and Red, stumbled out, tipsy and pouting.

'There you are, Harry.' She looked at the two men. 'Why the long face, boys?'

The model's timing was perfect. Tapper was raging and could have punched the other man in the face.

'Fancy a game of darts, Harry? Romford v Leyton. I'll fucking cane ya.'

'Why not?' Tapper desperately needed a distraction and Phoebe was one of the few guests in attendance that he actually liked. Despite her porcelain skin, pampered hair and haute couture clothes, she was still a foul-mouthed Eastender.

As he and Phoebe walked into the kitchen, he shot the other man a withering, silencing look. The conversation was over. Wallace had his orders. This thing was in motion and they had no choice but to pursue it to the bitter end.

Chapter 18

Stamford Hill, north London

Wallace sat in a battered red Corsa just up the road from the hotel.

He had been driving past Keddie's house that morning, hoping to spot the elusive shrink, when he saw a police car parked outside. He'd seen the vans in the street in the early hours, the tape stretched across the gate as the snow slowly fell.

Wallace drove by slowly. As he did, he saw Keddie emerge from the front door clutching an overnight bag, accompanied by a policeman. Neither of them looked up at the passing red car.

He parked outside a corner shop. In his rear-view mirror, he saw Keddie get into the police car, and the vehicle accelerate away. Wallace waited till it had gained a little distance, then began to follow. The car ended up at the hotel, which Keddie entered with his bag.

Wallace spent the rest of the day drifting from café to pub to his car, anywhere he could keep tabs on the hotel entrance.

There was only so long he could maintain this kind of scrutiny. And of course there was just him. He'd visited the toilet a handful of times. Moved his car. So he couldn't be sure that the shrink was even still in the building.

It was 10.30pm. A cab drew up outside the hotel. Wallace, slumped in the driver's seat, watched the entrance with weary eyes. Seconds later, Keddie emerged and jumped in the car. Wallace sat up straight, drowsiness banished in an instant. Where the fuck was Keddie going?

Wallace started the engine and followed. The cab did a U turn and then hung a right on to the A10, heading north. Wallace put his foot down, keeping a respectable distance.

An hour later, he was on the M11 heading towards Cambridge, the cab a few cars ahead. The banks either side of the motorway were thick with snow.

When the taxi indicated it was exiting, Wallace, who'd been nursing a theory ever since he'd joined the motorway, became certain.

Ten minutes later, Keddie was dropped outside the terminal building at Stansted Airport. Wallace broke into another sweat. He'd had this problem ever since he was a kid but it had become much worse since Iraq. He tried to keep a lid on it with after-shave but in moments like this – when a rapid decision was required under stress – the odour began to get the upper hand.

Wallace watched Keddie enter the building and followed the road to the nearest car park. It was ten minutes before he'd found a space, paid, and was jogging back to the terminal.

Inside, he paused to take in the scene around him. Every seat was taken and people were lying on the floor, heads propped against luggage, while long queues snaked out from check-in and various information desks. The snow, Wallace concluded, had brought the airport to a standstill. Perhaps Keddie wouldn't be going anywhere after all.

An argument broke out to his right. Wallace turned to see a group of people surrounding a kiosk that belonged to a budget airline. He could hear a man's voice from within the throng. It was strained, angry: 'There's no bloody information. I don't know whether to stay or head home.' Then Wallace heard a woman's voice, calmer, conciliatory:

'As soon as we know anything sir, we will let you know. But the weather has made everything unpredictable.'

Wallace continued to scan the room, more slowly now. A 'bing-bong' sound heralded an announcement. A female voice intoned: 'Ryanair regret to announce the cancellation of Flight FR4135 to Milan.' The rest of the announcement was drowned out in groans and jeers erupting from a far corner of the terminal building.

It was then that Wallace caught a glimpse of Keddie. He was in a short queue by the desk of another airline. Was he buying a ticket?

Wallace found a vending machine and bought himself a can of Coke. He then perched on the edge of a shallow wall bordering a bed of plants. It was narrow and, with his weight pressing down, uncomfortable. He stood, rubbing his buttocks. He was tired, hungry. What the fuck was the shrink up to?

Wallace watched as Keddie handed over his credit card. Minutes later, he was given a piece of paper. Then he was on the move again, walking with purpose across the hall in Wallace's direction.

Wallace froze, then as quickly calmed down. There was no reason why the shrink would recognise him. Besides, Keddie had veered off and was now joining another queue, this one about twenty people deep, for a check-in desk. Wallace's eyes followed the queue to its head, noted the flight number at the desk then looked up to the departures board.

At least ten flights had been cancelled and most of the others delayed. Keddie's flight was among the latter ones. Wallace felt a fresh dampening of sweat at his armpits. The shrink's flight was scheduled to leave in two hours.

Tapper had asked him to keep an eye on Keddie. Which meant only one thing.

It would take about three-quarters of an hour to get home and pack a bag. He'd make it. But only if he shifted it.

Chapter 19

Amsterdam

The plane touched down just after 4am with a slight skid, prompting a collective gasp from the passengers.

It was a miracle that they'd even taken off. While countless other flights had been cancelled due to the weather, the Amsterdam plane had remained stubbornly delayed. Waiting in the airport, Sam called Susan, Eleanor's aunt, who told him there was no change in Eleanor's condition. He explained that he'd be away for a short while but got the impression that Susan was too preoccupied to really take in what he was saying. He dozed fitfully, unable to close his eyes and not see Eleanor or Fitzgerald. Eventually they were called to the departure gate. He watched through a window as ice was blasted from the body of the plane and a path was dug through the snow from the terminal to the steps.

Extreme weather and the prospect of being confined inside a narrow space were perfect conditions for an attack of his claustrophobia, which asserted itself whenever he was under stress. But his body had felt charged, as if a fierce electric current were running through him.

His success reaching Amsterdam against all odds should have been cause for celebration, but as the plane taxied, he felt his resolve take a dive. He had a clue, that was all, and a city to search. And what if Zahra had decided at the last minute not to make the journey? Or maybe she had tried, but been apprehended. He shuddered at the thought of her being sent back to Creech Hill.

Outside the terminal, in a wind that was brutally cold and unforgiving, Sam joined the queue at a taxi rank, his head buried deep in the collar of his coat. The cab that eventually took him into the city, its interior a warm, damp fug, travelled slowly along an untreated motorway, sliding occasionally in a grey cocktail of ice and snow.

He asked to be dropped just off Dam Square and walked a short distance down Spuistraat – his toes numbing in his shoes – to a hotel he remembered from a previous stay, when he was attending a psychotherapy conference.

The doors were locked and Sam had to press a bell three times before a woman wearing a sweat top, leggings and flip-flops trudged to the entrance to let him in. She looked unimpressed, her face as severe as the weather outside.

The foyer was as he remembered it – a large bland place of plastic plants and leather seats. The woman checked him in quickly, clearly keen to get back to sleep.

In the hotel room, he dropped his bags on the floor. It was nearly 6am. There was nothing he could do right now. He flopped down on to the bed.

His sleep was disturbed by dreams of him chasing Eleanor and Zahra through a foggy cityscape – the women visible for brief tantalising moments, before they vanished.

He woke in the afternoon, feeling groggy and disoriented. He peeled open his curtains and saw that it was going dark already. Ideal. He was fairly certain the place where he planned to start his search didn't really come alive until this time of day. He showered and headed down to the hotel restaurant, where he ate a greasy burger and chips. Outside, a high-pitched whine of brakes announced a slowing tram, which stopped outside the nearest window to disgorge passengers before moving off, sparks from overhead cables illuminating the wintry gloom. Across from the hotel, in a tapas bar with bare brick walls, a man was hanging a leg of ham on a hook. He paused to look out the window and seemed to fix his stare on Sam's face. Sam turned away.

Just before 5pm, he drained a coffee and went to reception. He picked up a map of the city and sat briefly to work out his route. He'd done some exploring during his previous visit and had a sense of the city's layout – the horseshoe-shaped pattern of canals rippling out from the centre – but he'd never visited this evening's destination. Satisfied, he folded the map in his coat pocket, and left the hotel.

As his foot hit the pavement there was a ping of a bell and a cyclist swerved round him. Sam felt his pulse quicken, the anxiety lying close to the surface. He moved at a pace, hoping the energy would generate some heat. He crossed a main road then headed east down a narrow alley, passing an antique shop and the tempting, candle-lit interior of a bar.

This was the city centre, a tourist-friendly area of well-lit streets, with windows giving on to restaurants, hotel lounges and department stores, yet Sam couldn't escape the feeling that he was being watched. Twice he turned to look round and both times he saw nothing. There were people about, but they were heading in the opposite direction, emerging from buildings or walking arm in arm with partners. No one seemed interested in him.

About ten minutes later, he emerged from an alleyway on to a canal. It was, at first glance, a classic wintry view of Amsterdam. A canalside fringed with leafless trees; tall, handsome houses with gables like upturned boats; bikes chained to the railings of the bridges. But the inky water of the canal amplified the subtle difference in this area – its surface shimmering with reflections of red lights and neon.

Sam turned north, past a sex shop, its windows crammed with skimpy plastic uniforms, whips, handcuffs and so many dildos he felt his eyes water. Then a theatre with a big neon sign that flashed with the promise of live sex. A poster of a black man wearing little more than a thong, a blonde in thread-like underwear bent double at his waist, gave a taste of the show inside.

Bar the odd couple and a handful of solitary men, punters were thin on the ground. Perhaps it was still too early. Perhaps it was too cold.

Sam moved on, then, passing a narrow alley, doubled back on himself. This, he realised, was as good a place as any to start.

He began down the walkway, aware of eyes watching him from a full-length window to his left. He looked briefly at the girl, trying to take in her features with the eyes of a detective, not a leering punter. She was Asian, her white bra and panties luminous thanks to fluorescent lighting, and she was pressing both hands against the glass and locking on to Sam with glazed eyes. The next booth was empty but the one after contained a blonde girl in pink underwear and furry Moonboots. She sat on a shiny plastic chair, legs parted, beckoning slowly with her forefinger.

Sam heard jeering and laughing. Ahead, a group of six men were walking in his direction. The noise and the way they swayed suggested they'd been on a bender. Here was the next stage of the day's entertainment.

As they reached Sam one of them spoke up: 'Any recommendations, mate?'

Sam smiled and shook his head, moving on. There were two more occupied windows, an older woman in a long, tight t-shirt stretched over large breasts, and a stick-thin, pale girl with red hair, who might have been a teenager.

Sam turned back on himself, prompting a rapping on the glass from the Asian girl as he passed her booth, then returned to the canal. He tried three more alleyways and was beginning to lose hope when he passed the entrance to another show. According to a sandwich board that sat in a pile of snow, the theatre promised a 'United Nations Sex Show'. The poster on the board featured a group of pouting women. There were about ten of them in all, all clichéd sexual fantasies from around the world. Among them was a tall, too-perfect Scandinavian-looking blonde, a petite Thai girl in hot pants, and a rangy black woman with an afro.

The black woman shared the same fine, almost Arabic features, as Zahra. Sam felt himself flood with hope, an emotion that was as quickly doused in despair. The woman might, just might, be from Eritrea or Ethiopia or Somalia. And she might, just might, know of the community of women Zahra had once lived with. But it was tenuous stuff, not least because he was in the Red Light District on a hunch, no more.

That Amsterdam was the last place Zahra had felt safe, Sam was certain. Her life since had been defined by a terrifying cross-Channel journey, and then the fear, frustration and uncertainty of life inside Creech Hill. But about the sex worker angle, Sam was on less solid ground. He remembered Zahra describing two women – a nurse and a teacher back home in East Africa – who were now doing what she called 'other work'. Uttering that phrase, her eyes had filled with sadness. Did that mean they worked here? He couldn't be sure. But all he had to do was think of the man who'd put Eleanor in a coma and Fitzgerald in the freezing canal, and his mind was made up.

He stepped inside. The cold was immediately replaced with a thick warm wall of perfumed air-conditioning. Sam dreaded to think what the smell was covering up. There was a ticket booth from which a woman, all low-cut top and dyed blonde hair greying at the roots, looked up at him with dead eyes.

'I need to talk to one of the girls.'

The woman blinked slowly, then spoke in a thick Dutch accent: 'No one speaks to the girls. No one touches the girls.'

'Just five minutes. I'm looking for a friend who's gone missing. She may be in danger.'

'I told you –'

'I'm not looking for sex. I'm looking for a friend.'

Behind the woman, a door opened and a short, wiry man emerged. He looked North African, and had bulging eyes and oily skin.

He muttered something in Dutch to the woman and she grunted a response.

'You don't talk to the girls,' he said.

'I don't want to cause trouble,' Sam said. 'I want to find a friend.'

He slipped his hand in his coat pocket, pulled out his wallet, flashing it in the man's face. 'I have cash.'

The man looked him hard in the face with his bug eyes. 'Fuck off.'

Sam felt the blood rush to his face. 'Listen! A friend of mine's in danger. All I want is a few minutes with the African girl on that poster –'

He was still holding the wallet aloft when he felt his arm yanked behind his back and pushed upwards. A shot of pain coursed up his arm and the wallet slipped from his grasp. He caught a glimpse of a large man behind him, a black face, before he was being marched to the entrance. He was pitched forward, his upper body over-reaching and legs scrambling on the icy wet cobbles for purchase. He lost his footing and fell forward, his arms breaking the fall.

'Fuck!' Sam cried out. He was lying on his front on the cobbles, the pain in his arm now eclipsed by a burning sensation in his right hand. With his left, he pushed himself up into a kneeling position. He then gingerly lifted his right hand from the ground. It must have caught the rough edge of a cobble. It was bleeding from a large cut to the fleshy part of his thumb.

He turned to shout some abuse at the man who'd flung him to the ground but he'd already disappeared and the woman in the booth was now serving a customer.

'You OK?' said a woman's voice behind him.

Sam, still on his knees, turned to see a tall figure wrapped in fake fur, a bobble hat pulled low over her head.

'I'm fine.'

He felt an arm cup his elbow and he was being pulled, as if he weighed no more than a bag of shopping, to his feet.

'I think this is yours,' she said, handing Sam his wallet.

'Thank you,' he said, stuffing it in a pocket.

'You don't want to mess with those fuckers.'

Sam realised her face looked familiar. His eyes darted to the sandwich board, then back to his Samaritan. Though shorn of make-up, she was definitely the Scandinavian blonde on the poster.

The woman was moving away when Sam spoke. 'Do you work in there?'

She turned, giving him a weary look, as if already regretting her good deed.

'I'm looking for a friend. She may be in danger.'

The woman sighed.

'She's Eritrean. That girl on the poster might be able to help.'

'I doubt it. She's from Sudan.'

Sam's hand pulsed with pain. He winced.

'You need to get that seen to,' said the woman. Her face softened. 'Listen, there's a café in Rembrandtplein. The Schiller. We go there after the show. Just after eleven. My Sudanese friend might be there.'

Chapter 20

Amsterdam

The Café Schiller had a discreet frontage among the tourist traps of Rembrandtplein, but opened up inside into a large brasserie, with wood panelling and subdued lighting.

Sam visited the toilet to wash his injured hand then applied a dressing he'd bought at a pharmacy en route. He then settled into a booth in a far corner of the room, ordering a coffee. The café was half-full, people having dinner or playing board games while nursing hot drinks or Amstels.

It was 7pm. Four hours to kill.

He should have felt calmer. He had a lead, of sorts, but that episode at the theatre had left him trembling with anger and frustration. He signalled to a waiter for another coffee.

*

Sam glanced at the clock hanging on the wall above the bar. It was 11.15pm. He was on his third coffee and feeling edgy, the caffeine coursing through his system.

The bar's patrons had thinned to about ten people. Another couple were just leaving, the open door bringing bitter air into the café.

The barman, a young, handsome guy, was leaning against the polished mahogany of the bar, playing with his phone.

Another blast of cold air invaded the room, this time accompanied by a group of people, obscured by thick coats and hats. The barman looked up and smiled. He called out a greeting in Dutch.

Sam recognised the Scandinavian woman, who was first to the bar. Then, tensing in his seat, he caught a glimpse of the figure by her side, the large black bouncer who'd flung him to the pavement.

The others in the group had disappeared to the toilet. The Scandinavian blonde was chatting to the barman and then glanced round, seeing Sam. She elbowed the large black man and gestured in Sam's direction.

Sam readied himself to move fast. Although there was a lot of floor to cover, he reckoned he had speed on his side if he went now. But it was too late. The bouncer was already moving towards him, a lumbering mass who seemed to get bigger with every inch he covered.

Soon he was looming over the table, his face impassive.

'Hey,' he said, his voice containing some trace of West Africa, 'sorry, man.'

Sam just stared, overwhelmed with relief.

'Just doing my job.'

To Sam's huge surprise, the bouncer then sat next to him on the banquette, the leather sighing as the man eased down. He turned to Sam and grinned like a child.

Next to join them was the blonde, who held two steaming mugs of hot chocolate in her hands. She placed them on the table then peeled off her coat and hat.

'It's the crazy fucker,' she said. 'How's the hand?'

Sam held up the bandaged hand for her inspection. 'Fine.'

Up close, even in the soft light, her face was far removed from the sexualised fantasy of the poster outside the theatre. Cleared of make-up, it was lined and tired, her lips chapped and the skin around her nostrils pink and raw.

The others were coming to join them. As they discarded their coats, scarves and hats, Sam made out the Sudanese girl. Like the blonde, she was markedly different to the promised woman of the poster. There was no afro, just cropped peroxide hair and an angular, hardened face. Behind her was an almost skeletal man with long black hair, the Thai girl, and a short, dumpy woman. Sam found himself hemmed in on the banquette, an instant member of the gang.

'You're lucky,' said the blonde. 'Leyla's gonna talk to you.'

Leyla tipped her head to one side and frowned at Sam. She then muttered something in Dutch to the blonde.

'She wants to know who you're looking for.'

'An Eritrean woman, Zahra Idris.'

The blonde translated. Leyla started to laugh, then spoke.

The blonde translated again. 'She says, "You must think we're all one big family, us African girls".'

Sam protested. 'That's not what I meant. Zahra said she lived with a community of women – some Europeans as well as Africans. They looked after her. I think some of them may have worked in the Red Light District.'

Even as it was escaping his lips, he realised how pathetically tenuous it all was. But there was no chuckle this time. Leyla was speaking in more hushed tones now, her face deadly earnest. The blonde muttered back. She then spoke to Sam.

'She thinks she knows the group you mean,' said the blonde. 'But where they live is not a place for someone like you.'

'Why's that?'

Leyla emitted a short, mirthless laugh.

It was the skinny man's turn to speak, his voice deep and Italian sounding. 'The commune you're talking about is in Bijlmer.'

'Right.'

The skinny guy exchanged glances with the others. 'It used to be a total shithole, a place where they dumped everyone they didn't wanna see in the pretty streets round here. Junkies, blacks. Then a plane crashed into one of the tower blocks.'

Sam had a vague recollection of the disaster. Some time in the 90s. An image of a tower block sliced in two surfaced in his mind.

'It was a 747, wasn't it?'

The skinny guy raised his eyebrows, as if impressed. 'You got it. An El Al flight. That 747 took out a whole section of one of the tower blocks. Killed fifty people.' He paused, laughing. 'But at least the demolition had started.'

'They started to tear the other high-rises down. Build more expensive, low-rise stuff. Pull in the yuppies.'

The word 'yuppies' seemed to tickle everyone in the booth, whatever their grasp of English. A chuckle rippled around the table.

'The yuppies came to see Justin Timberlake and Beyoncé at the arena,' continued the skinny guy, 'but they never moved in.' He scratched one of his hollow cheeks. 'The place is better. I mean, you're not gonna get mugged in daylight. And kids play in the park and shit. But there are still corners I wouldn't visit.'

'Like the one we're talking about,' interjected the blonde. 'It's right by the crash site. Got a bad vibe.'

'I need to go there,' said Sam. 'I've got to find her.'

The skinny guy rotated a finger at his temple.

'What's so special about this woman?' asked the blonde.

Sam looked round the table, at faces he barely knew. He didn't have the energy for an abridged, safe version. 'My girlfriend was attacked,' he said. He could feel a stab of emotion behind his eyes, sadness and anger balled into one. 'Whoever did it is after me too. Zahra may know why.'

There was an audible intake of breath, as if the group were reassessing the stranger in their midst.

'Catch the Metro to Bijlmer Arena,' said the blonde quickly, as if she now wanted rid of Sam. She muttered something to Leyla, who pulled a biro from her bag and began drawing on a napkin.

The blonde handed the napkin to Sam. He stood, indicating to the bouncer that he wanted to get out.

'Tell me you're not going there now,' said the skinny guy.

'The metro's still running, right?' asked Sam.

'It's worse at night, man,' said the bouncer. 'Even I wouldn't go there now.'

But Sam remained standing and eventually the bouncer got up to let him out.

'Thanks for your help,' he said to the group. They stared silently at him and as he walked to the door, he could feel their eyes on his back.

Chapter 21

Bijlmer, Amsterdam

Of course he could have gone back to the hotel, had a good night's sleep. Gone to Bijlmer in the morning.

He knew the people in the café thought he was insane to be going at any time. Given what they'd probably seen of human nature, it would have been sensible heeding their advice. But Sam didn't feel sensible. He felt mad, as if a fire were burning in his stomach, fuelled by anger and a sense of denied justice.

When the Metro train pulled into Bijlmer ArenA, he briefly wondered what all the fuss was about. The station was a state-of-the-art building of concrete and steel, well-lit and spotlessly clean. But then he stepped outside and slowly the illusion ebbed away.

The wind had dropped and snow was falling, attempting to coat the neighbourhood with a sugary white layer. But it was clear that it would take more than a snowstorm to transform Bijlmer.

He'd studied the map on the napkin before getting off the train and knew he had to walk down a long straight road to the north of Bijlmer before he entered the estate. The bulk of it now lay to his right side, broad tower blocks that zig-zagged across the landscape, endless layers of walkways lit up by bright lights.

The odd car or lorry moved slowly past him, spraying arcs of icy sludge on to the pavement. The side of the road had been used as a dumping ground, a graveyard of the unwanted and discarded. A mattress, snow slowly obliterating its stains and the stuffing spilling from its ripped surface. The rusting skeleton of a shopping trolley, its frame bent and distorted. A small hill of rubble, topped with empty paint cans and tubes of filler. Sam side-stepped a dead fox, a shadow of blood stubbornly darkening the snow that was trying to cover it up.

There was clearly a desire to improve things for the residents of Bijlmer. In front of one tower block, the grounds had been landscaped, soft undulating mounds interspersed with young saplings, paths lit by street lamps. The ghost of a new playpark, equipment dusted with snow.

But the development had only gone so far. Large pockets were still ringed with wire fencing and hoardings, the surfaces daubed with angry messages sprayed in black.

A little later, Sam cut down a narrower road, heading for the 'X' marked on his napkin map. The snow was falling more heavily now, blurring the line between pavement and road. Only the odd parked car, ancient bangers no one would have wanted to steal, showed where one ended and the other began.

He passed more of the zig-zagging tower blocks, the occasional walkway appearing and disappearing in the gloom as lights blinked on and off. A distant scream in the darkness punctured the still night, followed by a man's voice, ranting and shouting.

He was near the site of the crash now and saw, to his left, a gap in the snake of a building. Had the other tower blocks not been longer, it would have been impossible to spot the difference here, but Sam knew that this was the spot where a huge 747 had crashed.

It was the far building he was heading for, no more than a dark mass in what was fast turning into a blizzard. With a complete absence of parked cars, the pavement and road were no longer distinguishable. Sam moved in the direction of the building, hoping that the ground beneath the snow was solid.

Another cry went out. Somehow it sounded nearer, yet more muffled. The building in front of him was around twenty storeys high, a long hulk of concrete that might once have seemed a good idea to an architect or city planner. Now, cast adrift from an already isolated place, it was like a foreboding castle in an abandoned landscape.

Sam paused in the snow to plot his next move. He fished with a gloved hand for the napkin in his pocket and squinted at it in the half light. His feet had long ago numbed, his shoes wet through. Underneath his coat he was sweating, not just from the exertion, but from a fear he dared not acknowledge.

The building ahead was barely illuminated. Whole floors were blacked out while others were partially lit. Were people living in there? Sam shoved the makeshift map back into his pocket and moved forward, heading for the far right of the building. It was here that the map had suggested there was an entrance. He needed to find the seventh floor where, according to Leyla, a handful of apartments had been knocked into one makeshift living space.

Sam approached the entrance and saw two figures huddled under a light. He could feel the blood thumping in his ears, his torso damp with sweat.

As he drew closer he saw, to his slight relief, that it was an elderly man and a young woman. The man was wearing a long overcoat. He had a mass of wild grey hair and pitted skin covered with several days' worth of stubble. He was drawing on what looked like a joint. The woman was black, with hair pulled back in a tight pony tail. As Sam got closer, he realised that there was a child clinging to her leg.

They turned when Sam was just feet from them, his arrival muffled by the snow. If they were surprised to see someone out at this hour, they didn't show it. Their eyes were dulled and disinterested and Sam moved past them unimpeded, nostrils filling with the herby, resinous whiff of marijuana.

In the dimly lit entrance, its walls scribed with graffiti, a strong stench of urine drifting up from the wet floor, he made out two lifts. But there were no lights to either side and he could tell they'd long ago broken and were probably never going to be fixed. To the left of the lift banks was a staircase.

The brief relief he'd experienced when he'd realised how little threat the two figures posed now evaporated as he began to mount the stairs. What light there'd been in the entrance was now snuffed out. Sam moved upwards with a hand on the wall for guidance. The surface he felt with his fingers was rough but somehow slick with liquid. He hoped it was melted snow or rainwater that had found its way in, but in his mind he had an image of a building that was, like him, sweating with anxiety.

He moved upwards, past the first and second floors, long galleries of concrete lit by the odd strip of lighting or glow coming from a window or doorway. Noise came at him in brief waves: pounding drum & bass, an argument between two men. His throat had contracted, the familiar sensation of claustrophobia slowly tightening its grip on him.

He turned a corner and placed his foot down on the next step when he felt something that made him freeze on the spot. He had brought his shoe down, not on hard concrete, but something softer, that gave under pressure. He glanced down. His eyes had become more accustomed to the darkness but all he could see was a mass of dark material stretched across his path. He leaned down to get a closer look, to see if there was a way round the lump, when he heard a groan. Sam reared back, his whole body rigid with fear. Desperate to put distance between him and the figure, he leapt over the body, moving up the stairwell at a pace.

If he'd had any illusions about the place up until this moment, they'd now been shattered. This was a building stripped of basic amenities, devoid of any sense of community. God knows what had happened to that person. They could have been mugged or simply collapsed drunk. One thing was for sure. In sub-zero temperatures, they'd probably be dead by morning. As soon as he found someone who wasn't pissed or stoned themselves, he'd get help.

He moved on upwards, hands still tracing his route along the rough, damp walls. Finally he reached the seventh floor. He stopped, his heart now pounding. He was grateful for the sensation of physical exertion which had, for a brief moment, replaced his mounting terror.

Ahead of him was a long gallery identical to the ones he'd passed on the other floors. He looked down at the white-out of the ground below, the horizon obliterated by the blizzard.

There were more lights on this floor than any other he'd passed – some sense of life, whatever that might mean. He inched forward slowly.

The first flats he passed had long since lost their doors and windows. The dull white of the storm suggested interiors but was soon swallowed up by the darkness. His feet crunched over broken glass. He smelt the acrid stench of burnt rubber.

Ahead of him was the first of the lights, a blaze by the block's standards, flooding out of a window. He approached slowly, his mouth dry and knees weakening with every step. He'd come too far to give up but a large part of him longed to be back on the ground, running as fast as possible back to the Metro station.

The sight that greeted him at the window was not what he'd expected. A woman, white with a bob of black hair, was stirring a steaming vat over a portable camping stove. The 'kitchen' around her was a mass of wooden crates, slabs of timber propped between them acting as shelves, which sagged under the weight of food in boxes and cans. Behind her he glimpsed more space, candles illuminating small pockets in the darkness, mattresses on the floor.

Just then, the woman looked up. It took her a moment to take in what she was seeing, the reflection of the glass perhaps distorting her view of Sam, and then she screamed.

Suddenly she was joined by three other women. The first one pointed at Sam with an accusatory finger. The others stared out of the glass at him, eyes narrowing, and then they moved. Seconds later, a door a little further down was flung open, a rectangle of faint light laid down on the dark walkway floor, and the three women were charging out, abuse pouring from their mouths in what sounded like Dutch.

Sam stepped back, hands raised. 'I'm not here to cause trouble.'

'Fucking pervert,' spat one of the women, who was thick-set with short red hair. 'You know the rules. No guys on this floor.'

'I don't know any rules,' managed Sam. But the thick-set woman was suddenly right in front of him. Sam glanced down and realised too late that she was clutching a short knife, which she held just beneath his jawline.

'I've come to find someone,' he stammered.

'You're a fucking perve. We should throw you over the edge.'

'I'm looking for an African woman. A friend of mine.'

'Show him who's boss, Ruby,' said one of the others.

'She's called Zahra.'

Sam sensed the tension drop a fraction, though the knife was still at his throat.

'Zahra Idris,' Sam managed to splutter out. 'She's from Eritrea.'

'The rules are simple,' said Ruby. 'No men allowed on the seventh floor.'

'She's in trouble. We both are. I need to talk to her.'

'She's safe here,' said one of the others, prompting a sharp look from Ruby. Until that moment, Sam hadn't been certain she was even in the building.

'My girlfriend was attacked. She's in a coma. I think Zahra can help.'

Sam thought that mentioning the plight of another woman might soften Ruby. He was wrong.

'Fuck you,' snapped Ruby. 'It's your problem.'

There was a pause, during which Sam considered his likely fate. At best, an escort from the building. At worst, a knife across his throat and his body flung from the balcony.

But then he heard a voice. It was coming from a group of women that had gathered at the open doorway. It was soft, yet commanding.

'Leave him.'

Chapter 22

Bijlmer, Amsterdam

The stoned old man at the corner of the building shrugged when Wallace asked for help. So Wallace pulled out his wallet and opened it to reveal a wad of English cash. The woman giggled in a manic way. The man became more alert.

'I'm looking for a friend,' said Wallace. 'Another Englishman.'

'Yeah,' drawled the old man. 'Me and Anita saw another guy earlier.'

'Where did he go?'

The old man moved his head lazily in the direction of the stairs. 'Up there.'

'And what's up there?'

The old man paused. Wallace knew it was time to pay. He opened his wallet and pulled out a twenty-pound note.

'What's this worth?' asked the old man, staring suspiciously at the note held out before him.

'About thirty Euros.'

The old man grunted his approval and snatched the note from Wallace.

'Up there?' he said, taking up where they'd left off. 'There's not much up there. This place is just somewhere to get stoned. Or maybe disappear for a while. There's a commune on the seventh floor. But your guy won't be there.'

'Why's that?'

The old man chuckled and this set the woman off, her giggle a high-pitched, childish sound that set Wallace's teeth on edge. 'No guys allowed,' he said. 'The place is run by ex-hookers who used to work in the city. They don't like men.'

'And is it all hookers up there?'

The old man sniffed in a slightly hurt way.

Wallace opened his wallet again and handed over another twenty-pound note.

'No,' said the old guy, once he'd taken the money. 'Immigrants too.'

'Any Africans?'

The old man's face scrunched up, as if he were attempting some feat of thinking the joint severely impeded. 'Thought you were worried about your friend.'

The wallet opened and one more note was handed over. Wallace wished he could have got a receipt. He wanted this cash back from Tapper.

'Yeah, lots of Africans.' He leaned forward conspiratorially, as if this were man-to-man stuff, not for his companion's ear. 'A few of those hot women from Somalia. You know, tall with beautiful faces.'

Wallace had no idea where Zahra Idris was from. But that description fitted her.

'What's it like up there?'

The man looked puzzled.

'I mean, let's just say my friend is up there. Could someone like me get in and pull him out? Or would I need a bit of help?'

The old man looked Wallace up and down. 'You're a big guy. You look like you can take care of yourself. But there's a lot of them up there. A lot of angry lesbians, women built of concrete.'

Wallace knew he could go up there himself, but he doubted he'd get in, let alone deal with Keddie and Zahra Idris, if indeed she was there.

'I know some guys,' said the old man. 'They could help out.' He paused, then smiled broadly, his remaining teeth brown and rotten at the gums. 'For a price.'

Chapter 23

Bijlmer, Amsterdam

Candles lit the table, casting dark shadows across Zahra's face. Behind her, the space was difficult to quantify. A brazier was lit somewhere in the distance, and Sam could see a handful of figures gathered round it. There were other lit candles. Sam made out clusters of bedding and areas partitioned by drapes, rough edges of walls where a bit of impromptu demolition had opened up a room.

It was a fraction less cold in here than outside. He got the impression there was a water supply of sorts, and enough power in the building for the few lights he'd encountered on his way up to the seventh floor. But that was probably a generator, not something provided by a utility company. No, this place was effectively on its own. A safe haven for women escaping some form of persecution or exploitation. Or, seen from another viewpoint, a hellhole of unimaginable poverty just outside an affluent European city.

Seated at the far end of the table, Ruby was jabbering on about rules. She'd been talking for twenty minutes. But she had at least accepted Zahra's assurances that Sam was no threat.

She finally wound up. 'You've got half an hour to talk. But I'm listening in.' She fixed her small eyes on Sam. 'After that, you're leaving. Understood?'

Sam lifted the palms of his hands in assent. After the reception committee and Ruby's monologue, he had the message loud and clear. Men were not welcome. The fact that it was now the middle of the night and a blizzard was raging outside was immaterial.

'How did you find me?' asked Zahra.

Sam told her about his visit to the Red Light District, and the people who'd directed him to Bijlmer.

'And what about you, Zahra? How did you get here?'

She massaged her forehead. There were bags under her eyes and the skin around her nose and mouth was dry and flaky. 'I went to Harwich. Did what I've done so many times before, found a way into the back of a container. It was easier than Calais. Less guards.'

Sam had been right about the port. And her abilities.

Zahra's face darkened. 'I've only been here a few hours, Sam. I need to sleep. Why did you come?'

'I didn't tell you the last time we spoke – I didn't get the chance. My girlfriend was attacked shortly after the riot at Creech Hill.'

'I'm sorry.'

'I believe it's the same man who attacked Fitzgerald.'

Zahra's eyes flared briefly. 'And the man who threatened me at Creech Hill.'

'What do you mean?'

She told Sam about the events leading to the riot.

Sam listened, felt his pulse quicken. When she finished, he took a breath, tried to calm himself. 'All the more reason to speak to the police.'

'I told you, I'm not talking to the police. Maybe now you understand why.'

At the other end of the table, Ruby bristled. 'All you're doing is upsetting her. She came here to get away from this shit.'

Sam swung round. 'Let me spell out "this shit" for both of you. Because of it, my girlfriend is in a coma, a man is dead and my life is in danger. And Zahra is the only person who can identify the attacker.' He turned to her. 'I know you can't remember why the man in the suit terrified you. But you can at least help bring this thug to justice.'

'Even if I came forward, I can't prove it was the same man. I've never seen his face clearly.'

Ruby rose from her seat. 'OK,' she snapped. 'That's enough. You need to go now. Now you know why we don't have men here.'

They were interrupted by a sound outside – a noise that made the hairs on the back of Sam's neck stand up. People were running down the walkway outside. It was like the charge of an invading army.

Before Ruby could react, let alone bark out an order, there was a loud thud swiftly followed by the noise of crunching wood. Suddenly a gang of men – at least ten of them – were pouring through an open doorway from the walkway.

Sam felt a shot of adrenaline course through him. He grabbed Zahra's hand and ran in the opposite direction.

Shouts rang out. Ruby had recovered enough from the shock to resume control. As Sam and Zahra moved swiftly past her, she was reacting with lightning speed, tipping the table over to make a barricade, while screaming for support.

Chapter 24

Bijlmer, Amsterdam

As they darted into the darkness, Sam gripping Zahra's hand and leading their retreat, the inhabitants of the commune were rousing around them. He heard groans as he stumbled over bedding, screams as people woke more fully and realised they were under attack.

Behind them, chaos was quickly taking hold. They heard objects being thrown, metal hitting the concrete floor, cries of pain from both men and women as weapons or fists made impact.

Sam's eyes were well adjusted to the gloom now and he could see they were at the far end of the space, away from the floor's residents. They moved through a graveyard of household objects – battered fridges, freezers and ovens, old sofas and armchairs. If they could make it out on to the walkway, there would, he hoped, be another stairwell to descend to the ground below – and freedom.

They reached an opening in a wall, softly illuminated by the white light of the blizzard. Zahra slowed, then inched out, followed by Sam.

To their right, there was a short stretch of walkway. But where there should have been a concrete wall at the end, there was nothing, merely a view of the next building, some fifty metres away. Sam felt his mouth go dry.

They heard a shout from the other end of the walkway.
'There!'

There was a sound of boots on concrete. Zahra turned. She was panting, her face balled up in fear. And then she was rushing forward, rounding the corner. Sam followed, willing his body to speed up even as another part of him wanted to glue his feet to the floor.

Turning the corner, it was far worse than Sam had expected. There was still a staircase, but no wall beyond. The stairs below them, deep with snow, were of uneven length, as if something had ripped random chunks from each step. Occasionally there were pieces of remaining wall, but then nothing again – and the certainty that, if you slipped or mistook an overhang of snow for concrete, you would fall to your death seven floors below.

In an instant Sam realised what he was looking at. It was damage caused by the air disaster. A plane had crash-landed on this very spot and all the authorities had done was to demolish the worst-hit portion, leaving the rest standing.

'There's no time to stand there!' shouted Zahra, who was already stepping gingerly down the stairs. It was when Sam followed that he first got a sense of the drop to his left. The ground below was covered with snow but where it met the base of the nearest tower block gave him a stomach-contracting sense of scale.

Zahra was descending with haste, a speed Sam was too terrified to match, clinging to the building on her right. He could see her occasionally slip and quickly correct herself.

Sam inched downwards, placing a foot on each step and then, once it had gripped, moving to the next. The wind was whipping across the estate, sending flurries into his face so that he had to constantly wipe his eyes with a sleeve to see clearly. He felt a gust tug at his coat, as if to drag him off the building into the soft but deadly cushion of snow below.

Zahra was already at the base of the first landing and moving on to the next when Sam realised he wasn't descending fast enough. From behind him, at the head of the stairs, he heard a voice.

'He's there.'

Sam speeded up, slipping as he put a foot down too quickly. He reached out to the jagged concrete on his right for some grip. He winced as his injured hand made contact. Looking down, he realised Zahra hadn't waited. He pressed on, increasing his pace and hoping to God his shoes gained some traction.

Finally he was at the next landing. He stole a glance upwards, saw two men moving surprisingly quickly towards him, then turned to negotiate the next leg.

Zahra was nowhere to be seen.

Chapter 25

Bijlmer, Amsterdam

Where was she? She couldn't have made it to the bottom of the flight below already.

Then he understood. She'd fallen.

His heart stopped. This was all his doing. He'd killed her.

The men were closing fast and he knew that whatever thoughts he had to face would have to wait. He pressed on, the anguish like a lead weight. About three steps down, he slipped.

His right foot lost its grip and suddenly his lower body was pitched forward. He reached out for the wall, hand grabbing in vain at coarse concrete, and then he was landing, a painful crunch of elbows and lower back making contact. With a sensation of pure unadulterated terror, he realised he was still moving – a bed of icy snow like a slalom – towards the drop on his right. He scrambled with his hands for something to grip, his fingers merely combing through powdery snow. It was his right foot that saved him, finding some obstacle below the snow, and bringing the rest of his body to a halt. He closed his eyes for a second, then opened them. To his right, about six inches away, was the edge.

From behind him, a voice called out. 'He's fallen. We've got him!'

Sam glanced back. The nearest man was just above him. He was caught. There was no way he'd be able to get up and move with enough speed to escape.

And then the man above Sam slipped. He watched in horror as he stepped forward and, like him just moments before, lost his footing. But unlike Sam, this man's trajectory was less staggered. He tipped headfirst, as if a hand had given him a firm shove. There was no time to reach out to grip the wall. In a matter of seconds, he went from stepping forward, to stepping into space. There was a brief flash of dark hair, terrified eyes and flailing arms as he shot past Sam, and then he was gone, a bloodcurdling scream piercing the dense, snow-filled air.

Sam's heart was thudding in his ear – his own near-death experience put into true perspective by what he'd just witnessed. He wanted to move, to lift himself up off this man-made precipice, but he couldn't. He was consumed with terror. And completely rigid.

It was then he heard a soft voice to his left. A voice he thought he'd never hear again. He turned and realised that what he'd taken to be solid wall was in fact a dark hole. An opening in which he could just make out Zahra's face.

It was the hope he needed. He found strength again, scrambling with his hands to crawl left, climb through the hole and drop to the floor, some two feet below.

His eyes took a moment to adjust but then he made out Zahra pressed against the wall next to him, her body crouched below the opening, a finger to her mouth.

They sat, as still as headstones, Sam's heart galloping. And then a figure appeared at the hole. Sam held his breath. As the man crossed the opening – his bulky figure clad in a bomber jacket, head encased in a hoodie – the grey light of the storm briefly dimmed.

The man muttered to himself. 'Fuck this. Fuck this.' It was an English voice; an Essex accent, maybe South London.

Zahra threw a hand to her mouth.

The man was moving slowly, taking his time, all too aware of his colleague's fate. He was so close, Sam could hear the man's laboured breathing, each intake of air an expression of fear.

Sam was conscious that the man was probably using the wall to steady himself. Which meant that, were he to probe it in the right place, he too would discover the opening – and them.

But he didn't. He moved past, the darkness lifted and once more the subdued light of the storm seeped into their hiding place. Sam finally exhaled.

Zahra was mute beside him. When, a moment later, she turned and her mouth opened to speak, it was as if she were choking on her words. Eventually she managed to whisper a short, croaked sentence.

'That was him,' she croaked. 'That was the man who threatened me at Creech Hill.'

Her eyes blazed and her voice returned, quiet but raging. 'And you brought him here.'

Chapter 26

Bijlmer, Amsterdam

'How was I to know I was being followed?'

'I was safe here,' she hissed.

'Christ,' muttered Sam, angry at a society in which a frightened immigrant might consider a tower block without amenities of any sort – the kind of place where people lay dying of hypothermia on stinking stairwells – 'safe'.

His mind rapidly processed the implications of the man's arrival, how the tables had suddenly turned. How he'd gone from amateur investigator to hunted quarry. That man wouldn't give up till he'd found and eliminated them both.

'This doesn't end until we find out why that man is after me,' he said. 'After us. What he thinks we know.'

'I told you, I have no idea.' Her voice had changed tone. It sounded broken.

Even if she didn't know why they were being pursued, Zahra was confident about the identity of the man who'd just come within a whisker of their hiding place. But as Sam weighed that up, Zahra reminded him of a more pressing issue.

'We need to get out of here,' she said. Her survival instinct, which had served her so well, was kicking in. 'That man will be back.'

'I'm sorry, but what's your plan? We can't just keep running.'

She lifted herself from the floor. 'What else do you suggest?'

'We have to find somewhere safe,' said Sam, pushing himself up to a standing position.

Zahra gave him a withering look. For her, there was nowhere safe.

Sam had another thought, and not a pleasant one. The attack might have been crude but the fact was, the man had found him here. Which suggested a level of sophistication, an ability to trace. They had to disappear below the radar.

'There is somewhere,' Zahra said, interrupting his thinking. 'In Rome. An Eritrean community. I know people there.'

This would do, thought Sam. A place that was familiar to Zahra, which was important. And one that gave them distance. 'I have money,' he said. I can help you get there.'

Zahra nodded, almost imperceptibly. It was not an agreement as such. But Sam sensed that at least she recognised his worth. He was needed, if only as a wallet in the short term.

Zahra moved into the shadows, Sam following. The building had stilled around them. Where, Sam wondered, was the man? Was he waiting in the dark, hiding behind one of hundreds of pillars to pounce?

They inched towards the walkway. Sam had no idea what floor he was on. It mattered little. If you discounted the exposed steps on the outside of the building, there was only one way down – and that was via the stairwell he'd climbed.

'We can't go out the way I came in,' Sam whispered. 'He'll be waiting at the bottom.'

Zahra shot Sam a look. He couldn't make out her expression in the darkness but the message was clear. She was making the decisions.

Sam sensed that this floor was all but uninhabited. Beyond the traces of former residents – the crunch of glass underfoot, a sweet-smelling cocktail of alcohol, rotting food and piss – it was near silent.

The light was changing, a ghostly white slowly leaching into the building as they neared the walkway.

Zahra was first through the nearest opening, moving, for Sam's money, too fast as she headed down the walkway. Unlike the cleared seventh floor, this one was covered with snow, Zahra's footsteps making tell-tale prints in its pristine surface, each step a soft squeaky crunch that made Sam tense with fear.

She was at the stairs a moment later, Sam just behind. Zahra was now descending with way too much speed. Did she know something that he didn't? Was she leading him straight to the man – and then planning to run? How far would she go to survive?

As the stairwell closed in around him, Sam sensed another companion by his side, the suffocating presence of claustrophobia, a cold hand gently but surely encircling his throat.

A couple of floors down, by which time Sam's breath was coming in shallow gasps, Zahra cut back on to a walkway. She turned to jerk her head quickly, urging him to follow.

A glance over the balcony to his left told Sam that they were now on the second or possibly first floor. He saw Zahra dart across the snow-covered walkway and then disappear through an opening.

He followed her through the gap. The floor was lit with a soft white glow, as if the walls were emitting their own light. Zahra moved with speed towards the rear of the building. Her haste sent a bottle flying across the concrete floor to hit a concrete pillar, the noise amplified in the cavern-like space. Sam heard a distant voice – a man shouting what sounded like instructions. At this early hour in the morning in a place as dead as a tomb, it had to be their pursuer. Fear coursed through Sam. The chase was on again.

Zahra was at the far wall, her torso a silhouette against a window that had long ago lost its glass. He was a few paces behind when he saw, to his horror, her climbing on to the ledge and then, without a second's hesitation, jumping.

With the sound of footfall gathering behind him – one, maybe two, people moving up the stairwell at a pace – Sam rushed to the window. He looked below. Here was the source of that eerie white glow. Snow, catching the first of the morning's light – a brightness that disoriented, obliterating horizon and depth. Sam squinted. A snowdrift had gathered at the base of the building, a bed of white ten feet, maybe more, below the ledge. A figure was emerging from what looked like a burrow. It was Zahra, her landing cushioned by the depth of the snow. She turned to look up and shouted one simple instruction: 'Jump!'

Sam heard his pursuers getting closer, knew he had to leap before they saw him at the opening. He lifted his right leg and left hand to the ledge, pulling his body up, crouched long enough to taste a rush of bile in his mouth, and jumped.

Chapter 27

Bijlmer, Amsterdam

Sam landed in a belly flop, his whole front making contact. He felt a jolt ring through his body, like he'd just been given a large electric shock. Underneath the first foot or so, the snow went from pillow-like to hard and compacted.

A figure was at his side. 'Run!' shouted Zahra.

Sam's feet scrambled in the snow for purchase, his eyes dazzled by the brightness. As he rose from the ground, he saw Zahra plod away from the building, as visible against the white of the snow as a smudge of charcoal on white paper, each step slow as her feet sunk deep. He wanted to shout at her to hide, tell her to cling to the side of the building, but then he saw the prints her feet had made and, looking back, the huge patterns their falls had created. Whichever way they headed, their trail was there for all to see.

He moved forward, each step ponderous as if the snow were trying to drag them downwards, suck them into a deep frozen grave. It was then he heard a voice behind them. 'They're there!'

Sam turned. The building was hard to make out now that his eyes had adjusted to the brightness. But he recognised the voice. The man was at the empty window. 'Jump!' he was shouting. 'Go and get them!'

Sam turned round, tried to move faster, but the snow protested at his new pace. With each step, the soles of his shoes gathered more snow, slowing his movements further.

Behind him, an argument had erupted.

'I'm not jumping, man!'

'I paid you to find them. Now jump!'

'Fuck off! I've had enough.'

'For Christ's sake!'

There was a moment's pause and then Sam heard the crunch of a body making contact with the ground, followed by a groan. A quick glance confirmed his worst fears. The man was now about fifteen feet from him, currently lying on the ground and still cursing, but before long he'd be up and moving after them. The blood pulsed in Sam's ears. He pushed on, his legs like lead weights. Ahead, Zahra was moving faster now, as if on more compacted ground.

There was another groan from behind and Sam turned again to see the man's bulky frame rise from the ground. There was a skid of legs, another expletive and then he was up. The head hidden inside the hoodie appeared to lock on to Sam.

A few feet on and Sam hit the ground that Zahra was on. Snow that was compacted, less giving. He broke into a jog, putting more ground between him and the man. Up ahead, Zahra was about to round a corner, to disappear behind the nearest block. A glance over her shoulder and another flick of her head confirmed to Sam that she still wanted him to follow.

Sam ran faster, chasing Zahra round the side of the building. The light was changing fast, a bright day dawning on a white landscape. Sam could hear the man grunting behind him. Sam thanked God for the man's bulk, which would be working against him in this sprint for survival. He turned for a second. Another mouthful of bile rose in his throat. He was wrong. The man had actually gained on them.

Zahra was now crossing open ground, heading back in the direction of the road. If they cut left in a minute or so, they'd reach the Metro station.

Sam's lungs protested, as if he were ascending a mountain and the air were thinning. Zahra had reached a fence and crawled through a small hole at its base. Sam was at the opening seconds later, ducking down to move through. Exposed lines of wire snagged at his coat. He turned to free himself and saw, with sickening clarity, that the man was now a matter of feet from him, so close Sam could see his eyes, framed by a black ski mask under his hoodie.

It was as if a starting pistol had been fired in his head. Sam lurched forward, hearing a rip of material and feeling a brief slash of pain from his back. He pelted after Zahra, who had left the slippery pavement and was running in the middle of the empty road on a surface of watery slush.

As Sam chased after her, he turned to see the man struggling with the same exposed pieces of wire, his larger frame too big for the narrow opening. He was caught momentarily, giving Sam and Zahra a vital few seconds.

The Metro station loomed ahead, a big lump of concrete, steel and glass, an oasis of urban civilisation. A building where others would be around, where the man wouldn't dare follow them, let alone attack. Surely.

Zahra was at an intersection in front of the station. The first traffic of the morning was moving through a soup of melted snow, sending arcs of grey slop either side. Zahra darted across the road, Sam following the path she'd carved in a gap in the traffic. A car that had been moving quicker than Sam realised slammed on its brakes and he looked to his left to see it sliding towards him, the driver's eyes wide with alarm. The car came to a halt inches from an immobilised Sam. An angry chorus of horns rang out. Sam's heart was beating so fast he thought it might burst from his chest. Then, seeing the man about to cross the road behind him, he felt a fresh shot of adrenaline and began running again.

Seconds later, he was inside the Metro station, Zahra just ahead and darting up an escalator. Sam followed, barging past a handful of sleepy commuters. He looked back. The man was inside the station. He had slowed. But then he glanced up at Sam, and picked up the pace.

Zahra had reached the barrier and leapt over it in one graceful movement. By contrast, Sam's attempt at a vault was a mess of stumbling limbs followed by a clumsy landing. The man was seconds behind but by now, a Metro official was at the barrier, shouting in Sam's wake. Their pursuer swotted the official aside with a shove of his hand and clambered over the barrier, dropping heavily the other side.

A train was pulling in, accompanied by a protesting screech of brakes and an engine whirring to a stop. The doors opened with a hiss and Zahra was in, swiftly followed by Sam. They watched through the opening as the man limped towards the train. He appeared to have twisted an ankle and was wincing with every fall of his right foot. But he was now feet from them.

'Close,' hissed Sam, willing the doors to shut. 'For fuck's sake, close.'

A pinging noise heralded the imminent departure of the train. The doors began easing shut just as their pursuer reached them. Sam's heart was in his mouth. The man stretched out, his fingers getting trapped as the doors closed against them. He now stood inches from Sam and Zahra. The hoodie and balaclava still hid everything except his eyes, but these bore into Sam with a look of utter hatred. Zahra reared back in terror.

The man tried to slide another hand into the gap but, as he did this, the fingers already trapped in the door, the tips shiny with sweat, lost their grip and, seconds later, the train eased out of the station with a heavy sigh of surging engine. The man stood motionless in the train's wake, his eyes rooted on Sam, until he disappeared from view.

Chapter 28

Amsterdam

Zahra and Sam sat side by side, panting like dogs. Sam's lungs felt like they were on fire.

He knew what would happen. That their pursuer would catch the next train, resume his hunt. But for now, they were safe. There was time to think.

The man had clearly been following Sam ever since he'd arrived in Amsterdam, perhaps before. Which meant that, in all likelihood, he knew where he was staying. Depending on the frequency of trains the man was, at worst, minutes behind them. Perhaps they had longer, but Sam had to assume not. He had his passport and wallet in his coat pocket. That would have to be enough. Going back to the hotel was too dangerous.

He looked at Zahra. Her dark skin glowed with sweat, but her breathing had slowed. She was staring ahead through the window, the suburbs of Amsterdam flying by. Apartment blocks and snow-covered streets, cars and people moving slowly through the awakening cityscape. Her face looked mask-like, numbed.

The train was whizzing through stations and Sam realised that they'd caught an express. Perhaps luck was on their side. He sniffed derisively. If staying a few minutes ahead of a violent predator was luck, then he needed to take a long, hard look at the situation he'd got himself into.

He felt a stinging pulse from his back and remembered how he'd got caught on the wire of the fence. He sat forward, reaching an arm behind him. The coat and shirt beneath were torn. He touched ripped flesh and winced at the pain. When he examined his hand, he saw blood on his fingertips.

The train was slowing, an automated female voice announcing the next station in Dutch. There was a pause, and then the same voice intoned: 'We will shortly be arriving at Amsterdam Centraal. Next station, Amsterdam Centraal.'

Zahra stood, moving to the doors, readying to run. Sam followed, bracing for more after the brief respite of the journey. Through the windows, the dark walls of a tunnel were replaced by a platform thronged with people, a city awake and ready to work.

The train stopped, the doors slid open and Zahra was instantly out and pushing through the wall of bodies. Sam followed.

Zahra jogged ahead of him, moving towards another barrier that they'd have to negotiate without tickets. She nudged in behind a woman, slipping through the barrier in her wake. Sam spotted an elderly man and took his chance. The man was fumbling with a ticket, struggling to feed it into the slot in the gate. Sam approached, touched the man gently on the shoulder. The man turned. Sam smiled and nodded towards the gate, as if offering to help. The man looked puzzled but Sam didn't wait for consent, gripping the shaking hand and guiding it to the barrier slot where the ticket was drawn inside. The gate opened and Sam, pressing into the man's back, moved them both through.

He and Zahra ascended an escalator into the square in front of the station. It was a bright, sunny day. A day for tourists who wanted to wander the pretty snow-covered streets and canals, to break for coffee or hot chocolate in snug cafés. But all Sam felt was a desperate need to hide, as if the light made them more visible, more of a target.

He spotted a queue for the cabs, decided this might be the best way to gain some proper distance from their pursuer. Where they went was immaterial, they just needed to get away. Sam rushed to the front just as one cab sped off and another car moved into place. The two people at the head of the queue, a pair of men in suits, were reaching down to pick up bags and Sam took advantage of the moment, opening the back door of the cab and jumping inside. Zahra swiftly followed Sam, climbing in the opposite side.

'That's our cab!' One of the men had appeared at the side of the vehicle, grabbing the door handle before Sam could pull it shut. He directed his next comment at the driver. 'They jumped in front us!'

The driver turned to the rear of his cab, gave Sam a weary, irritated look. He signalled with a jutting hand and outstretched thumb.

'I'll pay double,' said Sam.

The driver's face paused momentarily in thought. But then the suited man's voice cut into the car again. 'This is our fucking taxi.'

'Get out,' said the driver.

Sam knew that the more they argued, the more time was lost. He signalled to Zahra and they got out. As he passed the man in the suit, Sam was shouldered out of the way. Sam's fist clenched then slackened. This idiot was not the problem.

They began running away from the station. There was no logic or thought to the direction, just a need to clear ground.

They'd barely got twenty metres across the slippery, snow-covered cobbles when Sam turned and saw, to his horror, the bulky form of the man who'd been hunting them like animals since the early hours. He'd clearly emerged from the station, noticed the commotion by the taxi rank, and zoned straight in on them.

'Oh Christ,' said Sam, his parched throat reducing his voice to a croak.

The man was jogging, like a robot that never tired, in their direction.

Sam saw a break in the traffic and sped right, across the road, Zahra close by.

On the other side they darted down a narrow street of shops, windows filled with huge, wax-covered wheels of cheese, wine, mannequins in winter fashion.

'There!' shouted Zahra, pointing across the street. Two bicycles were propped against the window of a gift shop, its frontage twinkling with fairy lights. Zahra grabbed one of the bicycles and mounted it, skidding on the cobbles as she moved off. Sam pulled the other bike from the window and climbed on. He pedalled in standing position, pushing down hard on the pedals, accelerating away.

It was only when they'd reached the next junction that he dared look back. Their pursuer was pulling frantically at a bicycle that was obviously securely chained to railings, his means of chasing thwarted. For now.

Chapter 29

Amsterdam

They abandoned the bicycles in a backstreet in Jordaan, leaning them against a garage door. The house next door had window baskets filled with shrubs dense with plump red berries. The colour caught Sam's eye and he thought immediately, not of life in the midst of winter, but of blood and death.

Zahra paced up and down the street, muttering to herself. She then turned, her face flushed with rage and rushed at him, both fists raised. She brought them down on his chest like she was beating a drum, one fist after another. Caught unaware, Sam took three powerful hits to his chest before he was able to bring his hands up and grab her wrists. He could feel the strength in her arms, the tension ready to explode.

'I'm sorry,' he said.

'It was OK before you came!' she shouted.

'No,' said Sam, as calmly as possible. 'It was OK before you saw that man at Creech Hill.'

A voice called out from a window above. A woman shouting angrily.

Sam felt some of the pressure in his hands subside as Zahra calmed. Her arms dropped and he let her wrists go. Her head sunk into her chest, the fight gone out of her.

'You've upset someone,' said Sam. 'Someone who has ordered that man to find us. You've seen him. He's a machine, who doesn't care about the law. He will do whatever it takes to locate us. And, I'm guessing, whatever it takes to silence us.'

'I'm frightened.'

'So am I,' said Sam.

'I can't help,' her voice cracked. 'I can't remember.'

'I know,' said Sam. 'And I understand.'

She looked up at him, eyes glassy with tears, but jaw set hard.

'I need to get out of here.'

Sam knew that another plea to talk to the police would fall on deaf ears. She was terrified – convinced, more than ever, that men in uniform were not to be trusted. Maybe he could call Emery when he had a chance – tell him that the man hunting them was, so Zahra believed, the same person who'd threatened her at Creech Hill and therefore in all likelihood the man who'd pushed Fitzgerald to his death. But the fact was, the police would still need to talk to Zahra and the moment she discovered he'd made the call, she'd bolt.

So his only hope lay in staying by her side. But now it all hinged on her accessing lost memories – trying to figure out the significance of the suited man.

The problem was, retrograde amnesia caused by head trauma was only eased by time and, more importantly, rest. Zahra wouldn't be remembering anything any time soon.

Sam had another idea. Maybe, just maybe, there was someone in this Eritrean community in Rome who remembered what happened on her voyage – someone who could help them fill in the moments leading up to Zahra's 'waking' in Catania.

'I'll take you to Rome,' he said. 'But I need to ask for something in return.'

'I'll find my own way if it involves the police.'

'Nothing to do with the police. I just want you to ask around the community you mentioned, see if anyone knows anything about your journey across the Med.'

Zahra shook her head. 'You think I haven't asked? I got separated from my husband, Abel. I've asked everyone.'

'Surely the community changes all the time. People coming and going. There might be someone new who knows something.'

Zahra closed her eyes. When she opened them, it was with a look of resignation. 'I'll ask. But I can't promise anything.'

Sam experienced a swell of hope. 'We need to find transport.'

As soon as the words escaped his mouth, he felt his morale take a dive. As their recent experience had demonstrated, the people after them had the means to track their movements, which meant he and Zahra had to be careful. 'We cannot travel on trains and buses, or hire a car. Names will be taken, passports checked.'

'You don't think –' Zahra's voice was tinged with fear.

'Who knows? We just can't take any risks.'

'So how exactly are you going to help me get to Rome?'

As Sam tried to think of an answer, Zahra came up with one of her own. 'Ruby has a car. She lets the girls use it. If you fill it up, we've still got a deal.'

It sounded good, but Sam had a reservation. 'I don't think we should go back.'

'It's not on the estate. It's just north – in a garage that belongs to a friend of hers. We used to go to the supermarket in the car, drop off our shopping then take it back there. The key is kept hidden in the garage. We can get a cab there.'

'I don't think Ruby will be too pleased,' said Sam, a smile breaking across his face.

'Ruby's a dictator. I don't like dictators.'

They visited a bank. Zahra hung back while Sam withdrew a thousand Euros. The cashier chatted breezily to him. Was he on holiday? What did he think of the weather? Had he visited the Rijks Museum or Anne Frank's House? Sam played along – telling the woman he'd liked the Vermeers in the Rijks (which was true, from his previous visit) but that he hadn't visited Anne Frank's House – as his stomach churned with acid and his feet strained inside his shoes, as if readying for another sprint.

The cashier counted out the notes, placed them in a plastic envelope and passed it, along with his passport and credit card, under the plate glass separating them.

Outside the bank, Sam noticed that Zahra was shivering. Her cheeks had a grey tinge to them.

'We need to get you some more clothes,' he said. 'You'll freeze to death.'

Despite the shivering, Zahra shot Sam a look. 'We get the car first. If someone else takes it out, we've got no transport.'

They caught a cab to an area north of Bijlmer. They were dropped on a high street of sorts. A handful of stores were open – a kebab shop, launderette and grocer with a window clad in steel mesh – but the others were boarded up, the surfaces covered with Dutch graffiti – not, Sam guessed, messages of love and peace. Zahra led him down a narrow alley between two shops, the ground slippery and shiny underfoot where the passage of cars had flattened the snow.

The garage was one of a row of six. Zahra lifted the door, which swung upwards with a high-pitched screech, as if crying out for lubricant. As the light of day penetrated the space inside, a rat, its long, worm-like tail giving it away, scuttled for the nearest hiding place.

Inside, between walls stacked with shelves that groaned under the weight of paint cans, cardboard boxes and rusting tools, sat the Opel, the dark green of its bonnet spotted with water, melting snow from a recent journey. Patches of rust were creeping up from above the front bumper. A piece of black gaffer tape had been attached to a corner of the left front light where the glass was broken – just about discreet enough, Sam hoped, to avoid attracting the attention of the police.

Zahra reached for a shelf just to the left, lifting a can of varnish and pulling a set of keys from underneath. She handed them to Sam.

'I never learned to drive,' she said, a sheepish look on her face.

The car had a heavy gearbox and brakes that were – whether due to the road conditions or because they were worn out – reluctant to bring the car to a standstill unless Sam pressed his foot to the floor. And the rear window only partially defrosted, offering him an oval of visibility. But the interior soon warmed and Sam got used to the car's idiosyncrasies.

They visited a hypermarket south of Bijlmer, where Sam bought Zahra some extra clothes and basic toiletries. Then they stopped at a garage and he filled the tank and bought a European road map and a dressing for the wound on his back. In the toilet, he peeled off his jacket and shirt and used a dampened wad of toilet tissue to clean the cut. Staring at his torso in a dirty mirror, Sam saw that the gash, wiped clean of blood, wasn't as large as he'd expected. But it was still a deep cut, and bleeding slightly. It probably needed stitching, but that would have to wait. He peeled open the dressing and placed it, as well as he could given the angle, over the wound, pressing down the edges.

He balled his right hand. The cut sustained outside the theatre still hurt. But he figured the sensation would prove handy, keeping him awake on the journey ahead.

In the car park, he rested the road map on the roof of the Opel, plotting a vague route that amounted to a shorthand of cities they would pass as navigation points – Antwerp, Brussels, Reims, Dijon, Lyon, Grenoble, Turin, Bologna, Florence, Rome. The route wasn't arrived at with any skill on Sam's part, merely some sense that the alternative – travelling through Germany and then across the Alps – was a journey the Opel might not manage.

He closed the map and climbed back in the car, anxiety biting in his stomach. Rome might have represented a haven of sorts to Zahra, but at that moment – his body battered and tender, and terrifying images of their machine-like pursuer still replaying in his mind – Sam felt anything but safe.

Chapter 30

Romford, East London

The Haven Nursing Home was in Romford's Gidea Park, an area of immaculate large detached houses, manicured gardens and neat drives boasting two or three shiny new cars.

It was a far cry from the council flat, less than a mile away, in which Harry Tapper had grown up with his mother and father, a cramped, damp hole of dark memories. Tapper would dearly have loved to move his mother nearer his place in Notting Hill, but while Mary-Beth Tapper's dementia made her confused, frustrated and forgetful, she managed to hold on to one certainty. That she'd been born in Romford and she would die in Romford.

So it was that Tapper made weekly pilgrimages to the home to see his increasingly muddled mother. Today, she'd mistaken him for an old neighbour from the 1950s and had reminisced fondly about a street party to celebrate the Coronation. It was obvious that she remembered it more lucidly than yesterday.

They were in her ground floor room, the heating cranked up full so that, even after discarding his overcoat and jacket, Tapper still felt like he was in a sauna. Mary-Beth Tapper sat small and bird-like in a large, high-backed chair. She held on to her son's hand tightly as she spoke.

'It was a lovely day, wasn't it Teddy?'

'It was,' said Tapper wearily.

'All them flags and the lovely sandwiches and cake. And we got a telegram from the Palace.'

'Did we?'

'Don't you remember, Teddy? It was the talk of Romford.'

He felt his mobile vibrate in his trouser pocket and reached for it with his free hand. The name flashing on the screen was Wallace.

''Scuse me for a moment, Mum.'

'I ain't your mother, Teddy, you silly arse. It's me, Mary-Beth. From Number 12.'

Tapper exited his mother's room. The corridor outside led to a conservatory where there was a door into the garden. He opened it and the cold rushed into the room as if trying to devour the air inside. He put the phone to his ear.

'Pat.'

For the next couple of minutes, Tapper focused on the garden – the evergreen shrubs poking out from a blanket of white – as Wallace reported back. It was all he could do to stop himself screaming.

'So where are they now?' he asked.

'I went back to the flats,' said Wallace. 'To see if I could find anyone who knew anything. I was told about a junkie who'd overheard them speaking.'

'And?'

'He said they were talking about Rome.'

'Right.' Tapper felt the enormity of the disaster on his hands. The two of them now together. Aware of each other's plights, aware that others wanted them dead. The shrink and his client, with her incendiary secret.

There was nothing to discover, of that he was sure. But she was a witness.

Despite the bitter cold, Tapper felt a bead of sweat escape an armpit and trickle down the side of his torso as he remembered the night.

'I can't do this on my own, Harry,' Wallace said. He was calm, stating a fact. 'This operation needs another body on the ground.'

'Know anyone you can trust?'

'Not with this kind of thing. We need people we can rely on one hundred per cent.'

'Let me have a think,' said Tapper. 'I'll call you back.'

The firm was a no-no. Systems in place to track every appointment. He wondered about ex-employees. God knows, Tapper Security didn't always employ angels, especially for low-level stuff. But he didn't know any of them. He was too far removed from operational matters.

He rubbed his forehead with the heel of a hand. Perhaps he could pay a visit to Tapper Security's HR department, do the hands-on CEO routine again. He couldn't think of a reason right now, but there was probably some way he could get his hands on previous employee records, find someone with services experience, and a less-than-perfect past. But it would take time, and with Keddie and Idris escaping across Europe, they had little to spare. Besides, with another team member, the circle widened a little more. Wallace had latterly more than proved himself, rising above their initial setbacks with some exemplary tracking. Tapper could hardly believe he'd ever doubted him. But could a new team member be trusted?

He breathed in through his nostrils then exhaled, his breath condensing in the freezing air.

Wallace needed someone by his side who he could depend on. Tapper closed his eyes, felt a decision rise, with certainty, to the surface, drowning out every other thought.

He pressed '1' on speed-dial.

'Sir Harry,' said Jenny, his PA, her voice bright and cut-glass.

'Jenny, I'm taking some time off. Mum's not well. Can you clear the diary? Sure the board can cope. I don't want any calls, understood?'

He called Wallace back. 'I'm coming out, Pat.'

'But you can't do that, Harry. You've got a company to run.'

'Right now, I'm not sure I have a choice.'

Tapper promised to call back when he'd sorted a flight to Rome. It had been years since he'd had to deal with bookings. Normally Jenny took care of such matters.

The cold was now penetrating his skin, inching its way to his vital organs. How long would someone survive standing still in such temperatures, he wondered?

He thought of the task before him. Of tracking two people, one effectively a ghost, in a large European city, if indeed they were in Rome.

There were plenty of dangers. Logically, it made sense for him to stay as far away from Zahra Idris as possible, for the hunt to have no connection to him at all. What if it all went wrong? What if they were caught as they tried to deal with Keddie and Idris? Arrested. It would all be over.

But then it was all over if he didn't act.

Tapper thought of the last time he and Wallace had been together for any length of time. He thought of the violence that he might inevitably witness, possibly even be a part of. He shuddered with fear. And also, he realised, with pleasure.

Chapter 31

Belgium

Sam watched in horror as the traffic ahead slowed at the Belgium border crossing. It hadn't occurred to him that they'd have any problems passing through what were meant to be the open borders of the Schengen Zone. But Europe was a twitchier place these days. Sam cursed. He should have anticipated this.

'Get in the back now!' he hissed. 'And take that blanket with you to pull over your body.'

Without hesitation, Zahra unbuckled her seatbelt and climbed into the rear, taking the blanket she'd had wrapped around her.

The car inched forward, the air thick with condensed exhaust fumes. The border was comprised of a line of booths. He looked at the car at the front of the queue, watched as the driver handed his passport to a border official. The man examined the passport for less than thirty seconds, then handed it back. The barrier rose and the car departed. How hard could it be?

But Sam was harbouring an immigrant who'd escaped from a detention centre in the UK. A woman without a passport.

Sam could hear his pulse thudding in his ear.

There were now just two cars between him and the booth. He glanced behind at the backseat. Zahra's feet were sticking out from the bottom of the blanket. Sam undid his seatbelt, removed his coat and draped them over the protruding limbs.

A car horn sounded. The driver behind was urging Sam to move forward into the space that had been freed up ahead. Just one car between him and the booth.

Sam re-buckled his belt, accelerating into the gap.

A minute passed. The barrier rose and the car ahead moved off. Sam came to a halt by the booth. The man to his left wore a blue uniform, a colour that almost matched his complexion.

'Passport,' he said disinterestedly.

Sam handed it across to him. The man flicked through the pages, pausing on the final one where Sam's image appeared next to his details. He scrunched up his eyes as he studied it, then glanced at Sam and the vehicle.

'Moment,' the man said.

Sam's heart was in his mouth. The man had placed the passport down on his desk and seemed to be tapping at a keyboard. He scratched his stubble. This hadn't happened to the other drivers. What the fuck was going on? Had he spotted the tell-tale lump in the rear? Was there a problem with the car? Had Ruby reported it stolen?

The man looked up. The passport was handed back. The barrier rose. Sam thanked the man, then slowly accelerated away, finally letting go of his breath.

'You can come out now.'

On the back seat, there was a movement – a blanket rising up – and Zahra emerged, climbing from the rear into the front.

'God, that was close,' said Sam, the words escaping on a sigh.

Zahra glanced at him, a look of mild incredulity on her face. Of course, thought Sam. Crossing borders illegally was what she did, and that last one was probably child's play compared with most.

A sign above the road read Antwerp, Brussels and Maastricht. He hoped the next crossing was open.

Zahra opened the vanity mirror above her, brushing a few stray hairs from her face. She then reached for a bag in the footwell, pulled a packet of wipes from it and began cleaning her face, closing her eyes as if the cool tissue afforded her a rare moment of pleasure.

She threw the used wipe back into the bag, then turned to Sam. 'Do you mind if I sleep?' she asked.

'Be my guest.'

*

Sam was driving around the outskirts of Brussels when he noticed that Zahra was sweating. She'd also begun twitching, her face screwed up in a grimace. The tics became more pronounced and soon she was tossing her head from side to side, moaning to herself in a language Sam couldn't understand.

He needed to pull over, convinced that her movements would become more dramatic, endangering them both. But then they came to an abrupt and blood-curdling stop.

Zahra woke, eyes wide, and screamed, the car filling with an ear-piercing, primal noise. Sam flinched as the sound was repeated again and again, like an alarm of pure terror. As he tried to pull the car across two busy lanes of traffic and bring it to a standstill on the hard shoulder, Zahra finally stilled. Sam found a way to enter the far right lane then pulled over, skidding as he came to a halt on the untreated road surface.

He turned to Zahra. Her face was glistening with sweat.

'It was a snake,' she said, her voice trembling.

'What?'

Zahra was staring ahead, as if in a trance.

'The belt.'

'I don't understand.'

'I dreamt that I was on a beach on an island. It was a perfect place. The kind you see in magazines. White, powdery sand, palm trees. I got up and began to walk towards the trees. The air smelt sweet. But then my foot brushed against an object and I looked down to see something buried in the sand.' She shuddered. 'I began digging with my hands. When I'd pulled the sand away, I could see it was a leather belt, with a metal buckle. I held it in my hands and that was when it turned into a snake. A snake that reared up and opened a mouth full of fangs.'

Zahra shook violently, as if desperate to eject the repellent image from her mind.

Was this connected to her lost memories, Sam wondered? Was it some way in? He glanced at Zahra as she sat upright in her seat.

'Does that remind you of anything?' he asked gently. 'Any feelings you've had?'

She turned to him. 'It reminds me of every time I have felt frightened.'

'In it, you're somewhere perfect.'

'I haven't been anywhere perfect for a long time.'

Zahra had turned away, her face pressed to the glass as the traffic sped by. Sam decided to let it drop. It was a possible angle to explore, nothing more. The dream might have been a link to a lost memory, or simply a reminder that the woman by his side carried a headful of darkness.

Chapter 32

Ragusa, Sicily – the previous summer

Ispettore Guido Reni parked his car in the courtyard of the police headquarters. Opening the door, he felt a wall of oppressive heat and knew he'd be sweating before he reached the air-conditioned interior of the building ahead.

He unlocked the boot, lifted out a case of Santa Cecilia, an over-priced red with an almost blood-like consistency, and placed it gently on the ground while he slammed the boot shut. His chest felt tight, and he knew he'd need a hit on the inhaler as soon as he could put the box down.

Reni had been told that it was his asthma that had held him back for well over a decade. He had the right qualifications for promotion – a degree, in his case forensic investigation, from the University of Naples – but was constantly passed over. He'd tried to question this reasoning – after all, higher ranks spent more time behind desks and less time running around – but was always palmed off. At first he thought it was because the Mafia still had influence in the town and, as a result, honest, incorruptible men could not thrive. But then it slowly dawned on him that the real reason he languished at Ispettore was even less palatable.

Although his father's forebears had lived in Siracusa for centuries – his father a fisherman, like his grandfather and great-grandfather before him – his mother was Tunisian.

He'd come to realise that the Arab blood that flowed through his veins counted against him. He knew about his nickname, 'Arabo', though it was never used to his face.

And so, over the years, confident that he'd remain an Ispettore forever, he became the outsider they all thought he was. He stopped going for drinks after work, was less collaborative and more intransigent, happy to plough his own furrow.

Lugging the case of wine, he walked to a glass door, turning the handle with an awkward sideways stance, then stepped into blissful air-conditioned chill. He nodded to the officer behind the desk, and moved down the corridor, passing under a suspended sign that read 'Obitorio'.

The first room was a waiting area. A slim, dark-haired woman in a fitted white shirt – a welcome sight for grieving men, Reni thought – looked over the lip of spectacles and tipped her head in the direction of the next room.

Reni pushed through a set of swing doors into a larger area. Down the far end a rotund man in a white coat was standing over a body on an examination table. Observation benches climbed the wall behind him. Opposite were steel-fronted cabinets, the temporary homes of those bodies that required a closer examination following death.

'Ciao Guido!' called out the rotund man. He had a scrubbed appearance, his face pink and shiny.

'Ciao Simone.'

'What have you brought me?'

'Don't play the innocent, Simone,' said Reni, lowering the box to the floor. 'You wouldn't have looked at the corpse if I hadn't bribed you.'

The pathologist pretended to look affronted. 'Come on, Guido. You know how busy it gets in here. Besides, no one's interested in your man. He should be signed off and released for burial.'

Reni shook his inhaler then pumped it into his mouth, drawing in deeply. He felt his lungs relax. 'It's a sad world when we stop caring about people like him.'

The pathologist opened the lid of the box and carefully lifted a bottle out. He held it with all the love of a father for their new-born child. Bending to kiss the bottle's breast, he then placed it back in the box.

'So, what have you found?' asked Reni.

The pathologist peeled back a white sheet to reveal the head and torso of a man. Once again, Reni, who'd seen plenty of murder victims, was struck by the marks on the corpse's chest.

'The wounds are no great mystery, as we've already discussed. But I've jotted down my findings so you have it on paper.'

Reni was beginning to wonder whether the wine hadn't been an expensive mistake.

'However,' said the pathologist, his voice rising in enthusiasm, 'the contents of the stomach are interesting. Here,' he said, handing Reni a sheaf of stapled papers. His report. 'Read.'

Reni cast his eye over the report. As he turned to the second page and found what the pathologist was referring to, he felt a small charge of electricity run up his arms, as if the report itself held a live current. The pathologist's findings cast the body in a whole new light. Not that it would make any difference to his commanding officers.

But Reni knew that, unless he could solve this mystery, it would haunt him to his dying day.

Chapter 33

Heathrow Airport, London

Instead of his usual airport haunt – the bar of the nearest executive lounge – Tapper opted for the anonymity of a faux Irish pub in the terminal building. The people he normally encountered in airports would never bump into him here, or indeed in Alitalia's economy section (ordinarily he flew with BA or Virgin). He couldn't wholly disguise the fact he was heading to Rome – flights had been booked, passport details taken – but there was little point advertising it loudly, or inviting awkward conversations about where he was heading.

Tapper bought himself a large gin & tonic and sat in a quiet and shadowy corner of the room. He took two large gulps. He soon felt the alcohol go to work, flooding his veins, settling the uneasy mix of fear and anticipation that swam in his gut.

He opened the BBC news web page on his phone, scanning distractedly through the headlines.

The big story was that the Foreign Secretary had made a surprise announcement, that he was resigning due to ill health. Tapper opened the accompanying footage. It showed the Cabinet Minister briefing reporters at the Foreign Office. 'I will shortly be undergoing an operation for prostate cancer,' the man said, his face grey. 'This will be followed by several weeks of radiotherapy, which I'm told will be debilitating. As a result I have no choice but to resign the job I have been so proud to carry out on behalf of Her Majesty's Government.'

Tapper noticed a red banner across the top of the page with the words: 'Latest: Prime Minister pays tribute to Foreign Secretary and announces successor.' Tapper clicked on it.

There was another video clip, this one showing Gillian Mayer outside Number 10, flanked by about ten men and two women. Tapper knew three of the men personally. In fact, they'd all attended his Valentine's party.

'I want to thank the Foreign Secretary for his work,' the PM was saying, 'and, in particular, his efforts to spearhead international agreement on the need for destruction of chemical weapon stockpiles, as well as his pivotal role in the Anti-ISIL Coalition Conference, held here in London last year.'

Mayer's voice, once known for its piercing tones, had been given a Thatcher-style make-over. She'd learnt to soften it, to slow and deepen her enunciation.

There was an incoming call from Wallace. Tapper paused the clip and answered.

'Pat.'

'I haven't got long. The Rome flight's leaving soon.'

'Fire away.'

'I've accessed the laptops.'

'And?' Tapper tensed.

'Fitzgerald's machine had a dense file on Zahra Idris, but it's all harmless stuff, correspondence with the barrister who was going to represent her in court, legal notes and brief write-ups of his meetings with her at Creech Hill. Nothing that mentions you.'

Tapper felt himself relax a fraction.

'The date on the last entry was the day before we first spoke, so I'm thinking that Zahra Idris hadn't talked to Fitzgerald about you until their final meeting in Islington.'

After which, thought Tapper, Fitzgerald wasn't writing any more entries. 'What about the other laptop?'

'No case notes about Idris. But there are no notes about any client. So he either has them on another computer or writes them all up by hand.'

Wallace's voice was drowned out by a tannoy announcement. He stopped to let it finish. Tapper drummed the fingers of his free hand against the arm of the chair.

'All I found were his emails. There's no reference to Zahra Idris apart from some information-only exchanges with some woman at Creech Hill. But there is one thing that might be worth a gander.'

'Oh?' Tapper's pulse quickened.

'Turns out Idris is from Eritrea,' said Wallace. 'Keddie's done some research on the country. A while back, by the looks of thing. Stuff about Eritrea's history, the government, refugees. I'll send you a link to one item. Might be a good place to start.'

Tapper felt another wave of relief wash through him. The file was clearly nothing to do with him.

There was another tannoy announcement.

'It's my flight,' said Wallace. 'Gotta go. I'll see you at the airport.'

Seconds later, Tapper's phone pinged with the arrival of Wallace's message. He opened it and clicked on the link. It was a short video on YouTube, an Al Jazeera news report about a ghetto on the outskirts of Rome known as Salaam Palace. An abandoned office building, it was now home to hundreds of African immigrants, among them large numbers of Eritreans. The commentary claimed that the place was now so well known in Africa that many migrants leaving Libya had already decided to make it their destination, more often than not as a place to stay before they continued their journey to northern Europe. But some got stuck, caught in limbo by the Dublin Regulation, designed to clamp down on multiple asylum applications by forcing migrants to stay in the country they first enter. Salaam Place was now so overcrowded that the underground car park was filling up, with new arrivals sleeping on soiled mattresses.

Tapper closed the clip and sat back. He cast an eye over the room, at the people waiting for their flights in this corner of the airport. A ruddy, overweight man barking into his mobile; a sullen, rake-thin woman plastered in make-up; a couple in their early twenties leaning into each other, faces hidden by sunglasses.

Would this building in Rome be where they'd find Idris and Keddie? It was a possibility. Hotel bookings, certainly in Tapper's experience, demanded passports, and he doubted Zahra Idris had one.

Even if they weren't there, it was a place to start, to gather intelligence from other Eritreans. It was, he realised with a feeling of dread, the only place to start.

He returned to his phone and the story about the Foreign Secretary, watching Mayer's speech again, this time to its conclusion.

His stomach rose and fell with a wave of nausea.

The stakes in this operation had just been upped tenfold.

There was no longer any margin for failure. Idris and Keddie had to be found and destroyed.

Chapter 34

Rome

Sam drove through a dense sprawl of light industrial parkland and characterless apartment buildings, balconies strung with washing lines – clothes hanging limply in feeble winter sunshine – and rusting satellite dishes. Pausing at some traffic lights, he saw a wall covered with layers of graffiti. Artful tagging and colourful imagery had been consumed with messages and symbols in black. One read 'Contra la crisi' – no arguments there, thought Sam – while another read 'L'unica famiglia e' quella tradizionale'.

His eye was caught by one message in stark, angry capitals: 'Immigrati cazzo'. Sam knew enough Italian to know that it translated, simply, as 'Fuck immigrants'. There were other aggressive symbols sprayed hastily in black – a circle with a cross, and several swastikas. He turned to Zahra, but she was fast asleep in the seat beside him.

It was just over twenty hours since they'd left Amsterdam. Aside from filling up, they'd stopped just once, at a service station north of Lyons in the late afternoon. Sam was hungry and exhausted and needed to eat and rest. They parked some distance from the only building on the site, a large cafeteria serving dead-eyed truck drivers. Sam went in to buy sandwiches and coffee and returned to the car, half-expecting Zahra to have run away. But she was still there.

They consumed the sandwiches and coffee in silence. Despite the hit of caffeine, the overwhelming sensation was of a full belly, and Sam's eyes dropped. He woke with a start about an hour later. It was now much darker, orange street lamps casting a miserable glow over trucks and cars. He turned to Zahra. She was watching him, her face in darkness but her eyes catching the glow of a distant light. 'We should go,' she said.

The lights turned green and Sam moved forward. He noticed a large supermarket to his left, a cut-out cartoon figure of a jolly, smiling chef on the roof. He hastily indicated and pulled left, prompting a honk of horn from the car behind.

He drew into a space in the empty car park, killing the engine. The lack of motion woke Zahra. Her eyes blinked open and she shot Sam and her new surroundings a nervous glance.

Seeing her, Sam felt something gnawing at his insides. Now that he'd got her to Rome, would she still choose to help him, as she'd offered in Amsterdam? Or would she decide to go her own way? Evaporate. She was probably safer doing that. The sight of them together was far more memorable than the two of them apart.

'We're here,' he said. 'Rome.' Though he had to admit these grim suburbs were a far cry from the backstreets of Trastevere, which he and Eleanor had explored when they'd visited in the autumn. He felt a sharp pain in his chest.

'Where do you want to go now?' he asked.

Zahra rubbed the back of her fists against her eyes and then turned to look straight at him. 'The centre,' she said. 'There's a camp there.'

When Zahra had talked about a community, Sam had not envisaged a camp, let alone one that had taken root in the heart of a major European capital.

'I'll ask around, Sam. And then you must go home.'

Sam nodded, though he had no intention of returning home without answers.

They left the car in the supermarket car park. Sam had the feeling that they would not be returning to retrieve Ruby's battered old Opel.

The windows of the Metro train were covered with more graffiti, giving the interior a dark, gloomy feel, despite the bright winter sunshine outside.

Twenty minutes later, the train pulled into Circo Massimo. Sam held a hand over his eyes as they emerged on to a busy street, the daylight momentarily blinding. The air was filled with the hum of engines and a cloud of exhaust fumes. Ahead, at an intersection, a traffic policeman in dark blue uniform, white gloves and hat was directing cars, vans and mopeds with agitated waves of his arms and shrill bursts of a whistle. It seemed the lights were out.

A black man in a thick coat moved languidly between the vehicles, offering to clean windscreens with a sponge and squeegee.

'This way,' said Zahra, pointing to an area of parkland just north.

They waited for the policeman to halt the traffic and then crossed, moving up a narrower, quieter road. On their right, a couple of coaches were parked bumper to bumper, their sides inscribed with the names of French and German tourist companies.

The camp was obvious from some distance. It was concentrated on the edge of the park on a terrace just below road level, its borders makeshift walls of tarpaulin and plastic sheeting flapping in a slight breeze. Sam passed a line of smart apartment buildings and houses that enjoyed an uninterrupted view of the camp. Two worlds, poles apart, separated by a strip of tarmac.

Sam followed Zahra as she crossed the road. A sign ahead offered visitors information about the park in a number of languages. As he passed the sign, he noticed a brief phrase in English explaining how the Circus Maximus was once a place of entertainment, where Romans had come to watch gladiatorial contests, chariot races and beast hunts. He was reminded of the man who'd chased them in Amsterdam, and swallowed hard.

As they got closer to the camp, Sam saw a group at its edge, one which had been concealed by the coaches. There were about twenty men, all white. They wore a mix of bomber jackets, combat fatigues and black leather coats. Some had shaved heads – the back of one was tattooed with an image of a Viking wearing a horned helmet. A pile of banners and flags lay to one side on the pavement. One flag had unfurled and Sam saw a white circle against red. Inside the circle, there was a symbol in black – a ring over a cross – the same one he'd seen on the wall earlier in the day. The men were huddled in conspiratorial circles, as if planning their next move.

If Zahra was upset or frightened by their appearance, she didn't show it. About ten metres from the group, she stopped and turned to Sam.

'We need to separate,' she said.

He knew this was coming, but now felt fearful, suddenly convinced she'd disappear inside and slip away. The presence of the men merely exacerbated his feelings.

'There's a church at the end of this road.' She pointed down the street. 'I can meet you there at 4pm. It's quiet at that time. We can talk.'

Behind Zahra there was a gap in the walls of tarpaulin and plastic, what appeared to be a narrow alleyway. Sam caught a glimpse of an old canvas tent, its front open to reveal a floor of dirty old mattresses – blankets neatly folded at the ends – and a small pile of soup cans. People struggling to live a form of existence in the midst of chronic uncertainty. A cold breeze picked up and a high note of raw sewage caught in Sam's nostrils.

'What about them?' asked Sam, pointing to the men.

Zahra shrugged nonchalantly, as if she'd seen worse. She nodded at Sam, then entered the gap. He watched her for a moment before she turned a corner and disappeared, swallowed up by the camp.

Chapter 35

Rome

Wallace was waiting at arrivals as Tapper emerged from customs. He felt a surge of warmth in his gut, and an eagerness to get going.

Tapper deposited his bag in left luggage and they caught a cab outside the airport, giving the driver an address in the north of Rome. Tapper saw an eyebrow rise in the rear-view mirror.

'Giornalisti?' asked the driver.

'Si,' replied Tapper, nodding to Wallace. 'Giornalisti.'

As they headed north, Tapper realised that being journalists might be the only way to explain their presence at the building. And if that was their story, then at least he looked vaguely convincing in his bland ensemble of grey cotton trousers, navy wind cheater and the fawn hiking trainers he'd bought at Heathrow. Wallace, in his tight stone-washed jeans, bomber jacket and close-cropped hair, looked more like a night club bouncer, but there was little he could do about that right now.

Within half an hour, the cab was pelting down a busy four-lane highway, high walls of graffiti-clad concrete to their sides blocking views of the city. The warm interior of the taxi had filled with Wallace's odour, his unmistakeable cocktail of after-shave and armpits. Tapper found himself transported back in time to their cell in Ipswich.

Before he could reminisce, the driver indicated and the cab peeled off, rising up a slip road. As they emerged above ground, Tapper saw an area of scrubland, a handful of pinched looking trees and grass that suggested it might once have been a park. It was now most definitely a waste ground, the rusting hulk of a burned-out car the only play equipment.

The cab drove round the edge of the scrubland. To their left were rows of office blocks, tatty and uninspiring lumps of concrete. Then, up ahead, was a larger building, its façade one of steel and brown-tinted glass. Many of the windows appeared to be broken. Curtains billowed in the wind, as if signalling for help.

The driver pulled up. 'Salaam Palace,' he said, indicating to his left with a contemptuous flick of his hand.

Tapper handed the driver a wad of cash. 'Aspetta, per favore,' he said.

Wallace and Tapper stepped out on to the pavement. There was a fence of thick steel railings and a bank of overgrown shrubs and weeds behind that divided the block from the street. They moved closer to peer through a gap. Six cars were parked haphazardly in front of the building, their windows thick with dust. Two had no tyres. A skip overflowed with detritus – old desks, chairs and office partition walls, concrete building blocks, smashed toilets. As if a gutting of the building had started and then been abandoned.

They moved on down the pavement towards an opening in the fence. Just inside the building's perimeter there was a ramp that dropped down to what was obviously an underground car park. There were two white vans parked – or more probably abandoned, given their rusting, dirty state – at the bottom.

Near the vans two black boys were playing football. Tapper gestured for Wallace to follow him down the ramp.

At the sound of Tapper's trainers squeaking on the tarmac, the kids stopped kicking the ball and looked up.

'Ciao,' said Tapper, as he got closer.

'Ciao,' said one of the boys. He was a tall, skinny lad of around eleven or twelve, a crusty layer of dried snot around his nostrils.

Tapper's Italian stretched no further than basic phrases, so he reverted to English, hoping the kids understood.

'I'm looking for an Eritrean woman.'

The boys looked at each other without expression. Had they understood? Or were they weighing up what information like this might be worth?

The snot-nosed kid flicked his head in the direction of the underground car park. And then gestured with his hand, inviting Tapper and Wallace to follow.

They trailed the boys into subterranean gloom, the air bitterly cold and tinged with the smell of ammonia. The bays of the car park had been divided up by large walls of material – plastic sheets or cloth roughly stitched together, scant protection against a damp chill that was never lifted by sunshine. The kids turned right between two of the blocked-off areas. Tapper heard a crunch underfoot and looked down. The floor was strewn with food wrappers, empty plastic milk cartons and broken glass. Ahead, the boys had moved through a set of swing doors into a dimly lit stairwell. Wallace, as if acting like Tapper's bodyguard, went first.

The stairwell was marginally warmer than the car park, a difference that was clearly key to a handful of the building's residents. Four or five mattresses were arranged on the landing. At their feet were dozens of candles of different sizes and states glued with blobs of wax to the floor – clearly the only source of light when darkness fell.

On the next floor, Tapper and Wallace moved through another door into a long corridor. Through sepia-tinged windows Tapper saw the rusting vehicles at the front of the building and, across the road, the scrubland. It was like some image of a post-apocalyptic world. Not that things were much better inside.

More mattresses were lined up against walls, a narrow footwell left for human traffic. As the kids led the way, it became obvious that there were people on the mattresses. Tapper looked down in horror at two or three bundles of body-shaped blankets huddled up in the foetal position against the cold.

At the end of the corridor, the kids side-stepped a bright red child's tricycle and pushed through more swing doors into what had once been a large office. There was a sound of chanting. Arranged to their right were neat rows of shoes – hundreds of sandals, flip-flops and trainers. Tapper turned and saw several lines of men on their knees, heads rising and falling.

The kids moved on across the abandoned office, down a narrow path carved through an indoor refugee camp filled with yet more mattresses and tented 'rooms'.

Their men at prayer, women sat in clusters on the floor, looking up listlessly as they passed. They were clearly not the first visitors.

'What if she's in there?' whispered Wallace. 'What if she makes a fuss?'

'One step at a time, Pat,' said Tapper, who had no strategy if things kicked off. 'We don't even know she's in the building.'

The boys had stopped and were indicating another set of doors. It was as if they'd reached a border which they were reluctant to cross.

'Piccola Asmara,' said the tall, snot-nosed kid. A cupped hand reached towards them. Tapper opened his wallet and peeled out a twenty Euro note. The kid snatched the cash and the two boys disappeared back the way they'd come.

There were small windows in the top half of the doors and Tapper and Wallace peered through them. It was another room like the one behind them, littered with mattresses and partitioned rooms, with figures shuffling around or seated on the floor. Tapper guessed that, if other floors mimicked this one, the building contained thousands of refugees. Who fed them? How did they live?

He pushed the doors open and stepped inside. Here, for once, their presence was noted. A group of men sitting on the floor – dressed in dirty puffa jackets and threadbare wool overcoats, beanies and woolly hats pulled low over their heads –looked up with a mix of fatigue and suspicion.

Tapper smiled feebly at the men as he approached. Beyond, the room seemed to stretch for two hundred metres. A terrace outside that overlooked the scrubland could be seen through some double doors. There were two dome tents pitched outside.

'Hello,' he said. 'Do you speak English?'

'Little,' one of them muttered. His voice was muted, as if the volume had been turned down in every aspect of his life. A defeated human being.

Tapper crouched down so he was at their level. He saw one of the men glance at his new trainers.

'I'm looking for a woman from Eritrea.' He paused as he realised the journalist story wouldn't wash at this stage in their enquiry. Why would a hack be looking for a specific refugee? Another idea came to him. 'I'm a lawyer. I was helping her in the UK.'

The man he'd been addressing lifted himself, with some effort, off the mattress and stood. He was roughly the same height as Tapper but at least two stone lighter, the trousers at his waist bunched tight with a length of twine.

'Come,' he said.

Tapper and Wallace followed the man through the centre of the room. Large windows magnified the heat of the sun and with the slight lift in temperature came the unmistakeable smell of unwashed bodies, of soiled bedding. They passed, he guessed, nearly a hundred people in the space of less than a minute – a group of mothers chatting while their toddlers played on the floor with battered old plastic toys; children in a makeshift classroom, a teacher pointing to a map of the world with a stick; four old men, cheeks pinched and hollow, playing cards in silence at a table; a man with his arms round a silently sobbing woman.

Finally the man stopped and pointed at an old canvas tent to their left.

'Immigration,' he said. Then he grinned, a mouth full of perfectly straight and very white teeth.

Some in-joke, thought Tapper. He and Wallace stepped inside the tent. There was a portable gas fire in one corner. In the other, two women – one black, the other white – sat at a large table. The white woman had a pile of scrappy papers before her. She was reading aloud from the one in her hand while the black woman typed the information into a laptop. That done, the white woman placed the scrap of paper to one side and reached for the next one in the pile. Behind them, tacked to the walls of the tent, was a banner that read 'Caritas – ending poverty, promoting justice and restoring dignity'.

The women were so engrossed in their work they hadn't noticed the presence of the two men. Tapper coughed gently. The women looked up, giving the visitors a once-over.

'Yes?' the black woman said. She wore a denim jacket over a dark t-shirt, a necklace of brightly coloured beads. Framed by a cloud of curls, her face shared the same high forehead and penetrating eyes as Zahra. Tapper felt a slight tremor. She could have been her older sister.

'I'm looking for a former client, Zahra Idris.' The lie began taking shape as he spoke. 'I was working on her case in the UK. Helping her with her application for asylum. I think she might be here.'

The two women exchanged puzzled glances. 'You came all the way here to find her?' said the black woman, her English lightly accented with Italian.

He could sense the disbelief. The hole in his lie. Why would an overpaid lawyer bother with a poxy asylum case if the client had done a bunk?

He felt exposed suddenly. He'd uttered her name. Made his visit here more conspicuous.

'I think she's in trouble,' he said. Which was, of course, true. 'I want to help.'

He shaped his face into a look of genuine concern, even if it was only for his own skin. The black woman softened a fraction. She tapped the laptop with the nail of a finger.

'We try and keep a record of who comes in and out of Salaam Palace. Just in case family or friends turn up, looking for others. And people also make contact when they've settled in other countries in Europe. They tell us where they are – and whether there's accommodation and jobs that others can go to. It's like a database. A very basic one. What did you say her name was?'

'Zahra Idris,' said Tapper, with a cough. His throat had gone dry. With its permanent chill, shifting migratory population and lack of sanitation, this whole building had to be rife with germs, a breeding ground for dysentery, malaria and god knows what else.

The black woman was typing at her keyboard. The other woman looked at Tapper. She seemed to be drinking him in. She was bigger than her colleague, clad in a tent-like dress of white cotton, badly dyed blonde hair pulled tightly back from a round face.

'Ah yes,' said the black woman. 'We have three women called Zahra Idris. Two are living in Germany. Moved there in 2014. The other stayed here earlier last year and then made contact in the autumn from an immigration detention centre in the UK.'

'Any news since?' Tapper could feel the whole operation slipping like sand through his fingers.

The woman looked up from the screen. 'Nothing. If she was here, we'd know. Piccola Asmara is a tight community. People look out for each other.'

It was then the larger woman muttered something in Italian.

Her colleague sighed. 'She could be in the city centre. Some people choose to stay in a camp there.' She leaned back in her seat, ran both hands through the curls of her hair. She looked tired all of a sudden. 'Some find life in this building a little claustrophobic. Which I can understand. And if you're in the city centre, it's easier to beg. But life in the city is not any easier. There are many residents who do not like immigrants. Who do not even like black people. It's not always safe.'

Tapper's feet were straining inside his trainers.

'And where might we find this camp?'

Chapter 36

Rome

The cab circled the Colosseum and then, minutes later, came to a halt on a street corner opposite the camp. Tapper paid the driver, and they stepped out.

It was evident that they'd walked straight into tension.

A group of about thirty men chanted angrily and waved placards and flags. It didn't take a linguist to understand what their overarching message was. It was the clothes they wore, the scattering of shaved heads, and the black and red colours of their banners that gave the game away. Now was clearly not the moment to make enquiries.

Tapper and Wallace positioned themselves on the opposite side of the street. A group of immigrants emerged from the camp and began shouting back at the protestors. This immediately prompted the men to stop chanting the same message and begin hurling individual insults, accompanied by angry jabbing fingers.

A battered transit van pulled up. The back doors were opened and more protestors jumped out. Additional banners and flags were raised, the angry noise swelling as extra voices joined in. Tapper sensed that things were reaching a peak. That, sooner or later, there would be violence. He wondered whether this might serve his purposes. If Idris and Keddie were in the camp, they'd be flushed out.

One of the protestors, a man dressed like Wallace but wiry in frame, sprung from the group and charged at the nearest shelter, kicking ferociously at it with the sole of a Doctor Marten's boot. From across the street, Tapper and Wallace watched as the shelter began to collapse, its skeletal structure able to withstand wind and rain, but not the angry and relentless kicks of a man possessed. A plastic sheet tore and fell, exposing timber supports and an interior of mattresses that sat on top of wooden pallets. The man was inside in an instant, dragging blankets and plastic bags full of belongings from the shelter and flinging them on to the pavement.

The immigrants outside the camp, who'd been concentrating on the main body of the group, spotted this destruction and ran at the wiry skinhead.

A battle soon broke out. It was clear to Tapper that the undernourished and fatigued immigrants were no match for their well-fed opponents. He watched as one African was head-butted and collapsed to the ground; another was punched in the stomach, bending double in agony. More immigrants emerged from inside to the point where protestors were outnumbered. But Tapper knew this would make little difference.

More shelters were brought down, the protestors slowly eating their way through the flimsy structures with their hands and boots. Tapper heard the sound of a woman screaming as a wall of tarpaulin was ripped from its frame, exposing a mother and two small children.

It was then he saw the fire. It was just to the left of the protest, a spot far enough away to go unnoticed, at least until the flames caught. One of the protestors had clearly lit something – perhaps the dry timber of a palette – and now a fire was spreading with extraordinary speed. The fight stopped as everyone turned to stare at the latest development. Then, as if a switch had been flicked, the immigrants rushed back into the camp to raise the alarm.

The protestors were now standing back to admire their work. Tapper watched with some fascination at how indifferent they were to the peril of those inside the camp. It was as if they were enjoying a bonfire in the garden.

Two shelters were now engulfed with flames, great black plumes of smoke climbing into the sky. Tapper could smell the sharp, acrid whiff of burning plastic. He heard shouts from inside the camp, screams of alarm.

Immigrants were emerging from the camp by the opening nearest the protest. An old man coughing, a women clutching a child protectively to her chest, others stumbling into the light, a look of shock on their faces. Tapper sensed that this spot was the main way in or out – that everywhere else, the outer walls of the camp were tacked tightly to the ground to create some security. Understandable, but fatally flawed when it came to an emergency like this.

Tapper had a thought. If there was just one way out, Idris and, with luck, Keddie, would soon emerge if they were inside – or be burned alive. But he had to be sure. He turned to Wallace. 'Can you check round the back?' he said. 'We need to know if they're leaving the camp at any other point.'

Wallace moved off at a pace.

At the camp's exit, shock was quickly turning to anger. Some of the immigrants were turning on the protestors, a barrage of abuse flying between them.

The fire was spreading, the flames climbing higher to lick the lower branches of the umbrella pine trees that lined the street, the resinous foliage catching with a crackling noise.

Against this backdrop, Tapper heard the sound of sirens. Moments later, four police cars and two vans turned into the street. They parked across the road to block any traffic. Police spilled out, wading into the commotion and peeling apart the two sides. Tapper watched as a truncheon was raised and then swung down with force, whether on an immigrant or protestor, he couldn't be sure. Finally the two sides were separated. Another policeman stood by the exit point, ushering the immigrants out with rapid hand gestures. To anyone on the outside of the camp who could see how quickly the fire was spreading, it was clear those inside had limited time.

Everyone was being asked to move across the road away from the edge of the camp. Tapper found himself surrounded by protestors, and inched to their right to make sure he wasn't lumped in with them if and when arrests were made.

The line of people exiting the camp had dried up and Tapper was certain that Idris and Keddie hadn't emerged. A fire engine turned into the street. Soon the place would be overrun by the authorities.

Tapper was in a no-man's land between immigrants and protestors. With a sense of detachment, he glanced at the people to his right. There were about seventy, maybe eighty of them. Some of the men had bloodied faces. All shared a look of exhausted defeat.

His phone rang. It was Wallace.

'I'm following a woman,' he said. 'She crawled out on all fours and started running away from the camp.'

'Is it her?'

'Can't be sure.'

'Has she seen you?'

'Don't think so.'

Tapper scanned the group to his right once more. He couldn't see Idris, or Keddie for that matter, among the faces.

'I'm right behind you.'

Chapter 37

Rome

Having spent the afternoon wandering aimlessly around the Palatine and dodging selfie-stick salesmen and overweight men dressed as Roman soldiers at the Colosseum, Sam wasn't feeling optimistic as he walked under a carved archway into the porch of the church. Back in the UK, his counselling room was designed to be free of unnecessary distractions. In his experience, Catholic churches, with their loaded imagery of mutilation, pain and bloodshed, were exactly the opposite.

A gaggle of chattering Japanese were queuing to reach the far end of the porch. From there, camera flashes filled the space with blazes of white light. In a gap between two tourists was a ghostly and immediately recognisable circular carving. A man's face, bearded, his mouth partially open to form a hole large enough to fit a hand. The Mouth of Truth. How ironic, Sam thought, that he should find himself here now, as he searched for an elusive truth of his own.

He pushed a heavy wooden door open, its hinges creaking and groaning, and stepped inside. He was struck immediately by an eerie stillness. Ahead of him there was a small nave bordered by pillars and, above, pale walls that rose to tiny arched windows sitting beneath a roof of painted timbers. Instead of pews, there were about twenty wooden chairs arranged in rows on the floor, all facing forward. There was a marble altar at the end and, in the shadows beyond, the curved back wall of the church, some hint of fresco in the darkness.

Behind him, the door closed with a loud bang and Sam flinched. He exhaled and moved down the nave. He now reckoned that the only distraction that might cause a problem was not visual. It was the heavy smell in the air, the sweet and spicy whiff of incense.

Beyond a reference to Zahra's religion as Catholic in her referral notes, they'd never discussed the subject. Did she find this church somehow comforting, a reminder of a calmer period in her life?

He sat. Just ahead was a stand on which dozens of votive candles flickered. Individual prayers – hopes, wishes and fears climbing into the air.

Sam's mind drifted back to the first time that he and Zahra had met. He'd arrived early at Creech Hill, the visiting room reverberating with noise around him. He was always slightly anxious before meeting a new client, but this time his nerves were exacerbated by a concern about the far-from-ideal conditions – that he'd not be able to hear her or that, if they over-compensated and raised their voices, others might over-hear what should have been confidential. But in the end, none of that had mattered. Her voice was soft but clear, her manner immediately friendly, as if she recognised that Sam was there to help. There was, however, a slight shyness and inhibition, which led to a brief moment of friction. Hoping to find a starting point for the therapy, Sam referred to the notes Linda had given him, and gently mentioned the scars on her back – the reason she'd been referred for counselling in the first place. It was a stupid mistake. It was up to her to decide what they talked about and he should have left that emotionally loaded detail out. Her head dropped and he thought he'd upset her. But she was not upset, or at least not in the way he expected. A second passed, then she pulled her head back up and spoke, her voice firm: 'I'll talk about anything. But not the scars.' The subject never came up again.

Out of the corner of his eye, he saw a dark shape move to the right and his head darted in that direction. An old lady, clad in black, was sweeping the marble floor of the aisle to his side. She looked up at him, eyes magnified behind thick lenses, then resumed her work.

Sam relaxed, aware now of how nervous he really was.

He was clutching at straws. As he understood, every summer, thousands of migrants crossed the Mediterranean. What were the chances of anyone in that small camp knowing what happened on Zahra's voyage? Her fellow passengers would have been scattered to the far corners of Europe by now.

Sam heard the door's hinges creak and turned. A figure stood in the doorway, instantly silhouetted as a flash went off in the porch behind. Sam blinked but found he had the silhouette imprinted on his eyelids. He blinked again and realised the figure was now moving towards him. He tensed. It had to be Zahra but recent experience had made him decidedly edgy.

The gap closed between them and Sam breathed a sigh of relief.

'Hi,' said Zahra, as she sat down next to him.

She seemed unnaturally calm, as if something had broken inside her.

'How are you feeling?' he asked.

She shrugged. 'OK.'

The light from the windows above was dimming. The votive candles glowed in front of them.

'I used to come in here when I was staying at the camp,' said Zahra, her eyes staring ahead to the altar, dark shadows playing across her face with the movement of the candles' flames. 'Not to pray. Just to remember. It reminds me of home. There's a big cathedral in Asmara. We went there every Sunday when I was a child.'

She looked down to her lap. 'Now I'm not sure God even exists.'

In therapy, Sam would have explored this feeling, but today's conversation was about one thing only, information.

'Did you talk to people in the camp?'

'I asked if anyone knew anything about the boat. And whether anyone had heard from Abel.'

She closed her eyes.

Sam could see how hard this was for her. In the UK, she'd been living in a state of permanent uncertainty, waiting for news of her asylum claim and the possibility of bringing her son over from Eritrea, while hoping that her husband made contact. Despite sending out feelers, joining Eritrean forums online, setting up a Facebook page, there was nothing. Sam could only conclude that Abel was either in some form of trouble, or didn't want to make contact. But now, of course, there was even less hope to cling on to. And she would not see her son again unless she returned home.

Zahra reopened her eyes, turned to Sam. The votive candles danced in her watery pupils. 'No one knew anything.'

Sam was about to say something. Attempt some words of comfort. But he was interrupted.

There was a sound of creaking hinges. Followed by someone running.

Chapter 38

Rome

Sam froze in his seat as the figure rushed towards them but then, as her features became visible, his shoulders dropped. By the look of her face, lit up now by the candles, she was from East Africa, like Zahra. An immigrant. She wore a red patterned scarf over her hair, an overcoat drawn tightly across her body.

The woman looked at Zahra's tear-filled eyes with concern, but clearly whatever was on her mind trounced everything. Her voice was breathless as she spoke rapidly in a language Sam couldn't understand.

The woman's words brought Zahra abruptly back into the moment.

'She's just come from the camp. She says it's on fire.'

They stepped from the church into the street, the woman leading them round the corner and back on to the road that led to the camp. Sam heard sirens. He looked up the street. The evening gloom pulsed with blue lights, while umbrella pine trees stood silhouetted against the glow of flames.

Zahra looked stunned. The safe haven she'd hoped to return to was now destroyed.

The woman was muttering something. And trying to pull Zahra by the arm. Clearly she thought Zahra was safer with her own, rather than the strange white man.

Zahra screamed. A noise that rose above the din of traffic and sirens. She held an arm up, pointing ahead of them.

It took Sam a moment as his eyes adjusted to the dark foreground. But the heavy-set figure closing on them – perhaps no further than twenty metres away – was unmistakeable. Not least when a car passed and headlights lit up his hooded face.

Sam's reaction came from the gut. He grabbed Zahra's arm and yanked her in the opposite direction. Enough adrenaline was coursing through her system to override the shock. She was off like a gunshot, pulling free of his guiding hand. She cut right at the church and then began across a road without pausing as she weaved through cars driving in both directions, their speed mercifully slowed by the street's cobbled surface. Sam was right on her tail, pausing for one brief moment to avoid a small van that was about to cross his path.

Zahra was already on the opposite side. There was a small area of trees and then a busier road that ran along the raised banks of the Tiber. By the time Sam reached the trees, Zahra was running in a northerly direction along the road. Sam looked back and saw the heavy-set man crossing the road in front of the church, a mobile phone clamped to his ear. Were there others in the city? The taste of bile rose in Sam's mouth. If there were more men as determined as the one on their tail, then what hope did they have?

As Sam pursued Zahra, the traffic to his left slowed for a red light and he watched her dart across the road towards the river. He snatched at his chance and ran between cars slowing for the lights to the pavement opposite. To his left in the gathering gloom, he could see the dark waters of the Tiber below.

Zahra turned left, crossing a bridge. Sam glanced back and now saw two people on his tail. Just behind the big man was another figure. There was no time to think.

He reached the bridge and cut left after Zahra, his heart pounding in his chest. She was now about half-way across and he thought, for one sickening moment, that she would stop and fling herself into the river below. God knows, she had little enough to live for. But to his relief, she continued on.

A glance behind confirmed that the men were not gaining on him. They were still about thirty metres away, though the other man – a leaner figure – had now caught up with his bulky partner.

Headlights illuminated Zahra ahead as cars moved past them, people leaving work to return to homes and families while they ran for their lives from a pair of assassins.

Suddenly Zahra disappeared. Sam had looked away for a moment and when he glanced ahead again, she was no longer there. She couldn't have gone far, but the fact that he might have lost her made his body, hot from exertion, chill in an instant.

As he reached the end of the bridge, he realised where she'd gone. To his left was a barely lit stone staircase that led down to the embankment. In the darkness below him, he could hear someone descending the steps. It had to be her. He began down the stairs.

In his haste, he nearly slipped, steadying himself with a hand on the wall to his right. The steps were greasy, ancient stone worn smooth by centuries of footfall, made worse by clusters of wet leaves.

He heard a cry from below. It was Zahra, without doubt. And the sound she'd made spoke of fear and frustration in equal measure.

A moment later, as he reached her at the bottom of the stairs, he knew why. A gate, taller than both of them and topped with razor wire, was closed shut and padlocked. There was no way to get to the embankment.

As Zahra pulled frantically at the gate and let out another anguished cry, Sam looked over the wall to his left and felt a fresh wave of fear course through him. The black Tiber lay below, how far the drop or how deep the water, it was impossible to gauge. But Sam was aware of an audible roar, as well as the agitated reflection of street lights from the road above. The river was moving fast, its surface chewed up by currents.

He heard voices from above.

'They're there!'

Sam looked up and saw two dark forms at the top of the stairs. He was sure the voice he'd heard belonged to their pursuer from Amsterdam. The men had slowed and were now descending the stairs at leisure, the larger one in front. They'd heard the sound of Zahra pulling at the gates, her cries. They knew that the two of them were trapped.

Zahra turned. On seeing the two men slowly descending towards them, her reaction was animal-like. She spun round and began pulling at the gates with even greater frustration, screaming out repeatedly. 'Come on! Come on!'

Sam heard the other man speak out: 'Be careful, Pat.' This hint of concern – of humanity – did nothing to calm Sam. The man to the rear might have been protective towards the larger figure, but they were still in grave danger.

As the men continued to descend, Sam realised there was only one option if they were to avoid a violent death at the foot of a dark stairwell. He grabbed Zahra by the shoulders, pulled her round to face him.

'We have to jump,' he said quietly, convinced that if the men overheard, they'd speed up.

Zahra shook her head in the darkness.

'We've got no choice,' he whispered. 'They'll be here in seconds.'

He unclasped Zahra and glanced upwards. The bigger man was over halfway down the stairs. What chance did they have against him, let alone the pair of them? He railed against his choices – stand and defend Zahra or take the equally suicidal route and jump into the Tiber.

Zahra's hand gripped his arm. She was staring at the water, as if assessing her jump. Then she spoke, uttering a word Sam did not understand.

'Potzarni,' she said. 'Potzarni.'

With one swift movement, Zahra placed both hands on the wall to their side and swung herself up on to its lip. She lifted herself to a standing position, paused for a second, and jumped. There was a splash below, and she was gone.

The men reacted instantly, their cruel, leisurely descent transformed into rapid movement as they dropped, two steps at a time, towards Sam.

There was not a moment to lose. Placing his hands on the wall like Zahra had, he used his upper body strength to pull his knees up on to the lip. The bigger man was inches from him as Sam, with no time to stand or consider his leap, launched himself forward into the darkness.

Chapter 39

Rome

Sam hit the river head first. The shock of the icy water shot through him like an electric current as he surfaced for the first time, drawing in great hungry gasps of oxygen. Then another sensation hit him, of velocity. The river was carrying him downstream with speed. His ears were filled with the sound of water raging angrily, as if it were telling him, in no uncertain terms, that he was somewhere he did not belong.

Seconds later he felt as if great hands had grabbed his legs and yanked him under. It was inky black all around him, but quieter, the violent noises of the surface muffled. It was a terrifying vision of nothingness, a glimpse of his death. His lungs began to scream for oxygen, his arms flailed.

Then he was spat to the surface. He saw, for a brief moment, the streetlights that ran along the road above the Tiber. Would this be his last sight of life? He braced himself for another spell underwater, for the moment when he wouldn't re-surface. His clothes had become sodden and heavy, but at the same time, he was acutely aware of feeling light, like a feather being flung around by strong winds. He sucked in another breath, convinced it would be his last.

And that was when he hit something. A hard, long object that slammed into his side. Almost instantly, the river began to drag him away again. He tried to claw at the object with hands weighed down by water-logged sleeves, grasping but finding only more water. But as he felt himself pulled back into the currents, he also experienced a drag in the opposite direction. Some part of his clothing had caught on something. However flimsy, it was stopping him, perhaps even saving his life.

He was facing upstream, the water like a typhoon around him, itching to spin him round and fling him downstream. He could feel a hard point pushing into his right side above the waist. He let his hand drop to that place and discovered a slim, smooth object stuck in his coat pocket. He reached back and his hand met a larger body of material. It was wood. A branch that had fallen into the river. It was now all that stood between him and a watery grave.

If he could just turn himself around, he'd be able to grab the branch with both hands, cling on to it like a life raft. But he knew that would mean unhitching himself from the piece that had snagged in his pocket and that, surely, was all that stopped him from continuing his one-way journey. He took a deep breath. Waves were slamming into his face, forcing water into his nostrils, flooding his nose, making him choke and cough. It was as if everything were dulling, his sense of touch, the warmth of his body. The lights were slowly dimming. It was now or never.

His right hand began to pull at the pocket to release his coat.

It took seconds, much quicker than he'd expected. And then his body was ejected from the wood and spun violently round. And that was when he reached out with both hands and grabbed at the tree limb. They slipped at first, the wood smooth and glasslike in the icy water, but then he grasped one, then two, truncated branches.

He was now facing downstream, his body pressed against the gnarly timber, points of wood pushing into his chest and stomach. He knew now that another herculean task lay ahead. To find a way from the wood to dry land. He looked to the left. The embankment pathway was about seven feet away. It was like a cruel glimpse of freedom for a prisoner looking out from the barred window of his cell. Tantalisingly close, but Sam then noticed, with a sinking sensation in the pit of his stomach, that the branch, which jutted out at right angles from the bank, didn't quite reach it. So even if Sam could have negotiated its length, it wouldn't be far enough.

But then another thought formed in his brain, the idea coagulating with glacial sluggishness as the cold slowed even his ability to think. Something else was keeping the branch in place. He looked upwards. The branch was resting against a concrete pontoon that sat in the river. Above it was a timber construction, a riverside restaurant perhaps, or boat house. Sam craned his neck further up, and that was when he saw a light in a narrow window.

Summoning every last drop of strength in his body, he reached up with his right hand and hit the bottom of the building. His first attempt was feeble, a light rap. He knew he'd have to try harder – and repeatedly – if anyone inside was going to hear. But he also knew he was on borrowed time, the strength dying in his body with every moment he spent in the water.

He reached up again and hit the timber. Again. And again. And then he felt the cold blackness rise up from his toes, and the lights slowly went out.

Chapter 40

Rome

'What the fuck were you doing in the water, man?'

Sam looked up sluggishly, focusing on the giant above him, a man with cropped blond hair, wearing ripped jeans and an old grey sweat shirt with paint stains and the Harvard University logo on its front.

He was sitting in a chair close to an electric heater, warmth slowly bringing life back to his body while his brain remained numbed. The walls around the cabin were stacked with rowing boats and oars. One boat lay upside-down on a long table in the middle of the room, a paint brush and can of varnish by it. The air was thick with the changing room smell of male sweat, as well as a heady whiff of lacquer.

'You're seriously lucky Enzo was here. I always thought the cox was a waste of space but I have to admit he's just saved your life.'

'Vaffanculo, Kyle.'

Sam turned slowly to the other man in the cabin. Enzo was a shorter, leaner figure, with a quiff of dark hair. Italian, unlike his American friend.

'Enzo heard the knocking,' said Kyle. 'So we came out. You looked as if you were just about to slip under. This hero,' he said, pointing to Enzo, 'inched along the edge of the pontoon and grabbed your collar.'

Enzo dismissed the description of his heroism with a flick of his hand. 'It was a team effort. I couldn't lift you out of the water, so I dragged you along the branch till you were nearer the embankment and then we both pulled you from the river and on to the cabin's deck.'

Sam had barely been conscious at that stage and had a hazy memory of being helped into the cabin. How they'd peeled off his coat, shirt and trousers, dried him and given him a t-shirt, jeans and sweater.

His brain began to thaw. He remembered, with a sensation like a stab wound to his belly, Zahra leaping into the Tiber. 'Did you see anyone else in the river?' he asked, panic flooding his system so fast he thought he might be sick. 'A woman.'

'You're saying someone else was in the river?' asked Kyle. He shot Enzo a look. 'Call the police, man.'

Enzo reached for a mobile that sat on a shelf nearby and punched in three numbers.

'Polizia, per favore.' There was a pause. 'Una donna e caduta nel fiume, in vicino del Ponte Palatino.'

Enzo placed his hand over the receiver and said: 'Can you give me a description of the woman?'

Sam described Zahra and the clothes she was wearing. Enzo passed the information on.

'They're on the way. They're gonna want to talk to you too.'

Sam knew he couldn't hang around to talk to the police.

'Gotta ask,' said Kyle. 'Were you trying to kill yourself?'

'Madonna, Kyle,' said Enzo, 'and you're majoring in medicine. Unbelievable.'

'It's fine,' said Sam. He was now itching to get out of the cabin. He had to look for Zahra. And then he thought of the two who'd been chasing them. He was certain that they'd still be looking for them. Surely the cabin, with its lights on, was an obvious place to start.

Sam attempted to stand, but felt his knees give way and collapsed back in the seat, frustration coursing through him.

The two men were watching him closely. Sam realised he had to throw them something. 'Seeing as you saved me, you've got a right to ask. The answer's no. I wasn't trying to kill myself. It's complicated.' Sam was too tired to lie. 'There were two men chasing me and the woman. People who mean to harm us.'

Kyle screwed up his face in disbelief. 'You sure about that, man?' he said. 'I mean, this is Rome, not Detroit.'

'I'm sure.'

Out of the corner of his eye, Sam saw Enzo's eyebrows rise.

Sam's wet clothes were in a pile at his feet and he began rooting through the pockets of his jacket for his wallet and passport. He found his phone first. Its surface was wet, the screen clouded with condensation. He was wary of using the mobile anyway, so it was no great loss.

Looking up from his searching, Sam said: 'I should get going. I've taken up enough of your time. I'll return the clothes.'

'You really are crazy, aren't you?' said Kyle. 'You gotta sit tight.'

Just then there was a loud rap on the door. Sam tensed in his seat.

'Who the fuck is that?' said Kyle, moving towards the door. 'You don't see a soul all winter and now suddenly the Tiber Rowing Club's like the Trevi fucking Fountain.'

'Wait,' said Sam. The fear in his voice halted Kyle in his tracks. 'If it's the people who are after me, you cannot tell them I'm here.'

Kyle stared Sam hard in the face, studying him.

'Sure, man. Whatever.'

Sam was sitting close to a wall that was partially hidden by a row of lockers. But he wasn't taking any chances. As Kyle moved to the door, Sam pulled himself up with difficulty and pressed back against the wall, as close to the lockers as possible.

The knocking came again. 'Chill out, man!' shouted Kyle. He then opened the door.

When Sam heard the voice, his blood chilled all over again.

'We're looking for a friend,' the man at the door said.

It wasn't the voice of the larger man, but Sam was certain it was his companion – the figure who'd spoken on the steps.

'He's had an accident and fallen in the river. We're very worried about him.'

'I'm real sorry, man,' said Kyle. 'Haven't seen or heard a thing. Me and Enzo have been inside all evening. We should come out and give you a hand. We got torches.'

'No, that's kind but we're – .'

'Guessing you called the police,' interrupted Kyle.

'I –'

'No worries, man. We'll call them now.' His voice projected into the room. 'Enzo, would you do the honours?'

'Thank you,' said the man at the door. 'We best get going, carry on looking.'

'Enzo and I will help.'

'No, really.' The voice was already getting quieter. The man was moving away from the door, Kyle's persistence clearly discomforting.

'It's no problem,' shouted Kyle into the darkness outside. He then shut the door.

Sam exhaled, his tense shoulders dropping, and moved away from the wall.

Kyle crossed the cabin to him. 'Gotta say, man. I thought you were mad. But that guy was very shifty. I'm thinking you might be telling the truth.'

Sam slumped back into the seat before the heater. 'I am.'

A dark cloud descended over him, as he began considering the terrible possibility that the only thing the police would find was Zahra's body.

'You've gotta talk to the police, man.'

'I can't do that,' said Sam.

He watched as Enzo and Kyle exchanged suspicious glances.

'It's not what you think,' said Sam. 'I've got nothing to hide. It's just that I've got to get moving. Those guys you just spoke to – one my build, the other big and broad, I'm guessing?'

Kyle nodded.

'Well they won't give up until they've found me. So if they see the police arrive and I leave with them, they'll just follow the police and then they'll know exactly where I'm being questioned – and where I will eventually emerge.'

'This is fucked up,' said Kyle.

'That's exactly what it is.'

'Listen,' said Enzo. 'Take the clothes. We don't need them.'

'Thank you,' said Sam, who'd resumed rooting through his jacket for his passport and wallet. He pulled them out of a pocket along with a handful of coins. The passport was limp with damp and would be buckled when it dried out, but Sam reckoned it might just pass muster if requested. As for the cash in his wallet, that would dry out.

'Take my coat too,' said Kyle. He reached for a parka that hung on the wall to his side. It was as if they wanted rid of Sam now. He'd gone from crank to liability.

'I couldn't.'

'Fuck that,' said Kyle. 'Just take it. Unless you wanna freeze all over again. And there's some sneakers that one of the guys left behind.'

Kyle pulled the shoes from a locker and passed them to Sam. He then opened the door and stepped out. Re-emerging a moment later, he said. 'All clear. There's a staircase up to the bridge just to your left. Better get going before the police arrive, or your two buddies come back.'

'Thank you for everything you've done,' said Sam as he moved to the door.

'Hey,' said Kyle, briefly slapping Sam on the back outside the cabin. Sam winced as the hand narrowly missed his wound. He suspected the gesture was not meant affectionately, but as a nudge. 'It's no problem.'

Sam began walking left towards the bridge then, when he was sure Kyle had closed the cabin door behind him, turned back on himself. Zahra would also have been pulled downstream which meant this was the only direction in which to search.

The path ahead, dimly lit by the streetlights above, seemed clear, but that didn't stop Sam's heart from racing. Aside from the sanctuary of the rowing club cabin, the riverbank was deserted. The steep stone walls to the street above were at least twelve metres high, giving the embankment a sunken, isolated feel. There were shadows everywhere, countless places for two men to hide. Sam edged forward.

Seconds later he heard a sound ahead, and froze. A familiar voice called out.

'No sign of them, Harry. They could be miles from here by now.'

Then: 'Fuck it. Let's get out of here.'

It was hard to tell what distance the voices had carried. They could have been far away, or close by. But Sam's reaction was immediate. He turned, and as fast as his weakened legs would carry him, ran towards the stairs. It was like jogging through thick mud but eventually he reached the open gate.

Again he heard a man's voice from somewhere down the embankment. It sounded fainter, further away, but it still acted like an injection of cold, undiluted fear to his system. He tried to climb the steps quickly. But he couldn't manage haste. His feet felt leaden.

Back on the bridge, he followed his original path across the Tiber, but this time on the far side so that, if the men were walking back towards the bridge along the embankment, they would not spot him. His head was sunk into his chest. He felt cold to his bones.

At the end of the bridge he glanced behind him. Two women were walking arm-in-arm in his wake, their chatter and laughter carrying towards him. But otherwise there were no other figures.

Sam crossed a lane of traffic and moved down an alleyway of crumbling ochre-coloured walls and black cobble-stones. He passed a trattoria, its entrance overhung with creepers. Inside, a waiter was lighting candles on the tables as he prepared for the evening. Sam realised where he was. This was Trastevere, where he and Eleanor had stayed. He remembered how she had tripped on the uneven, undulating surface of a cobbled alley and he'd caught her. He felt his eyes well with tears. He had to call Eleanor's aunt. Find out how she was.

As the dark of the alley began to close in on him, he couldn't shake a pair of images from his head. Eleanor lifeless in a hospital bed. And Zahra dropping to the inky and perishing depths of the Tiber. A horrible knowledge surfaced in his head. It was all his fault.

A single word disturbed his dark thoughts. What was it Zahra had uttered before she jumped?

'Potzarni,' she'd said. 'Potzarni.'

What had she meant? Was it a word in her native tongue, some message from the gut as she faced the terror of the river? He had no idea.

He would search for its meaning, but he had little hope of finding any. Little hope at all.

Chapter 41

Rome

Tapper and Wallace sat at a table in a bar, a brightly-lit place decorated with framed photographs of football teams. A handful of men were gathered in one corner, eyes glued to a football match on television. Tapper and Wallace had the opposite corner to themselves. They could talk undisturbed.

Wallace had a pint of lager in front of him, Tapper a brandy. He craved a shower. He was a fit man, but chasing after Keddie and Idris had left him damp with sweat, his shirt clinging to his back.

Whatever he'd expected from this trip, he never thought he'd be hounding his quarry through the city. He let Wallace take the lead, hung back to keep his face hidden from Keddie and Idris. But when they'd cornered them at the river, he felt both fear and dark pleasure, as if he longed to push them into the river, to watch them gasp for breath. The sensation surprised him yet at the same time felt quite familiar, like he'd bumped into a long-lost relative who shared the same physical features and mannerisms.

But now those contradictory feelings were eclipsed by doubt, which had crept into the bar to sit by his side like an unwanted guest.

'No one could have survived the river,' Wallace said, reading his thoughts. 'It's not just the cold, but the currents.

They'd have been dragged under and either drowned or passed out. The river's got 'em, I tell you.'

'I want to believe you, Pat. It's just that, in my experience, the woman has a knack of surviving.'

'She's dead, Harry. I tell you.'

Wallace's solid certainty was comforting. Tapper felt himself relax a fraction.

The big man took a gulp of his lager, wiping his mouth with the back of a meaty hand. 'It was weird what she said before she jumped, wasn't it?'

Tapper felt a prickle of electricity. 'I didn't hear anything. I was further up the stairs.'

'She turned and grabbed Keddie's arm before she leapt. Looked a bit possessed. Then said something like 'Botzarni or Potzarni.'

The colour drained from Tapper's face.

'What's up, Harry? You look like you've seen a ghost.'

For Tapper, the mere mention of the word conjured up nightmares and brought on cold sweats. He thought again of water, of faces in the darkness crying for mercy.

'How did she say the word?' he gabbled, his mind in overdrive. 'Like she was repeating it for emphasis, or using it for the first time?'

'I dunno, Harry.'

Tapper took a sip of brandy. It was like rocket fuel. He felt the alcohol burning in his stomach.

'We need to go to one more place, Pat,' he said. 'I know the chances are slim, but if they have survived, it's where they'll head. We must be there to greet them.'

Chapter 42

Rome

The receptionist on duty smiled at Sam as he entered the hotel. It was the place where he and Eleanor had stayed and Sam remembered that there were two laptops for guests' use just off reception. If he could get past the desk without being challenged, he figured that one was bound to be free.

'Can I help?' asked the man on duty.

'No, thank you,' said Sam, walking purposefully towards the laptops. The receptionist returned to his work.

Both laptops were in use. A thin, older woman was looking at TripAdvisor on one, while the other was occupied by a boy playing a video game, his father sitting on a nearby sofa tapping at a BlackBerry. When the man looked up and saw Sam waiting, he barked some German at the kid. The boy immediately vacated the machine. Sam thanked them both and sat.

Opening Google, he tried countless derivations of what he thought Zahra had said – Potzarni, Port Zarne, Potzarny, Potsarni, Pozzarni – and was rewarded with results that included an Italian American congressman, an opera singer from the 19th Century, a town in Bosnia, a hotel in southern Spain, an S&M site, reams of results in Russian and Polish, and one page with zero results. He was despairing, convinced he'd misheard Zahra, when he saw a suggestion just below the search box. 'Did you mean: Pozzani?' He clicked on the word.

The screen filled with results, all referring to the same place.

Pozzani was a town in Sicily. There was a map to the right of the page, images of a sandy beach, and a square-looking citadel perched on the water's edge. There were Wikipedia pages in English and Italian and, as subsequent results revealed, dozens of links to pensiones and campsites. A holiday resort. Hardly murky but then, as Sam knew all too well from countless clients, the most innocuous façades could hide the darkest truths.

Sam clicked on the map. Suddenly Pozzani was seen in context. A town close to the southern-most point of the island. West was Tunisia. South was Malta and then, as Sam tracked down the map, the coast of Libya.

He revisited the search box and typed in: 'Pozzani immigrants'. The results told a more immediate story. It was clear that Pozzani was a favoured landing point for naval and coastguard vessels who'd picked up immigrants in trouble. The town had temporary accommodation in dedicated buildings and large tents and had, it appeared, seen thousands of immigrants pass through in the last year alone. There was talk of tension in the town between different groups of immigrants, as well as resistance from certain parts of the community. Sam had seen enough to know that he'd found the right place, and clicked the window shut. A screensaver – a bland landscape of rolling green fields and bright blue sky – filled the screen.

He paused, thinking of that moment on the staircase, the sudden unlocking of memory – the fragment that had burst to the surface of Zahra's mind. He knew of cases where patients with retrograde amnesia remembered snatches of lost memory when they were exposed to smells, sights, textures or sounds similar to those experienced during the original trauma. But what was the prompt in Zahra's case? Water? And if Pozzani was where the injury occurred, how come she started remembering in Catania? Retrograde amnesia was the loss of memory prior to an injury. Sam was confused.

Stepping out of the hotel, he felt a chill wintry wind whip down the alley from the piazza at the end. He thought of the men on his tail. Now that there were two of them, the larger man was thrown into context. He seemed like a hired grunt, while the slimmer man – of whom Sam had seen little more than a silhouette – was somehow more polished. He tried to remember his voice. A trace of Essex, but less pronounced than the other man. And what had he said on the stairs? 'Be careful.' And then a name. Sam racked his brain, but couldn't remember what it was. But he did recall the tone, the hint of concern for the other man. While it hadn't suggested a merciful stance when it came to him or Zahra, there was some hint of friendship between the two men.

And then there was the calling out on the embankment. The sense that a search was being abandoned. And a name that Sam had heard clearly. Harry. But who was Harry?

Another thought occurred to him. How the hell had they traced them to Rome? Had the bigger man somehow managed to pick up their trail back in Amsterdam, and follow them here? Sam was sure they'd shaken him off in the city. Then, with a sinking feeling, he remembered. That brief conversation in the building in Bijlmer, when he and Zahra were hiding from their pursuers. When Zahra had talked about Rome. They'd clearly not been alone in the dark. There must have been someone listening, someone willing to pass on a scrap of information in exchange for some cash. Thanks to them, the two men had turned up here and, by sniffing around an immigrants' camp, had picked up their trail again.

He reached the piazza and saw a church. Remembering the spiel Eleanor had given him about the building – how the campanile and mosaics were 12th Century – he wanted to weep again. He needed to call Eleanor's aunt.

There was a phone booth directly across from where he stood. He looked around the piazza. There were people about, but no sign of the heavy-set man or his companion. He crossed the piazza and stopped by the booth, pulling a handful of change from his pocket. His hand was shaking when he lifted the receiver. He wanted to put it down to the cold, but knew it was fear.

He fed coins into the slot, dialled the international code for the UK, and then Eleanor's aunt's number. It began to ring, a soft purring noise. Perhaps he'd got the wrong number. But then a familiar voice answered.

'Hello.'

'Susan, it's Sam.'

'Sam! Where are you? I've been trying to get hold of you.' Clearly she hadn't been listening when they'd last spoken.

'I had to get away. A conference.' The lie sat in his stomach, acid burning away at his insides.

Susan sighed. 'It's not good, Sam.'

He said nothing.

'She's had the MRI.'

Sam felt his mouth go dry. 'And?'

'It's complicated, Sam. They think her brain moved during the attack.'

The phone was hot against his ear, but otherwise Sam was enveloped by the cold. His legs felt weak again, as if he might drop to the ground. He wanted to find a corner to hide, a place to pull himself into a tight ball and forget everything.

'Sam. Are you still there?'

'Yes.'

'There may be severe damage.'

Sam had a brief vision of the large man flinging Eleanor aside. A sudden flash of violence. Her head smacking against the radiator. 'Surely there's something else that can be done? She's young, strong. They can't have exhausted every treatment.'

There was a persistent beeping sound, the phone demanding more change. Sam fumbled in his pocket but by the time he'd pulled enough coins out, the phone had gone dead.

He stood like a statue, phone still clamped to his ear, eyes fixed on the stone work of the building behind the booth. He saw Eleanor as clear as day in front of him, ached to be by her side.

Laughter from a passing couple woke him from his trance. The Eleanor he ached for had been torn from his life. He felt his blood heat, the anger rise from his stomach to his chest. He burned for justice.

Had Zahra survived the river? Or had she been pulled, lifeless, from the water by the police? He shook the darkness from his head. She was a survivor. He had to believe that.

And if Zahra was alive, would she head to Pozzani or disappear for good, convinced that he just brought trouble to her door? All he knew was that he had a clue, one he felt compelled to pursue.

Chapter 43

The Strait of Messina

Sam lay on a hard couchette in the hot compartment. The curtains were drawn but a crack in the material revealed the ferry's bowels – metal trusses and steam ducts covered in the same grey paint, and the orange of a life buoy.

The train had boarded the ferry shortly before dawn and was now easing across the water to Messina. From there, according to the map he'd briefly consulted at Rome's Termini Station, it was less than an hour to Catania and then possibly the same to Pozzani.

He turned on his bunk. The wound on his back protested and he winced. But at least he was warm.

The other three Italian passengers in his cabin – a woman and two men in their early twenties – had got off the train and were on the ship somewhere, possibly sobering up with coffee after the two bottles of Chianti that had been consumed on the journey. Sam had taken a few sips to be friendly, lied about his intentions in Sicily – he was, as far as they were concerned, heading for a language school in Palermo – and then feigned sleep while the others continued imbibing. Had they not been so keen to get pissed, he reckoned they would have questioned him a little more. He was, after all, unshaven, travelling without baggage and wearing clothes that were a size too large. There was a lot about him that didn't add up.

The boat groaned and Sam felt a drop in his stomach as the vessel pitched downwards. Despite being cocooned in the train, layer upon layer of dense metal between him and the water, he still sensed a storm outside, imagined water lashing against the side as the ferry battled forward through a wintry sea.

He thought of the journey Zahra had made through the same waters. From what he'd read, there was a window of opportunity for immigrants in the warmer months to make their way, most often from Libya, to Italy. But even kinder weather did not guarantee safety. They were travelling in overcrowded, flimsy and often faulty vessels, with limited supplies and pilots who rarely had anything other than profit on their minds. Thousands drowned every year. The lucky ones were those who limped, dehydrated and malnourished, into Lampedusa, or who were rescued by coastguard, naval or NGO vessels.

There was another groan from the ship, followed by a clang of a door being slammed. Moments later the sliding door of the cabin opened and his three fellow passengers returned.

'We've arrived in Messina, Sam,' said one of the men.

'Buono,' managed Sam.

There was movement suddenly as the three of them began shoving belongings back into the mouths of rucksacks. The boat's horn sounded.

Sam lay still on his bunk. There was no space to move while this was going on and besides, the train wouldn't leave without him.

The groaning increased, a noise that was joined by the sound of announcements in Italian and English urging passengers to return to the train. The horn sounded again.

He could feel the motion of the boat more keenly now, sensed it turning in the water. And then the anchor being dropped, its chain clanging and rattling as it plunged beneath the oil-streaked surface of the harbour's water.

There was a shift in the light. The woman had opened the curtains fully and Sam peered down the train. The bow door was slowly opening. A locomotive would be waiting on the quay, ready to couple with the carriages and pull them on to Sicilian soil. Sam felt his stomach flutter with nerves. One way or another, this was the end of the journey.

Twenty minutes later, the carriage shunted. There was a brief pause, then the train began to ease out of the boat's insides on to a quayside slick with water. Dense, menacing clouds pregnant with more rain moved with speed across the sky. Sunlight briefly broke through, lighting up small pockets on the harbour before plunging them back into the gloom. A harbour guard clad in a dark wind-breaker and heavy boots, cap pulled tightly down over his face, guided vehicles spilling out of another ferry. In the distance were two more boats; beyond them a long loop of road running along the waterfront, a ribbon of white and red car lights stretching into the distance. A regular day beginning in Messina.

*

At Catania, he and his fellow passengers parted ways and Sam bought a ticket for Pozzani on a train that was leaving at midday. He sat on a bench in the station by a newsstand and ate a baguette stuffed with ham and tomatoes, washed down with a double-shot espresso. He felt like a wreck. He'd barely slept for days. Even now, the chances of drifting off were slim – the fire burning in his chest and stomach would surely prevent that – but to lie his head on a pillow and his body on a half-decent mattress seemed, at that moment, to be the most desirable thing imaginable.

The train arrived in Pozzani shortly after 4pm, the journey he thought would take an hour prolonged by endless stops at tiny provincial stations. A landscape of rocky hills and fields of vines cut back for the winter sat under the same brooding sky. Heavy rain broke out intermittently, reducing visibility to a matter of feet. An old man in a grey tweed jacket and coppola slept opposite him for the whole journey.

Sam reckoned that the most likely location for the town's hotels was the front. He consulted a map on a notice board outside the station, then set off. He walked for five minutes down a broad avenue before reaching the sea.

There was a line of palm trees bending in the wind and, just beyond, the sea wall. Sam could hear waves crashing angrily on the beach and the lone cry of a seagull. In the distance, a dark silhouette loomed over the seafront. It was, Sam realised, the solid, square-looking citadel he'd seen on the internet, a fortress designed to repel invaders.

The sea front was curved like a bow and, as Sam reached its proudest point, he saw the sea-facing wall of the citadel. A tremor ran through him. It was crowned with a sign lit up by dozens of light bulbs. Benvenuti a Pozzani.

He stopped and stared at it. He thought of how the sign might appear to someone out to sea, reflected on the surface of the water, like the street lights in Rome had appeared on the Tiber. Had the sight of this been the memory that broke to the surface in Zahra's mind? And if she had seen that sign out to sea, she was tantalisingly close to land. So what had happened?

He plodded on, conscious of his aching need to find a place to bed down. His guess was right. The front was home to the town's hotels and pensiones, but as he walked wearily along its length, occasionally exploring side streets when he saw a sign hanging from a building, he began to realise that Pozzani had shut up shop for the winter.

The light was fading fast, streetlights and a handful of shops guiding his path. When he was almost despairing of finding anywhere to stay, he reached the junction of another narrow street off the front. A little distance down, lit up like a beacon, was a sign for the Hotel del Mare. He felt his spirits lift.

A short walk brought him to the hotel's entrance. Through a glass panel in the front door, he could see a corridor, a reception desk lit by a single table lamp, and a staircase rising to the first floor. He tried the door, but it was locked. He pressed the bell. A moment later, as Sam was beginning to give up hope, a short old woman wearing black appeared at the end of the corridor. Sam raised a hand wearily. The old lady shuffled in slippers down the hall, unlocked the door and ushered him in.

'Momento,' she said, raising both palms to emphasise her point, before she moved back down the hall and disappeared through an open door. Somewhere in the distance a television was on, the sound of lines being hammily delivered in sing-song Italian, followed by canned laughter. Sam imagined standing beneath a hot shower, finally washing the sweat and River Tiber grime off his body.

Minutes later a man in his fifties, the same short rotund frame as the old woman, came out of the doorway.

'You want a room?' he said.

'Please.'

'Well, you have the hotel almost to yourself,' he replied, smiling.

'Any room will do.'

'I can give you a room on the second floor. The balcony has a partial view of the sea. But maybe you won't be standing outside much in this weather!' He laughed and Sam attempted to laugh along with him.

'Where's your baggage?'

'The airline lost it,' said Sam.

'Madonna,' the man said, lifting and dropping his balled fists in a gesture that conveyed annoyance and disbelief in equal measure.

He moved behind the desk and asked Sam for his passport. Sam pulled his now buckled passport out and placed it in front of the man.

The hotelier opened it and let out a short chuckle.

'Inglese,' he said. 'It's amazing. The third today.'

Sam felt like he'd been given an electric shock. There were, possibly, other reasons why a pair of English travellers might be staying in Pozzani in the depths of winter. But he could think of only one.

And then another thought struck him. Just as he'd heard one of his pursuers speak on the stairs by the river in Rome, they could have easily heard Zahra's parting words. In which case, they'd have known his next move had he survived the water.

Sam's mouth was dry when he next spoke and he had to swallow hard before he could get the words out. 'Is one of the men staying here called Harry?'

The man at the desk pulled back as if struck by an invisible hand. 'Incredible! You know him.'

'Maybe.' Sam's voice was barely audible, fear reducing it to a whisper. It was possible that a different Englishman called Harry was staying at the hotel, but Sam knew that was simply wishful thinking.

'Harry Tapper,' continued the hotelier, 'and a big guy called...' he flicked through the register in front of him, 'Patrick Wallace.'

Sam just found the courage to ask the next question. 'Are they in?'

'They got here an hour ago,' the man said, beaming, as if he'd personally facilitated a wonderful reunion of old friends. 'They're on the same floor as you.'

There was a pause, a moment when Sam railed against what he knew he had to do. Then he snatched his passport and ran for the door.

Chapter 44

Pozzani, Sicily

'I'm in Sicily,' said Tapper.

There was silence at the other end of the phone.

'Pozzani. Does that name ring a bell?'

'I cannot talk about this now.'

'I think you need to.'

Tapper was sitting on his hotel bed, an old, spongey mattress sagging under his weight. The room was plain, save a faded print of the sea front and, close to the basin in the opposite corner, a wardrobe and a framed photograph of Pope Francis.

'It's not a good time.'

'Oh, I'm sorry,' said Tapper, voice dripping with sarcasm. 'Perhaps I should have scheduled this call.'

'For Christ's sake, spell it out.'

'Zahra Idris's psychotherapist left London and made contact with her in Amsterdam. We found them but they fled to Rome. They may now be heading here.'

'May?'

'If they're alive.'

There was silence. Then: 'What do you want from me?'

'Some sign that we are in this together.'

'Believe me. I never stop thinking about it.'

'Good. Because if this goes south, I am not taking sole responsibility.'

'Of course.'

There was a knock on the door. 'Hang on a minute,' said Tapper.

He opened the door. It was Wallace, dressed in jeans and a t-shirt. Tapper was struck by his old cellmate's powerful chest and shoulders. He found himself distracted, suddenly lost in a memory that made him feel giddy.

'Got to go,' said Tapper, ending the call. He steadied himself with a hand on the doorframe.

'I just went down to reception to get a towel,' said Wallace. 'And guess what the owner told me?'

'Keddie?'

Wallace nodded. 'He said a man just tried to book into the hotel. He told him he had other English guests. When he mentioned our names, the man legged it.'

'He told him our names?' Tapper felt his insides chill. 'We're sure it's him?'

'The owner saw his passport.'

Tapper swallowed. 'This ends now.'

Minutes later, they were passing through reception. The hotelier poked his head out as they passed. 'Try Al Barrocco for dinner. There's not much else open.'

Tapper waved a hand in response but kept moving.

Outside, the wind had picked up, bringing with it a cold, salty taste that Tapper felt on his lips. 'You go into town, I'll check the front and side streets. Ring if you spot him.'

They parted ways. Tapper moved off and was on the front moments later. It was now dark. Picking up his pace, he moved left first, scanning down each of the side streets in turn, before retracing his steps and peering down the other roads that fed the sea front. By the time he reached the end, the only people he'd passed were two lanky youths and a pair of old women in thick coats being buffeted by the wind.

He suspected that if Keddie wasn't now running from Pozzani, he would sleep rough in the town. Even if there was another hotel open, he doubted whether the shrink would book in. He was a sitting duck if he did.

Tapper's phone buzzed in his pocket.

'I can see him. About a hundred metres ahead of me.'

'Where are you?'

There was a pause. 'Via Andromeda.'

Tapper touched the map app on his phone and, after briefly studying the town's layout and the position of Via Andromeda, broke into a jog in Wallace's direction.

Chapter 45

Pozzani, Sicily

Sam had sprinted from the hotel but now slowed, exhaustion and despair sapping the last remaining energy from his body. It was over. It had to be. They were in Pozzani. Two men who never gave up. While he was alone and all but finished.

What had he expected? To discover Zahra waiting for him at the hotel? Her memory miraculously restored? Her secrets laid bare and Eleanor's attacker brought to justice before she, equally miraculously, emerged from a coma?

The wind picked up again, cold air clawing at his back. There was a promise of rain in the air, another drenching of his already damp and grimy clothes. He caught a glimpse of himself in the window of a closed butchers. Eyes hooded, face unshaven, oversized clothes hanging from him. He looked like a lunatic, a homeless madman. Inside the shop, slabs of meat were laid out in a cooler unit. Sam shuddered.

It was then he caught a glimpse of the larger man out of the corner of his right eye. He was some distance off, with his back turned as he looked up the same street in the opposite direction. In a shot, Sam pulled himself into the entrance of the butchers, hiding in the shadows but still able to keep the man in his sights. It was him, Sam was certain. He had the same lumbering gait and hooded face.

A minute passed. The man moved off in the other direction. Sam exhaled.

He slowly emerged from the shop's entrance and began inching down the street, keeping tight to the buildings. Apart from a handful of shops, the streets were dominated by houses and apartments. Some were old, with tiled roofs, exteriors of stone or peeling plaster, shuttered windows and iron-work balconies. Others were modern buildings made of concrete. Lights were on inside. Bodies moved past windows, families gathering for an evening meal.

But just ahead on the opposite side of the road was a darker building. As Sam got closer, he realised it was unfinished, a carcass of unplastered blockwork and open doorways and windows. He might be able to hide there, keep an eye on his pursuers, then escape at first light.

It wasn't a plan, but then he didn't have the brain power to construct one in his head. He looked down the street again. The big man seemed to have paused and was standing with his back to Sam. Now was his chance. With his heart in his mouth, Sam darted across the road and through the open doorway of the building.

He stepped in a puddle of water, felt the wet penetrate his trainers. As his eyes slowly adjusted to the dark, he saw a crude stairwell in a corner of the room. Perhaps he'd have a better vantage point up there. Some warning if his pursuers were getting close.

He climbed the rough stairs carefully, steps emerging from the gloom as he rose up. On the next floor it was just as dark, and Sam felt his way along a wall to try to find a corner to hide in. He heard a creature, most probably a rat or mouse, scuttle across the dry, dusty floor away from him. Somewhere on the floor below, a cat meowed.

His foot hit a hard lump and he felt with his hands in front of him. It was a pile of unused concrete blocks, about waist high. He continued probing with his fingers and discovered it was about six feet in length. Somewhere to hide behind. But for now, he wanted to be near the balcony, keeping an eye on the street below. The exhaustion was a distant memory. All he felt now was his heart, sprinting in his chest.

*

Wallace had watched as Sam crossed the road then disappeared. If he was trying to hide in that building, then he'd just signed his own death warrant. Tapper arrived on the scene minutes later, slightly out of breath.

'He's in the dark building there,' said Wallace, pointing up the street.

'Check the rear, Pat,' said Tapper, 'see if there's an escape route. If so, one of us needs to be positioned there if he tries to make a run.'

They split up, Tapper staying put while Wallace checked the back of the building.

Minutes later, Wallace returned.

'There's a high wall. No way out. The only exit point is the front door.'

'He's trapped,' said Tapper, feeling the same rush of fear and unsettling pleasure he'd experienced at the Tiber.

'I'll go in first,' said Wallace. 'You stay by the door, just in case he gets away from me. But he won't.'

Tapper was reassured by Wallace's brute confidence. The chances were, Keddie was about to be extinguished. As a pair of detainees at Ipswich – two feral psychopaths who'd made Tapper's early days at the young offenders' institution a particularly brutal experience – had discovered, when Pat Wallace swung one of his meaty fists, you didn't get up.

They moved slowly up the street, keeping close to the houses.

*

Inside the building, Sam watched with utter horror as the two men gathered at the end of the street. He tried to calm his mounting terror. Perhaps they were just plotting the next stage of their search. When they split, he exhaled and felt the relief flood through him. But then he realised the lean man wasn't going anywhere. What the fuck was he hanging around for? Then his worst fears were confirmed. The larger figure returned and they started up the street in his direction.

He'd screwed up. Been spotted. How the hell had that happened? He was sure the large man hadn't been watching.

Sam moved back from the balcony and into the shadows of the room. It began raining. A light patter that soon turned into a downpour. He found his hiding place in the dark and crouched down behind the wall. Sweat covered his body, which was now coiled tightly. He reached out to the wall, tried to move one of the bricks and quickly realised that lifting it would require two hands. As a weapon to strike out with, it was no use. He needed to find something lighter. He had a sudden fleeting image of David and Goliath.

All he could hear now was the rain driving down on every surface. The roof above, the street outside. The only other sound, a car speeding by, tyres hitting a puddle, the splash of water.

There were other people around. This place wasn't a ghost town. Could he have screamed out for help? Not now. No one would have heard him above the din of the rain. It was the perfect blanket under which to stifle the noise of a murder.

He combed the floor with his fingers for something to defend himself with. But other than dust, the odd nail and a pile of powder, he found nothing. No broken lump of blockwork that he could use to strike out with. And of course, even if he had found something, he might never get the chance to use it. If the men had torches, they'd quickly spot him and be able to close in on him slowly.

Then he realised that what he needed was right by him.

He crouched and waited, the rain hammering against the building. Such was the noise, the men might already have been inside for all he knew.

The darkness, the threat to his life, closed in on him, bringing with it his oldest friend, claustrophobia. His throat felt constricted, his breath shallower. He felt now, more than ever, that he might become consumed with panic, start hyperventilating. He had to resist it. If that happened, he was theirs for the taking.

*

Wallace mounted the stairs. Having swept the ground floor and the small yard outside, he was confident that Keddie was upstairs. Tapper had offered him his phone, shown him the powerful torch it had. But Wallace had declined. His eyes would adjust to the dark and, while a torch worked for him, it also worked against him, showing his prey exactly where he was. Surprise would be everything now. Giving him the chance to strike once, rather than get involved in a messy and unnecessary struggle.

He reached the top of the stairs. He moved stealthily into the space, each footfall slow and gentle. He was confident that the rain was masking his movements, but still didn't want to take any chances.

Wallace became aware of the opening that led on to the balcony. The subdued light and the sound of the rain. His eyes moved around, taking in a handful of shapes. One of them was where Keddie was hiding, of that he was certain.

*

Sam was desperate to move. He felt the darkness was like a wall, slowly closing in on him, ready to bury him. He had a sudden image of the courtiers and slaves of an Egyptian emperor, entombed with their master inside a pyramid.

And that was when he smelt it.

It was the odour he'd encountered in the house when he'd found Eleanor slumped against that radiator.

Her attacker was in the room with him. And close.

His hand tightened, ready to strike.

The smell was gathering strength, getting closer. Sam held his breath, aware now that his next move was critical – quite possibly all that stood between his survival, and death.

Sam heard the man shouting over the din of the rain. 'I know you're in here!'

It was all that Sam needed. While the smell suggested proximity, the voice confirmed it – as if the man were compensating for the noise of the rain and trying to throw his words as far as possible. In doing so, he'd given Sam the best clue yet as to his position. It was now or never.

Sam shot up from his crouching position and saw a dark shape before him. He paused for a second, hoping his sudden movement would get him noticed, saw the figure swivel in his direction, then flung the contents of his hand at the man's head.

The effect was instant. The man cried out. 'Argh! Fuck! Fuck!'

As the cement powder burned into the man's eyes, Sam charged out from his hiding place and ran at the shape before him, his right shoulder hitting the man hard in the chest. Sam felt the pain shoot from his shoulder and down his arm. It was like ramming a wall. He saw the shape drop away, arms flailing, and heard a mighty thud, accompanied by a crack. There was another cry of pain, but more truncated, like the man's breath was being forced from his lungs at the same time.

As Sam rushed to the stairs, a voice came up from below.

'Pat! Pat! Are you OK?'

He paused, aware now that he was sandwiched between the two men. There was a groan from behind him, a shift in the light as the large man began to lift himself off the floor. Sam made a rapid calculation. He had to get away from the big man. But the only escape route he could see took him directly into the path of the other man. There was nothing for it.

He bolted, taking the stairs two steps at a time. He hit the ground floor running and surged forward, aware now of a figure silhouetted in the doorway. Sam pelted at him, right arm pulled back and ready to strike.

As the man's features loomed out of the dark, Sam flung his hand forward, smacking into the face in front of him, following through with the full weight of his charging body. The man fell back, but instead of tumbling to the ground, he slammed into the side of the doorway, effectively blocking Sam's path.

Sam crashed into the man. Skull met skull and Sam felt a searing pain in his forehead. The sudden and violent full stop had an instant effect. Though he managed to right himself, Sam felt his balance floundering, his feet stumble. The man was similarly disoriented, but was pulling himself away from the doorframe, and moving into Sam's path to strike out. Despite feeling as if someone had branded his forehead with a hot poker, Sam did not hesitate. As the man moved into his orbit, he swung his right fist, driving it into the man's stomach. There was a sharp intake of breath – he'd winded him – and his adversary bent over double.

With the man disabled, Sam pushed past him. A hand grabbed at his parka as he passed but Sam lashed out with his left arm, beating the man's hand away. He was, quite suddenly, free of them both.

He stumbled down the street, dizzy with pain, his legs threatening to give way at any minute. But he was also aware that although he'd possibly injured them both, there was only a brief window of opportunity before they rallied and began chasing. And now they'd be raging as well as murderous.

Still running, Sam glanced back at the dark building. Seeing no one emerging from it, he turned his head in the direction of travel. Which was when he saw the headlights of a car about to cross his path. Sam tried to stop but it was too late. The car was suddenly in front of him and he flung himself on to the bonnet.

He landed on his side, the metal crunching beneath him. Brakes screeched and he was pressed against the windscreen as the car jammed to a halt. He knew he'd had a lucky escape. Had the car arrived milliseconds later, he would have been hit.

Behind the glass a man was staring wide-eyed at Sam. He knew he couldn't hang around – that he had to get moving. He slipped off the bonnet and landed on the ground to move off. But the driver was as quickly out of his vehicle and shouting at Sam. As Sam began to run, a hand grabbed him by the collar. Sam tried to push him away, striking the man in the face. But the hand held tight and then another was on his shoulder, pulling him back and then to the ground.

Chapter 46

Pozzani, Sicily

Sam was left in an interrogation room, given a cup of strong, black coffee. He suspected that, with his unshaven face, and dirty, oversized clothes, he cut a pathetic figure. But he no longer cared. He was safe. If only temporarily. And his next course of action was clear. He was alone – a foreigner in Sicily, with two men out to kill him. He had to tell the police what was happening.

But first, he needed to close his eyes for a short while. He folded his arms on the table and rested his head against them. He felt exhaustion weigh down on him like a cloak.

There was a cough. Sam looked up, blinking rapidly. How long had he been asleep? The man opposite him was wiry, with grey, dishevelled hair and an untrimmed beard. He looked down at some notes on the table.

'Signor Keddie.'

'Yes.'

'I am Ispettore Guido Reni. Do you understand why you have been arrested?'

Sam nodded.

'Today you assaulted a resident of Pozzani, Signor Massimo Fazzino.'

'I didn't mean to hurt him.'

Reni brushed aside the comment. 'Of more interest to me is that you were running through the streets of the town in the middle of winter. We don't get many English tourists here in the summer. We don't get any at this time of year.'

'I can explain.'

Reni lifted an outstretched hand. Be my guest.

Sam spoke for half an hour, the story pouring out in an exhausted babble. His account moved from Creech Hill to London, from Amsterdam to the camp and riverbank in Rome. He then shifted to Sicily, pausing to rack his brain for the names the hotelier had mentioned. Reni did not interrupt, but Sam got the creeping sensation that he did not believe a word.

When he finished, the policeman stared at Sam for an uncomfortable minute. Finally, he scratched his beard.

'Here's what I think, Signor Keddie. You haven't really broken any laws. Massimo Fazzino doesn't want to press charges. He isn't hurt. He's just angry. You were running without looking where you were going. He could have killed you.' Reni paused. 'So we will take a few more details and then you are free to go. As for your story, we will need to speak to the other people involved.'

'You're not going to arrest them?'

'You have told me an extraordinary story. I need more evidence before I arrest two men. And what will I be arresting them for? Attacking you? Killing a solicitor in London?'

'What about me?' asked Sam, fear layering itself over the anger he felt. 'There are two men out there who are trying to kill me.'

'I suggest you book into the Pensione Vesuvio on Via Spugia. It's the only other place I can think of that might be open.'

Sam rose from his seat. His legs ached and head pounded. Sweat had freshly salted the wound on his back. He felt himself sway with dizziness.

'You OK?' asked Reni, an arm reaching out to steady him.

Sam swatted him away. He paused for a second, steadied himself.

Reni walked Sam out of the police station, giving him directions to the pensione he'd mentioned.

Sam descended steps to a yard filled with vehicles. It was the rear of the station. Perhaps Reni was looking out for him making him leave this way, rather than sending him out the front like a lamb to the slaughter. No, that was hardly likely. If the policeman really intended to protect him, he'd still be inside.

He felt drizzle against his face and a cold, biting wind that whipped his skin. Dread tightened like a clamp around his chest. He was more alone than ever, disbelieved by the one person he should have been able to trust. He longed for a hole he could crawl into.

Behind him, at the back door of the station, he heard Reni talking to another man. There was the sound of a car blinking to attention, an engine starting and the vehicle accelerating away.

He turned, saw the car's red tail-lights. If Tapper and Wallace were back at the hotel, the conversation Reni had in mind might take an hour, if not longer. That's if they were there. If they were still on the streets, the deadly game of cat and mouse started as soon as they spotted him.

He needed to leave town. But then he had a thought that halted him in his tracks.

What if Zahra had also come here to find answers? What if the town brought more memories to the surface? And if she was here, she'd have no idea of the danger she was in.

But where would she be? As far as he could see, nearly every hotel was shut for the season. And besides, she was without cash and passport.

And then it struck him. In a town like Pozzani, there was a place that was always open. A place where he might, just might, find Zahra.

Leaving by the back door had, he hoped, bought him some time. But not long.

Chapter 47

Pozzani, Sicily

Wallace dabbed at the corners of his eyes with a tissue. They'd been weeping constantly since cement dust had been flung in them. He needed to get some drops. But in the meantime, medicine of a different kind was heading in his direction. Keddie, and he was alone again.

He and Tapper had witnessed the arrest from the darkened entrance of the half-finished building, Tapper relaying most of what was happening because Wallace was temporarily blinded.

They found the police station and holed up in a scruffy workers' bar just down the road. Wallace rinsed his eyes in the basin in the toilet and joined Tapper at a table in the bar. His boss was fidgeting in his seat.

'This is getting complicated, Pat,' he whispered, drumming his fingers on the table's surface. 'God knows what Keddie is going to tell the police.'

Wallace wiped the tears from his bloodshot eyes. He noticed the barman looking in their direction.

'Fuck, my head hurts,' muttered Tapper. His boss had an injury of his own, a lump from his collision with Keddie. Fortunately, it was just inside the hairline so all but invisible. Just as well given the barman's interest in them both.

'We need to split,' said Tapper. 'I'll take up a position at the front of the station, you watch the rear.'

Tensing in the darkness, Wallace waited as Keddie passed on the other side of the road. In a moment or two, he would step out of the shadows and begin tailing him. Then it was just a question of finding somewhere dark and quiet, and beating the man to a pulp.

Just as he was moving out of the alley, he saw another man behind Keddie. He pulled back into the shadows. Was the figure on Keddie's tail? Wallace couldn't be sure. He watched the man's footfall. It was very deliberate, as if he were trying hard to match Keddie's pace. The man was walking quietly and keeping to the sides of buildings. He was following the shrink, all right. Which meant only one thing. Keddie had excited the interest of the Old Bill.

Wallace stood immobile in the alleyway, no longer sure of what to do. Eliminating Keddie was one thing. But putting a copper down was out of the question.

Tapper was right. This was getting more and more complicated. He stepped from the shadows, hoping that he was mistaken, and the figure ahead was not a policeman. Because opportunities to resolve this were fast running out.

Chapter 48

Pozzani, Sicily

Sam glanced at the roofline of the town as he walked away from the police station and immediately knew where to head. The two tallest buildings in Pozzani jutted above the tiled roofs – a dome to the west of the station and another nearer the sea front.

The first church presented itself in minutes. He turned into a piazza and saw it in front of him. A modern building, shorn of decoration bar a statue of Mary in an alcove above the entrance.

Sam climbed a short set of steps and pushed the door open. Inside, the church was brightly lit and, at the front, filled with around twenty people, who turned in unison at the sound of Sam's entrance. A man and woman stood at the front. Behind them, a priest, not in gowns, but a black suit, officiating. A wedding rehearsal, by the look of things.

Sam backed out of the church, his heart heavy, expectations dashed.

He moved on towards the sea front down an alleyway of buildings clad in crumbling plasterwork. A cold wind blasted up the street like a warning.

There was a banging noise above him. Startled, Sam looked up to see a shutter swinging in the breeze. He momentarily lost his footing on a slippery, loose cobble, stumbling forward.

He passed a café, its interior panelled and shadowy. A man stood at the bar, hunched forward in conspiratorial conversation with the barman.

The alleyway opened into another piazza. Leafless trees and empty benches around its edges, a fountain in the middle, the water turned off. A group of men stood near the fountain clad in thick coats and hats. As Sam moved past them, he saw black faces. They looked back at him with empty gazes.

The church was on the opposite side of the piazza. As the building emerged from behind the trees' branches, he shuddered. The façade was lit from the side by a streetlight, casting theatrical shadows from every elaborate Baroque swirl, pillar and statue. As he got closer, he saw grotesque faces in the stonework, stains of algae, weeds sprouting from damp recesses.

He ascended the steps, the stonework cracked and loose beneath his feet, and tried one of the large doors. It was locked. He tried another, rapidly losing heart. This one eased open with a groan.

Like the unadorned church in Rome, the interior was lit by banks of votive candles. But that was where the similarities ended. Every inch of wall was crammed with stucco, frescoes and sculptures. This continued up the walls until the light petered out and darkness took over.

It was cold inside, a chill that seemed to emanate from the floor. Sam moved cautiously down the centre of the nave, his trainers squeaking damply on the marble floor. As the pews in front materialised from the dark, Sam saw they were empty.

A rustle to his side made his heart leap and he turned sharply to his left. There was a figure asleep on a pew, a head of matted hair the only sign of a human being.

Heart now hammering in his chest, he reached the transepts. Ahead was an altar of blood red marble fringed with sections of whiter stone. Laid over the top, a covering of lace, yellowing and threadbare. His eyes moved right and then left. And that was when he saw someone sitting in the front pew.

The person was lit from the side by a bank of candles. But at this distance, all Sam could see was a body clad in a thick coat, neck wrapped in a scarf, a baseball cap pulled low over a brow.

He moved in their direction. The person appeared to flinch.

Sam felt fear and excitement in equal measure. The figure on the pew had looked up. Sam saw a jawline, mouth and nose – dark skin, or was it just the light?

And then the figure stood, began inching towards him. Sam froze on the spot.

He could have turned around, run, but he no longer wanted to. With his body close to collapse and no other plans up his sleeve, what else could he do but have faith?

The figure was closer now and Sam saw that they did indeed have dark skin. Another of the immigrants in town? A hand reached for the baseball cap, pulling it free to reveal a head of curls tied back tightly in a ponytail.

Sam gasped. The person before him was Zahra. Alive.

Chapter 49

Pozzani, Sicily

They hugged tightly, Sam certain that, if he let her go, she would evaporate.

'You survived,' said Sam, as they peeled apart. 'I should have stayed at the river. Found you. I tried to look but the men were there. I'm so sorry, Zahra.'

There were tears running down her cheeks. She beckoned him to sit down.

'How did you make it?' asked Sam.

'I was thrown downriver,' she said, drying her cheeks with a sleeve. 'I was sure I was going to drown.' Her voice trembled with recollected fear. 'Then I hit a metal grille. It was right across the river. There were bits of wood and plastic caught in it. I used the metal to pull myself to the embankment. I could hear the men on the other side. So I waited till they'd gone. Then made my way back to the camp.'

'You must have been freezing.'

'I tried to run, get some warmth back into my body, but I could barely walk. Eventually I got back to the camp. There were people there, sifting through the remains, looking for belongings. A couple of tents were still standing. They found me some dry clothes.'

'How did you get here?'

He saw her smile, a brief moment of levity play across her face. 'Same as before. Containers. But not cabbages this time. Toilet roll. Much more comfortable. And warmer.'

There was a sound of creaking timber. Sam shot a look down the church and saw no movement. But given the darkness, visibility was down to about ten metres. They sat in silence, listening out for any other sounds. But there was nothing more, and Sam concluded that it was the sleeping figure. He relaxed a fraction.

'You remembered Pozzani,' he said.

She nodded. 'It was the lights –'

'– reflected on the water?'

'How did you know?'

'I saw the sign lit up on the front. You saw that out to sea, didn't you?'

'I think so.'

'Still no other memories?'

'Nothing.'

'But you came back.'

'I have nothing left, Sam. I have to get my memories back. Find out why they want us both dead. I hoped you might be here to help me.'

There was a click from further down the church, like the sound of a shoe's heel on marble. Sam's eyes darted down the nave again. Nothing. But he sensed that the noise was close.

He felt Zahra's hand grab his, the cold fingers grip hard. He braced himself. Ready to run again. But where, this time?

The next sound they heard was a vibration. Followed by another. Then another.

A mobile phone was ringing.

Zahra was off first, pulling Sam's hand as she darted into the darkness behind the altar, heading for the rear of the church. Sam hoped to God there was a doorway at the back, otherwise they were trapped. Footsteps – slow and deliberate, not a run – echoed down the church. Someone was on their tail.

Shapes emerged from the shadows. Choir stalls to their sides and, ahead of them, the rear wall of the church, a crucified Christ surrounded by cherubs and angels in plasterwork, disturbed candles causing ghostly shapes to flicker across its surface.

There was a door off to the right. Perhaps to a vestry and then out the back. Zahra was first to it, turning the handle and pulling it open. A cold, fungal smell escaped like a sigh.

There was no time to pause. Zahra was through the door first, fumbling for a switch in the darkness. Lights blinked on to reveal a staircase dropping away, damp stonework lit by a series of bulbs that hung from a loose cable overhead. Zahra turned to Sam, her face stricken.

'Go!' he shouted.

Zahra moved down the steps, her initial speed tempered by a fresh terror. Sam was not exactly keen to rush headlong into this part of the church. The low ceilings and stench of decay were already pressing in on him, bringing that familiar sense of breathlessness.

There was a cry from below. Zahra had reached the base of the staircase and frozen on the spot. Catching up, Sam saw what had caused her reaction.

A narrow corridor lay ahead, off which were small chapels. The string of light bulbs lit the corridor – and the interior of each chapel – in a cold, yellow light.

Sam had read about catacombs like this in Palermo, huge underground chambers filled with what he could now see at the lip of each chapel. Coffins framed in timber but cased in glass. Just to the right, a man's face, skin stretched parchment-like over his skull, eyes closed, a waxed moustache above dry lips. Elsewhere, those who'd not been afforded the luxury of a coffin. A figure hanging on the wall in the chapel to their left, head twisted in deathly curiosity, eyes black hollows, skin like brown leather, hair carefully parted to one side.

They heard footsteps on the stairs.

Sam saw his fears mirrored in Zahra's face, which was creased with terror, her forehead beaded with sweat.

'We have to hide,' he whispered.

As the noise on the stairs gathered strength, Sam and Zahra inched into the crypt. Each chapel was lit by a single bulb, one that cast its grisly contents in a horrifyingly harsh light. There were shelves of bodies stacked to the ceiling, as well as rows of suspended corpses. Men and women in their Sunday best. Two toddlers in night dresses, hands still clutching dolls, mouths agape as if they'd died screaming.

To their left was a chapel in which the light bulb had gone. Sam pulled Zahra into the darkness. Something cold and brittle brushed his face and he shuddered. His free hand reached forward in the darkness. He felt the timber of a shelf to his right and, moving his hand up, cold, hard bone beneath a thin layer of dry cloth. He moved his hand down to waist height. Another skeletal corpse greeted him, this time with dusty, bony fingers. He was certain he was seconds away from a panic attack, a bout of breathlessness that would leave him gasping for oxygen in a place that only offered dust.

Sam let his hand drop further and found a cavity. A place in which two bodies could have been stacked. They could, he reckoned, both squat in the space. He let go of Zahra's hand and, summoning the last residue of courage he could muster, crouched down and tucked into the space till his back met stone. Dropping his backside to the ground, knees drawn into his chest, he reached out for Zahra's trembling hand and pulled her towards him.

She dropped down, crouching by him. Now he'd found a place to hide, Sam's mind let loose on the imagined horrors all round him. Faces without eyes stared at him, skeletal hands reached out for him. He felt death in his nostrils, enveloping him in a cold embrace from which there was no escape. His breathing was accelerating, reaching the point of panic. Next to him, Zahra was shaking uncontrollably.

The footsteps, slow and steady, were getting louder. Could they spring from their hiding place, use the element of surprise? But of course there was no element of surprise. Their pursuer had them trapped in this hellish place. He could take all the time he wanted.

And it was then that Zahra began speaking. Not whispering, but speaking.

'They were lined up on the beach. Body after body.'

'Please,' hissed Sam. 'Not now. You mustn't speak.'

But Zahra was deep in her memories, oblivious to the danger closing in on them both. 'They were all dead.'

She stopped and Sam saw that the light in the corridor was disturbed by the silhouette of a man.

He was about to die. He was certain of it. To die in a ready-made tomb.

Chapter 50

Pozzani, Sicily

The silhouette spoke. 'It's OK,' he said. 'I won't hurt you.'

Sam knew who it was, even if he couldn't see the man's face against the harsh light of the corridor. It was Reni, the policeman who'd just interviewed him.

'I'm sorry I scared you both,' he said. He glanced around the crypt. 'But your choice of hiding place does not help either. Here.' He reached into the darkness and took Sam's hand. Zahra was still cowering in the alcove.

'It's OK,' said Sam, his heart racing and throat tight, offering his hand to her.

Zahra took the hand and Sam pulled her off the floor.

Reni led them up the stairs. At the top were two uniformed officers. When Zahra saw them she flinched.

'They won't hurt you,' said Sam.

She shot him a wide-eyed look.

'Please,' he said. 'We need an ally.'

The eyes relaxed a fraction, as if she realised they couldn't run any more.

There was a brief exchange of Italian between Reni and the men. Then the policeman turned to Sam.

'Perhaps you should come back to the station with me.'

They were not handcuffed or strong-armed out of the church. Reni simply walked in front with the two other men,

Sam and Zahra behind. As Sam's breathing began to slow, he wondered why the policeman was so calm. His recent behaviour must surely have aroused their suspicion. Unless Reni knew something he didn't.

Reni invited them to sit in the back of his car then, without locking their doors, walked round to the front of the vehicle, got in, and drove back to the station.

They were led to the same interview room Sam had sat in earlier, given coffee, then left alone.

'What does he want?' asked Zahra, her voice still quivering with fear.

It was the first time she'd spoken since the crypt. Since she'd recalled the sight of bodies lined up on the beach. A memory triggered, without doubt, by the corpses arranged around them in the darkness. There were more questions to ask. Did Zahra now remember anything else, how those bodies – her fellow passengers, of that he was sure – ended up on the sand? But now wasn't the time.

'I may be very wrong,' said Sam, 'but I think he wants to help us.'

The door opened and Reni came in, clutching a laptop. His face had lost the look of scepticism it had worn during the first interview. He smiled gently.

'And this must be Zahra Idris, the woman you mentioned,' he said. Reni placed the laptop on the table and sat down. He smiled gently at Zahra. She nodded hesitantly, her hostility towards the police still evident.

'I spoke to this man earlier,' Sam said to Zahra. 'He knows everything.'

Zahra's face flashed annoyance.

'I had no choice. They're here. The men who tried to kill us in Rome. They nearly succeeded this time.'

Zahra visibly tensed.

'Your story intrigued me, Signor Keddie,' said Reni. 'And what you spoke about in the church, particularly what Signorina Idris said in the crypt.' The policeman looked saddened for a moment, as if it had struck a chord within him. 'My colleagues visited the hotel to talk to the other men. But they were not there. The hotelier said they were out. In fact, that was the news I received in the church when my phone rang. Causing you to run.' He smiled again, as if apologising.

'Then I suggest you find them as soon as possible,' urged Sam.

'My men are returning to the hotel as we speak.'

Reni ran a hand through his hair, which seemed to do nothing but further increase its dishevelled appearance.

'I need more if I'm going to take this further.'

'So where do we start?' asked Sam.

Reni reached for the laptop. 'Harry Tapper.'

Chapter 51

Pozzani, Sicily

Emerging from behind the church's organ, Tapper dusted down his coat and began to breathe again.

- Following a call from Wallace, he'd joined his old cellmate outside the church. They moved stealthily through the building, discovered the policeman standing at the top of the staircase.

But before they could make any decisions, they heard a car screech to a halt outside, knew they'd soon be outnumbered and caught. There was no option but to hide.

Tapper was now pacing the marble floor.

'I'm fucked!' he cried. 'Completely fucked! They've found a sympathetic policeman, and they're going to fucking talk.'

'You've got to calm down, Harry,' said Wallace. 'You know how police investigations work. They don't go anywhere without evidence. What do they have?'

Tapper's brain raced with the implications of what had just happened. All Keddie needed to do was finger them for assaulting him, and that might be enough to get the ball rolling, to start a trickle of suspicion that turned into a flood. He knew how it worked, how shit blossomed. At the very least, the police were going to be curious as to why he, Harry Tapper, CEO of Tapper Securities, had booked into a one-star hotel with a former cellmate in some backwater in out-of-season Sicily. It was a bloody good question.

And that was looking at the whole matter in an optimistic light. Idris and Keddie were back together, a potentially credible team. And while they were probably not in possession of any real evidence – after all, what did they have without a murder weapon or a body? – they did have a story. And what a bloody story it was. It took an infamous event and added a grisly and horrifying angle to it. Who wouldn't be curious?

Maybe they hadn't talked. They'd certainly had opportunities before – back in the UK, and in Amsterdam – and not taken them. He would have heard by now.

He quickly discounted that crumb of comfort. They were with the police now. Two terrified, hunted people. They were bound to be talking.

Bile rose to his mouth. He spat the yellow saliva on to the marble floor.

Evidence.

Despite their best efforts after what had happened – the scrubbing, the disposal of clothes and the knife – there was one way to link him to what had happened.

It was unlikely – so unlikely – and he knew his mind was off again at a hundred miles an hour, but there might, just might, be a body. And if Zahra could identify that body and the murder scene, then there was evidence. Evidence that no amount of cleaning into the small hours could ever completely eradicate. He knew how people were sent down thanks to the existence of a single hair, or a fleck of blood. And there'd been a lot more than a fleck.

His mind was suddenly filled with the images of that night. The horror that had so quickly unfolded.

As he paced past Wallace, his old cellmate's hand shot out and grabbed his arm. The grip was strong, almost painful. But its effect was instantly calming. He was held, protected, just as he'd been back at Ipswich.

Tapper fixed Wallace with his eyes. Saw the solidity there. And knew then, as his brain slowed, that there was something they could do to end this. The evidence they could destroy. And if, after that, the police kept coming, then he'd set Tapper Security's legal team on them.

He was sure there was a way to explain his presence in Sicily. Perhaps he was paying an incognito visit. Discovering more as he prepared for his next role. With Wallace's hand still gripping his arm tight, and an alternative narrative growing in his head, he started to rally, to feel a surge of confidence.

He placed his free hand on Wallace's arm. 'One last stop, Pat. Then it won't matter what shit they throw at us.'

Chapter 52

Pozzani, Sicily

Reni angled the laptop so that all three of them could see the screen, then typed the words 'Harry Tapper' into Google.

The screen began to flood with search results. Sam zoomed in on an image to the right of the page, of a well-groomed man in his fifties with grey hair.

He turned to study Zahra, wondering whether she'd crumble or, worse, be consumed with terror. He thought of the memories that were beginning to emerge, how fragile she was. Was this blunt technique wise?

It was too late.

'That's the man I saw at Creech Hill,' she said, pointing to the screen, finger quivering.

'Is there anything you can remember about him?' asked Sam.

Zahra shook her head emphatically.

Reni clicked on the first link, Tapper's biog on the Tapper Security website.

'Big cheese,' muttered Reni. 'So what's he doing having fights in the street in a place like Pozzani?'

Sam scanned through the copy. 'His company runs Creech Hill. Which at least explains how he managed to get Wallace into Zahra's cell.'

He thought about the two men. The friendship that seemed to exist between them. Which was odd, given their social divide.

Reni had returned to the search results and was now looking at a bank of images of Tapper. There were photos of him pressing the flesh with various political figures, another of him standing outside Creech Hill, a smug look on his face. Then a picture of him dressed more casually, with what looked like a marina in the background.

Reni broke away from the screen. 'Can I ask, Signorina Idris, when you crossed the Mediterranean?'

'Last summer. It was August.'

'And how many were travelling with you?'

'About one hundred.'

The policeman paused, weighing up Zahra's words. He looked at them both. 'You may already have gathered that Pozzani is getting a bit of a reputation as a place where immigrants arrive. Immigrants whose boats have drifted from their intended destination, which is normally Lampedusa. They are rescued by the coastguard or the navy. Sometimes by voluntary organisations.' He turned back to Zahra, smiling gently. 'The lucky ones, that is. There are many who don't make it. Lots of sad stories.'

The policeman scratched his beard. 'I need to show you something, Signorina Idris. But I should warn you now. It will not be easy.'

Chapter 53

Pozzani, Sicily

Tapper left the engine of their hire car running. Wallace entered the hotel by a side door. Tapper watched his silhouette move through the unlit dining room before he disappeared through a doorway and up the stairs.

Minutes later he re-emerged with their luggage. He opened one of the rear doors, flung the bags on the back seat, then climbed in the front. He pulled two passports from an inside pocket and deposited them in the glove compartment.

Tapper accelerated away. The hotel would not be a problem. They had his credit card details.

According to the sat nav, it was less than an hour to their destination. He hoped to God that left them enough time – and they could do what was necessary without being disturbed. If that happened, Wallace would have to act.

A part of him hurt at the prospect of what he intended to do. But did it really mean anything to him? He doubted it. The Leopard was in the same category as the interior designer crap Yvonne had filled their homes with. It was all meaningless. It was only ever about the money for him. The distance it bought from his father. From the poverty that had made him into a monster.

The car had filled with Wallace's scent. Tapper felt a wave of deep comfort. Out here, away from everything that was expected of him – husband, businessman, father, and friend of the rich and powerful – he dared to admit what he was feeling. A part of him didn't want to return.

Sure, he still needed Keddie and Idris eliminated. But there was an undeniable sense that he felt more alive than he had for years.

He glanced at Pat briefly. His old cellmate was looking ahead, readying for the next task.

Pat had been his protector at Ipswich. He'd saved his life when those two inmates had decided that Tapper was fair game, someone to unleash their violent frustrations on. The screws had turned a blind eye and Tapper often found himself bloodied and bruised on the floor of the games room, showers, even his cell – that particular time, clothes damp with his tormenters' urine. He knew he wouldn't last long. He was taking kickings to his chest with already fractured ribs. Sooner or later a boot to his head would have given him brain damage.

And then one day his cellmate moved out and a new one – Pat Wallace – arrived. And within days, his two attackers understood that they could never bother Harry Tapper again.

A thought occurred to Tapper as he left the streetlights of Pozzani and the landscape around them darkened. Wallace didn't know the full story. Beyond that initial question he'd asked following the riot, he hadn't returned to the subject. He just served, unquestionably.

'Pat,' said Tapper. 'I need to tell you what happened. I owe you that.'

'There's no need, Harry.'

'Really, there is.'

And so he told Wallace what had happened the previous summer. And why seeing Zahra Idris in Creech Hill had triggered such a gruesome turn of events.

Wallace listened in silence. Then finally, when Tapper had finished, he spoke: 'I appreciate that, Harry.'

And with that uncomplicated comment – again free of all judgement – the unsettling feelings that had been conflicting him for the past days evaporated, and a sensation of warmth and solidity enveloped him.

Chapter 54

Sicily

The car slowed as it approached another hairpin bend. The road had been zig-zagging uphill for the past hour.

They were sitting in silence, Sam relieved that, for once, they were safe. But the feeling seemed tenuous, fragile.

They passed a sign for Ragusa, which was two kilometres away. Zahra's eyes were fixed on the road, staring at red tail-lights and the oncoming beams of vehicles on the opposite side. Sam sensed that she was girding herself.

They entered the city, the road still winding its way upwards but now past shops and apartment blocks, municipal buildings and churches fronted with elaborate Baroque decoration. The street opened out into a large piazza and Reni swung left through an open gateway, pulling up in a near-empty courtyard. He killed the engine and turned to his passengers. 'We're here.'

They followed him across the courtyard and through a modern glass door that had been set incongruously into the opening of an old building.

Inside, Reni asked Sam and Zahra to sign a visitors' book on the reception. Sam penned his name then turned to Zahra. She shook her head, clearly reluctant to sign anything official. Reni saw her expression and waved a hand dismissively, taking the pen from Sam. He and Zahra were then handed badges on ribbons by an officer behind reception, which they draped round their necks.

Reni moved down a long corridor of grey lino flooring and white walls, passing black and white photographs of the local police force from the last century. Uniformed officers standing by old model Fiats and Alfa Romeos, graduation ceremonies, medals being pinned on chests. Up ahead, Sam saw a suspended sign that read 'Obitorio'.

When Reni reached the corridor's far end, he stopped and turned. 'OK. I didn't tell you where we were going because I didn't want to frighten you. But now I need to be honest.'

Zahra stiffened.

'This is the mortuary,' said Reni. 'Where we keep the bodies of crime victims – or those whose deaths require further investigation.'

A hand shot to Zahra's mouth.

'Signorina Idris. This will take a few minutes. Nothing more. With your help, we may be able to secure justice for someone you knew.' He looked at Sam. 'And for the others.'

The hand was still held tightly over her mouth. But very slowly, Zahra began to nod.

'Va bene,' said Reni, rewarding her bravery with a warm smile.

He pushed through a set of swing doors and into another room. There was a distinct smell to it, an odour of industrial-strength disinfectant that Sam could taste in his mouth, as well as a noticeable drop in temperature. There was a sofa by a table with a vase of silk flowers and a pile of glossy magazines – an attempt to replicate the mood of a surgery waiting room. Reni nodded at a woman sitting at a desk tapping at a keyboard and moved through a further set of doors.

The next room was vast, more the scale of a school gymnasium. At the far end was a row of stainless steel examination tables, equipped with sinks, tall taps and industrial-style hosing. Sam spotted a large floor drain in front of the nearest table.

Down the length of the room was a long wall of steel-fronted cabinets, each with a small framed label just below the handle.

They followed Reni as he moved down the room and stopped in the middle. He fixed Zahra with a sympathetic look.

'I'm going to pull this cabinet open and show you the body of a man, Signorina Idris. I need you to tell me if you know him.'

Zahra was now rigid with fear, her upper lip and forehead glowing with sweat.

Reni pulled a handle on the cabinet. It eased open soundlessly. The policeman stepped backwards, continuing to pull. A long drawer was slowly revealed and, lying on its base, the unmistakable shape of a body shrouded in a white sheet.

With the drawer fully extended, Reni stood on its far side, Sam and Zahra opposite him. Zahra reached for Sam's hand. Her palm was cold and clammy.

Then Reni pulled back the sheet from the man's face.

Zahra gasped. The man before them was, Sam guessed, in his early thirties. He was handsome, strong featured, but his dark skin was tinged with the blue pallor of death.

'You know this man?' asked Reni.

Zahra was still for a moment. Then she nodded.

'Can you tell me who he is?'

The hand tightened, nails digging into Sam's flesh.

Then she spoke. 'It's Abel,' said Zahra. 'My husband.'

Chapter 55

Ragusa, Sicily

The room was silent for what felt like minutes. Sam could feel Zahra's hand trembling in his. He wanted to cry out to Reni to stop, to cover Abel's face. But Sam knew it was too late. This moment could not be undone.

With Abel's continued lack of contact, she must have wondered. But that was very different to knowing.

Reni peeled the sheet further back to reveal a series of wounds on Abel's chest. Puncture marks barely half an inch in width.

'You saw Abel murdered, didn't you, Signorina Idris?'

Zahra was crying, sobs accompanied by heaves of her chest as if she were gulping her last breaths. Then she began howling, her damp hand slipping from Sam as she crumpled to her knees and then dropped to the floor.

Alerted by the noise, the woman from the reception area next door rushed into the room. The three of them lifted Zahra's ragdoll-like body from the floor and gently led her, her face devoid of life, through the doors to the sofa in the next room. The woman opened a closet behind the desk and pulled out a blanket. It clearly wasn't the first time this had happened in the mortuary.

Reni cupped Sam's elbow and gently pulled him back into the examination room.

'She's in shock,' said the policeman.

They stood just inside the door. Sam could see through a small window into the reception area. Zahra was rocking backwards and forwards, sobbing uncontrollably. The woman sat by her side, an arm wrapped tightly round Zahra's shoulder.

'I should help her,' said Sam, about to push the door open.

He felt a hand lightly grip his arm.

'Wait,' said Reni.

Sam turned to face the policeman, saw something in his eyes.

'What is it?'

'I need to tell you something.' Reni grimaced, his face suddenly stricken with anguish. 'When Zahra mentioned the date she crossed the Mediterranean and how many she travelled with, her words rang an alarm bell. Something happened in Pozzani that month and I thought there might be a connection.'

'Are we talking about Abel's death?'

Reni nodded, his eyes hollow and sad. 'His cause of death is significant, which is why I showed her the corpse. But sadly he's not the only one.'

Reni released Sam's arm. His face darkened. 'Last August a fishing boat from Pozzani was returning to harbour. It was close to dawn, the sun just coming up over the water. The helmsman saw what he thought was debris in the sea ahead. The boat was sailing right through it when he realised that, in addition to chunks of splintered wood, there were bodies. Everywhere.' Reni shook his head, as if trying to remove the image from his mind. 'The coastguard was called, and the navy. And slowly, the bodies were pulled from the water and brought to Pozzani. It was the worst tragedy the town has ever seen. Ninety-six bodies in total, ten of them children. Even those voices in the community that normally shout the loudest about the dangers of immigration fell silent. The whole community was in deep sadness.'

Reni paused, glancing back up the room in Abel's direction. 'And then someone noticed him. And I was called. Now, as you can imagine, our budget is tight these days and there are many in the police who might have chosen to ignore the wounds on his chest. But I decided to investigate. I brought Abel here and we performed an autopsy. What we found surprised even the pathologist. And believe me, he's seen everything.'

Reni massaged his forehead. 'This man, Abel, had not drowned like his companions, but bled to death following a frenzied stabbing.'

As Sam struggled with the image in his head, Reni went on.

'It gets stranger,' said the policeman. 'Before Abel was killed, he ate a rather unusual meal.'

'What?'

'Lobster.'

'I don't understand.'

'Neither do I, Signor Keddie. But if anyone does, it's Zahra.'

Chapter 56

Ragusa, Sicily

Sam was starting to feel nauseous, whether from the smell in the room or the implications of what Reni had said.

'We can't talk to Zahra now,' he said.

'We have to.'

'Look at her.'

They peered through the door again. Zahra was still rocking. Still in shock. Even if Sam had been willing to talk to her – which he wasn't – they'd have got nothing out of her.

'She's going to be in that state for some time. I would guess her pain is as raw now as it was when she witnessed Abel's death.'

'We must try.'

Sam rubbed his face with both hands. His jaw was covered with stubble. His skin was dry. He ached for this to end.

'I can see she's in agony,' said Reni. 'But we need to discover the connection between her and those two men. They are trying to shut you both down, which makes me think they have something very big to hide. If that secret is murder, then we must find out what else she can remember.'

Sam knew Reni was right. He noticed that Zahra's rocking had slowed. But this meant nothing. She might simply be going into deeper shock, catatonic even.

'My mother is Tunisian,' said Reni, looking at Zahra. 'So even though my father's family has lived in Siracusa for centuries, I'm an outsider here in the police headquarters. Crazy, but true. So I have sympathy for Abel. For anyone who is treated differently because of the colour of their skin, or country of origin.' His face darkened. 'But that is as far as my knowledge goes. I cannot imagine what these people go through. And I'm sure you know, the immigrants who cross this stretch of the Mediterranean are now very low down on the government's list of priorities. And the EU's. Thousands drown every year. That is one tragedy. Being brutally murdered is another thing altogether. It is a terrible crime.'

'Come,' said Sam.

They pushed through the doors, moving as quietly as possible.

Sam sat by Zahra. Reni nodded at the woman and she got up and left the room. Zahra was staring into the middle distance. Reni perched on the arm of the sofa.

They sat in silence. Minutes passed. Sam looked up at Reni, could feel the policeman's impatience, feel him itching to question Zahra.

Then she spoke.

'I always knew this was possible. That Abel might have died. But I never believed it. Even in the worst moments, I thought he would call, make contact. But now I know the amnesia was fooling me.'

Fresh tears spilled down her cheeks. Sam placed a hand gently on her shoulder.

'What do you mean?'

She turned to him, face stony, despite the tears. 'I remember,' she said. 'I remember what happened at sea.'

Unlike the triggers of the lights on the water and the bodies in the crypt, which were similar to her memories and had acted like reminders or nudges, this was the real thing. Her memory – her darkest memory – had just been laid out before her. And a door in her mind, closed for months, had been violently kicked open to reveal a room that Sam suspected was choked with horrors.

'Can you tell us now?' asked Reni, no longer able to contain himself.

Zahra swung round to face the policeman. 'Can you find those men?'

'The more I know, the more I can do.'

She closed her eyes, raised her head and breathed deeply. When she reopened her eyes, she seemed to have drawn on a reserve of strength. How long this would last, Sam did not know.

Chapter 57

Ragusa, Sicily

Abel and I had paid smugglers $1,000 each to travel from Libya to Lampedusa. After the journey from Sudan, we thought the worst was over. But we were wrong.

We were kept waiting for a week in a warehouse. There were hundreds in there with us, people from all over Africa. There was some water, scraps of food. It was sweltering, even at night. After dark the men came, grabbed women from where they lay. I heard screams, but Abel held me tight.

One morning, about a hundred of us were herded from the buildings by men clutching machine guns, and driven in pick-up trucks to a beach. There were boats in the water, RIBs, old rusting vessels. Our group was led into the surf towards a wooden fishing boat lying at anchor. I thought the men were joking. The boat looked ancient. But they were not. A man came on board with us. Showed us bottles of water. Told us we were one, two days maximum, from Lampedusa. He started the engine, and we set off.

We sailed for most of the day and then we saw a bigger boat. It came close and, before we knew what was happening, our pilot had jumped into the water and was swimming for the larger boat. We shouted at him but the pilot just climbed aboard the other vessel and then it motored away. We were on our own.

Abel and another man went to the wheelhouse to take over. But I could see from his face that something was wrong. I joined him and he showed me the fuel gauge. It was close to empty.

The weather changed that evening. The wind dropped. The sea became still. Abel and the other man took turns at the helm. We knew that if the sun was to our left at sunset, we were heading north. We were sure we were close to Lampedusa.

But we were dreaming. Lampedusa is a dot in the sea and we must have missed it as we sailed north.

The next day, the fuel ran out and we began to drift. It was hot. There was nowhere to shelter. That morning, an old man who had made it from Somalia died in the boat. He just gave up. We had to throw his body into the water.

People began to pray, to cry out to God for help. By the afternoon, the water had nearly run out.

We drifted for three days. The weather did not change. It was hot, still, with no wind. We rationed the water, small drops every few hours. By the evening of the fourth night at sea, most people were slipping in and out of consciousness. They were dehydrated, malnourished, beyond desperation.

And that was when Abel and I saw the sign lit up. My spirits soared. I didn't know where Pozzani was, but I knew it meant land.

But the sign disappeared. We weren't getting any closer. We were getting further away. People began to weep and wail. A boy of around fifteen or sixteen, who was dying of thirst, dropped a bucket into the sea and scooped up seawater, which he began to gulp down. Someone grabbed the bucket from him. He was sick minutes later.

We drifted more. I fell asleep, my throat raw and dry. And then I thought I heard music. I opened my eyes and saw a big white boat, lit up. We were heading towards it. The music was loud, like disco music. I woke Abel and showed him the boat. Abel stood, began shouting. I joined in. But whoever was on board couldn't hear us. We drifted closer. Abel and I went to the front of our boat as we neared the yacht's rear. Abel was soon close enough to jump on to a platform at the back. I threw him a rope and he tied it round a metal loop. He then helped me aboard. The other passengers were too weak to do anything but lie in the shadows, staring at us with dead eyes. They were all close to death.

My legs were weak but I followed Abel up a small set of steps on to the main deck. I couldn't believe what I saw. A dinner table with two empty chairs. Silver cutlery, empty bottles of Champagne and wine, plates with half-eaten slabs of steak, the remains of a lobster on a large dish in the middle of the table. I almost passed out at the sight of the food.

Beyond the table were some glass doors that opened into a lounge area. And there, sitting on a long sofa, were two naked men. One was Harry Tapper. They were watching a film on a large screen. At first I couldn't work out what they were looking at. It just looked like a mess of limbs and flesh. Then I realised it was three men having sex with each other.

Tapper was chopping up white powder on the glass table and then he rolled up some money and snorted the powder into his nose. The other man did the same.

Abel and I stood watching. It was like we had stepped into a different universe.

Then the other man turned and saw us. First he looked shocked, which I can understand. But then he glanced around him, at the drugs on the table and the film playing on the screen, and started looking panicked.

He reached for a remote control and the TV screen went blank and the music died. He grabbed a towel and stood, wrapping it round his waist.

'What the fuck are you doing?' he shouted.

Abel spoke first, but his throat was so parched he could barely get the words out. 'We need water,' he finally managed. 'Food.'

The man marched out of the lounge and on to the deck. Tapper followed.

The man began shouting. 'Get off the boat, you fucking parasites!'

Abel's English wasn't as good as mine, but he understood the man's sentiment. We were nothing to him, worse than nothing. Bloodsuckers who weren't even worthy of a cup of water.

Abel knew the man was serious, but I could see he was angry that someone could be so hateful. And of course he was starving and dying of thirst. He grabbed at a bottle of water on the table, took a long gulp, passed it to me. Then he snatched a lump of lobster flesh, took huge hungry bites.

The man went insane. Started screaming at Abel. Abel responded by eating more lobster, scooping up the remains of the flesh and stuffing it into his mouth.

That was when it happened. The man grabbed a knife from the table and ran at Abel, plunging it into his chest. Not once, but again and again.

Abel collapsed to the deck and I must have screamed, it's hard to remember. But the next thing I knew was that the man was coming for me with the same knife. I stepped backwards, completely terrified, and missed the steps down to the platform. I was suddenly falling backwards. I remember a crack and a brief moment of unbelievable pain. Then everything went black.

Chapter 58

Ragusa, Sicily

Zahra stopped talking. She looked exhausted. As if the telling of the story had sucked the life from her. She bent forward, cupped her head in her hands and began sobbing quietly.

Sam pressed a hand to her back, felt her shuddering. Inside he was reeling.

She would soon long for the amnesia to return, to blot out the horrific visions that had just been unleashed. He would help her all he could, but this was her pain to endure, one that would take a long time to process, and even longer to recover from. Christ, he thought. She'd dreamt of a new life in Europe and this was what had greeted her.

Reni's mobile rang.

'Pronto.'

He listened, then fired off a couple of questions before ending the call with an angry punch of his thumb.

He turned in Sam's direction. 'The hotelier has just called the station. The two men have disappeared. Taken their bags and passports, and gone.'

'Does that matter?' asked Sam. 'We have Zahra's testimony.'

Reni looked pained. 'We need evidence. A murder weapon. DNA. We have nothing.'

Sam had a fleeting memory. 'I need a laptop.'

'There's one on the desk over there.'

Sam gently removed his hand from Zahra's back and propped some cushions in the corner of the sofa, gesturing for her to lie down. She responded like a pliant child.

At the desk, Reni fired up the laptop.

'Search for Tapper again,' Sam said, his voice charged. 'But this time, just the images.'

Reni typed the words and pressed 'Enter'.

The screen was filled with images. Sam took the mouse from Reni and scrolled through the pictures. He stopped, scrolled upwards. There it was. The image he remembered from the station. He double-clicked on it.

'Look,' he said.

It was a picture of Tapper at a marina. The aft of a large white motor yacht behind him, nestled between two other similar craft. The name of the boat and the port in which it was registered sat beneath a British ensign.

The Leopard, Southampton.

Sam opened the page and began reading, his voice gathering pace.

'It's from a superyacht magazine. "Sir Harry Tapper chose to moor his new 50-metre superyacht, The Leopard, in Siracusa Marina. He praised Siracusa for its intimate feel and spacious berths. 'It gives me access to some stunning cruise grounds', Sir Harry said. 'The southern coast of Sicily and the Egadi Islands are close by and The Leopard is also within a day's reach of the Amalfi coast and Capri.'"'

'I know the marina well,' said Reni. 'It's just by the harbour where my father's boat is moored. We can be there in less than half an hour.'

Chapter 59

Siracusa, Sicily

Reni's foot was pressed to the floor as the car roared down a wide avenue in Siracusa. Sam pushed himself back in the seat, certain that, if a pedestrian decided to step into the road and Reni braked, they'd been flung violently forwards and no airbag would save them. But the policeman was clearly not in the mood for caution.

The road narrowed and Reni eased off the accelerator a fraction as the car sped down a thin strip of cobbled street between homes with delicate Baroque balconies. Suddenly the houses on the right disappeared and there was the sea. And what should have been a dark mass stretching out into the distance under thick stormy clouds was broken by a sight that made Sam gasp.

Reni braked and pulled the car over, mounting the pavement. He and Sam climbed out of the vehicle and stood by a shallow wall just above a quayside. There were a handful of large motor yachts moored, noses pointing out to sea. There was a conspicuous gap between two of the boats and directly in front of that gap, about one hundred metres into the water, a stationary vessel.

It was on fire, great angry flames that crackled and spat and seemed to be eating the vessel alive.

As Sam looked closer at the burning boat, he saw something that made him recoil in horror. At the rear of the vessel was a figure, a bulky man moving through the blaze with the stumbling gait of a drunkard, as if he were no longer sure of which direction to go in.

From a distance, the flames seemed to dance playfully around him, licking him. But his body movements told a different story. His arms reached out in front of him, groping desperately, searching in vain for relief from his torment. His mouth was open in a silent scream.

He was being burnt alive.

Sam wanted to look away, but he was drawn to the scene like a motorist to a pile-up on a road. The man looked like a guy atop a Bonfire Night pyre, his whole body surrounded by a halo of flame. Still he stumbled forward, arms raking the white hot air.

Then, whether because of the pain or the smoke in his lungs, he fell to his knees and tipped forward. He briefly lifted his head and opened his mouth. At that moment, the spit and crackle of the inferno around him seemed to quieten a fraction and Sam heard the animal-like roar of a man in unbearable pain, a man seconds from the most agonising death imaginable. Then he collapsed to the deck, not to rise again.

Chapter 60

Siracusa, Sicily

Reni made a call. There was a rapid exchange of Italian.

'It's already been called in,' he said to Sam. 'But the harbour master's vessel is in dry dock, the coastguard are at least twenty minutes away and the island's only police launches are in Palermo and Catania.'

The policeman shook his head in frustration. Then his eyes widened with an idea. He made another call. Sam heard the word 'Papa' used three times.

The policeman gestured to Sam to get back in the car. Reni did a three-point-turn and then accelerated back up the alleyway. When the lane widened he yanked the wheel left and pulled into a small piazza that overlooked the edge of the same quayside. But where previously the boats were large, sleek and luxuriant, here there were more tightly clustered vessels, a mess of wheelhouses, aerials, winches and lines.

Reni descended a staircase that dropped to the quayside and then sprinted across the tarmac towards the boats. Sam followed, his eyes darting to the left where the almost white flames of the burning superyacht drew his gaze. It was then he saw the solitary car parked on the quayside. Sam halted in his tracks and strained his eyes. There was someone at the driver's seat. A head resting against the window. Something wasn't right.

'Reni!'

The Ispettore had reached a fishing trawler and was standing by the vessel looking expectantly down the quayside. He turned at Sam's call.

'There's a car,' shouted Sam, pointing at the vehicle, 'and someone in it.'

'Leave it!' shouted Reni. 'Back-up's on its way. Stay there!'

Sam stood on the quayside, watching the inferno out to sea, a fire accompanied by the crackle and pop of burning fibreglass. But his eyes kept returning to the car. What if one of them was in it? To his right, Reni had been joined by his father and he was now untying ropes on the quayside, readying to set off.

He looked at the car again. After everything that had happened, everything that these men had done to him, he could not simply stand by.

He approached the vehicle slowly. When he was about ten metres away he saw that the figure inside was either unconscious, or dead.

A small explosion on the water made Sam jump. Something on board the superyacht had gone up with a bang, sending a ball of flames into the night sky. The fire had now spread forwards and every inch of the boat seemed engulfed by angry white flames. The cold sea air had become tainted with a sharp, choking stench that caught in Sam's throat. There was no longer any sign of the figure that had collapsed on the deck, which was now a bed of flames.

Sam returned his gaze to the car. As the flames from the boat lit up the quayside, Sam realised, with a mix of nausea and rage, who was behind the wheel. Tapper.

He was feet from the vehicle. Was this some kind of elaborate trap? He had to assume not. The head resting at the window was still. It struck him then that Tapper might well be dead.

At this thought – and the prospect of denied justice – rage engulfed Sam. He marched to the car, grabbed the door handle and wrenched it open. Tapper dropped out on to the tarmac, his body limp and lifeless.

Sam lent down and fumbled for a pulse in the man's neck. He was alive, alright. Just knocked out. Just then there was the juddering sound of a diesel engine and Sam turned to watch a small fishing vessel, with Reni and an older man at the helm, starting out towards the burning yacht.

He heard a cough from below and turned to see that Tapper's eyes had opened. He stared up at Sam with a look of utter dislocation. But then he caught sight of the yacht.

'Pat,' he said gently. Then he cried out, his voice loaded with dread and panic. 'Pat!'

Tapper's anguish for his barbaric friend – a man who'd attacked Eleanor and drowned Fitzgerald – filled Sam with a visceral disgust. He felt hatred flood his veins.

'You bastard!' cried Sam, grabbing Tapper by the collar of his coat and pulling him off the tarmac before slamming his head down again. Tapper reached up with weakened arms to try and grip Sam's neck. But Sam beat him to it, moving his hands in a shot from Tapper's collar to his throat. He closed his hands around the flesh, tightening slowly. Tapper pawed at Sam's hands feebly.

With Tapper's face darkening, Sam felt a warped pleasure surge through him.

A siren was gathering strength behind them but Sam barely heard the noise. Staring down, he saw Tapper's face – his eyes bulging with both pressure and terror – and felt all his anger distilling to a single point in his hands. He poured all his strength into them in a final attempt to snuff out the man.

It was then that he felt strong arms on him, and his body being pulled away. He cried out in frustration as he was yanked backwards and pressed, face down, on the tarmac, his hands wrenched behind his back.

Chapter 61

Ragusa, Sicily

Sam sat in a small cell in the basement of the building he and Zahra had been in hours earlier.

As he got up to pace the cramped grey room for the umpteenth time, he heard a key being turned in the lock. The door opened. It was Reni.

The policeman sat on the narrow bed, sighing loudly. 'I'm sorry you were arrested,' he said. 'They were just doing their job.'

Reni's hair clung damply to his forehead. His eyes were bloodshot.

'You look terrible,' said Sam, leaning against a wall. He'd done enough sitting.

'I had an asthma attack out on the water. From the fumes. But that was preferable to what followed.'

Reni picked at the foam surface of the mattress. 'The boat incident has taken this whole case up the chain of command. There are other people involved.'

'But that's a good thing, right?'

'Not here,' said Reni, looking crestfallen.

The Ispettore stood and went to the open door, peering out into the corridor in both directions. He returned to the bed and coughed wheezily. He pulled an inhaler from a pocket, shook it and pumped it into his mouth.

He paused as his lungs relaxed.

'Tapper has given my commanding officers his side of the story,' he then said. 'The reason why he was in Rome and then here. He has told them that, as the CEO of a firm that detains thousands of immigrants, he wanted to learn more about their experience – their journey.'

'But that's bullshit.'

'Please,' said Reni, pleading with both hands. 'Tapper said he wanted to do this discreetly, not as part of some big trip accompanied by other important people. He brought along a man he says he has known for years, a trusted employee. But he claims the man had been acting increasingly strangely. He attacked another British visitor – you, who Tapper says he does not know – in the street in Pozzani. He alleges that his associate forced him to come to the marina and demanded the start code of the yacht. When Tapper refused, his associate hit him repeatedly till he gave in. Tapper was then knocked unconscious. The next thing he knew, he was being strangled by the man who his associate had attacked in Pozzani. You, in other words.'

Sam's blood boiled. He began pacing the room again. 'So they're being sold a story that Wallace was some kind of obsessive. And that he went mad, took Tapper's boat out into the harbour and set it on fire.'

'It seems that way.'

'But that's all lies.' He stopped pacing and looked Reni in the eye. 'I mean, your superiors have heard your side of the story, right? They know that I was with you. And what I told you.'

'They know, yes.'

And then Sam understood. For whatever reason, Reni was being sidelined.

'Look,' said Reni. 'Tapper is a man with great influence. His firm, under a different name, runs the custodial transport system here. As far as my superiors are concerned, he has committed no crime. In fact, he has been the victim of one. So my involvement – your story – is just an inconvenience to them.'

'Even though it's plausible? I mean, why would anyone make something like this up?'

'I honestly believed that the boat might provide the answer I needed to make my superiors finally take an interest in Abel's strange death. But the vessel is gone now. It was set on fire with diesel. At the rear, where there were no sprinklers. The fibreglass caught, the flames became white hot. The sprinkler system in the next area to catch – the main saloon – was completely overwhelmed. I think Wallace must have intended to escape but became trapped by the flames. The fire was only extinguished when it reached the water line. By then the vessel was a blackened, distorted mess.'

Reni coughed again. 'If there was any evidence, it's gone now. The deck was teak. If a murder had occurred on board, there would have been blood in the timber's grain. But there's no hope of finding that now.'

Sam leaned back against the wall, sliding down it to sit, defeated, on the floor. 'Tapper must have come to the same conclusion, that the murder scene still held a clue. And with Zahra and me talking to a police officer, there was a risk we'd come looking.' He paused, a thought occurring to him. 'And where is Tapper now?'

'He's been checked into a private clinic in Palermo to be observed. There are some worries about concussion – and swelling around his neck – and then he's flying home.'

None of this surprised Sam. As he was only too aware, the rich and powerful had a gift for extracting themselves from all manner of sticky situations.

'And what about me? The man with the ludicrous story? The man caught with his hands around the throat of Sir Harry Tapper?'

'Tapper has graciously decided not to press charges. You are free to go. To be honest, my superiors would prefer you did not exist. You do not fit with what they have decided to believe. I imagine my statement will be destroyed. I strongly urge you to leave the island as soon as possible. And not return.'

'But what did your superiors make of Zahra's positive identification of Abel?'

Reni hung his head in shame. 'I'm afraid that, in telling the whole story, I have alerted them to the fact that Zahra has escaped from a detention centre in the UK. She will be flown back to your country, detained and most likely deported to Eritrea. So what she says or thinks is immaterial. She is a non-person as far as they are concerned. As for Abel, they've never been interested in him. Nothing has changed.'

Sam had a sudden lurch of panic. 'Has she been taken already?'

'No,' said Reni. 'She's still with Francesca, the lady from the mortuary.'

It was a crumb of comfort. But they had lost. Spectacularly. Zahra would be returned to a country that would imprison and perhaps even torture her. Reni was ruined. As far as his superiors were concerned, he was an embarrassment – a reminder of an episode they wanted to make disappear. And the men who'd set in motion Eleanor's attack and Fitzgerald's murder had escaped justice.

'What a fucking mess,' he said.

Sam put his head in his hands and attempted to shut the day's disastrous events out of his mind. But it was impossible. He remembered, with a shudder, the moment he'd arrived in Pozzani and discovered Tapper at the hotel. He had followed Sam and Zahra all the way to Sicily to destroy them. He peeled his hands away and looked up at Reni.

'You can't send Zahra back.'

'Please,' said Reni, his voice full of exhaustion. 'No more requests. I need my job. A couple more years at this rank won't hurt me. Then I can collect my pension and slip away.'

'Listen,' said Sam, his voice pleading. 'You've seen how powerful Tapper is. If Zahra ends up back in a detention centre – especially one run by his firm – she will not be safe. He's still dangerous.'

'But she's got nothing on him now.'

'Except the ability to identify the other man – the murderer. That's got to worry him.'

Reni was silent.

'Look,' Sam said, pulling himself off the floor to face the policeman. 'There must be a way to finish this.'

Reni placed his hands flat on the mattress, then clenched and unclenched them.

Sam pushed on. 'You were so close to solving this case. But instead of siding with you at the most critical moment, your superiors have dismissed your work. They have accepted the concocted story of a millionaire with influence on the island. They have colluded with him to cover up a murder.'

Reni grimaced, as if he'd just swallowed something sour.

'You're on the side of the outsiders, Guido. You always will be.'

'But what can we do?'

Sam thought of his break, the moment he'd remembered the picture of Tapper at the marina. And that was just a general search. 'We search again,' he said, 'but this time with different criteria. Tapper's allies, business associates, political friends. Show Zahra the images.'

Reni looked up, his face registering renewed hope. He nodded. 'If she identifies one, then I can cross-check with flights from London – possibly ferries, though I doubt these two would stoop so low – that arrived before the disaster. Tapper and the other man probably travelled together, or certainly round about the same time. We need to be absolutely sure we have the right man.'

Reni's brow furrowed. 'We haven't got long. You need to leave the island soon. They've made that very clear. Given how much they bent over for Tapper, they may even be running an exit check at airports and ports. We need to do this now.'

He paused in thought. 'The station is pretty quiet at this time of night. I can arrange to have Francesca called away. And then get Zahra out of a back door. Make it look like she's escaped.'

'Where can we take her?'

Reni looked upwards, eyes searching for a solution. A moment passed, then he turned to Sam. 'My father has a cabin near Vizzini. Zahra can stay there. My mother will look after her. Mama has a big heart.' He winked. 'And she's an outsider, like Zahra.'

Chapter 62

Hyblaean mountains, Sicily

Reni drove into the night, heading north along more switchback roads. Zahra slept, her head resting on a blanket propped against the window.

If nightmares didn't intrude, sleep would be the one place she might briefly escape this. But their plan had at least given her focus.

On a road that spanned a ridge, the lights of two small villages in the valleys either side, Reni peeled off left and began down a bumpy, rock-strewn track. Pine trees appeared either side of the car.

Minutes later, the car's lights swung into a clearing and Sam saw the cabin. It was a simple stone building, single-storey, with a tiled roof.

Reni parked the car, then unlocked the old wooden front door with a large key, ushering them inside. Sam had expected a more basic place, but Reni flicked a switch and lamps blinked on to reveal a homely space. There was a galley kitchen off to their left, a rustic dining table and chairs, and an old sofa and two armchairs ranged round a fireplace. A few yellowing photographs hung on the walls, images of men hunting, and a couple on their wedding day.

Their breath condensed in the cold air. Reni busied himself lighting a fire in the hearth and cranking up a stove in the kitchen. He then showed Zahra one of the cabin's two bedrooms, which was basic, but comfortable, with a soft mattress and a pile of blankets.

They ate tinned soup in silence, watching as the fire gathered strength, the flames dancing and leaping.

'Shall we start?' said Reni, once he'd cleared the bowls.

Zahra tipped her head backwards, then swung it from side to side, like an athlete preparing for an event. She nodded.

Reni fired up his laptop at the table, plugging a dongle into the side.

'There's a mobile phone mast in Vizzini,' he said, grinning. 'The signal's better than Ragusa sometimes.'

They started with 'Sir Harry Tapper friends'. The search results seemed to be dominated by image after image of a party Tapper and his wife had hosted in Venice the previous year, a costume ball at the Cipriani. Endless pictures of gurning people, their eyes hidden by carnival masks. Next to useless. Eventually these gave out and there were pictures from various newspapers and society magazines of his parties in the Cotswolds. Men in dinner jackets and women in long gowns. Reni scrolled slowly through them, Zahra shaking her head.

Maybe, thought Sam, this man was an outsider. Not a public figure or from Tapper's circle of friends or associates. Publicly, Tapper appeared to be a happily married man. Maybe this mystery figure came from a secret part of his life. In which case, they might never find him online.

They started another search, typing in 'Tapper political allies'. There were dozens of images of Tapper and Gillian Mayer in India, both sporting garlands of white flowers round their necks at what looked like the opening of some big facility in the sub-continent. Another of him and the Home Secretary standing outside the gates of Creech Hill. Sam looked at Zahra, but she shook her head again.

Soon the image results became less focused. There were no more pictures of Tapper and the screen filled instead with one mug shot after another of politicians. It was hopeless.

'Let's start again,' said Sam. He typed in 'Harry Tapper' and was about to add 'business associates' when Google suggested a list of other criteria: 'yacht', 'homes', 'children', 'helicopter' and 'shoot'.

Slowly they went through each suggestion. Sam learned that Tapper's yacht was built in Poole, that he had homes in Cape Town, London and New York, in addition to the property he already knew about in the Cotswolds, that his two beautiful children – like their dad, all tan and good grooming – attended a private school in Somerset, and that he had a helicopter on standby to take him on short-haul trips round the UK.

'Try the last one,' said Zahra. While Sam's eyes had begun to droop she seemed wide awake. Probably firing on adrenaline, he guessed, as she fought the images of Abel lying in the mortuary.

Sam typed in 'Harry Tapper shoot'.

The images were grainy, taken from some distance, but showed Tapper and a group of others standing in a field. They were dressed in classic country pursuit gear – flat caps, Barbour jackets, plus fours or wellies. They clutched shotguns, while Labradors stood to heel. There was a picture of Tapper aiming his gun into the air. Another of his wife taking a pot at some defenceless bird.

'Him.'

It was Zahra, her finger pressed to the screen. The room seemed to close in around them. There was a crackle and hiss from the fire. Sam and Reni exchanged a glance.

Her voice was barely a whisper. 'That was the other man on the boat.'

The picture showed Tapper and another man, also wearing a flat cap, walking and talking. Their guns were lowered to the ground. It was grainy, but Sam could make out a lean figure, slightly taller than Tapper, broad-shouldered with a square jaw. He clicked on the image.

The picture was from the Daily Mail, the article titled 'Sir Harry Tapper's January shoot – the first unmissable date of the year'. Sam scrolled through the article, trying to find the image Zahra had pointed to. The screen froze.

'For fuck's sake,' he muttered.

Finally it moved on. And there was the image. Sam read the caption out loud. '"Sir Harry Tapper with Home Office Minister, Adam Thorpe MP".'

He opened another window, typed in 'Adam Thorpe MP', and pressed 'Enter'.

The page loaded. To the right a clear head-and-shoulders shot of Thorpe. Sandy-coloured hair, blue eyes, strong symmetrical features.

Zahra reared back, her mouth agape. A hand shot out and grabbed Sam's arm. If she'd had any doubts before, she was certain now.

'It's OK, Zahra,' said Sam. 'He cannot hurt you.'

Her breathing accelerated, rapid intakes as if she were convinced the oxygen in the room was running out.

Sam slammed shut the laptop.

'Look at me, Zahra,' he said, his voice authoritative and calm. 'Look at me!'

Zahra turned to face Sam. She was still panting like a dog, her eyes bulging.

'That man cannot hurt you here, do you understand?'

The breathing would not slow. Sam took her hands, squeezed tightly. 'Guido and I are here. We will not let anyone hurt you.'

The pressure of Sam's hands seemed to work. There was a slight nod from her.

Sam shot a quick look at Reni. 'Have you got anything to drink?'

'My father has brandy.'

'Get it.'

Sam remained with Zahra, her hands held tightly in his.

Reni returned with a bottle and a glass. He poured a measure.

'You need to drink this, Zahra. It will help calm you down. Help you sleep.'

Zahra, still breathing like a sprinter after a race, shook her head.

'Please,' said Sam, 'drink. It will help.'

With a shaky hand, Zahra lifted the glass to her mouth. She took a sip, grimaced, then took another.

Her breathing began to slow. Sam sat with her, still gripping her hands, until it returned to normal. Without being asked, she then stood and retreated to the bedroom Reni had shown her. She lay down on the bed, eyes drooping almost immediately. Sam draped three blankets over her. He didn't expect her to sleep well, but right now any rest was better than nothing. One thing was for sure, if she was staying here indefinitely, she needed sedatives.

'She's asleep, for now,' said Sam, returning to the table. 'Let's have a slug of that brandy and take another look at this bastard.'

Reni fetched a couple more glasses and poured the brandy. Sam drank, felt fire trace a path down his throat, and opened the laptop.

He clicked on the top search result, Thorpe's Wikipedia entry. He skim read then summarised out loud.

'Born in 1972 in Shropshire, educated at Shrewsbury. Studied law at Bristol then took a job at an international law firm. Married to The Hon. Fiona Cruickshank; two children, Rory and Sophie. Stood successfully for Staffordshire East at a by-election in 2003. Rapid rise through the ranks at the Ministry for Energy and Climate Change, before a move to the Home Office where he was appointed Minister for Security and Immigration.'

Sam paused. 'Shit.'

'What is it?' asked Reni.

'There was a reshuffle days ago. The Foreign Secretary resigned due to illness. The Home Secretary was given his job.'

'What's that got to do with Thorpe?'

Sam looked up from the screen. 'He was promoted,' he said. 'Adam Thorpe is about to become the UK's new Home Secretary.'

Chapter 63

Hyblaean mountains, Sicily

Sam exited the Wikipedia page and scrolled through the rest of the results. He had a vague sense of the man, must have heard his name mentioned on the news at some point, but now Adam Thorpe came to life.

There were dozens of references to him in the media. Plenty about his ascent to the top job at the Home Office. A piece that praised him for his role in negotiating with the Bahraini government to secure a promise that an extradited man wanted for inciting terrorism would not be tortured when he returned to his native country. An article in the Wall Street Journal that talked of his visit to the IMF to urge better co-operation in the freezing of bank accounts associated with terrorist activity. Thorpe was also mentioned in an editorial about alleged failures at the Border Force. The MP was quoted as saying: 'I am incredibly proud of the work of the Border Force but it has to be acknowledged that there is only so much they can do with a problem that mushrooms year on year.'

Reni got up to throw another log on the fire. He leaned against the mantelpiece, looking beaten. Abel's murderer, it turned out, was one of the most powerful politicians in the UK.

Sam carried on reading, gorging on the endless material online. There was the inevitable Twitter feed. He groaned as he read a mix of bland, earnest and achingly inclusive statements and platitudes from the politician's office.

Great to meet the young people of @Somalicommunity today and talk openly about refugee integration. Some spirited debate

Thinking of my Jewish friends and colleagues as they celebrate #Purim

But now and then, there were tweets with a little more bite.

Looking forward to voting today on strengthening #counterterrorist laws. People of UK need protecting.

Deport first, appeal later works. 1,250 foreign criminals exited UK last year, making country a safer place for all.

There was a retweet of a Refugee Council post – Thorpe was apparently personally looking into the alleged abuse of a Sudanese woman detained at Creech Hill. He had also responded, in a roundabout way, to a query from a lawyer about potential changes to international extradition treaties.

The man was clearly a skilled player, able to use the media to push himself, if not, at this stage, a particular agenda. There were shades of liberal and more right-wing leanings in his work and pronouncements, making him difficult to pigeon-hole.

Reni had promised to cross-check with flight manifests – confirm that Thorpe did indeed enter and leave Sicily in August the previous year – but Sam sensed that was a formality. Zahra had positively identified Adam Thorpe MP, the next Home Secretary, as Abel's murderer.

Sam pushed the laptop to one side. How the hell did they get to someone like him?

Reni was rummaging around in the kitchen. He came back with cheese and biscuits.

'Leave this for tonight,' said the policeman.

They drank another brandy, ate the food. Afterwards, Reni found a towel and some clean clothes belonging to his father that Sam could wear the next day. At the door of the bedroom, the policeman clasped him on the shoulder, then headed back to the sofa by the fire.

Sam felt anaesthetised by the brandy. In the bathroom, he slowly peeled off the filthy clothes he'd been lent at the Tiber Rowing Club.

Standing before a small mirror, he was shocked by his appearance. The gaunt look of his face seemed to be matched by his body. Ribs that showed through his skin. He turned and caught sight of the wound on his back. It seemed swollen, as if slightly infected. But when he peeled the dressing off his hand, he discovered that it had, miraculously, begun to heal.

Under the shower, he let the hot water run over him for ten minutes before he began to slowly soap himself free of sweat and dirt.

Finally, with a towel wrapped round his waist, he shuffled like a man twice his age towards the bedroom, pulling back the covers to collapse on to the sheets.

His body sunk into the bed, as if desperate to become one with the mattress. But Sam soon realised his mind was not ready to switch off.

He was, he knew, safe. At least for now. Tapper was in a clinic. Wallace was dead. But the day's events kept replaying in his head. Running from the hotel when he discovered Tapper and Wallace were staying there. The fight in the half-finished house. His arrest. Hiding in the crypt – the very thought of which made Sam's throat tighten. And then the sight of the burning motor yacht, and Tapper coming to on the quayside.

In that instant Sam felt his exhausted body prickle.

Wallace. It was all about Wallace.

He sat up, propping himself on pillows. They had identified Thorpe but, as yet, had no means of getting to him. But Sam could see a way forward. By starting with Tapper.

Tapper had not hired killers to eliminate him and Zahra. Which suggested he trusted no-one when it came to the job. Except the man he brought with him.

Wallace was no sophisticate like Tapper. Yet there was a bond between them. Something that went beyond friendship. Tapper had expressed concern for Wallace on at least three occasions, and was distraught at the time of his death. Given what they now knew of Tapper and Thorpe's relationship, was it possible that he and Wallace had once been lovers?

In the end, the exact nature of their relationship was not the point. The fact was, Wallace was dead and that left Tapper, judging by his reaction on the quayside, bereft. A condition that Sam, as a therapist, could exploit.

Doubt crept in. Even if Tapper cracked, it was highly unlikely he'd just spill the beans to the police. No, they needed some other form of leverage.

The doubt solidified. Sam began thinking of the return home. Seeing Eleanor again. He swallowed hard, as a tsunami of emotion threatened to overwhelm him.

It was too much. He returned to Tapper.

An hour later, Sam climbed out of bed, pulled a blanket round him, and went into the main room, where Reni was snoring on the sofa, the fire dying before him.

Sam jolted the policeman's shoulder.

'Guido,' he said. 'Wake up. I've got it.'

Reni peeled open his eyes, groaned. 'Got what?' he mumbled.

'A plan,' said Sam. 'Do you think Zahra can stay here for a little while longer?'

Reni sat up, rubbed his face. 'You're so damn persistent. You would make a great policeman.'

'In the short term, she'll need tranquilisers.'

Reni nodded. Then his forehead creased. 'So, what's this plan?'

Chapter 64

'Did you know you were a brief viral hit?' asked Thorpe, leaning across the table.

A plate of insalata tricolore, the ingredients swimming in olive oil, sat untouched before Tapper. They were lunching in a near empty Italian restaurant, a place that hadn't been decorated since the 1980s. Tapper didn't want to go anywhere he'd be recognised. He wanted, in truth, to crawl under a rock and never re-appear.

'I mean, not you personally, although you are getting very favourable press. The boat. It was all over the net. Someone must have filmed it on their phone. It shows that man in flames on deck. Like some bloody horror film.' Thorpe took a bite of garlic bread and began chewing. 'It's been pulled now,' he said, through the contents of his mouth. 'Bit grisly.'

Tapper felt a great well of sadness rise from his chest. He thought he might cry, be sick, or both.

'You OK?'

'That man you're referring to was the only person I could trust. He was invaluable. He gave his life to save us. You do realise that? I notice you didn't come rushing out to Sicily to lend a hand.'

'You know I couldn't risk it. My every move is scrutinised these days. And what with my new diary commitments, it was just impossible. Christ, I would have been there in a shot if I could have.'

Tapper wasn't listening. He took a swig of wine, something he'd been doing a lot of recently. The only way he could blot out the pain.

Thorpe tilted his head. 'Forgive me. I'm being insensitive. You've been through a lot. And believe me, I'm incredibly grateful. You saved us both. And the deal.'

Tapper nodded numbly.

'Do you know,' Thorpe continued, 'when the whole boat story emerged, I read the papers with huge admiration. You were a genius to come up with that when you were talking to the police. All that stuff about going under the radar to learn more about immigrants. It's very helpful, you know. And even though the whole boat business is drowning some of that message out – at least for now – it still paints you in a very favourable light. It will make our announcement seem somehow more,' he paused, searching for the right word, 'thoughtful.'

Tapper was staring at a faded print above Thorpe's head, an image of Roman ruins and a coastline sweeping away in the distance. He looked closer and saw the caption: Taormina, Sicily. He felt the sadness in his chest again.

'Can I ask,' went on Thorpe, 'was it your idea to get knocked out? Make it look like Wallace had gone mental?'

The mention of Wallace by name merely accentuated the ache in his chest. 'No. His. He said it was the only way we could make it look believable. He planned to jump. Then disappear. I would have provided for him.'

Tapper felt his voice break.

Thorpe reached out and patted Tapper's hand. 'There, there, old boy. Don't get upset. Must have been bloody traumatic.'

'You have no idea.'

Thorpe raised his glass. 'Well, no use looking back now, is there? Not when the future looks so rosy.'

Thorpe raised his glass to clink with Tapper's. The CEO lifted his reluctantly. Glass met glass, and Tapper drank long and deep.

A cloud seemed to pass in front of Thorpe's face. 'The boat,' he said, sotto voce.

'What about it?'

Thorpe looked to either side. The restaurant's other diners were some feet away. 'You said you destroyed it because you thought the police were getting close. That perhaps, in addition to any statement Idris might have issued, they also had a body?'

'It struck me as a distinct possibility. I mean, of all the bodies that might have floated ashore or been fished out of the water, his would have seemed a little conspicuous.' Tapper felt a perverse pleasure reminding Thorpe. 'He hadn't exactly drowned, had he?'

'But you're not sure?'

'Of what?'

'That there's a body.'

'I've no idea. But I do know that they're not interested in pursuing the case. They mentioned an inspector – a loner, some obsessive.'

'The one Keddie and Idris had hooked up with?'

'Yes.'

'So he's discredited.'

'That's my impression.'

Thorpe looked dissatisfied. 'And you say they plan to send Idris back to the UK?'

'That's what they told me.'

'In which case, I will personally ensure that, as an escaped detainee, she is deported forthwith. Unless you have a more fitting solution in mind?'

Tapper gave Thorpe a withering look. 'I'm not a fucking hitman, Adam,' he hissed.

'And I never meant to suggest it,' Thorpe said quickly. He paused. 'What about Keddie?'

'He can't be deported to Eritrea.'

Thorpe laughed nervously, now unsure of Tapper's mood. 'Quite. But what do you think his intentions are?'

'I haven't got a fucking clue, Adam. All I know is that he will be very pissed off still.' He shrugged. 'Who knows? Maybe he and the Sicilian policeman will try and pull something together.'

'You don't sound all that worried.'

'I'm tired, Adam. I can't think straight. The point is, even if there is a body, there's no murder weapon and no crime scene. And the only witness will soon be on a plane to Africa.'

Thorpe exhaled. 'You're quite right. And we have our announcement coming up at the end of the week. Time to look to the future, I believe.'

Tapper drained his glass in a hollow display of agreement. The future meant nothing. The past was all he'd be thinking about.

Chapter 65

Heathrow Airport

Sam's flight touched down shortly after midday. As soon as the plane came to a halt at the terminal and passengers got up to pull bags from overhead lockers, Sam stiffened.

He walked slowly, as calmly as his racing heart would allow, down long corridors towards passport control.

The queue was moving fast. Soon Sam was at its head, being beckoned forward by a tired, overweight woman with peroxide hair. She glanced at his passport, passed it under a sensor on the desk, then slipped it back to Sam with a forced smile.

He moved on, felt the tension in his body subside. He must have been crazy to think Thorpe would attempt to involve the Border Agency in his own personal mess. But Sam was tired, and Thorpe was an unknown quantity.

In the Arrivals hall, he bought a basic Pay-As-You-Go mobile. He found a quiet corner in a café, and called Eleanor's aunt.

'Susan, it's me.'

'Thank God.'

'I'm back in London. Can we meet at the hospital?'

'When can you get there?'

Sam glanced at the digital clock on the Arrivals and Departures board. Factored in journey time across London. 'Two hours? Maybe two and a half.'

'Let's say 4pm.' She paused. 'And Sam?'

'Yes?'

'The consultant wants to talk to us.'

*

Susan was waiting at the bedside with Mr Khan when Sam arrived. He smiled nervously at them, then looked at Eleanor. His breath caught.

Although the tube had been removed, Eleanor's cheeks had hollowed and her skin was pale and lifeless. He went to the bed and kissed her hair. It smelt unwashed. He whispered in her ear.

'Hi, it's me. '

They sat outside the room.

Sam was the first to speak. 'The breathing tube has gone. That's good news, right?'

'Her breathing is spontaneous now,' said Khan. 'But that's because we were using a general anaesthetic in the early stages to relieve the inter-cranial pressure. We're not now.' He smiled tightly. 'What's more significant is that the MRI revealed the presence of small haemorrhagic lesions on the brain's stem.'

Susan reached for Sam's hand and squeezed it tightly, which worried him enormously.

'This suggests something called Diffuse Axonal Injury, or DAI. We think that the attack may have rotated her brain, stretching or shearing axons.'

'Sorry,' said Sam, 'I don't follow.'

'Nerve cells, Mr Keddie. Axons are long extensions of nerve cells.' Khan sighed. 'DAI is very serious. It can be mild, but it can also be irreversible and, if extensive, lead to severe brain damage. Possibly death.'

Susan began to cry and Sam unclasped his hand and wrapped it round her shoulder.

'So what can you do to treat it?' he asked.

'All we can do is continue to run tests assessing her responses, and make sure we prevent long-term muscle damage or any infection from bedsores.' He paused, looking at Sam, then at Susan. 'We may need to think about transferring her to a hospital that can meet her needs more effectively.'

Susan had stopped crying, as if this bit gave her some comfort.

'Eleanor might be better off at the Royal Hospital for Neuro Disability in Putney,' said Khan. 'They have specialist physiotherapists there.'

'Is that it?' said Sam, his mouth dry. 'She's just going to stay like that?'

Khan tilted his head. 'Possibly. She may also deteriorate.'

'But she could recover. Come round?'

'It's unlikely.'

'But not impossible.'

Khan twisted in his seat. 'Not impossible.'

*

Outside the hospital entrance, Sam looked up at a grey sky, felt the chill envelop him. Traffic choked the streets. He found a vacant spot on the steps and sat, the stone cold beneath him.

He knew what had happened these past days. How he'd shut out the possibility that Eleanor might not recover, ploughed all his energy into finding the truth behind her attack, discovering what secrets Zahra knew. How all the activity had stopped him dwelling on Eleanor's condition. It was called denial. And as a therapist, he knew all there was to know about the subject. Pushing Khan to suggest hope was, in effect, more of the same. He could see how the consultant preferred to err on the rational, the medically likely. While Sam could not even contemplate it.

But if he had to be in a state of denial to have hope, then so be it. Because hope was what Eleanor deserved.

Sam lifted himself off the step. It was time to get to work again.

Chapter 66

Paddington, London

Sam took the Tube to Paddington – close, but not too close, to his target – and booked into a large bed & breakfast on Sussex Gardens. He then went straight out.

First stop was an internet café. He bought a cappuccino, and returned to the searches he and Reni had conducted the previous night. One result, in particular, had caught his eye. A picture of Tapper's London home, in Notting Hill. It took him less than a minute to find the shot he'd seen before, but now it was time to take a closer look.

The image was part of a long, gushing piece in an interiors magazine, which featured lots of glossy shots of the inside of the house, and one telling picture of the exterior. Almost cropped out of view, the top half of the house number could just be seen inscribed in black on a white wall by the front gate. He skimmed the article and soon found the other nugget of information he required – the street name.

There was one more item to find, the contact number for Tapper Security's HQ in London. Sam had it in seconds.

Next stop was an upmarket stationery shop. Sam bought the most expensive plain white cards and envelopes available, and a good quality pen.

He then found himself a telephone box. He slotted a handful of coins in and dialled the Tapper Security number.

'Tapper Security, good afternoon.'

'I'd like to speak to Sir Harry Tapper's personal assistant.'

'One moment please, sir.'

There was a brief burst of ambient music, then a cut-glass voice came on the line.

'Sir Harry Tapper's office.'

'I'd like to make an appointment to interview Sir Harry for the FT.'

'Have you interviewed him before?'

Sam's pulse quickened. 'No, I'm a freelancer. Working on a piece about trends in the global security market.'

There was a pause. Sam considered killing the call.

'Sir Harry's schedule is blocked out for the next three weeks.'

'Can I ask if Sir Harry is in London?' persisted Sam, his throat parching.

'I don't follow.'

'Perhaps you could slot me in if there's a diary cancellation?'

There was an irritable sigh.

'He's in town for the next two weeks. Give me your number.'

Sam supplied a fictitious name and number.

'We will be in touch in the unlikely event of a cancellation.'

'Thank you.'

The final stop was a sports shop, where Sam bought running clothes and trainers. He returned to the bed & breakfast, dumped the stationery and got dressed.

It was 7pm and dark by the time he left in his running kit, a beanie pulled low over his forehead. The streets were busy with cars and buses, the pavements thronged with people.

It took him five minutes to jog to Notting Hill. By the time he cut on to Pembridge Crescent, his heart was beating fast, and not just from the exertion.

Sam jogged up the street on the left-hand side, slowly drinking in the neighbourhood and terrain. The houses were substantial properties of white stucco, the interiors hidden at this hour by drawn blinds or closed shutters and curtains. There were detached and semi-detached houses, stretches of terracing and regularly spaced trees. There was also a length of railings that edged a garden. Sam saw a notice attached to them: Pembridge Crescent Residents Garden. Strictly Private.

At the end of the street, he turned to make his way back on the opposite side. He slowed to a walk outside Tapper's house.

It was a huge double-fronted property. A path led from the pavement to steps that climbed to a portico and a front door painted in grey gloss. The right side of the garden was an abundant but carefully maintained area of shrubs, while the left was given over to a parking area. Sam noted the presence of a CCTV camera above the front door.

He then repeated the loop twice more.

It was on his third pass of Tapper's house when he saw a black Range Rover moving down the street towards him. As he got closer, Sam saw that Tapper was behind the wheel. At this rate, Sam was going to be crossing the threshold of Tapper's drive at exactly the moment the vehicle turned in.

The car indicated and Sam, trying to act as naturally as possible, halted. But Tapper paused and flicked his hand languidly, inviting Sam to move on.

Heart in his mouth, Sam waved back and jogged on. Behind him, the car turned into the drive. Sam was tempted to sprint away, but wanted to behave as normally as possible. Besides, had Tapper seen him, there would surely have been a look of recognition on his face. But it was dark and he suspected Tapper had not been examining the face of the runner outside his house that closely.

Despite all that, his pulse was still flying as he jogged away. He heard a car door clunk shut and half expected to hear Tapper call out. But there was no shout, and soon he was at the end of Pembridge Crescent, the first stage of his plan complete.

He was far from relieved. The most difficult part was still to come.

Chapter 67

Paddington, London

It was 6.45am and Sam, dressed in his running gear again, nodded at the sleepy man on desk duty before stepping out of the bed & breakfast's front door.

What had seemed do-able the previous evening now appeared the height of madness – and highly dangerous. What if Tapper saw him from the window or emerged from his house at the same time? He'd been lucky once. But his luck was sure to run out a second time round.

As a bus – empty save for a large black woman dozing on the bottom deck – passed him and filled the bitter air with a cloud of diesel fumes, Sam countered his fears. So what if he was caught? He had nothing left to lose. Tapper had taken the only thing of value from him already. With that thought came a surge of courage.

Figures passed him in the morning gloom, heads hunkered down into scarves and collars to fend off the Arctic temperatures. As he got closer to the real heart of Notting Hill, he counted around a dozen men out pounding the pavements like him.

By the time Sam reached Pembridge Crescent, he felt confident, the endorphins surging through his system. He carried on running, progressing down the pavement on the opposite side of the road to Tapper's house, so he had a better vantage point. To Sam's huge relief, the black Range Rover was still parked in the drive. There was a light on behind a window blind on the second floor of the house, as well as just inside the hallway. If the car was there, then Sam was confident Tapper was still inside.

Again, he turned at the end of the road, but this time stayed on the same side for the return journey to maintain an uninterrupted view of the property. In less than a minute, he was just across from Tapper's place.

As casually as he could manage, Sam crossed the road towards the house. Despite his earlier confidence, fear had now returned with a vengeance. His heart was hammering against his rib cage as he got closer. He glanced at his watch. It was 7am. What time did Tapper leave for work? God only knew.

He was now feet from the driveway, and the Range Rover. The front was facing outwards, which was perfect. Sam glanced around. At the windows of the surrounding houses, at the pavement across the street, then up and down his own. A man in a thick coat was moving at a pace some twenty metres in front, heels sounding out an impatient beat on the paving stones as he headed away from Sam. Otherwise the coast was clear.

Sam unzipped his jacket, took out the envelope he'd stashed in there and moved into the driveway. He then reached across the Range Rover's bonnet and carefully slid the envelope under one of the car's windscreen wipers.

The task completed, he broke into a jog and sped away. A few metres on, he moved between two cars, glanced up and down the street, and ran across the road. He reached the railings of the garden he'd spotted the previous evening and, after briefly looking round to satisfy himself no one was looking, placed his right foot on a flat gap between two spikes. He grabbed a spike in each hand and pulled himself up, dropping down into the greenery. Finding himself a shrub to hide behind, Sam crouched down and peered out from behind the dense leaves. It was the perfect place to study Tapper's house. The question was, for how long? At some point, certainly when it became too light, he'd have to exit his hiding place. And what if Tapper didn't come out? Decided to work from home? Or was picked up by a driver? Sam thought of Eleanor and was overwhelmed with a sense of failure – of letting her down. He couldn't let that happen.

Around fifteen minutes later – as the day was dawning bright and clear, the pavements were becoming busier and Sam was about to abandon his mission – Tapper's front door opened.

Chapter 68

Notting Hill, London

Sam held his breath.

Tapper pulled the front door closed behind him and strode down the steps. He wore an overcoat and carried a compact tan briefcase. A scarf was tied elegantly around his neck. He looked a little tired but otherwise, to Sam's irritation, tanned and untroubled, as if he'd just got back from skiing, not a manhunt in Sicily that ended in fiery destruction and death.

At the base of the garden path, he turned right towards his Range Rover. Up until this point, he appeared almost in auto-pilot mode. He unlocked the 4x4 with his fob and the vehicle blinked awake. But as Tapper moved round the front of the Range Rover, he caught sight of the envelope and halted.

Positioning the envelope on the windscreen, rather than posting it through the letter box, was deliberate. Not only did Sam want to avoid the CCTV camera above the front door, he also needed to see Tapper's reaction. And now he could, in delicious detail.

Tapper reached for the envelope, turned it over, then ripped it open, pulling out the card inside. Sam had chosen heavy stationery, something that Tapper might have used himself. He wanted the message to have gravitas.

The effect was electrifying. Even from his hiding place, Sam could see the colour drain from Tapper's face. As if he'd been confronted with news of a terminal diagnosis. Tapper looked up from the message, face full of panic as his eyes scanned the street in both directions. At one point they seemed to lock on to the very spot where Sam was hiding. Sam crouched down even lower, his body tensed to make a run, possibly deeper into the garden.

But Tapper looked on. He then returned to the message. He turned the card over, as if searching for something extra, some further clue. But Sam knew that the words contained all the meaning that was required.

He had written one short phrase:

You loved Pat, didn't you?

The wording was very deliberate. He had been tempted to rail at Tapper. But Sam knew that the way to really destabilise the man was to make him confront a loss that he could not afford to acknowledge.

That Tapper was gay or bisexual and did or did not conceal it from those around him was of no concern to Sam. It was about forcing him to look at pain he was trying to suppress, in the hope that it would make him unravel.

Looking at Tapper now, he sensed a rallying of strength in his nemesis. The man was a CEO after all. A survivor, as well as a ruthless hunter of other men. He stuffed the note back in its envelope, then the whole thing into a coat pocket. Got in his Range Rover, started the vehicle and accelerated away with an angry growl of engine.

Chapter 69

Notting Hill, London

The following day, mindful that Tapper would be on the lookout for the envelope dropper, Sam left three-quarters of an hour earlier.

When he reached the house, the Range Rover was nowhere to be seen. There were two possibilities. Tapper was away – possibly on some last-minute business trip – or he was trying to thwart Sam by parking the vehicle elsewhere.

Sam would not be defeated. Pulling the beanie low over his face, he opened the garden gate and dropped the envelope on the tiled path, several feet from the steps and out of shot of the camera. He then sprinted from the house as if someone had just fired a starting gun. At the end of the road, he crossed, slowly making his way back to his hiding place.

Tapper was out of the house ten minutes later. He looked less polished than the day before, some hint of stubble around his jawline, a greying around the eyes.

He saw the envelope immediately and stooped to pick it up. He ripped it open and tore out the card.

The effect, on reading Sam's short message, was subtly different to the day before, but just as satisfactory. He walked to the gate and looked up and down the street frantically. He dropped his briefcase to the pavement and ran a hand through his hair. He looked close to tears.

Sam felt a frisson of cruel pleasure at seeing his enemy so distressed. The messages were achieving their goal.

Today's was similarly short, and written on the same heavy card in the same pen.

You've never trusted anyone as much as Pat, have you?

Eventually Tapper deposited the message in his coat pocket, took one last look up and down the street, then walked with a slow, defeated gait, towards the junction with Pembridge Road. Sam watched him stop at the end, as if lost. Then he seemed to come to, lifting his arm at an approaching cab. A taxi pulled alongside and Tapper climbed in, soon disappearing from view.

Chapter 70

Notting Hill, London

Sam knew that a fresh approach was required for the next drop.

He'd been watching a homeless man who occupied the same bench in Sussex Gardens, whatever hour Sam passed. The man was broad and heavy set and seemed oblivious to the temperatures. And despite his life on the street, he was comparatively cheerful, belting out a greeting to people he knew.

That evening, Sam approached him.

'Sorry to disturb you,' he said. 'But I wonder if you could help me?'

The man, who was aged anywhere between twenty and sixty, his face a red, weather-beaten landscape of creases and pockmarks under a thick ginger beard, looked jokingly to his side and behind, as if suggesting that Sam had to be talking to someone else.

'Beyond giving you the time, I'm not sure how much use I am.'

Sam noticed with some relief that there wasn't a stench of booze on him. He needed reliability.

'I've got a job that needs carrying out. A letter I want delivered to an address round here.'

'And you're too busy to deliver it yourself.'

'It's complicated.'

'Sounds dodgy.'

'I'll give you fifty quid if you do it.'

One of the man's eyebrows arched.

'Sounds very dodgy.'

Sam was regretting even mentioning it to the man.

'So you want to pay me to deliver a letter.'

He nodded, ready to call it off.

'For fifty quid.'

'Look, if you don't want to do it, just say –'

'Done.'

'But no money until you've delivered it.'

'How do you know you can trust me, and I won't just fling it in the Paddington Basin?'

'I'll know if you've delivered it.'

The following morning, Sam left the bed & breakfast at 6.30am and took a circuitous route to his usual hiding place, avoiding passing Tapper's house. From his spot behind the hedge, he could see Tapper's Range Rover was back in position, as if he were now inviting messages, or laying a trap.

At 6.50am, Sam spotted his homeless friend walking up the street. He suspected the man had not been given much in the way of responsibility recently. He looked puffed up with importance, like he was delivering news of Napoleon's defeat at Waterloo.

The man stopped at the house and opened the garden gate. He hesitated at this point, as if the grand frontage had intimidated him. But then he pulled himself together and walked towards the portico.

Suddenly the front door opened and Tapper was out, dropping down the steps and racing to the man. He grabbed him by his lapels and began ranting. 'How dare you do this? Fucking with my mind, you bastard! I'll fucking kill you!'

Sam watched with horror and increasing guilt. The homeless man was a big guy but Tapper was like someone possessed.

He heard the homeless man mumble some kind of response and saw Tapper's rage deflate a fraction as he realised the figure before him was just a messenger. Still grasping the lapels, Tapper spoke again, his voice clear in the still morning.

'Who gave you this letter to deliver?'

'Some random guy approached me,' said the homeless man.

Sam tensed.

'Describe him.'

There was a pause.

'Bald, about 5'9". With a paunch.'

Sam exhaled.

Slowly Tapper let go of the lapels and the man handed over the envelope, before walking briskly away.

Tapper ripped the note open. It took a moment, and Sam wondered whether he was somehow hardening to the messages. But then he heard him cry out like a wounded animal. The homeless man looked back, then hurried on his way as if he'd just escaped the clutches of a mad man.

At the open doorway of Tapper's house, a slim woman appeared in a silk dressing gown. She called to Tapper but he turned round, snapping: 'Get back in the house, Yvonne! This is none of your business.'

The message Tapper still clutched in his hand was, again, short, to the point, and designed to hit him where it hurt the most.

Pat gave his life to save you both. But does Thorpe appreciate that sacrifice like you do?

Chapter 71

Notting Hill, London

Later that morning, Sam paid the homeless man.

'I owe you an apology.'

'Too right. He was a bloody psycho.'

'Which is why I'm paying you £80.'

'Oh, nice one.' He grinned, revealing a mouth that was missing a front tooth. 'Got any other dodgy tasks that require the sure hand of a homeless vagrant?'

'Sadly not.'

Sam headed next to the internet café. With Tapper crumbling, it was time to step things up.

Once settled at a monitor, one he'd chosen close to a back wall that couldn't be overlooked, he searched for 'contacting an MP'. Within three clicks of the mouse, he had Thorpe's email address. He thanked God for the machinery of democracy, even if it did allow the election of monsters like Thorpe. He then opened a long neglected Hotmail account, and pasted Thorpe's address into a new mail message.

Sam had rehearsed the lines in his head, but now that he came to type them, he found that his fingers were slipping with sweat on the keys.

Dear Mr Thorpe,

Given your current and future role, you are no doubt already grappling with the complexities of the immigration debate. I wonder, therefore, whether you can answer my question. Is there anything that can be done to stabilise the countries these immigrants are fleeing? As human beings, surely we must do everything we can to avert the catastrophes that have occurred in the waters of the Mediterranean, not least the tragedy that claimed the lives of 100 immigrants – men, women and children – close to the Sicilian town of Pozzani last summer.

Yours sincerely,

Sam Keddie

Sam took a deep breath, then pressed 'Send'.

Chapter 72

Westminster, London

The Home Office building on Marsham Street has three large atria and a central street, ensuring that, at any given time, no worker is more than six metres away from natural light. Which was exactly what Adam Thorpe didn't want right now. He craved a covering of darkness and an office that wasn't walled in glass, but thick stone.

He had been catching up on constituency and social media correspondence with a private secretary. Many of the letters, emails and tweets he received were easily responded to by a junior, but every Thursday afternoon, there was a brief get-together to discuss those messages the private secretary felt merited a more considered response.

'Finally, Minister,' said the secretary, an intense and rather humourless young man who'd been plucked from a glittering career at McKinsey & Co, 'there's this – an email that came in this morning.'

He handed Thorpe the printout. 'My sense is that one of the team could pen a response. That you're in agreement and the Foreign Office and Department for International Development have this in hand, etc etc.'

Thorpe grasped the sheet of paper, began to scan its contents and then felt his stomach floor give way at the mention of Pozzani. By the time he reached the end and saw the signatory, his body was covered in a cold sweat and the blood had drained from his face.

'Minister? You're looking a bit off-colour.'

'I'm fine,' said Thorpe, his mouth as dry as a desert floor. 'Give me a minute will you, Dominic? Need to make a call.'

Dominic exited the glass office like a dutiful dog and Thorpe dialled Tapper's number on his mobile.

'Adam,' said Tapper sleepily.

'Did I bloody wake you?'

'I'm sick. At home. What do you want?'

'Well sorry to fucking disturb you. I've just had an email from Sam Keddie.'

'Oh?'

'Is that all you've got to say?' Thorpe placed a hand flat on the printout, covering, for a brief, blissful second, the poisonous words. Then he removed his hand. 'He penned a bloody clever message. Dressed it up to look innocuous to my people, but struck the fear of God into me.'

'So what are you going to do?'

'Don't you mean "we"?'

There was silence at the other end, then an exhausted sigh. 'I'm not feeling great, Adam.'

'Well in case you've forgotten, this affects us both. You can't just zone out.'

Thorpe heard Tapper's slow breathing. The man sounded as if he were tranquilised. 'So what do you suggest?' he finally said.

'Maybe it's time to get a lawyer involved,' said Thorpe haughtily. 'Someone who'll point out to him what happens when you mess with a member of Her Majesty's Government.'

As soon as the words left Thorpe's mouth, he knew how scared he sounded.

'I guess a lawyer is an option,' said Tapper sluggishly.

Thorpe ended the call with an angry stab of his thumb. What the fuck was wrong with Harry? The Tapper of old would have simply engaged a thug from his former life of crime and snuffed the bastard shrink out. But today's Tapper was in fucking bed. Which left him to deal with it.

Dominic was hovering outside the office. Thorpe attempted to smile and lifted a hand, fingers splayed, miming the word 'five'. Dominic nodded.

Think, for fuck's sake.

Keddie was not going to give up. If the shrink did have evidence – and that was now a distinct possibility – then maybe he wanted something in return for not going to the police or press. A deal of some sort.

He had to reply. As much as it stuck in his throat, he had to correspond with Keddie. The time for a lawyer might come, but for now, there had to be a solution that didn't involve discussing the painful details with anyone else.

He opened his email and began typing, his ears throbbing with blood. Mindful of the fact that his correspondence could be scrutinised by others, he kept the language as polite and neutral as Keddie's first message.

Dear Mr Keddie,

Many thanks for your message and for your interest in the subject of immigration.

You are right about the need to stabilise the countries from which so many immigrants flee. To this end, the Foreign & Commonwealth Office and the Department for International Development work together to find ways of nurturing more settled conditions, both politically and economically, in a number of countries in Africa and the Middle East.

As you can imagine, it's a huge task and there are limits to our reach. In the meantime, we must find compassionate ways of dealing with increasing numbers of immigrants attempting to reach Europe, whilst also protecting our borders and the needs of our own citizens.

I hope I have addressed your concerns. If not, please feel free to contact me again.

Yours sincerely,

Adam Thorpe, MP

Pressing 'Send', Thorpe imagined himself dancing very close to a huge out-of-control fire.

There was a number at the bottom of Thorpe's email. Not a direct line, but one that connected the caller to his department within the Home Office. He felt sure Keddie would call.

Chapter 73

Paddington, London

His nerves frayed, Sam took a stroll up Praed St, cutting down a pedestrianised alley to the Paddington Basin.

It was another bitterly cold day and a wind cut right up the canal, tearing at Sam's coat. The windows of huge apartment blocks looked down on him, the glass reflecting the sun but no warmth. He looked down at the water, its surface rippling with agitation, and thought of the solicitor, Fitzgerald, and his death in the freezing depths of the Regent's Canal. His thoughts then turned to Eleanor and he felt an ache in his chest, followed by a dizziness that threatened his balance.

Ten minutes later, Sam pushed open the door of a different internet café, this one on Norfolk Place, nestled between a Costa and a launderette. Inside, he shrugged off his coat and bought a coffee as he waited for a terminal to become free. He was going to check his Hotmail account, though he doubted Thorpe would have responded.

He waited half an hour for a computer to become free. Finally a stick-thin girl with choppy hair vacated a terminal, glaring at Sam as she passed by on her way out.

Sam logged on. Seconds passed. Then his emails loaded.

He felt his body tingle.

Something had chimed. There were two messages, the first an autoreply acknowledging his email.

The second was from the 'Office of Adam Thorpe, MP'.

Sam took a deep breath and, with a trembling hand, clicked the mouse and opened the email.

As he read it, he felt the world around him – the assorted internet café users, the clatter of the kitchen – disappear. He re-read the message. With a thumping heartbeat, he wrote down the telephone number at the bottom of the email, then exited his account and stepped back into the street.

Thorpe was prepared to play ball. Hiding behind the polite language was a willingness to talk. Before Sam could think too hard about it and his fears took over, he headed straight for the nearest telephone box. He pushed a handful of coins into the slot and dialled the number he'd written down.

It was answered after three rings. An automated voice confirmed that he had got through to the Ministry of Security and Immigration at the Home Office, and invited him to enter the extension number of the person he wanted to talk to. Or say their name.

Sam swallowed hard. 'Adam Thorpe.'

There was a short burst of Vivaldi's Four Seasons, then a man's voice. 'Can I take your name, sir?'

'Sam Keddie.'

'One moment, please.'

More Vivaldi, then another abrupt cut. 'Mr Keddie, it's Adam Thorpe. How can I help?'

The voice, courteous on the surface, was edged with ice.

Sam had to assume the call was being recorded by Thorpe. It meant the same civil tone was necessary, as well as utterly neutral content. He couldn't threaten Thorpe. Depending on which way his plan went, this could hurt him as much as the MP.

'About our correspondence.'

'Indeed.' Thorpe sounded confident, as if he had the upper hand. 'So glad a member of the public –' the last word delivered dripping with disdain '– feels so passionate about the subject.'

'I'd like to talk further about it.'

'And me too. Emails are so perfunctory, don't you think?'

'Perhaps we can meet?'

'Very short notice, but I'm making an announcement tomorrow in Dover. 11am at The Cliff Hotel. Be delighted if you could come along. Perhaps we can have a chat afterwards. I'll get your name on the door.'

'Thank you.'

Sam began to panic. His plan was pointless without Tapper. He racked his brains, the adrenaline flying through his system. A flash of recent press coverage surfaced in Sam's mind. 'I thought Sir Harry Tapper's recent trip to Europe was an admirable attempt to understand the problem, didn't you?'

'Absolutely. Though tragic how it ended. You'll be glad to hear he's rallying by the day.'

'That's wonderful news.'

'As luck would have it, Sir Harry will be there tomorrow.'

'I'd love to meet him.'

There was a pause as Thorpe chewed on the irony. 'Then I'll ensure the three of us get together for a pow-wow. Until then, Mr Keddie.'

The line went dead and Sam replaced the receiver in the cradle. His ear pulsed with pain. He'd been pressing the phone hard against it.

Tomorrow. They were meeting tomorrow.

He had to get hold of Reni.

Chapter 74

Dover, UK

Out of Sam's hotel window, beyond a lip of harbour wall, the Channel stretched into the distance, a grey-brown sea that merged imperceptibly into a sky of the same colour. Stiff winds coming across from France churned its surface, whipping up angry waves.

To the left was the vast ferry terminal. There was room, he guessed, for around six vessels to dock. Two were in port now, their sterns open like gaping mouths. One was disembarking, spewing forth cars and trucks on to the tarmac to be slowly herded past steel containers stacked like building blocks towards customs and immigration buildings. Another ferry was consuming vehicles ready for the journey to Calais.

A horn rang out and Sam saw a boat out to sea, heading slowly for a gap in the harbour wall, and the calmer waters within.

It was strange to think of this as the place Zahra had finally reached the UK. He imagined her in the back of that truck, shivering as she hid among the Polish cabbages. Carrying her own cargo of nightmarish memories.

There was a knock on the door. He opened it to reveal Reni.

The Ispettore had flown into Heathrow late the previous night. Sam met him off the plane and they drove down to Dover in a rented car. They went over their plan on the journey.

Now the hour was approaching, Sam was thinking of it as less of a plan, and more of a fantasy. That Reni was willing to drop everything and head to the UK at such short notice did not seem like validation. The Ispettore seemed almost reckless the night before, as if the frustration he felt from years of being sidelined were bubbling to the surface. But if this failed, Reni would not just be finished. He'd be destroyed.

'Buongiorno,' said the Ispettore. He caught a sight of the view and moved to the window, his eye drawn to the dock. 'I think we should have something to eat. I don't know about you, but I'm more effective on a full stomach.'

They breakfasted in a café, Sam watching as the Sicilian drank two double-shot espressos and consumed as many pastries. Sam nursed a cappuccino.

'Your coffee's not as bad as I imagined it would be,' said Reni, grinning.

Sam attempted a smile in response. He felt sick, his stomach twisting at the prospect of their next move, terrified at the thought of being alone in a room with two killers.

But as Reni had repeated the night before, Thorpe and Tapper would not attempt anything at the hotel. Certainly nothing that might affect their precious careers. And as for any other form of action? Well, Thorpe had nothing on Sam. His correspondence had been entirely innocuous. And the fact was, the MP had made himself available far too quickly and amenably – actions that, under scrutiny, might seem slightly suspicious.

As for Tapper, there was the possibility that he could claim Sam was stalking him. Possibly bring up the incident on the quayside in Siracusa. But again Reni didn't think that would happen. It was extremely unlikely that Tapper would want to revisit that episode given that it did not fit with the tale he had spun to Reni's superiors – and subsequently sold to the media.

At 10.15am, they took a cab to the Cliff Hotel. As it climbed from the seafront and edged through the town, and the houses and shops began to thin out, Sam willed the driver to stall – to put off, indefinitely, the ordeal he was about to face. His stomach rose and fell, constantly threatening to fill his mouth with bile.

But the hotel, just off a roundabout outside town, finally came into view. A long, two-storey building, a bland slab of brick and glass. The cab dropped them at the entrance and Sam paid the driver, counting out the cash slowly. Finally the taxi drove off and they stood, Sam's feet rooted to the tarmac.

'Andiamo,' said Reni, a hand gently pressing into Sam's lower back.

The reception area was already heaving. Sam saw a BBC correspondent – a familiar face from the news – flicking through a notepad. There was a scattering of casually dressed cameramen and photographers, as well as about twenty suited men and smartly dressed women talking loudly. There was something distinctly metropolitan about them, a smug air that suggested they were Thorpe's team. Across the room, looking rather starstruck, the local mayor, a huge chain of office strung round his neck, and a coterie of supporters murmuring quietly to each other.

It was just as Reni and Sam had expected. This was a speech from the future Home Secretary. People wanted to know what Adam Thorpe had to say.

A notice pinned to an easel directed visitors towards a conference suite to the right of reception. They spilt, Reni remaining at reception until Sam made contact.

At the entrance to the Channel Suite, there were two uniformed police officers and an airport-style X-ray scanning machine. Sam's breath stalled but then he relaxed and exhaled. The police presence was expected. The future Home Secretary needed protecting.

Sam reached the front of a small queue. He gave his name to a woman clutching a clipboard. She scanned her list then looked up.

'Your name's not here, I'm afraid.'

'There has to be a mistake,' said Sam.

The woman flicked through the pages on her clipboard again. 'No mistake.'

'I'm meeting Mr Thorpe afterwards.'

The woman's head lifted. 'Ah,' she said. 'You're the one. Wait here.'

He stood to one side as more people filtered into the room, their names checked, belongings scanned, bodies frisked. He tensed. Did this conspiracy go higher? Had he just walked into a trap?

The answer had to be 'no'. There was nothing stopping him walking out the door, the only security a pair of police officers who were already busy checking arriving visitors.

In the room, rows of seats were arranged facing an elevated stage – those at the front taken up by the press. To the side, cameramen were preparing their equipment.

Ten minutes later, the room was full. The woman approached Sam. 'If you'd like to come with me.'

They exited the room and turned right, pushing through a door. It was another conference room, chairs stacked in one corner, in the other, a large television showing the stage from next door. Wires trailed across the floor from the TV to a table where two men sat in front of a monitor which showed a series of views of the stage and audience.

'This gentleman is going to watch the speech in here, if that's OK,' said the woman, already turning on her heel.

One man turned and shrugged. The other was staring vacantly at the monitor, a finger circling the inside of his nose. Sam's shoulders dropped. These guys were hardly jumping out of their chairs to pin him to the floor. He guessed they were techies, managing the recording of the speech for an outside broadcaster.

The private conversation might have been on, but until then, Thorpe was taking no chances. The last thing the future Home Secretary needed was someone shouting out claims of murder during a key speech, or indeed launching himself on either of them as Sam had on the quayside in Sicily with Tapper. This way, the loose cannon was contained.

Sam lifted a chair from the stacked pile and sat. On the television, a woman had arrived on stage. She tapped the microphone, making a dull drum sound, before introducing the mayor. On stage, the man Sam had spotted in the hotel reception seemed smaller, as if the event had somehow shrunk him. He spoke briefly of Dover's proud place in history as a town that had welcomed and, when necessary, repelled, before moving on to what he described as 'the unique challenges we face today.'

'And here to talk about those challenges,' he said, 'is a man we can now call the future Home Secretary. Ladies and gentlemen, please welcome Adam Thorpe MP.'

The clapping was frenzied and everyone rose to their feet. Sam watched as the mayor was joined by Thorpe.

If the future Home Secretary was worried about being exposed as a murderer, he certainly didn't look it. He shook the mayor's hand, before tilting the man round so that they faced the audience and photographers. Thorpe grinned broadly, as if there was nowhere on the planet he would have preferred to be but a grey and drizzly Dover at the tail end of a bitterly cold British winter.

Still gripping on to the mayor, Thorpe waved at the audience with his free hand. To Sam, they seemed to be responding like infatuated teenagers. The camera zoomed in on a woman whose eyes were glassed with tears.

The Minister was scanning the room, as if drinking in each and every member of his audience. He then locked on to a camera. Sam shifted in his seat, as if Thorpe's gaze were boring into him like hot pokers.

Chapter 75

Dover, UK

'How lovely to be here,' boomed Thorpe, still grinning. The clapping resumed. Thorpe could have belched at this point and they'd have gone wild.

'And how appropriate.' Now the dazzling smile was slowly dimmed. The clapping halted in response. It was time to talk business.

'As the mayor has already said, Dover has always been a defender. I'd go further. I'd say this proud town, beneath its iconic cliffs, is a frontline against invaders.

'Now the potential invasions we've faced over the years have been very different. In the 16th Century it was the threat of the Spanish Armada; in the 18th it was the French under Napoleon. Less than eighty years ago, it was the forces of Nazi Germany. Throughout that period, Dover has stood resolute, keeping watch, protecting.'

He smiled calmly, as if he knew what everyone was thinking. 'These days Britain is, thankfully, not at war. But we are, nonetheless, still facing a threat. A threat that I believe represents a major challenge to a way of life we all cherish. A threat I believe we no longer have the resources to defend against.'

Sam knew what was coming and felt himself screaming inside. But the audience was lapping it up, as if Thorpe were a comedian delivering an oft-repeated, but much-loved, joke.

'On any given day, there are hundreds, sometimes thousands, of immigrants gathering just across the water attempting to smuggle themselves aboard trucks to reach these shores. Now don't get me wrong, I understand what drives many of them to do this. What desperate circumstances force them to flee their home countries in search of a better life. But the fact is, we cannot take them all. Nor can we afford to let in those twisted individuals who are bent on destroying our way of life in the most violent way possible.'

There was another outbreak of applause. A smartphone was raised in the air to take a photo.

'Our Border Force do a marvellous job. But the truth is, they are overwhelmed. They simply cannot cope with the numbers passing through the port, or provide the necessary scrutiny. Not if they are to keep vehicles flowing, ensure that the Port of Dover remains commercially viable.

'Just across the water, the authorities in Calais are grappling with a similar issue. There, the French border forces are trying desperately to ensure that traffic into the port flows smoothly – that bottlenecks and standstills which allow desperate refugees to smuggle themselves aboard a vehicle are prevented.

'The issue is complex, but today I am delighted to announce two developments that will, I am certain, go a long way to addressing the problem.'

There was a pause, as the consummate performer teased his audience.

'The first, which I cannot claim credit for, is a dramatic expansion of the parking facilities at Calais, which will ensure more trucks and lorries can park within the port's boundary, rather than idle outside. This will be surrounded by a four-metre high security fence. To complement this, the authorities at Calais and Dover, through a joint Anglo-

French agreement, are investing in an additional border patrol force. A substantial body entrusted with the critical job of protecting traffic flowing into the port, keeping it moving smoothly, as well as inspecting many more vehicles within the port's boundaries. This contract went out to tender and I am delighted to announce today that it has been awarded to a trusted provider – and a British firm to boot – Tapper Security.'

Thorpe's voice had risen to a crescendo and the audience responded to the end of his sentence with another outbreak of enthusiastic applause. More phones rose in the air.

Sam seriously doubted that the tendering process Thorpe had mentioned had really scrutinised any other firms that closely. This was a done deal, one concocted by two friends, two lovers. A wave of nausea swept through Sam's stomach.

The Minister bathed in the adulation. Sam reminded himself that a good chunk of those assembled were acolytes Thorpe had brought from London, while another group – the locals – seemed simply grateful that a warm metropolitan light was shining on them in the midst of winter.

He thought of the rest of the country – how easily some people were whipped up by stories of leaky borders and immigrants crossing Europe in their thousands – and imagined that many would receive this news just as favourably. Thorpe's initiative – effectively the equivalent of a huge, impregnable border – suggested both containment, which made people feel safer, as well as a full stop.

And if, on the other hand, you were not moved by scare stories and felt that immigrants deserved sympathy, not to be treated like an invading army or members of ISIS, Sam suspected that Thorpe – the smooth operator – would eventually find some other way to win you over. Some announcement about multi-culturalism, maybe – something to show that he was Mr Inclusive. Or perhaps an enhanced airport security initiative. Something that made you feel safer – and who would disagree with that?

Sam's skin broke out in goosebumps at the thought of what lay under Thorpe's smarmy exterior. And how soon he would come face to face with the Minister.

Lost in his thoughts, Sam had missed a development on stage. Tapper had joined the MP. Sam saw, with a degree of pleasure, that Tapper had changed dramatically since he'd last seen him, when he was grabbing the homeless man by his lapels. His skin sagged, his eyes were ringed with grey. It was exactly what Sam had hoped for.

The two men were shaking hands, Thorpe beaming, Tapper managing a wan smile, his eyes dimmed and empty.

Thorpe could see his partner in crime was not well, and disengaged from the handshake to let Tapper sit down.

He invited questions from the assembled press.

'I see a familiar face,' Thorpe said, pointing into the pack with a flirty look on his face. 'How can I help, Penny?'

The screen now showed a slim, pretty woman with long, flowing blonde locks. She gave Thorpe a coy smile.

'Tasty,' muttered the nose-picking man, who'd clearly selected this particular shot.

'Our readers will love this initiative,' said the blonde journalist. 'But what's it going to cost the taxpayer?'

'A lot less than the cost of detaining those who might arrive here and have no case for staying, I can assure you. But remember, we are funding this jointly with the French, so it's a shared cost.'

No doubt this new contract ensured Tapper Security was still quids in, even if the number of immigrants that needed detaining in their centres began to drop. Sam's fist clenched in fury, even as his stomach pitched with apprehension.

Hands clutching pens shot back into the air. Thorpe smiled again, pointing into the audience. 'Ahh, the Guardian.'

The camera remained focused on Thorpe, while a man's voice spoke up: 'Do you really think immigrants pose as great a threat as Napoleon's troops or the forces of the Third Reich?'

Thorpe tilted his head to one side and looked at the hack like a mother might at a toddler who's just tipped their food on to the floor.

'I can see the headline now,' he groaned. 'For the record, those were not my exact words. If you'd been listening, you would have heard me say that we are not at war. We are, nonetheless, facing a threat to our way of life. Listen,' he said, his voice morphing from mild irritation to conciliatory, 'immigration, as politicians from across the political spectrum agree, needs better management. And of course tighter border control goes hand in hand with the work of the Foreign Office and the Department for International Development, as they seek to stabilise the countries these immigrants are fleeing.'

The questions were wound up ten minutes later and the audience began to file out of the room, leaving Thorpe's coterie behind.

It was Sam's turn now.

He stood, felt his head pound with tension, and walked towards the door.

Chapter 76

Dover, UK

Sam waited as the audience filed out. Then, when the room was all but empty, he moved forward. The woman with the clipboard nodded at him, and Sam pulled off his coat and handed it to one of the police officers. As it glided through the scanner, the other officer ran his hands over Sam.

He wondered whether these men were trained to spot stress. If so, he'd be pulled to one side any minute. His body was rigid with it.

But the officer gave Sam the nod and the woman began escorting him to the front of the room.

Thorpe was chatting to a small group as he approached. The Minister noticed him immediately, and knew exactly who he was. He fixed Sam with a glacial smile, peeling away from his conversation and extending his hand. Sam, not wanting to draw unnecessary attention, shook it. The MP's hand was dry, firm, super-confident. Fingers dug into Sam's flesh.

Thorpe turned to another man. 'Dominic, I need ten minutes with this gentleman. Sir Harry will be joining us.'

Sam looked down at Tapper, who was still sitting in the front row, his face glazed, as people moved around him.

Dominic nodded and Thorpe led Sam into a side room. It was a smaller conference area, and a pile of bags and some coats suggested that this was where Thorpe had got ready. At the head of the room was a table with three delegate chairs and a tray laid with some glasses and a jug of water. The table faced about ten rows of seats.

'Come on, Harry,' said Thorpe, chivvying Tapper, who was moving sluggishly, like a crushed man.

Tapper entered the room and Sam noticed his eyes, which were clouded and dreamy, suddenly spark with interest when he saw him. He'd wondered whether Tapper was tranquilised, but now he suspected not. Which was just as well. He needed the man awake for what was coming.

Thorpe closed the door behind them. He then gestured for both men to move away from the door, which had a window of glass in its upper half. They made their way to the end of the room. Tapper perched on the table while Thorpe and Sam stood facing each other to his side. They were now out of sight to anyone looking through the door.

'You know Sam Keddie, Harry.'

'All too well,' said Tapper, with a voice that had a lot more life than his languid body movements. There was venom there too and again Sam felt a wave of terror at the thought of being alone in a room with two killers, men who had every reason to hate him.

'I wonder if you could do me a favour, Mr Keddie?' said Thorpe. 'Could you remove your phone from your pocket?'

Sam pulled the phone out.

'Please remove the battery.'

Sam opened the back and took out the battery.

'Now empty your pockets.'

Sam did as he was asked. He laid a pen and his wallet on the table by Tapper. Thorpe fanned out the wallet and then pulled the contents from it. A handful of notes dropped to the table, then a photo of Eleanor. Sam wanted to slam a fist into Thorpe's smug face.

'Do you realise who that is?' said Sam.

Thorpe ignored him as he examined the pen. It was a biro that Sam had picked up in the hotel he and Reni had stayed in. The MP undid the pen, pulling it apart, then dropped the pieces to the ground and brought the heel of his shoe down on them, crushing and splintering them.

Thorpe turned to Sam. 'Arms up, please.'

'For fuck's sake,' said Sam, raising his arms. 'They've already done this outside.'

Thorpe ignored him. He ran his hands over the coat then down the length of his arms. He then slipped them inside the coat, tracing his fingers in and around Sam's torso, before moving on to his buttocks, inside thighs and finally, legs.

He stepped away, looking him hard in the eye. 'Got to be on the safe side,' he said. 'Even rank amateurs like you can buy listening devices. So, what do you want?'

Sam edged back a little himself, keen for some distance from the man. There was something decidedly chilly about Thorpe, the way he'd coolly conducted the search just minutes after giving a Ministerial speech.

'A frank discussion about where we all stand,' said Sam, swallowing hard to stop his mouth drying out. 'I think we'd all benefit from that.'

It was a deliberately vague opener, suggesting that Sam wanted something, when in fact the point of this meeting was to drive an irreparable wedge between the two men before he attempted to scare the shit out of them.

'Then fire away,' said Thorpe casually. 'But bear in mind I only have ten minutes, fifteen max. So you'll need to spell out your demands sooner or later.'

'First, a question. I just need to ask Tapper something.'

Thorpe shrugged, as if he couldn't have cared less.

'Just out of interest, at what point did you decide Zahra Idris was trouble?'

'You don't need to talk about this, Harry,' said Thorpe. 'You're not under oath. This prick is just being nosey.' Thorpe was examining his nails, going out of his way to seem as nonchalant as possible.

Tapper looked at Sam, weighing him up. 'When I saw her at Creech Hill.' His voice was spiked with a trace of tension. 'I knew she'd recognised me.'

'Right,' said Sam. 'So on that basis, you thought it wise to threaten her. To set in motion a chain of events that had you running across Europe –'

'– Harry was right to act,' interrupted Thorpe.

'But all he did was enflame everything,' Sam said, his body now coursing with adrenaline, his voice gaining strength as the speech he'd prepared began to flow. 'If they'd never acted, Zahra would have been ignored. At that point, she had partial amnesia. She sensed Tapper was bad news, but couldn't remember what happened. She was vulnerable, and would have lost her grip on reality. Probably been hospitalised. A flaky immigrant with mental health problems. Hardly the ideal witness in an investigation.'

Thorpe shot Tapper a questioning look.

'And you would never have lost Pat Wallace,' slipped in Sam, almost as an aside.

'Sad though his death is,' sneered Thorpe, too quickly, 'I think Harry will survive.'

'You say that,' said Sam, 'but he's in a bad way.'

Tapper's eyes glassed. 'Because you've been bloody tormenting me, you little shit.'

'I admit my methods are a little crude, but I've simply been pointing out the truth.'

Thorpe looked rattled. 'The truth?'

'That your friend Harry Tapper loved Pat Wallace.'

Thorpe laughed mirthlessly. 'Don't be fucking ridiculous.'

'Tell him,' said Sam, looking at Tapper.

'Tell him what?' snapped Tapper. His face had creased up with disquiet.

'That you've lost a lot more than your henchman,' said Sam softly.

Tapper was momentarily disoriented, the concern in Sam's voice throwing him. He looked to his feet, as if deliberately avoiding Thorpe's face. 'Pat was bloody loyal.'

Thorpe snorted with derision. 'You can buy loyalty anywhere.'

Tapper's face lifted in a jolt, eyes zeroing in on Tapper with contempt. 'Pat saved my life at Ipswich, I'll have you know. Fended off some particularly vicious boys who'd targeted me. Who would have finished me off.' His mouth curled into a gentle smile. Sam might have had some sympathy for him at this point, were he not the man responsible for Eleanor's comatose state.

'We became lovers,' added Tapper.

'For God's sake, Harry,' said Thorpe. 'This is not the moment.'

Tapper would not be silenced. 'We went our separate ways after Ipswich. Until I got him a job at Creech Hill. And then he began helping me out with this, and I realised I still had strong feelings for him.'

'But he's a —'

'A what, Adam?'

'He's a no one. Just some guard at a detention centre.'

'I trusted him, Adam. He made me feel safe.'

Sam noticed that Thorpe's face had paled and was glowing with sweat.

'But what about us?'

It was Tapper's turn to sneer now. 'Us? We just had sex when it suited you, Adam. And we helped each other out politically.'

Tapper was getting stronger. Sam needed to take him back to his loss.

'Except it's him who's got all the advantage now, isn't it Harry?' said Sam. 'Adam Thorpe who's won. Who's about to become Home Secretary. Whereas you've lost the man you loved. And I suspect all the money you have will never compensate you for that loss.'

Tapper looked down and Sam wondered whether he hadn't gone too far. Made a false assumption. But when Tapper looked up, Sam saw he'd been absolutely right.

'Pat Wallace wasn't just my lover,' said Tapper, voice trembling but full of conviction. 'Being with him after all that time was fucking liberating. After years of denial, of sacrificing my true self to career and the front that Yvonne demanded of me, it felt like real freedom at last. I would have gone back to prison with him, if only to feel free.'

'You're mad, Harry,' railed Thorpe. 'Think of our project. Think of the money it's going to make. Think of the next stage. I'll be PM. You know I will. I'll elevate you to the Lords.'

'You don't get it do you, Adam? I don't want that crap any more. I don't want any of it.'

'Well you're a fool then, aren't you?' mocked Thorpe. 'Because this is the world you live in. You're not a vulnerable Essex boy in a young offenders' institute. You're the CEO of a massive bloody organisation. Wallace is gone. He's dead. And you made that happen. I never asked you to threaten that bloody woman. Or do the other things.'

Tapper looked Thorpe hard in the eye. 'No Adam. You made it all happen. You made it all happen by stabbing that man. By –'

'Enough!' snapped Thorpe, his face red with anger. 'Don't you ever repeat that again, you fucking idiot.'

'And why did you stab that man?' Sam piped up. 'Was it shame? Was it because he caught you out? Exposed you for what you really are, rather than the married man you pretend to be? Do you really think anyone cares these days?'

'Time's running out,' snapped Thorpe. 'I need your demands.'

'Then I need my phone,' said Sam. Behind the Minister, Tapper had begun pacing up and down in a state of high agitation.

'Why?' snapped Thorpe.

'I need to talk to someone,' said Sam. 'A Sicilian policeman called Guido Reni. He's here in the hotel. He has some evidence you might find interesting.'

Chapter 77

Dover, UK

The words drained the last trace of colour from Thorpe's face. He froze, eyes wide.

'I don't understand.'

'You will. And you'll need to tell the policemen at the door to let him in.'

Thorpe stared Sam hard in the face, trying to front it out.

'Why should I let you and your Italian friend waste my time with this charade?'

'Believe me, it's better this way.'

The inference hung in the air. Unless Thorpe dealt with Sam and Reni, the evidence would be handed over to the authorities.

'Well go on then,' Thorpe said, the nonchalance he was trying to affect deeply unconvincing.

Sam began piecing together his phone to call Reni. If the news had petrified Thorpe, it seemed to have had little effect on Tapper, who remained wrapped up in his own thoughts as he continued to pace up and down.

Sam switched his phone on and called Reni. It rang once.

'Hello,' said the Ispettore.

'He'll see you now.'

Anticipating Thorpe, Sam dismantled the phone again.

Thorpe moved to the door. Sam heard him calling to Dominic, his voice unsteady. 'There's someone else due at this meeting. A chap called Reni. Make sure he's allowed in.'

He returned to the table. 'You're playing with fire, Keddie. You do understand that, don't you?'

Tapper continued marching up and down a narrow path of carpet.

There was a knock on the door and Reni, without waiting for an answer, entered the room.

At last, thought Sam. An ally.

Reni went straight to Thorpe and, without bothering to shake hands, got straight to business.

'I am Ispettore Guido Reni, Provincia di Ragusa. I would like to discuss your involvement in an event that took place last August off the coast of the island.'

'Not so fucking fast,' said Thorpe.

'You're going to have to empty your pockets,' said Sam, pre-empting the Minister. 'And dismantle your phone.'

'You realise I'm a policeman?' Reni said to Thorpe.

'Don't come over all high-and-mighty with me. We all know what's going on.'

Reni shrugged his assent. He emptied his pockets, dismantled his phone, and let Thorpe conduct a search. Once the MP was satisfied, he said: 'Get to the point.'

'Very well,' said Reni. 'Last August, you entered Sicily on the same British Airways flight as Sir Harry Tapper. You then accompanied him on a brief trip on his superyacht. While at sea, you encountered a boat full of immigrants. You killed one. We have a witness.'

Thorpe stared coldly at Reni. Sam noticed his upper lip was sweating. 'The girl,' scoffed the Minister. 'Hardly a pillar of the community.'

Out of the corner of his eye, Sam saw that Tapper had stopped pacing and was now looking in Reni's direction, as if listening intently.

'We also have evidence. A trace of the victim's blood on a section of deck timber.'

Thorpe's voice quivered as he spoke. 'You're lying. The yacht was destroyed.'

'Not all of it.'

'So what does that prove?'

'That a murder took place.'

'But your witness will soon be on a plane to Eritrea. Your people have sent her back here. I'll bloody see to it myself.'

'She's still in Sicily.'

Thorpe laughed nervously. Sam noticed that Tapper, standing to Thorpe's side, was now clawing at the surface of the table.

'She's an illegal immigrant who's escaped detention. No one will take her seriously.'

'We still have the fragment of deck,' said Sam.

'All that will prove is that a man died on his yacht,' said Thorpe, jabbing a finger in Tapper's direction. 'But not that I had anything to do with it.'

What happened next was something Sam would replay for weeks after.

Tapper grabbed the jug of water and brought it down hard on the table. The jug shattered. Glass fragments went everywhere and water spilt across the table and on to the floor. In Tapper's hand was what remained of the jug, the handle attached to a jagged point of glass. Sam stepped back, convinced that Tapper was coming for him. To his right, Reni had done the same.

Thorpe, meanwhile, was still rooted to the spot, as if contemplating the noose that Reni and Sam had dangled in front of him. It took him a second longer to react. When he turned, it was too late.

Tapper moved with surprising speed. He thrust out, the handle still tight in his hand, plunging the point of glass deep into Thorpe's neck just below his left ear, before wrenching his makeshift weapon out.

Thorpe's face registered disbelief, and then utter horror, as blood began to pour from the wound Tapper had made.

Tapper stood before his old political ally and occasional lover, as if marvelling at his handiwork.

The Minister grabbed at his neck with both hands. Dark rivulets of blood began to flow between his fingers, gushing down his pale blue tie and white shirtfront, a crimson flower in rapid blossom.

Chapter 78

Dover, UK

It was Reni who acted first. He ran to the door, yanked it
open and screamed for help. Then he ran back to Thorpe.
The Minister had collapsed to his knees, hands still at his
throat. Reni grabbed his scarf from a chair where he'd
discarded it and tried to place it against the wound. But
Thorpe released one hand and pushed him away.

Sam stood stock-still, paralysed by the horror unfurling
before him. Behind Thorpe, Tapper stood equally
motionless, still clutching the jagged piece of glass, its tip red
with the Minister's blood.

The room was filling behind Sam. A woman screamed. A
man shouted out, 'Christ!'

The police who'd been taking care of security stormed in.
One rushed to Thorpe. The Minister fell backwards, his face
a deathly white, hands slick with blood as they scrabbled for
purchase at his throat, while Reni, utterly distraught, stood to
his side.

The other officer halted just feet from Sam, pulled a
handgun from a holster and aimed it at Tapper's chest.
'Drop it, Mr Tapper,' he shouted. 'Now!'

Tapper obliged, letting go of the jug handle, which
dropped to the floor, landing as one piece on the carpet. The
officer clutching the gun moved with speed to Tapper's rear,

holstered the weapon and then yanked the killer's hands behind his back to cuff them.

Chapter 79

Dover, UK

The policeman by Thorpe's side called for an ambulance on his phone, then screamed out: 'First aid box, now!'

He knelt by the Minister, who appeared to have lost consciousness, pressing a hand down against the wound, but soon there was blood seeping between his fingers.

Thorpe's coterie inched forward. A woman passed out, her body crumpling to the floor.

'Stand back!' shouted the policeman guarding Tapper.

A man in a black suit rushed into the room with a green box. The policeman with Thorpe yelled at him. 'Open it! Get me a dressing.'

The man wrenched the box open, ripping open a package. He handed a dressing to the policeman, who held it hard against the Minister's neck. But it was soon dyed red.

Sam's paralysis had given way to horror, as the true nature of this rapidly changing event became clear to him. The meeting they'd engineered and he'd manipulated, and its shocking climax.

Minutes passed. Sam heard the sound of sirens gathering strength. Paramedics in green were soon rushing into the room, and he and Reni were pressed back against a wall while they went to work.

And then the flurry of activity seemed to still, and Sam knew what that meant.

Thorpe was dead.

Whatever Sam had expected, it was not this. He felt despair creep over him. He despised Thorpe with every fibre of his being, but he'd wanted justice, not another corpse.

More police arrived. Thorpe's people were ushered out of the room. Then he and Reni were led out separately, out of the conference room and down the corridor to the hotel entrance.

The reception area pulsed silently with blue lights. Several police cars and an ambulance were parked chaotically outside.

They were placed in the back of a police car. They waited, too shocked to speak.

The two paramedics exited the hotel, carrying a stretcher. A sheet covered Thorpe's face. Sam was reminded of Abel.

He thought of how Tapper's simmering rage had built. He had cracked at the moment when Thorpe made it clear that he was willing to shaft him – to let Tapper take the rap for Abel's murder.

Anger had done this. A sudden, deadly burst of anger.

Sam shuddered as he contemplated what they'd done. What he'd done. How he'd helped push Tapper to that tipping point.

They were driven away, taken to a police station, and separated. It was when he was alone in an interview room – yet another interview room – that he realised he had not conferred with Reni. Discussed what to say.

Sam shivered. He reached out and touched a radiator. It was boiling hot.

A bearded man entered the room. Flicked on the tape recorder by the side of the table. Introduced himself, recorded the time, then scratched his head. Sam suspected that nothing like this had ever happened in Dover.

'Can you tell me what happened today?' he said.

'Sir Harry Tapper stabbed Adam Thorpe in the neck.'

'That's not in dispute. What we really want to know is how it happened, what precipitated the attack.'

'Then I need to start at the beginning,' said Sam.

Sam told the police officer what he'd told Reni when he first interviewed him, bringing the story up to date with what had happened since he'd returned to the UK.

The bearded man sat utterly still, his coffee undrunk on the table.

Finally, Sam finished.

'Fuck me,' said the policeman. 'That's a tale and a half.'

The one aspect of the story Sam had been tempted to omit was the envelope drops he'd orchestrated at Tapper's house, which had clearly contributed to the moment when he cracked. But Sam concluded that Tapper would without doubt talk about them. In fact, he fully anticipated being questioned again about what he'd done. When that moment came, Sam would say that taunts alone had not goaded Tapper to murder. The man had other demons.

'Interview with Sam Keddie terminated,' said the police officer, before giving the time.

He switched off the tape recorder.

'Don't you have any questions?'

The policeman shook his head, then exited the room in a flash, as if he couldn't get away from Sam fast enough.

The door shut. Sam took a sip of water from a plastic cup. He stared at the mug the policeman had left, its handle suddenly pregnant with dark potential.

Chapter 80

Dover, UK

Sam woke with a jolt from a deep sleep. He'd dropped off, overwhelming fatigue replacing the incessant shivering. He lifted his head from his folded arms.

The police officer had returned, accompanied by a shorter man clad in a double-breasted pinstripe suit that hugged his rotund physique. His face was smooth and cleanly shaven, thick grey hair neatly parted. He clutched a battered leather Gladstone briefcase.

The new visitor extended a hand. 'Strickland,' he said, with a plummy accent. 'I work for the government. I'm a lawyer.'

Sam shook the proffered hand.

Strickland nodded at the police officer, who left the room. The lawyer lowered his bag to the floor, removed his jacket and carefully draped it over the chair. Sam noticed a cerise-coloured silk lining. The lawyer sat, his hands clasped on the table's surface. He glanced briefly at the recording device, as if satisfying himself that it was switched off.

'That's quite a story you and Signor Reni have told the police.'

'All true,' said Sam, already mistrustful of Strickland.

The lawyer smiled broadly, disengaging his hands to place them palm-down on the table. 'Breathe a word of it outside this room and my department will be all over you like the Spanish flu.'

Sam felt the lawyer's eyes hard on him. The man then reached inside his Gladstone and pulled out a sheaf of papers.

'This is the Official Secrets Act.'

'I refuse to sign it.'

Strickland chuckled. 'Ah, bless. You don't actually "sign" anything. It's a law, not a contract. Once you're privy to information covered by the act – which you are, trust me – you are bound by law not to pass on that information to others, regardless.'

'You can't threaten me.'

'You're right. So let's put it another way. Your friend has already been sent packing back to Sicily, where his superiors are none too impressed by his extra-curricular activities, I can tell you. I doubt he'll be in employment for long. As for his pension, well, he can kiss goodbye to that too. The thing is, Mr Keddie, you haven't got a jot of proof. And your one witness, Ms Idris, will soon be deported directly from Sicily.' He patted his neat hair down. 'To be honest, it's a blessing. I would fillet her in court.'

Sam was stunned. 'What about Tapper?'

Strickland smirked. 'It's hardly in Tapper's interest to start bleating on about this. He's already in deep doo-doo. Besides, as I said before, you've got no proof.'

Strickland sighed, as if a dark cloud had drifted over a sunny picnic. 'Sadly, what we can't snuff out is speculation about why this happened. So we're telling everyone that Tapper was unhinged. That he was obsessive, infatuated with Thorpe.'

'So you'll crucify Tapper to ensure Thorpe's reputation – and that of the Government – is untainted.'

'Your words, not mine.'

The lawyer studied Sam for a moment longer, as if drinking in his defeat, then got up. He picked up the papers. 'I take it you've decided not to read this?'

Sam refused to acknowledge the question.

The lawyer shrugged, returned the papers to his Gladstone, slipped on his jacket and moved to the door.

Chapter 81

North London – two days later

Sam sat at his desk, running through his voicemail messages. There were three from an irritated Emery, asking him where he was and to get in touch, a handful from an increasingly anxious-sounding Susan, and the rest were clients who wanted to know when he was returning. If he wanted to stay in business, he needed to call them back. Reassure them. But he'd been putting it off. Putting everything off.

He had been drifting for the past two days. Moving from one room to another, trying to anchor himself. But the house was no longer a home. It was a tomb. A tomb constructed of memories. The perfume bottle on the dressing table, the photo of Rome in the hallway, the wardrobe full of clothes, the half-read novel by the bed. Eleanor was everywhere, but nowhere.

Sam couldn't sleep. If he did manage to drift off, he'd soon be wrenched awake by a nightmare. One particularly horrible dream began with Thorpe's murder, the Minister slowly dropping to the ground, before the blood from his neck became a sea of red in which thousands of immigrants were drowning. While he strongly believed that dreams had revealing content, Sam also knew that there were occasions when the unconscious needed emptying, like an overflowing bin full of rotting refuse. And then the dream was simply what it was. In his case, a replaying of two terrifying and interconnected scenes.

Much more significant was the nightmare that involved Eleanor. In it, she appeared recovered, but still weak and inactive. She sat in an armchair in their living room downstairs. Home, safe and alive. But in the middle of the room, Sam was building a wall between them. Methodically slapping on mortar and laying bricks down. Eleanor quietly pleaded with him, but Sam wouldn't listen. He slowly shut her out, till the last brick was slotted in beneath the ceiling.

If he ever managed to stop thinking about Eleanor, it was because he was haunted by another thought – a dark, disturbing vision of hell that wormed its way around his head, slowly corrupting every last corner of his mind. A vision he suspected was all too real.

He tried calling Reni. Left messages. But the Sicilian never returned his calls.

And he surfed the net for any new developments. It was an ongoing investigation, so beyond the tributes to Thorpe, there was nothing about Tapper on the main news sites. But away from them, it was clear the Government had started going to work on him. The more Sam dug, the more he found stories about Tapper's secret life, the rent boys and gay clubs. 'Former lovers' had suddenly emerged to speak of his violent tastes. The drip-fed insinuation that he was a psychopath had begun.

*

The doorbell rang. Sam leaned back in his chair and looked out of the front window. To his huge surprise, it was the smug lawyer, Strickland. What the hell did he want?

Sam opened the front door.

'Not disturbing you, I hope,' said Strickland.

'Even if you were, I doubt you'd give a shit.'

'Listen,' he said, his conceit tempered compared to their last meeting. 'I need you to come with me.'

'We've had the chat,' said Sam wearily. 'I understand the score.'

The lawyer looked sheepish. 'That's just it. I don't think you do. Things have changed somewhat.'

'What the hell's that got to do with me? You said, quite categorically, that I needed to keep my mouth shut. I get it. Now, if you please, I've got work to do.'

Sam began to close the door but Strickland stuck his hand out and pushed against it. Sam relented, pulling the door back open. The lawyer sighed. He seemed defeated and, Sam sensed, not a little humiliated. 'Can you spare an hour or so? Please. It's something that cannot be discussed on your doorstep – or indeed in your house. You'll understand why when you get there.'

'Where?'

Strickland looked pained. Sam was relishing the lawyer's discomfort and would gladly have let him squirm for longer. But he was also curious as to what had brought about the U-turn. And besides, the alternative was grovelling to clients or fending off images of Eleanor and Thorpe.

'I'll get my coat.'

The journey passed in silence, Strickland studiously avoiding eye contact as he stared out of the window at the Euston and Marylebone Roads. Ahead of them, the driver was equally taciturn.

Forty minutes later, on a side street off Edgware Road, the car came to a halt by a barrier manned by four policemen wearing black protective vests and clutching sub-machine guns. The driver flashed a card at the men and the barrier lifted. The vehicle dropped down a ramp into a subterranean car park. Sam caught a brief glimpse of a 60s tower block above them, before it disappeared from view.

Strickland and Sam were dropped by a set of doors. Two more identically dressed and armed police officers stood guard. Strickland nodded to the men and one punched a code into a keypad.

Sam had seen no signage at ground level. And when he factored in Strickland's guarded words and the heavily armed police presence, he felt a mounting tension. What the hell was this place?

Swing doors opened inward. Inside, for the third time in less than a week, Sam was subjected to an airport-style X-ray of his belongings and a body search. Strickland was enduring his own across the room, and gave Sam a defeated look.

They moved down a broad, faceless corridor. At the end, Strickland presented his face at a glass panel and a heavy metal door was opened by another officer. Ten more metres of grey corridor followed, strip lighting overhead, with no doors or windows. After another door was opened, they moved into a large seating area. It was like a doctor's waiting room. There were well-thumbed magazines to leaf through and some faded prints of Constable paintings on the wall. But apart from a Perspex dome in the ceiling, there was no natural light. The police officer who'd let them in remained positioned by the door.

Sam felt like he'd entered a secret chamber below the city. His stomach somersaulted with anxiety, though he sensed from Strickland's conspicuous daytime visit to his house and the amount of police around that he wasn't in any danger.

They sat on chairs upholstered with grey material punctured by cigarette burns. The walls were a shade of the same colour. Sam was struck by the total absence of information about the building they were in. No signage, flyers or posters. It was as if they were sitting in a vacuum.

He felt that familiar tightening of his throat, the gathering tension that came with being in a tight space and feeling highly stressed.

Moments later, another door opened and a short, strong-looking female officer nodded to Strickland.

They followed the woman into a corridor. Just inside on the left were some metal shelves stacked with a selection of rugs in different colours, and copies of the Bible and Koran. Ahead, he counted sixteen doors, regularly spaced along both sides of the corridor. Each was blue with a small window in its upper section.

Sam noticed that the female officer's belt contained a small armoury – cuffs, a baton and a can of what he imagined was CS gas. Another officer, a similarly beefy male, was positioned at the far end of the corridor.

The woman stopped by the fourth door on the left, looked through the window and, satisfied by what she'd seen inside, punched a code into a pad on the wall. The lock went slack and she pulled the door open.

She and Strickland then stepped back and the lawyer gestured for Sam to enter the cell.

Sam felt terror flood through him, like he'd been conned into being rendered. That he'd be taken from this anonymous chamber beneath London and dragged under cover of night on to a private jet and sent to a prison in some far-flung corner of the planet where his dark knowledge would be punished with beatings and torture.

But there was nothing coercive about the gesture. And when Sam looked into the cell and saw who was inside, he understood.

There, sitting on a low-slung bed, was Sir Harry Tapper.

Chapter 82

Edgware Road, London

'The door stays open,' said the female officer.

Sam watched her walk away, as if she'd been told to give them some distance, leaving Strickland at the door. Sam inched into the cell.

The walls were a cheery yellow and there was another Perspex dome overhead bringing a trace of natural light into the cell. Opposite the bed – the mattress covered in easy-to-clean blue plastic – was a solid-looking desk made of timber, its edges and corners rounded and smooth. On its surface, a wooden bowl overflowing with fresh fruit, and a manila file. Above the desk, well out of reach, was a wall-mounted television, and in the corner of the room by the bed, a small basin.

Sam stood against the wall, aware that, when he last saw Tapper, he'd just plunged a piece of glass into Adam Thorpe's neck. And, given how Sam had tormented Tapper, he hardly imagined the man felt warmly towards him. But there was also a repulsion, a deep hatred that went to his core, for the man who'd orchestrated the attack on Eleanor.

'I won't bite,' said Tapper. His voice was somehow more Essex than Sam remembered, as if he were reverting to a former incarnation. He wore a white t-shirt and jeans, but his feet were bare. 'Nor indeed stab. Sit down. We need to talk.'

Sam pulled a chair from the desk and sat opposite Tapper, out of striking distance.

He glanced at his former adversary. Tapper's tan was dying back and skin that Sam remembered being cleanly shaved now sported a layer of stubble.

'Do you know where you are?' asked Tapper, his back resting against a pillow propped against the wall. The cell was warm, too warm for Sam, and he shook off his jacket and hung it over the back of the chair.

'Somewhere they lock up very dangerous people.'

Tapper smiled. 'We're in Paddington Green. Where they lock up terror suspects for questioning. Although it's just me at the moment. They keep them for twenty-eight days in these cells if they want. They even have a forensic pod to examine suspects in sterile conditions. It's quite something.'

'You're that great a threat.'

'As bad as Al-Qaeda or ISIS.'

'You stabbed a Cabinet Minister.'

'I have to say that caught me by surprise. But the truth is, I was raging. Furious with him for starting the whole business, for being spineless, and for trying to shaft me at the ninth hour.' Tapper's eyes flared with recollected anger.

There was silence for a moment. Sam's shirt clung to his now sweat-damp torso. Tapper seemed to be studying him.

'You're wondering why you're here.'

'Just a bit.'

'I wanted to thank you.'

'I'm sorry?'

'You've set me free.'

Sam cast his eye round the small cell. 'You're kidding, right?'

'Not in the slightest. I can't tell you how free I feel.'

'But you're about to be sent away for life.'

'I think you're pre-empting the verdict a little,' Tapper said, the corner of his mouth curled in mischief.

'Well you're not going to get community service.'

'I'm sorry,' said Tapper, 'I'm being cheeky. You're right. I'll get life. But, in a sense, I was already on a life term. Prison, by contrast, will be liberating.'

Sam remained tense and alert. Tapper appeared genuinely calmer – happy even – but Sam suspected the anger was not far from the surface. He didn't want to be in the stifling, subterranean cell for a second longer than was necessary.

'I didn't know how much I hated my life until I was reunited with Pat,' Tapper continued. 'You saw how much he meant to me, helped cement that understanding with your little notes. But what you didn't see was the misery I already felt.'

Sam sensed that playing along was the only way forward. 'You mentioned it in Dover.'

'I always felt trapped in my marriage to Yvonne because I was gay. She knew, tolerated my little dalliances, but I was still living a lie. And then there was the whole lifestyle. The exhausting small-talk of drinks parties and functions. The front we presented. The knighted business leader and his pretty wife and their public-school-educated children. The houses in Notting Hill, Cape Town, New York and the Cotswolds filled with artwork that was meaningless to me. The money I could never have spent in ten lifetimes.'

'You're saying you'd prefer to be poor?'

'I made money because I never wanted to become my father. He was piss poor, and bitten so hard by poverty – by his shitty existence freezing his balls off in Romford Market – that he became angry and violent. But you shrinks know that no amount of money can change a man's DNA. My father will always be in me. I am a man of violence, like him.'

'And now it feels liberating to accept that part of him that's in you.'

'God, you shrinks have a nice way with words.' Tapper looked genuinely impressed.

'Yes, that part of my father that's in me. I might have killed him all those years ago, but he lives on in here.' Tapper pointed to his head. 'What was exhausting was the constant denial, the crime that had been buried by my slippery PR people. I'm tired of denying who I am. My violent nature. My sexuality.' He lifted a finger, almost in lecture mode. 'And while we're on that subject, let me just say that it's not just about the shagging, but about the possibility of love. I felt that for Pat, you're quite right. And, when I'm ready, I want to feel that again.'

There was a sigh from the corridor outside.

This was all clearly wonderful for Tapper – the great unburdening – but Sam was beginning to feel sick and breathless, as the tiny, airless cell began to close in on him. Just as he was ready to scream, Tapper got to the point.

'I owe you. And I want to shaft them.' Tapper nodded towards the open door. 'Grab that, will you.' He pointed to the manila folder on the desk.

Sam reached behind him and retrieved the file.

'Don't open it yet. I want to explain first. You see, I have something stored away in a private security box in one of my many bank accounts that has turned a cut-and-dry case on its head. Don't get me wrong, I will still go away for a long time, thank God. But I have a bargaining chip.'

'Which is?'

'A video I made on the boat.'

Chapter 83

Sam gasped.

Tapper continued. 'Thorpe liked to film himself in action, the little perve. So I've got him in flagrante. Which is bad enough. But then he went and stabbed that man.'

Strickland poked his head inside. 'Can you keep your fucking voice down?'

'Piss off!' Tapper hissed.

Strickland, like an admonished child, retreated back outside. Tapper clearly had them by the balls.

'You're right about Thorpe, by the way. Shame made him stab Abel. Shame and self-loathing. On the surface, he was a chiselled, upper-crust heterosexual, the future of the party. But inside, he was gay. And he hated that.'

He lifted his head, as if proud of his own honesty.

'Anyhow, like I said, people in the party had high hopes for him. And I can tell you, if he'd reached Number Ten, we would have heard lots more announcements like the one he made in Dover. He used to talk about reclaiming the right-wing agenda, re-packaging it in more palatable ways. Given his looks and persuasive manner, I think he could have got away with it. He had some pretty radical ideas.'

Tapper looked briefly wistful. 'The big one he wanted to drive through was privatising large chunks of the police force – something that would have swelled my firm's coffers, I can tell you. The Border Force – which he was slowly undermining – would have been the first to go.'

He laughed joylessly. 'He was a cunning bastard too. Always feeding his favourite hacks juicy details about race and religious hate crimes – stuff that had slipped below the media radar. Anything that gave the impression of a country overrun by minorities – and a police force overwhelmed. He was an expert at sowing the seeds of fear so he could present himself as the solution.'

Sam thought of the blonde journalist at the press conference in Dover. The woman had literally lapped up Thorpe's words.

'Anyhow, with his accession to the Home Office, he realised that his life was going to become a lot more scrutinised. So he went for it that night. Kind of a last hurrah. Brought a lot of coke he'd somehow managed to score in Palermo through an Italian pal of his.'

Tapper shifted on the bed. 'We had a slap-up meal on the sun deck. Champagne, lobster, a couple of bottles of Montrachet. Then we dismissed the staff. Told them to come back in the morning. We got high in the saloon. Thorpe put his favourite 80s dance tracks on – ghastly music – and some porn on the TV and, well, you don't need me to spell it out.'

It happened, like so many swings of mood, quite suddenly. It was the way Tapper so casually spoke of that murderous evening – the way he was so happy to paint Thorpe as the villain and him, somehow, as righteous – that made Sam snap. There were acts Tapper needed to take responsibility for.

'Blameless, are you?'

The nonchalant demeanour appeared to fade a fraction. 'I'm sorry?'

If Sam had just unsettled a man capable of murder, he no longer cared. 'You seem so confident sitting here – the newly liberated gay man, the newly liberated murderer – convinced of your own rectitude. That killing Thorpe was right. As justified as snuffing out nasty, wife-beating dad.'

Tapper shrunk into the room.

Strickland appeared in the doorway. 'Is this a good idea?'

Sam swung in his direction. 'Not now!'

The lawyer slunk back out, nervously scanning up and down the corridor.

Sam turned back to Tapper. 'And what about the solicitor, Fitzgerald? What about my girlfriend, Eleanor?'

Tapper's mouth moved but no sounds came out.

'What about the other immigrants?'

'What other immigrants?'

'Don't fucking lie! Abel tied their boat to The Leopard. Don't tell me you didn't notice them.'

Tapper's face crumbled. He buried his head in his hands.

'Let me guess,' said Sam. 'You kicked Abel and Zahra's bodies off the boat. And then, as you watched them float away, you turned to the other small problem ruining your evening. The witnesses sitting just feet from the murder scene.'

'It wasn't like that!'

Tapper had emerged from the cocoon of his hands. He was crying. 'You're right, we pushed their bodies off. But we never saw any boat. It was pitch-black beyond the rear of the vessel. But I did see the rope tied up at the back at that point. In all this time, I hadn't considered the possibility of other passengers. It was just too quiet.' The tears rolled down Tapper's cheeks. Sam felt his stomach churn with nausea.

'I grabbed the rope and gave it a tug,' Tapper continued, 'expecting it to be light. But it was incredibly heavy. So Thorpe helped, and slowly the two vessels came together.'

Sam was certain he was going to vomit. He was about to have the haunting images he'd been seeing for days made concrete.

'The boat emerged from the darkness. There were dozens of people staring at me. Vacant, skeletal faces, open mouths, hollow eyes. But alive.'

Tapper shuddered, his face shiny with tears.

'There was a pole lying on the platform, with a docking hook on the end. Thorpe grabbed it and began smashing the fragile timber of the boat with the hook. Weak hands emerged from the vessel to stop him but the pole was out of their reach. If anyone did get close, he just moved to a different section. Timber splintered. Screams rang out. I could see the boat sinking before my eyes.'

Chapter 84

Sam flung the file on to the bed and rushed to the basin, where he vomited.

Strickland reappeared in the doorway, his face white. Sam wiped his mouth on a towel. He returned to his seat, took a deep breath, trying to extract some oxygen from the dead air. Strickland remained in the doorway.

'You didn't think to stop him?' asked Sam finally.

'I knew I would lose everything. The firm, the money. All the stuff that once meant so much to me.'

'And so you stood by.'

'Well, not exactly.'

'What do you mean?'

'Thorpe untied the rope and gave the boat a shove with the pole and it began drifting off into the sea. The people on board were panicking. But with every frantic movement, they just made the boat more and more unstable. It capsized. And that's when some of them started swimming towards us.'

Sam thought to ask why it hadn't occurred to Tapper to throw a life vest into the sea, but he knew that was a silly question.

'By now Thorpe was screaming at me to move the boat. I did what he asked. I rushed to the flybridge, typed in the start code the captain always shared with me, and moved the boat forwards slowly. The last thing I saw when I turned around was flailing arms in the water. And Thorpe watching them drown.'

Sam had been certain the two men murdered the immigrants. Their boat had been tied to the rear of The Leopard but somehow, on a still, calm sea, it had ended up as splintered chunks of wood, its passengers all dead.

The images that had tormented Sam the past days had changed with every hour as he weighed up different grisly scenarios. But what Tapper had just described was worse than anything Sam could have imagined.

'You murdered them,' said Sam, barely able to breathe.

'We did. And believe me, it has haunted me ever since.'

'I thought you embraced your violent side.'

Tapper was silent, like a stunned animal.

'Reni said that ninety-six people died that night. Ten of them were children. Can you imagine the terror they experienced at that moment? Their hope of reaching safety dashed in the most vicious and heartless way imaginable. And as they started to drown, the last thing they would have seen was Thorpe coldly watching them from the deck. And you driving the boat away.'

Tapper blinked. Swallowed hard. 'That night will never leave me.'

The rejuvenated, born-again lag was long gone. His head had sunk into his chest, and he looked up at Sam as if begging for some forgiveness the therapist would never in a million years grant.

'That's why I'm using the tape.'

Sam stood. 'I'm not interested.'

Strickland pressed his hands together. 'Please. You should listen.'

'I can't.'

Still blocking the doorway, Strickland exhaled. 'They're not going to let us out till you hear what he has to say. I won't let them.'

Still standing, Sam reluctantly turned to face Tapper again. Strickland stayed at the door.

Tapper's voice was quieter when he next spoke. 'Thorpe thought I'd destroyed the tape. But I always sensed he might be slippery, might try and shaft me. So I kept it.'

Tapper took a deep breath.

'As you can imagine, the video not only incriminates him but, by association, the Government too. Imagine the reaction if this film got leaked. Most governments can survive the odd scandal, if they can be contained. But this would show a future Home Secretary with psychopathic tendencies, cold-bloodedly murdering immigrants.' His voice was gathering strength again, as if drawing comfort in once more apportioning blame to Thorpe. 'What does that say of those that promoted him to high office? Who allowed a man like that to run the Home Office? There would be multiple demands for justice from his victims' families. Column after column of all-consuming news coverage. The Government would never recover from a scandal of this magnitude.'

'Am I supposed to be impressed?' said Sam.

'For Christ's sake, Keddie,' muttered Strickland behind him.

'I've made a few demands,' said Tapper. 'Which have been met. There's something for you. It's all in the file.'

Sam flinched, felt the anger flare up in him again. 'What is this? An apology? My girlfriend is not going to recover from her injuries. Unless you have the power to reverse that, I'm not interested in anything you have to offer.'

'Please!' wailed Tapper.

Sam stood. 'I hope you rot in here.'

He barged past Strickland, out into the corridor. Behind him, he heard a muted exchange between Strickland and a tearful Tapper. Sam reached a locked door, and hammered on it with his fist. A moment passed. As he was about to beat the door again, the lawyer appeared at his side with the female officer, who unlocked the door. They walked in silence back through the building to the car park. He saw that Strickland was holding the file.

As the vehicle rose out of the gloom of the car park, Strickland spoke.

'That was news to me.'

'What?'

'The other immigrants.'

'There'll be no justice for those ninety-six people, will there?'

The lawyer shook his head.

There was a pause. Then Strickland said: 'I understand how you feel about Tapper.'

'Believe me, you have no idea.'

'If you can set aside your feelings, you should at least look at this.'

The file sat unopened on the seat all the way back to Stoke Newington.

As Sam opened the car door and stepped on to the pavement, he heard Strickland call out from inside the vehicle.

'The file, Mr Keddie. Just take a look. It really is in your interest.'

Sam pushed the gate open and walked the short distance to his front door. He could hear the car's engine purring behind him. Strickland wasn't budging.

Sam pulled his house keys from a pocket and inserted them in the lock.

As their first meeting had demonstrated, Strickland was a man with powerful connections. And now he was almost grovelling. Clearly Tapper had made them very frightened. What he'd extracted from them would be significant, of that Sam was sure. But how could it possibly benefit him? He didn't want money. He just wanted Eleanor back.

Clearly Tapper was desperate to somehow make amends. Sam felt his stomach turn at the thought of accepting anything from him.

A breeze, some hint of spring in the milder air, blew down the street, sending his thoughts off course.

He always encouraged his clients to look at problems from different angles. Nothing was ever black and white.

While Sam might have despised the person who'd achieved this turn-around, those who'd contemplated covering up Thorpe's heinous crimes were no less monstrous.

He paused, key in lock. Then turned around.

Chapter 85

Asmara, Eritrea – a month later

After a connecting early evening flight from Cairo, and then an endless sea of Sahara – undulating waves of golden sand that eventually disappeared at nightfall – the plane touched down at 3am. Sam stepped on to the tarmac by a small terminal building, the air cool and breezy.

At passport control, an official stared coldly and suspiciously at Sam, asking what the purpose of his trip to Eritrea was.

'Business,' Sam calmly replied.

The official held his stamp over Sam's passport, hovering it in the air as if teasing him with the prospect of denied entry. Then he stamped it, his little power trip over.

He caught a cab to a large monolith of a hotel not far from the airport. As he checked in, he noticed two willowy African beauties sitting on stools in the bar off reception. Both were cooing over their male companions, middle-aged white men, one wearing a UN peacekeeper uniform.

He woke the following morning and opened his curtains on to brilliant sunshine and an arid landscape dotted with eucalyptus trees giving way to the outskirts of the capital – a low-rise mess of new concrete housing and more basic constructions topped with corrugated iron roofs.

But the cab journey into the city slowly revealed a more beautiful place than he'd seen from the window. An NGO in the seat next to him on the flight from Cairo had described how, when the country was under Italian rule, Mussolini had used the city as a blueprint for his Modernist architects. Now Sam could see what the man had been talking about.

Long streets of bold 1930s buildings in pastel shades. A cinema designed to look like a large wireless radio, with big button shapes on the front. A garage resembling a futuristic plane, with two long wings of cantilevered concrete under which motorists filled up. A bank conceived like the prow of an ocean-going liner.

It was 8am and Sam was struck by something else. On the palm tree-lined pavements, a small regiment of women in blue tabards were sweeping the pavements clean, while neatly dressed children and their mothers were making their way to school. A scattering of other people moved swiftly, as if late for work. But otherwise the streets were empty. Traffic too was almost non-existent. A handful of buses belching out diesel fumes, some trucks and taxis, and the odd private car. This was a capital city, yet in appearance it was more like a small provincial town in southern Italy.

The taxi peeled off the main boulevard, climbing up an elegant avenue of crumbling villas clad in bougainvillea. The shutters on many were closed. Sam passed one that looked more spruce and open for business than the others, and noticed a polished brass plaque on the wall by the gate, with the legend 'Ambasciata d'Italia'.

The car continued to climb gently, then turned right and pulled up. They had stopped on a dusty lane. Ranged along each side were more villas, substantial homes that suggested they were still in a comparatively wealthy part of town. A couple of sentry boxes were positioned along the street. Sam saw a man in military fatigues appear from one, place an ancient-looking rifle against the wall and stretch his arms upwards.

The taxi driver pointed at the property by their side. The wall was about eight feet high, the plasterwork peeling.

Sam got out of the car. It was warm, like a summer's day in England.

He walked the length of the wall to an open gate which gave on to a gravelled drive sprouting with weeds. A stretch of lawn was overgrown and patchy, while the beds were a chaotic mess of rampant flowers and shrubs. Ahead was a long, low-slung 1930s bungalow that might once have been incredibly beautiful. Walls coloured earthy red, shutters sky blue, all now in desperate need of repair and repainting.

He moved past an old rusting Fiat and a discarded child's bicycle and climbed a short set of steps. He saw a bell pull and gave it a yank. He heard it peeling his presence inside.

Seconds later, the door was opened by a small boy dressed in shorts and a t-shirt. He smiled broadly. He had a handsome face, with a high forehead and eyes Sam had seen before.

'Are you Gabriel?'

The boy nodded.

A woman's voice called out from somewhere in the house in a language Sam didn't understand.

Gabriel shouted back.

The woman appeared at the door. She too had familiar features, though she was drawn and dangerously thin.

But she managed a smile that was as generous as Gabriel's, shook Sam's hand and invited him in.

He walked across the threshold and paused to savour the moment, to revisit the circumstances that had brought him here.

The manila file he'd reluctantly looked inside contained a letter from the Home Office granting Zahra UK citizenship. Her passport was also in the file, as was a print-out of a bank statement in her name – with five hundred thousand pounds lodged.

Sam remembered how he'd felt at the time. Manipulated, angered. What price did one place on the trauma she'd experienced?

He'd gone inside, slept on what he'd discovered, then called Strickland to ask Tapper to secure two further conditions. A passport for Zahra's son, and a generous pension for Ispettore Guido Reni. Sam suspected that the Government would have granted their most high-security prisoner anything at that point. Except, of course, his release. Which was, ironically, the one thing Tapper didn't crave.

He imagined the satisfaction securing those extra conditions would have given Tapper. The sense that he was pleasing a man who'd become, in his deluded mind, a kind of confessor or therapist. But it wouldn't last. Tapper would soon unravel. The loss of Wallace, as well as those crimes he'd initially sought to compartmentalise – his part in Eleanor's attack, Fitzgerald's murder, not to mention the ninety-six people who'd drowned – would, Sam was sure, consume him. He would certainly suffer depression which, in Sam's experience, was not something that received much in the way of treatment in prison, bar a prescription of tablets. Would that be enough, or would Tapper slowly come to the conclusion that suicide was the only way out? Sam did not care. He was cauterised to the man's pain.

With the citizenship secured, Zahra had returned to the UK shortly afterwards. and Sam had helped her find a place to buy in Seven Sisters, just north of Stoke Newington.

He remembered the moment she stepped inside for the first time as the flat's owner. The look of utter delight on her face.

'So this is mine?' she said, hardly believing the words.

'All yours,' said Sam, handing her the keys.

They walked through empty white rooms, light flooding in through large windows. But a dark cloud soon made its presence felt. It was a home bought by a murderer. And the passport in her possession was not a bribe exactly – she could not harm the Government – but still a pay-off.

She slumped in a corner, began to cry.

'I shouldn't have this.'

'You deserve it, after everything you've been through.'

Zahra looked blankly at him, unconvinced.

'And think who will soon be sharing this home with you.'

At this, a smile broke across her tear-streaked face.

It was decided that Sam would collect Gabriel from Asmara. Strickland, who was now available whenever they needed advice, said that, despite Zahra's status as a UK citizen, the authorities in Eritrea could not be trusted to treat her fairly. She had, after all, fled military conscription and was still the daughter of a known critic of the regime. There was even the possibility of temporary detention. Sam, meanwhile, could enter and leave the country unhindered.

*

Sam passed a sitting room of wooden furniture in need of polish. Faded photographs on the walls, one of a proud man standing in front of a stationery steam engine, an escarpment to the side. Another of a family get-together, possibly pre-Second World War. The men in suits, the women dressed in long, flowing white gowns. Had ancestors once held high rank under the Italians – civil servants or engineers?

He was directed to a dining room and asked to sit. Zahra's mother and Gabriel disappeared. A painting on the wall, of a grand country home, some glimpse of forest beyond, hung opposite him. He strained his eyes to read the caption on the frame. 'Casa Idris, Keren.' Former wealth too. Sam remembered Zahra talking about how the family's money had been appropriated by the regime after her father fell foul of it. Where was her father, for that matter?

There was a squeak from the hallway and Gabriel entered with a tray of cold drinks, followed by an old man in a wheelchair, pushed by Zahra's mother.

'This is Idris,' said Zahra's mother. Sam stood. 'And I am Ariam.'

Sam offered his hand to Idris. But the man's hands sat motionless in his lap.

'Idris had a stroke a year ago,' said Ariam. 'He has lost his speech and most movement. We do what we can.' She smiled sadly.

Idris's chair was drawn up next to Sam, and Gabriel and Ariam sat opposite. Ariam asked after Zahra, and Sam, who'd already formulated a new story with Zahra, told her a rose-tinted tale of how she'd reached the UK, won her case for asylum and successfully secured citizenship for her son. She had a job, Sam said, working for a local community centre, helping other immigrants. Which was true.

'Gabriel struggles to remember his mother,' said Ariam, her voice betraying a slight tremor. Talk of her long-lost daughter had clearly upset her. 'And his English is not good. He hasn't benefited from the kind of education his mother enjoyed.' Ariam's eyes glassed with tears. 'Everything has changed since those days.' But then she glanced in Idris's direction. 'Although some things are better.'

Sam sensed her eyes narrow, as if she were lasering in on the fragile man next to him. Sam remembered that he was a military man. Even in his wheelchair, he still had that deportment, some rigidity of the spine that refused to give up even when he'd lost control of his speech and body. His hair was cut short and neatly and he wore a khaki shirt and trousers, as if ready for service at the blast of a bugle. Sam glanced at his hands folded limply in his lap, just below an old belt. A strap hung loose from where it was buckled by a thick lump of metal, a prong piercing the leather.

They chatted some more, the old man a dull-eyed witness to their conversation, before Ariam wheeled Idris from the room and began readying Gabriel for his journey to London. Sam could hear the boy talking excitedly. He wondered how the child would feel halfway through a long flight with a strange man en route to a mother he barely remembered.

Finally they were ready for departure. Ariam walked them both to the taxi idling in the road outside, then wrapped the boy in a tight hug. Sam got the feeling that, for Ariam, the parting was unbearable. She'd already lost her daughter and now she was losing her beloved grandchild, even though Sam had assured her that Zahra now had the funds to pay for her to fly over and visit. Gabriel meanwhile was still in a state of high excitement, now sitting in the back of the taxi, his eyes drinking in the interior.

Ariam leaned in the open window and kissed his cheeks one final time then rose to say goodbye to Sam. She shook his hand, thanked him for his help.

'Will Idris miss his grandson?' Sam asked.

Her face darkened. 'The only thing Idris misses is power. Do you know what his name means in Tigrinya?'

Sam shook his head.

'Fiery leader.'

The cab departed. Gabriel waved through the back window until the vehicle turned a corner and Ariam disappeared from view.

The boy settled back into his seat and began examining the contents of the small bag Ariam had packed for the flight, which contained books, snack bars and fruit.

Staring out the window at the 1930s time warp city passing by, Sam found himself returning to the cloudy-eyed Idris. And his belt. An uncomfortable sensation crept over him. It was clear Ariam had little love for him, and made no secret of the fact he was easier in his incapacitated state.

In that instant, Sam recalled the nightmare Zahra had in the car. The island she'd found herself on. How she'd seen an object in the perfect sand of the beach. A belt, which morphed into a snake.

There was a suggestion of the snake in the Garden of Eden, which made sense given her Catholic upbringing. But Sam sensed there was an additional layer of meaning, one closer to home. Having escaped the tyranny and dangers of Eritrea, Zahra would have likened Europe to a paradise as she made her treacherous journey here. But instead she'd found it tainted by human nature, by a terror she could never have anticipated. And Sam wondered whether that belt was a reminder of the first person who'd terrorised her.

He thought of the scar above her eye. He knew she had more on her back. Had Idris beaten her with that old leather belt, the buckle prong scraping her back with every lash? Was that visible scar a record of the moment she dared defy him and he'd struck her, not on her back, but across her face?

He'd never know. She had refused to talk about the scars on her back when asked about them at Creech Hill and never wanted to discuss them in therapy. Was it because she'd realised that they had, unexpectedly, been the turning point in her claim for asylum? If a deeply unhappy period of her life suddenly gave her a modicum of good fortune, then he hardly blamed her for keeping silent about the truth. Given her experience of incarceration, Zahra had good reason to be fearful of deportation. Or was it just that those scars were mementoes of a period she was not ready to talk about?

They'd reached the outskirts of the city. Crumbling 1930s buildings had given way to the mess of concrete apartments and makeshift structures he'd seen from the hotel window.

Back in London, Zahra was seeing a therapist – not Sam, they'd shared too much – and finally piecing her fragmented memories back together in a contained, safe place. As Sam had suspected, she also suffered from some anterograde amnesia, an inability to form memories after the incident, which explained how she'd not 'come to' until Catania. But those memories had now come back. In addition to the horrific moment when she found herself among hundreds of bodies on the beach in Pozzani, she also recalled begging for a bus fare, before reaching Catania to attempt a crossing to the mainland.

Her therapy was going to be long and tough. Zahra had experienced more trauma in her short life than any client he'd met. But, with the security of a home and the company of her son, not to mention her exceptional resilience, Zahra would forge a new life – of that, Sam was certain.

Zahra shared much in common with Eleanor. He hoped that, one day, they might have the opportunity to meet.

The taxi passed a field of red earth peppered with rocks. In the middle stood a tree, lush green leaves seemingly in defiance of the dry landscape.

Sam would not give up. He had to believe that Eleanor, like Zahra, would emerge from her nightmare.

That she too would survive.

THE END

Acknowledgements

Before acknowledging those who contributed to Denial, I owe belated thanks to Hannah Keddie. My old work buddy, she kindly lent her surname to my hero, Sam. Given what he's been up to, I sincerely hope he's not let the family down.

I may live in the midst of rural Devon, but the lanes are packed with experts to lean on.

Samantha Knights, an immigration specialist at Matrix Chambers, patiently answered my questions and explained the complexities of the UK's immigration system, the Dublin Treaty and the tortuous processes involved in securing a foothold in Fortress Europe.

I am also indebted to Dr Barry McKenna, who helped me gain a better understanding of comas, as well as the treatments involved. If I've made any mistakes in that department, then please blame me.

Mike Harper proved an invaluable source of information on the workings of the UK police force. Apologies to Mike for a couple of liberties I've taken.

I'd also like to thank Steve Haines for once again spotting heinous typos, grammatical howlers and plot inconsistencies.

Honorary Devonian Eve Seymour provided her usual blend of wisdom and insight when it came to editorial support, helping turn my rough first draft into a much more polished effort. I would urge all thriller writers in need of an editor to beat a path to her door.

And frequent visitor to our home, Derek Nicoll, of the South London and Maudsley NHS Foundation Trust, helped me plot Tapper's mental disintegration.

Finally, huge thanks to a man who lives a million miles from Devon, in West Hollywood. When Chris McVeigh gave me a publishing deal with Fahrenheit Press, he made my dream come true. For that, and for all the energy and pizzazz he pours into promoting my books, I am eternally grateful.

In researching Denial, I drew on a number of accounts of immigrant journeys across the Mediterranean. These are voyages that frequently end in tragedy, notoriously in April 2015, when around 700 drowned south of Lampedusa. In 2014, the Italian government announced it was shelving Mare Nostrum, its search and rescue operation, due to lack of funding from other EU nation states (the UK had stated that such operations merely encouraged more immigrants). The replacement, Triton, is wholly inadequate. Voluntary organisations like Migrant Offshore Aid Station (MOAS), a crowd-funded NGO, attempt to fill the gap, while EU countries continue to talk options, including a depressingly short-sighted plan to take military action against the smugglers' boats.

Lastly, a word on Eritrea. Back in 2006, I penned an article about Asmara, the capital, for the Observer, celebrating the city's extraordinary Modernist architecture. Make no mistake, it is a gem. But what I neglected to mention at the time was the Eritrean government's appalling human rights record. Indefinite military service, severe restrictions on religion and expression, and torture and arbitrary detention are all commonplace. Little wonder that, like my fictional creation Zahra Idris, thousands flee every month. It's a tiny country that could have been a huge success story following independence in 1993. Tragically, it's the opposite. According to the Refugee Council at the time of writing, Eritreans now account for the majority of the UK's asylum applications.

March 2016

Printed in Great Britain
by Amazon